The Slaver Wars: First Strike

Raymond L. Weil

DEDICATION

To my wife Debra for all of her patience while I sat in front of my computer typing. It has always been my dream to become an author. I also want to thank my children for their support and of course to the thousands of fans who have read my books.

For updates on current writing projects and future publications go to my author website. Sign up for future notifications when new books come out on Amazon.

Website: http://raymondlweil.com/

Other Books by Raymond L. Weil
Available at Amazon

Dragon Dreams: Dragon Wars
Dragon Dreams: Gilmreth the Awakening
Dragon Dreams: Snowden the White Dragon

Star One: Tycho City: Discovery
Star One: Neutron Star
Star One: Dark Star

Moon Wreck: First Contact
Moon Wreck: Revelations
Moon Wreck: Secrets of Ceres
Moon Wreck: Fleet Academy
The story continues in
The Slaver Wars: Alien Contact
The Slaver Wars: First Strike
The Slaver Wars: Retaliation
Coming January 2014

Star One: Tycho City: Survival
Coming December 2013

Dragon Dreams: Firestorm Mount
Coming 2014

Chapter One

The 800-meter Hocklyn escort cruiser Kraken exited the swirling white spatial vortex in the next system of their exploration sector. The cruiser WarFire appeared out of a similar vortex two hundred kilometers distant. The two cruisers were far from their support base in search of a mystery and for future worlds for the Hocklyn Slave Empire to conquer.

"Jump complete," reported Second Leader Slith as the different departments began reporting in.

"Status on sensors!" barked First Leader Malken from the command pedestal, glaring impatiently at the sensor screens.

The screens were still covered in static, which was normal immediately after a jump. During those few brief seconds, his ship was vulnerable. Malken wore light body armor that was nearly gray in color as was customary for command officers. He stood nearly two meters tall, and the six digits of his right hand were closed tightly in a fist as he waited.

"Sensors are coming online," the sensor operator reported as data began coming in.

"The WarFire reports a successful jump," Second Leader Slith informed Malken as communications were established with the other ship. "They are moving into a support position."

"No other contacts showing on sensors," the sensor operator added calmly.

"Very well," replied Malken, glancing coldly at his second in command. "Begin standard scans and let's see what this system holds."

Malken sat down in his command chair and gazed about the War Room. His ship and the WarFire were on a special mission. For the last one hundred years, there had been numerous reports of strange sensor readings and mysterious ships on the fringe of the empire. These ships

1

had vanished before they could be engaged, and their system or systems of origin remained unknown.

There had also been a marked increase in the number of escort cruisers that had been sent out on exploration missions and failed to return. There was a growing unrest in the Hocklyn High Council that some new and unknown enemy was systematically probing the empire's defenses.

As a result, the Hocklyn High Council had ordered that all future exploration missions would consist of two ships. In the past, one ship would jump into a system and scan it while the other held back in a nearby system and waited for a report. Now, both ships jumped in so as to be able to engage any enemy they might encounter. The council was confident that two Hocklyn ships could easily handle any hostile ship. More pairs of ships had been ordered sent out on exploration missions to determine if there was an imminent threat to the empire.

It had been centuries since the Hocklyns had engaged a serious adversary. In that war, the Human Federation of Worlds had been destroyed at great cost to the Hocklyn attacking fleet. Now the Hocklyn High Council was worried that another powerful adversary was waiting in the near future and was behind these mysterious sensor readings and strange ships that had been detected. The numerous missing escort cruisers sent off on long-range exploration missions seemed to confirm this. If this continued, it would be necessary to notify their AI masters.

"Sensors continue to report nothing in our immediate area other than the WarFire," Second Leader Slith reported after speaking with the sensor operator in detail about the system. "The WarFire is ready to micro-jump farther in system on your orders."

"Very well," First Leader Malken answered as he stood up and gazed impassively at the large sensor screen. "Set both ships up for a micro-jump and let's get on with this exploration mission. The empire is growing impatient to find more worlds to bring us honor."

"This system holds no communications traffic," commented Slith, gazing over at the First Leader with his large dark eyes. "This system will hold no honor for us. Perhaps it is best for us to go on to the next system."

"Be it as it may, we have our orders," rasped Malken, impatiently. "We will scan all the systems in our search area thoroughly, even if they hold no new civilization to bring honor to our people."

A few minutes later, the two cruisers entered their respective white vortexes and jumped briefly into hyperspace, to appear several billion kilometers farther in system. The red dwarf system they were in contained seven planets, none of which seemed to be inhabited, even though there were three in the liquid water zone.

-

Aboard the Human Federation of Worlds light cruiser StarSearch, a warning alarm suddenly sounded. The commander instantly focused his attention on his second officer, his eyebrows arching in a question.

"What do we have, Mason?" demanded Commander Thomas, feeling apprehensive. It was very seldom that particular alarm ever sounded.

The alarm indicated that there had been an unauthorized hyperjump into a neighboring system. All the systems around Earth and New Tellus for twenty-five light years were equipped with sensor buoys that could detect hyperjumps. It had been discovered a few years back that hyperjumps gave off an energy spike when the spatial vortex collapsed. Since that time, numerous sensor buoys had been placed in all of the star systems around the new Human Federation of Worlds to detect such spikes.

The StarSearch was currently twenty-two light years from Earth on a standard patrol with two escort destroyers. The 700-meter cruiser was heavily armed and tasked with maintaining the security of New Tellus, Earth and the other systems of the new Human Federation of Worlds.

Glenn Mason, the StarSearch's executive officer, was standing by the holographic plotting table, which currently showed all the nearby stars within five light years of the ship. One of the stars was blinking a troublesome red.

"One of the hyper detection buoys in Gliese 667C is reporting two unauthorized hyperjumps," reported Mason with concern in his voice. He was worried as all Federation ships, both civilian and military, carried transponders that cleared them with the buoys.

"Gliese 667C!" Commander Thomas replied, his eyes widening in alarm. "How many planets are in that system?"

"Seven, Sir," Mason replied as he called up the information on his plotting table. "Only one is marginally habitable, Caden's World, and there are several large mining installations on the planet's surface. There are approximately twenty thousand people living in the two mining settlements. There are also twenty defensive satellites above the mining installations in geostationary orbits."

"Contact our escorts and set up a jump," Thomas ordered with growing unease showing on his face. "Send a message back to Fleet Command that two unauthorized hyperjumps have been detected in Gliese 667C, and we are proceeding to investigate."

A few moments later, the communications officer reported that the message had been sent. It would take a few minutes for the message to reach Earth and New Tellus. All the systems around Earth had FTL communication booster satellites that allowed quick communication between the planets of the Federation.

Thomas closed his eyes. For years, they had been expecting the Hocklyns to find the human worlds that Earth and the Federation survivors had settled. He opened his eyes and took in a deep breath as he watched his crew set up the jump. He hoped the hyperjumps detected by the buoy were just a couple of freighters off course with nonfunctioning transponders. If not, then the war the new Human Federation of Worlds had been preparing for might have just arrived. It the buoys had only detected one unauthorized jump he wouldn't be too concerned, but two were an indication of something troublesome and possibly dangerous.

"Destroyers Argyle and Swanson both report ready to jump on your command," Major Mason reported as he listened to the incoming reports over his mini-com.

Thomas nodded his head, knowing he might be taking his ships into a war situation. "I want the destroyers and us at Condition One when we exit the warp vortex. Have our two Talon fighters ready to launch if needed. This might just be a false alarm, but we will take no chances."

Major Mason nodded his head as he passed on the orders. He felt tense knowing what might be ahead. Almost instantly, red Condition One lights began flashing and a warning klaxon sounded. Mason spoke over the ship's com system announcing the setting of Condition.

Aboard the StarSearch, the crew raced to their battle stations, hoping that this was nothing more than a routine drill. In just a few minutes, all departments reported the setting of Condition One.

Thomas leaned back in his chair at the command console. He gazed at the large viewscreen on the front wall, which currently showed a myriad of beckoning stars. He hoped the hyperjumps detected were not Hocklyn exploration cruisers. Thomas knew that back at New

Tellus and Earth his message would cause quite a stir. Additional forces would quickly be rushed to Gliese 667C, but he couldn't afford to wait. If those were Hocklyn ships and they discovered the mining installations, they would know they had discovered a high tech civilization. If even one of those ships escaped, it could mean disaster for the human race.

"Jump," ordered Thomas, staring straight ahead at the viewscreen. "Let's find out what's waiting for us."

In front of the three ships, blue-white jump vortexes formed. Quickly the three ships entered the vortexes and jumped into hyperspace as the vortexes collapsed behind them.

-

First Leader Malken gazed in surprise at the latest data from the ship's sensors; the system was inhabited! They had detected several mining installations on the fourth planet.

"It's confirmed, Sir," Second Leader Slith reported as he turned to face the First Leader. "Long-range sensor scans have detected two large mining installations on the planet as well as numerous satellites in orbit. We may yet find honor in this system."

"It's those satellites that worry me," replied First Leader Malken, gazing suspiciously at the sensor data on the main sensor screen. "They are positioned directly above those two installations, and why are there so many of them? If they were just normal communication or weather satellites, they would only need six or eight to cover the entire planet. We are detecting twenty, and they are positioned extremely close together."

"Defensive satellites?" Second Leader Slith said warily, his dark eyes widening at the thought. "That would indicate they are expecting an attack."

"Possibly," Malken responded as he studied the data on the screen. "Move us in closer, but keep us out of the planet's gravity well. I want to get some more detailed scans before deciding on a course of action. We are too far out to be able to transmit a message to the nearest fleet base and I want to be prepared to run if necessary."

"Run!" blurted Slith in shock as he took several steps back from the First Leader. "We are Hocklyns; we don't run! We will gain no honor running from an enemy."

"In this case, we do," responded Malken in a grave voice, his cold eyes focusing on his second in command. "We have been losing ships mysteriously for years. Our orders from the High Council are clear; if we detect any advanced civilizations, we are to report back immediately. We will suffer no loss of honor in doing so. We will only be following orders."

Slith was quiet as he weighed the First Leader's words. There would be no honor in retreating. Orders from the High Council could not be refused, and severe punishments awaited those that disobeyed.

On the surface of the planet, long-range sensors had already detected the two Hocklyn cruisers. A frantic message had been sent to Fleet Command indicating that two enemy ships had been spotted and were approaching the planet.

"Put the defensive satellites at Condition One and order all personnel to the deep bunkers," Lieutenant Krandle ordered as she studied the data coming across the sensors in the operations center. "Order all marines to their defensive positions in case the Hocklyns land Protectors."

"Surely the Fleet will arrive before that happens," Sergeant Simmons responded as he quickly passed on the orders. He knew they were ill prepared to stop a Hocklyn attack.

He had never been in combat before, and those two approaching ships worried him. Counting the lieutenant and himself there were only forty marines on the entire planet. Twenty were stationed at each of the two mining installations. The area they had to protect was too large for the forces they had on hand. All they could hope for was to fight a delaying action until help arrived.

Lieutenant Krandle glanced down at her watch. "We're twenty-one light years out from Earth and fifteen from New Tellus, which means we're on our own for at least an hour unless we have a patrol fleet close by."

"Our people are making their way to the bunkers," Adam Severson reported as he walked up to the lieutenant. He was a civilian and in charge of the mining operations. There were a number of other people in the operations center operating the different consoles that monitored the settlements and mining operations. "It will take nearly an hour to get everyone safely inside the bunkers. The miners are going to the deeper sections of the mines until we sound the all clear."

"That's all we can do for now," responded Lieutenant Krandle, wishing she had more marines to protect the civilians. Why had the Hocklyns chosen her system to show up in? Krandle let out a heavy sigh as she weighed her options.

If the Hocklyns landed Protectors, they would lose a lot of people. From what she had been told by her superiors, the Hocklyns showed very little mercy toward civilians. She just hoped they didn't get nuked from orbit. The Hocklyns had a propensity for using nukes against civilian targets.

"Hocklyns," Severson spoke with fear and worry in his voice as he looked at the two threatening red icons on the main sensor screen. "How did they find us?"

"Probably one of their standard survey missions," replied Krandle, wishing the doors to the operations center were armored. If they got through this, that would be one of the first things she would recommend. This room would not be a good place to defend; it was extremely vulnerable to attack. "They have been coming nearer to our space every year, and it had to happen sooner or later."

"Multiple hyper traces being recorded in the outer system," Sergeant Simmons suddenly reported as three more red threat icons suddenly appeared on the long-range sensor screen. The three red icons suddenly turned green, indicating friendly ships.

"I guess today's our lucky day," Lieutenant Krandle breathed with a sigh of relief. "A patrol group must have been close by."

"Thank, God!" spoke Severson, looking with renewed hope at the sensor screen. He didn't relish seeing his mining operation turned to rubble in a battle with the Hocklyns. "Can they handle the Hocklyn ships?"

"We will know shortly," replied Krandle, her eyes focusing on the screen. "Make sure everyone continues to the bunkers until this is over. Communications get me a line to whoever is in charge of those Federation ships."

Commander Thomas had felt the normal queasiness associated with a jump and waited expectantly for the long-range sensor screens to come online. In just another few moments, he would know what the two unidentified ships in the system were.

"I have a communications from a Lieutenant Krandle on Caden's World," the communications officer reported. "She is reporting that they have two Hocklyn escort cruisers inbound. She has placed the planet's defensive satellites at Condition One and is sending everyone except the operations center staff and marines to the deep bunkers."

"Sensors online, and I confirm two Hocklyn escort cruisers," the sensor operator reported in a calm voice. "They are 20 million kilometers distant from the planet and moving inward at approximately 10,000 kilometers per second."

"We have less than an hour before they hit the planet's defenses," Major Mason commented as he studied the data above his holographic plotting table. "If they don't jump out before then and report back to their fleet base."

Thomas shook his head as he weighed his options. "We can't let them do that. We have our standing orders to destroy any Hocklyn ships that appear in our space."

"Yes, Sir," Mason replied. "We need to engage them immediately before they detect us."

"Plot a micro-jump to intercept the Hocklyns," ordered Thomas, taking a deep breath and walking over to the plotting table to gaze at the display. "They are already in range of the planet, and their sensors should have detected the mining operations as well as the defensive satellites by now. I want to be in combat range when we come out of the jump."

"They are either moving in to attack or still gathering data," suggested Mason, glancing over at the commander.

"Designate the two Hocklyns ships as Hostiles One and Two," Thomas continued as he planned what to do next. He folded his arms across his chest and contemplated the best strategy to use in this situation. "The destroyers Argyle and Swanson will engage Hostile One, and we will engage Hostile Two. Argyle and Swanson are to concentrate on disabling their target's jump drive. I doubt if they have the firepower to take out the cruiser on their own."

"That will be tough on those two destroyers going toe to toe with a Hocklyn escort cruiser," Major Glenn warned, his eyes showing deep concern. "We could lose one or both of them, even with our better shielding."

"I know, Glenn," Thomas said, knowing Mason was right. "But we have no choice. We can't let them report back with what they have discovered. Get the jump set up."

Major Mason spoke to Navigation and the two escort destroyers. It didn't take long to have the micro-jump plotted and ready to implement.

"Ready to jump and engage the Hocklyns," he reported, his eyes on the holographic display which had been changed to tactical mode. He could feel the increased tension in the crew of the Command Center.

"Jump!" ordered Commander Thomas, returning to his command console and buckling himself in.

In front of the three Federation ships, blue-white spatial vortexes appeared. Moments later, the ships were gone.

First Leader Malken was watching the viewscreen, which was focused on the planet ahead, when the warning klaxons started sounding. His head moved sharply to gaze at the sensor operator.

"Three ships have just jumped into extreme combat range, First Leader," the sensor operator reported, his large eyes narrowing as he studied the data on the sensor screen.

"I want the size and identification of those ships now!" snapped Malken, his eyes turning into dark slits. Perhaps this was the opportunity the High Council had been hoping for to identify who was responsible for the missing ships. Great honor could be forthcoming with that discovery. "Stand by to jump on my command once we have their identity."

"Incoming fire," Second Leader Slith warned as his board lit up with inbound threat icons.

He quickly passed on the order to return fire without consulting the First Leader. He was surprised that the aliens had attacked without warning. That seemed to indicate the aliens already knew who the Hocklyns were.

The Hocklyn cruiser rocked as missiles and explosive rounds struck the energy screen. First Leader Malken was nearly thrown to the floor from the ferocity of the attack.

"Put one of their ships up on the viewscreen," ordered Malken, angrily. How dare someone attack his ship without warning!

"Screens are holding," Slith reported as he listened to the reports coming in from the various stations. "Weapons stations are returning fire. The WarFire is also under attack. We have one ship of 700 meters and two of 400 meters engaging us."

"Turn and engage with our energy beams," ordered Malken, knowing that very few alien warships could withstand the Hocklyn's powerful energy weapons. If the attackers could not knock down his screens, then the energy beams would make short work of them. His two ships were larger and more powerfully armed. "I want boarding teams ready to go. Have our Protectors prepared to board the enemy ships as soon as they are disabled. They are to secure all computers and any star maps they can find!"

If his Protectors could board the enemy ships and find information leading to their home worlds, then much honor would come his way. Malken felt pleased with the good fortune that had suddenly been thrust upon him.

-

Commander Thomas watched the sensors as reports began to come in on their first strike. As he had suspected, the Hocklyn's energy screen was holding up to the initial attack. On the main viewscreen appeared one of the Hocklyn escort cruisers. It was wedge shaped and covered with weapon emplacements. Some of these flickered with light, indicating they were firing. There was no doubt in his mind that the StarSearch would be on the receiving end of that weapons fire. He looked back over at the tactical display.

"Hocklyns are firing railguns and missiles, Sir," Major Mason reported as the StarSearch began to shudder from the weapons fire striking their energy screen.

Commander Thomas nodded as he kept his eyes focused on the holographic tactical display above the plotting table.

"Continue to close the range. Focus bow lasers and pulse lasers on Hostile One," ordered Thomas, grimly. This battle needed to be short! "Follow up the laser strike with two Devastator missiles programmed with a five second impact separation."

"Yes, Sir," Major Glenn replied as he carried out the order.

"Destroyers Argyle and Swanson are both engaged. Swanson is reporting minor damage from missile fire," reported Communications.

In space, exploding missiles and explosive rounds were going off in dazzling flashes as they found their targets. Both sides were using defensive missiles to destroy inbound ordnance. Occasionally, a heavy missile would strike a ship's screen brightly illuminating it in a fiery explosion.

"Activate defensive lasers," Thomas ordered Tactical. "It's time we show the Hocklyns just what we have." So far, the Hocklyns were using the same types of weapons as they had in the past; nothing new had been detected.

Instantly, eight of the sixteen defensive laser batteries the StarSearch was equipped with opened up, destroying enemy missiles in bright explosions almost as soon as they were launched from the Hocklyn escort cruiser. Their advanced computer targeting systems made misses few and far between.

The helm officer turned the ship slightly, bringing the heavy bow lasers to bear on the Hocklyn cruiser. The tactical officer quickly entered the coordinates in his weapons console and gave the order to fire. Two other tactical officers were next to him, operating the ship's other weapons.

Moments later, the main laser weapons fired, sending out powerful orange-red beams striking the Hocklyn's energy screen. The screen wavered and shimmered as it struggled to resist the sudden onset of energy from the lasers. Gaps appeared in the screen, allowing several of the laser beams to penetrate and strike the ship's hull, carving deep holes that glowed cherry-red. On the StarSearch's main viewscreen, several explosions could be seen as compartments inside the Hocklyn ship were suddenly exposed to vacuum.

-

"Lasers!" Malken oathed as he read the data coming in on the sensors.

Instantly, warning alarms began to sound and red lights began flashing on the damage control board. He knew that his ship was suffering serious damage and now realized he was facing a very advanced enemy. The plan to disable and board the attacking ships would have to be abandoned; they would have to be destroyed instead.

"Firing energy beams," Slith reported as the Kraken finished its turn and brought its heavy energy beams to bear on the attacking ship.

Two bright blue beams speared out from the Hocklyn ship, striking the attacking vessel. The enemy ship's energy screen wavered, but held.

"Focus all weapons on that same point," Malken ordered loudly, angry that the ship was still there. "We must knock that screen down! Honor is at stake!"

Malken felt a serious vibration spread through the Kraken as more red lights lit up on the damage control board. The energy beams should have penetrated the attacking ship's energy screen. He started to feel uneasy as he realized the enemy cruiser was much more powerful than he had originally believed.

"We're taking serious damage from their lasers," warned Slith, worriedly. "We have numerous compartments open to vacuum and several fires that are out of control. We won't be able to keep the energy screen up much longer."

"I have a tentative identity on the attacking ships," the computer operator reported. "They are Human Federation of World's ships!"

"Impossible!" Malken bellowed in growing anger and frustration as his ship continued to take damage. "We destroyed them centuries ago. The humans are all dead!"

A panel shorted out, throwing a cascade of bright sparks across the War Room. Smoke was becoming prevalent in the air as the ship's ventilation system struggled to keep the air clear.

"Evidently not," Slith retorted as more red lights appeared on the damage control board. The ship was starting to come apart around them! The damage control board was indicating numerous compartments in vacuum and spreading fires; the ship wouldn't last much longer. "Those are human ships out there, and our jump drive is offline. Engineering is reporting the drive core has suffered heavy damage, and we can't jump until repairs are made. The WarFire is reporting their drive is also offline."

"Intensify our attack then!" Malken hissed, his cold, dark eyes gazing at the tactical console and the four Hocklyns who sat there. "We must destroy them!"

There was no doubt in Malken's mind that they had found who had been destroying their ships and was responsible for those mysterious ship readings: it was the humans! He had to get this information back to the Hocklyn High Council! If he could escape and take this information back, then honor might yet be forthcoming. He felt his ship shake violently, and more red lights appeared on the damage control console.

Thomas felt the StarSearch shudder as an enemy missile penetrated a weak spot in the energy screen and detonated against the ship's hull. Glancing at the damage control board, he saw that only minor damage was being reported. The new energy screens were holding up against the Hocklyn weapons fire. However, the Hocklyn energy beams were causing the screens to fluctuate and allowing some ordnance to penetrate.

On a side viewscreen on the front wall, he watched as the two Devastator missiles launched. The two were separated by a five-second firing interval. More missiles erupted from the other six missile tubes, targeting the same location on the Hocklyn ship's shields. The six Klave class missiles contained high explosive penetration warheads. The shield was already wavering under the intense fire from the lasers.

Occasionally a laser or an explosive round would strike the Hocklyn cruiser, causing even more damage. Large areas on the

Hocklyn ship's hull were showing heavy damage with deep jagged holes. Weapon emplacements had been blasted away, and numerous fires were burning inside.

"Swanson is reporting severe damage," the communications officer reported, looking over at the commander. "They have numerous fires that are out of control and heavy casualties. They are requesting permission to withdraw."

"Denied," Commander Thomas spoke with pain in his voice. "He had to keep the pressure up on the two Hocklyn warships even if it meant sacrificing the destroyer.

It was at that moment that the first Klave missile detonated against the Hocklyn's shields, followed seconds later by one of the Devastators. The ten-kiloton warhead finished what the lasers had nearly completed; the Hocklyn's energy shield went down. The second Devastator missile and the rest of the Klaves detonated against the Hocklyn ship's hull and the resulting nuclear explosion washed over the main viewscreen. When it cleared, the Hocklyn ship was gone.

"Hostile One destroyed," reported Major Mason.

"Target Hostile Two," Commander Thomas ordered, his eyes shifting to the two green icons on the tactical display that represented his destroyers. They had to help them before he lost one; they were not designed to take on a Hocklyn escort cruiser by themselves.

"Swanson is down," the sensor operator reported suddenly as a brilliant flash covered the main viewscreen. "Argyle is reporting that they are taking on heavy weapons fire and their shields are close to failure."

"Bring our heavy lasers to bear and fire two more Devastator missiles," ordered Thomas, feeling numb at losing one of the destroyers and over two hundred men and women. This was the first time he had lost anyone in combat.

Moments later, the second Hocklyn vessel vanished in multiple nuclear explosions as it activated its self-destructs.

"Hostile Two is down," the sensor operator reported with obvious relief in his voice.

"Communications, contact the Argyle and see if they need assistance," ordered Thomas, allowing himself to take a deep breath. Looking over at Major Mason, the commander continued, "Check on our casualties, Glenn; we lost some good people today."

"Yes, Sir," Mason replied. He let out a long breath and glanced around the Command Center. Everyone looked shaken but were going about their assigned duties.

Thomas looked over at the communications officer. "Communications, after you have contacted the Argyle, send a message to Fleet Command in the New Tellus system. Inform them that the two Hocklyn ships have been destroyed, but we lost the destroyer Swanson."

-

Down on the planet, Lieutenant Krandle stared with open relief at the long-range sensors that showed both Hocklyn ships had been destroyed. She also noticed with sadness that one of the green icons representing the Federation ships was also missing. The battle hadn't been without losses.

"Sergeant Simmons, tell the people they can come out of the deep bunkers. Set the defensive satellites to Condition Two. This is over with for now."

-

Commander Thomas had moved his remaining two ships over Caden's World. The StarSearch and Argyle had just gone into orbit when the sensor operator reported more contacts jumping into the system. The tension in the Command Center went up as everyone wondered if it were more Hocklyns.

"What do we have?" demanded Thomas, focusing his eyes on the large sensor screen next to the plotting table. He watched nervously as over a dozen red threat icons appeared, and then visibly relaxed as they turned to a friendly green.

"I have the battlecruiser WarHawk and two battle carriers, the Liberty and Independence, as well as two Monarch heavy cruisers and eight light cruisers reporting in," the communications officer replied.

"They sent a full fleet," Major Mason commented surprised at the number and size of the ships in the quick response force. "They were not going to take any chances with what might be waiting for them here."

"I have Rear Admiral Tolsen on the com, Sir," the communications officer reported. "He is requesting our current status."

Thomas took a deep breath and then activated his mini-com, putting him in instant contact with Admiral Tolsen. "Admiral Tolsen, this is Commander Thomas of the StarSearch. We are currently going into orbit over Caden's World. Both of the Hocklyn ships have been destroyed and from what we can tell were not able to get word out as to what they had found."

"That's good news, Commander," Admiral Tolsen's strong voice responded. "What are the conditions of your ships?"

"The Swanson was destroyed in the battle, the Argyle has moderate damage, and I have sent additional repair crews over to assist. The StarSearch received some minor damage and should be back to full operational status within two hours."

Admiral Tolsen was quiet for a moment before replying, "We will be micro-jumping in system and will rendezvous with you in a few hours. Once there, I want you and your executive officer to come aboard the WarHawk for a meeting. I want to go over the battle with you in detail as well as all the data that you collected. If the Hocklyns found this system once, it's only a matter of time before they find it again."

Commander Thomas looked out of the shuttle's cockpit windows as they neared the WarHawk. The ship was massive at 1,200 meters. The battlecruiser was covered with weapon emplacements, including offensive and defensive turrets that dotted the hull. However, Thomas knew that the WarHawk's most powerful weapons were the new power beams that had been installed in the bow. Rumor had it that they were much more powerful than lasers.

"I wonder what will happen next?" Mason commented as he stared at the massive warship and the open flight bay that they were rapidly approaching.

"We prepare for war," Thomas replied in a sad voice. "We knew this day was coming, it's just here earlier than we expected."

After the shuttle landed in the bay, Commander Thomas and Major Mason made their way to one of the small briefing rooms next to the Command Center. Two heavily armed marines allowed the two to enter. Once inside, they found Rear Admiral Tolsen and several of his aides.

"Have a seat, gentlemen," said Tolsen, motioning for them to sit down. "I want to go over this battle in detail before sending a full report to Fleet Command."

For the next hour, they went over every aspect of the battle, from the weapons used in the opening salvos to the end when the heavy lasers had been used as well as the four Devastator missiles.

15

"I'm concerned about one thing," Admiral Tolsen commented as he watched the last Hocklyn escort cruiser explode in a series of nuclear explosions on the large viewscreen. "The Hocklyns screens seemed to hold up surprisingly well to our initial attack. Even when the lasers were used, the shields didn't go down instantly."

"Is it possible the Hocklyns have strengthened their shields?" asked Major Mason, worriedly.

For years, the Federation had been basing their strategy on the fact that the AIs had not allowed the Hocklyns to further develop their weapons. For untold centuries, the Hocklyn ships and weapons had remained the same.

"I guess it's possible," Tolsen surmised not looking pleased. "We need to get this data back to Fleet Command and let the experts analyze it. I've already sent shuttles out to check the wreckage, but I don't expect to find anything meaningful."

"So what's our next move, Admiral?" Commander Thomas asked. "How soon will it be before the Hocklyns realize that two of their escort cruisers have gone missing and send a fleet out searching for them?"

Admiral Tolsen leaned back in his chair and thought about the commander's words. "No one can know what their response time will be. It may be a few months to a few years; all we can do is get ready. I have already requested two military transports from Earth. They will be bringing twenty more defensive satellites as well as six missile platforms. There will be an additional company of marines assigned to Caden's World as well. Fleet Command will also be assigning two destroyers to the system to support the orbital defenses."

"We have over thirty systems with mining operations in them," pointed out Thomas, wondering if additional defenses were going to be added to all of them. "The Hocklyns could show up in any one of them."

"I know," Tolsen responded with a nod. "I suspect all of their defenses will be beefed up. We need those mining systems to stay intact for the raw material they are providing for the future war effort."

"What are my orders now, Sir?"

"Return to New Tellus to have your ship checked. I suspect the Argyle will need some yard time. You have just successfully fought off two Hocklyn escort cruisers, and I wouldn't be surprised if a promotion were forthcoming. Good job, Commander!"

Chapter Two

Two blue-white spatial vortexes formed suddenly in the outer regions of the New Tellus system. The battle cruiser WarHawk, along with the battle carrier Liberty, flashed into existence. The battle carrier Independence and the rest of the fleet had remained behind in Gliese 667C to give support until the military transports arrived with additional defense satellites. The FTL messages had been hot and furious from various commands demanding to know what had happened above Caden's World. Already, word was spreading across the Federation that a battle involving Hocklyn warships had occurred in Federation space.

Admiral Tolsen was in the Command Center as the screen cleared and the sensors began functioning. Looking around, his eyes focused on the communications officer.

"We are being hailed by the light cruiser Crescent," Lieutenant Judy Davis reported from Communications. "It is the normal request for ship identification."

"Send it," Tolsen confirmed, satisfied with the quick detection by the light cruiser.

This was standard operating procedure in all of the ten inhabited systems of the new Human Federation of Worlds. The Federation consisted of thirteen inhabited planets plus Ceres with the government centered on Earth.

A few monuments later, Lieutenant Davis turned and looked toward the admiral. "We have a message from Fleet Command on New Tellus Station."

"That was quick," Colonel Beck commented with arched eyebrows.

"Everyone's on edge now," commented Tolsen, knowing it was only going to get worse. "The Hocklyns have finally made it to Federation space."

"What's the message?" asked Colonel Beck, looking back over at Lieutenant Davis.

"We are to micro-jump to New Tellus, and Admiral Tolsen is to report to Fleet Admiral Johnson with the details of what happened in Gliese 667C."

"Commander Thomas kicked the Hocklyn's collective asses is what happened," Colonel Peter Beck commented with a smirk.

"Set up the jump, Peter," ordered Tolsen, taking a deep breath. He knew that Fleet Command was anxious for a firsthand report of the battle. "We won this round, but round two will be coming at some point in time. We have to be ready for that one. This time we took the Hocklyns by surprise; that won't be the case next time."

Tolsen looked up at the large holographic image above the plotting table, which was now displaying the eight planets of the New Tellus system. New Tellus was planet number four and located almost dead center in the system's Goldilocks zone. There were currently twenty-two million humans living on the planet, the majority of them direct descendants from the original survivors of the first Human Federation of Worlds. There were an additional two million living inside the huge manmade caverns inside the asteroid Ceres in the Sol System.

The holographic image was full of different colored icons. Each icon represented a planet, ship, defensive satellite, or other manmade object; the image was blanketed with them. The New Tellus system was the most heavily fortified system in the new Human Federation of Worlds. The reason was simple; someday the plan was to lure the Hocklyns into attacking the system in overwhelming numbers. If they did, the Hocklyns would walk into the biggest trap ever built. New Tellus was also the closest system to the Hocklyn Slave Empire.

"Ready to jump," Colonel Beck informed the admiral as Navigation and helm reported their readiness.

"Then take us home," ordered Admiral Tolsen, leaning back in his command chair. Admiral Tolsen had been born on New Tellus and was well aware of the massive defenses in the system.

In front of the WarHawk and the Liberty blue-white vortexes of swirling light appeared. The two ships maneuvered into the center of the vortexes and vanished as they made the transition to hyperspace. Behind them the vortexes collapsed, leaving no trace of ever being there.

A few moments later, Admiral Tolsen felt the familiar wrenching sensation as the WarHawk dropped out of hyperspace and exited the vortex. The Liberty appeared off her port side and moved slowly into supporting position. Several Talon fighters took off from her flight bay and took up CAP positions around the two ships.

"Put New Tellus Station on the screen," Colonel Beck ordered as he adjusted the holographic image above the plotting table to show the area around New Tellus only.

It was covered in blue and green icons. The blue icons represented defensive satellites and the green icons represented ships. There were also eight large violet icons, which represented the massive asteroid fortresses that were in orbit around the planet, as well as six yellow icons, which represented the large orbiting shipyards. The Federation survivors had spent the last four hundred years preparing the system for the coming war with the Hocklyns.

"Take us in to New Tellus Station and contact Docking Control to see where they want us," ordered Tolsen, looking at the viewscreen, which showed the massive shipyard. New Tellus Station was the largest shipyard in the Federation. "I will be in my quarters getting ready to see the Fleet Admiral. Contact me when we're docked."

"Yes, Sir," Colonel Beck replied as he walked over to the command console to take over operations in the Command Center.

It was nearly three hours later when Admiral Tolsen made his way into the large briefing room in the station to meet with Fleet Admiral Johnson. New Tellus station was sixteen kilometers in length and eight in width. It contained six massive construction bays, which could produce any size ship the Fleet required, as well as twelve repair bays. It had been necessary for Admiral Tolsen to take a transit tube to reach the center of the station, which was four kilometers distant from where the WarHawk was docked.

"Good to see you, Race," spoke Admiral Karla Johnson, rising to her feet.

"Good to be back, Admiral," Tolsen replied as he saluted.

"Have a seat," Johnson said, indicating a chair close to her.

Tolsen took the indicated seat, noticing there were ten other people sitting at the conference table. They were all part of the admiral's staff or scientists.

"We have a lot to discuss and some plans that need to be made," Admiral Johnson said as she sat back down. The admiral was 56-years-old and had been born on Earth.

"There is some disturbing data in Commander Thomas's sensor readings," Admiral Freeman informed the group, looking over at Tolsen. Freeman was Admiral Johnson's chief of staff and in charge of all Federation shipyards. The man was efficient and knew ship construction intimately.

For the next few hours, the group went over the Hocklyn incursion into the Gliese 667C system. They went over the data recorded by the StarSearch and the effect their weapons had on the Hocklyn escort cruisers.

"I don't like how their energy shield managed to resist the StarSearch's lasers," Admiral Freemen commented with a heavy frown, leaning back and gazing at the others. "Those shields should have failed quicker than they did."

"It looks like some type of possible upgrade," Josh Sayth added as he studied the data, his forehead creased in a frown. He was a scientist and well versed in Hocklyn weaponry. "From what I am seeing from these scans, I would guess there has been a twenty to thirty percent increase in the strength of the Hocklyn's energy shields."

"Why?" asked Fleet Admiral Johnson not liking the news. "Why would they strengthen their shields suddenly? They have gone centuries without any improvements in their weapons or shields."

"It may be our own fault," suggested Admiral Arnold Bennett, leaning forward and looking around the group. Bennett was in charge of the six shipyards orbiting New Tellus. "Over the last sixty years, we have engaged and destroyed twenty-four Hocklyn escort cruisers that have ventured close to our space. We have also sent hundreds of stealth scouts into their empire keeping an eye on their advance toward us. They may suspect something or someone is out here, and this may be part of that response."

Admiral Johnson tilted her head and spoke softly. "Let's just hope their shields are all that has changed. We can deal with that."

"We have another problem you need to be made aware of," Sayth commented with a deepening frown. "I spoke to Doctor Reynolds at Ceres earlier today, and the cryosleep units are starting to show signs of failure."

"They're failing?" Fleet Admiral Johnson spoke, her eyes focusing intently on Sayth. "What do you mean they're failing? I thought they were good for years yet. We need those people!"

"I don't mean the units are about to quit working, it's the people in them. Their bodies are starting to degrade."

"Admiral Streth and the others?" Admiral Johnson asked with deep concern in her voice, her eyes looking intently at the scientist. "Can they be saved?" She knew it would be a deep morale blow to the

Federation if Admiral Streth were to die. Everyone knew he had gone to sleep to be awakened in the future to lead them to victory over the Hocklyns.

"Doctor Reynolds is suggesting waking up all ninety-two people who are currently in cryosleep within the next two weeks," answered Sayth, recalling his brief conversation with the cryosleep specialist. No one's body has yet reached the point of no return."

"It's just as well," said Major Ackerman, entering the conversation and opening a thick folder he had brought with him. He was from military intelligence and his department was tasked with keeping track of the Hocklyn Slave Empire's advance. "From our latest reports and considering the events of today, I am afraid the Hocklyns are ahead of their projected time schedule to make contact with us."

"How far ahead?" asked Admiral Johnson, fearing the answer. They were not quite ready yet with all their preparations. She could feel her heart start to beat faster as she waited for the answer.

"Close to thirty years," Ackerman replied, his eyes focusing on the Fleet Admiral.

"That puts full contact at any time," Admiral Johnson responded, her face turning pale. "Why wasn't I told about this sooner?"

"We only became aware of it recently ourselves," Ackerman replied in a calm voice. "The latest reports from the stealth scouts indicate the Hocklyns are constructing some new forward bases that will be within easy striking distance of our space. You were to be briefed on these developments next week."

"Why did they build these new bases?' asked Admiral Johnson, feeling aggravated with military intelligence for not telling her sooner. She would have a word with their commanding officer once this meeting was over. "What does military intelligence believe the Hocklyns response will be to the destruction of these two cruisers?"

"They will undoubtedly send a fleet to investigate the disappearance of the ships that Commander Thomas destroyed today. We believe they have begun sending their ships out in groups of two in order to find out if there is a threat to their empire. That may also be the reason for the new bases we discovered. We should have been more careful in engaging their exploration ships in recent years. There is also the possibility that they have been able to partially detect some of our stealth scouts that have been operating in their space."

Admiral Johnson leaned back in her chair in deep thought, crossing her arms over her chest. None of this news was good. It looked as if the war they had been preparing for over the past few centuries was nearly upon them. Fortunately, her staff had already discussed plans as to what would have to be done in case the Hocklyns were to arrive early. She had several options available to her even though she was leaning toward a third, particularly since the people in cryosleep were to be awoken.

"I need to go to Earth and brief the Federation Council," she said after a moment. Then, turning to Major Ackerman, she asked in a serious tone, "How soon before this response fleet of the Hocklyns arrives once they realize that their two cruisers are missing?"

"I would need to talk to some of our strategists, but I would guess we have maybe three to four months."

Admiral Johnson nodded her head. "Very well then. I will suggest to the Federation Council that we go to a state of readiness for war and take the appropriate actions."

"That won't be very popular with all the Federation senators," commented Admiral Freeman, shaking his head.

"Only a couple," responded Admiral Johnson, knowing the two Freeman was talking about. "The rest will support us; they know what's at stake."

"Admiral Freeman, I want our stealth scouts searching all the nearby stars between us and the Hocklyns for any trace of a war fleet. Search all the way to known Hocklyn space if necessary. I also want to know where all of their new bases are and their estimated fleet strength!"

"I will send the order to Rear Admiral Stillson," Freeman replied with a nod. "He has over three hundred stealth scouts at his disposal."

"I want all of them out searching," stressed Admiral Jonson with narrowed eyes. "If the Hocklyns are out there, I want to find them!"

She then turned her attention to the shipyards. "Admiral Freeman, what is the current status of new construction in the shipyards here at New Tellus?"

Admiral Freeman glanced at a computer pad he had brought with him. "We have one fleet command Vanquisher class battleship, two Conqueror class battle cruisers, and two strike cruisers currently under construction in the main bays here," he replied. "We have an additional four light cruisers and six destroyers being constructed in the other shipyards."

Admiral Johnson leaned forward and spoke. "I want all shipyards prepared to go to full military production once I return from Earth. I also want all the repair bays brought to full standby."

"Why the repair bays?" asked Freeman, confused. "The only damaged ship we have is the Argyle."

"It's simple," Admiral Johnson replied, her eyes focusing on Admiral Freeman. "I am going to recommend to the Federation Council that the entire Ready Reserve Fleet be activated and updated."

The Ready Reserve Fleet were all the ships that had been deactivated in the past twenty years. The Inactive Reserve were ships deactivated from twenty to forty years. After that point, a ship was taken to the breakers to be disassembled and its parts or metal used for new construction.

"The Ready Reserve," repeated Admiral Bennett, surprised. "Why activate the Ready Reserve? Those ships are to be used to replace fleet losses that can't be made up by new construction in case of war."

"Because the Hocklyns are coming and we're not quite ready for them yet," Johnson replied, her eyes focusing on Admiral Bennett who was in charge of the New Tellus shipyards. "How long will it take to update all the ships in the reserve and have them ready for combat?"

Bennett leaned back and closed his eyes in thought. Leaning forward, he opened them and asked a question. "How long do I have?"

"Six months," Johnson replied, her eyes deadly serious. "That should be after the Hocklyn response fleet arrives and before they can launch a major attack our planets."

"Can I use all the shipyards in the Federation, including those in the Sol System?" He asked, looking over at Admiral Freeman and Fleet Admiral Johnson.

"I will have it approved by the Federation Council," Johnson promised. "They will agree to it once I tell them what I have planned."

"Very well," replied Bennett, knowing he had a herculean task ahead of him. "It will be close, but I think it can be done. Can I ask why?"

"Its simple," Admiral Karla Johnson replied with a mystifying smile. "Admiral Streth will need a fleet to command, and I am giving him the entire Ready Reserve."

"Admiral Streth!" several of the staff member spoke aloud, their eyes growing wide. Everyone knew of the legendary admiral and that he was waiting in cryosleep to lead them in the war against the Hocklyns.

"He will need a flagship," commented Admiral Freeman thoughtfully, his eyes focusing on the Fleet Admiral. "I don't think you want to give Admiral Streth a ten or twenty year old battle cruiser as his flagship."

"Of course not," Admiral Johnson replied with a nod, and then she smiled. "We have a new fleet command ship under construction here in our own bays. I intend to turn that ship over to Admiral Streth to act as his flagship."

Everyone was quiet. The fleet command ship was of a new design. It was a Vanquisher class battleship, the largest warship ever built by the Federation. It had originally been planned for use by Admiral Johnson to command the Federation Fleet.

"It's fitting," Admiral Freeman spoke in agreement after he thought it over. "He should have the best ship we have."

"A Vanquisher class battleship," Admiral Tolsen spoke, his eyes widening at the thought.

He could only imagine what it would be like to command a ship as powerful as this one was supposed to be. Some of the ship designers even claimed it could take on an AI ship and win. Tolsen wasn't so sure about that. The ship had not even been tested in combat as of yet.

"What name shall we give the new ship?" Freeman asked. It was only right that Admiral Streth be given the most powerful ship in the fleet as his flagship. If it wasn't for the admiral, none of them would be here.

Admiral Johnson smiled. She had already thought of the name. "We will name the ship after the most famous ship ever to serve in our fleet. The ship will be named the StarStrike!"

-

Two days later, Admiral Johnson gazed at the multiple viewscreens on the front wall of her flagship the Conqueror class battle cruiser Victory. They were approaching Earth and her meeting with the Federation Council. The Sol System was the only other system with defenses that compared to New Tellus. Karla knew that a big reason for that was due to Ceres being there. Ceres was where the Federation survivors had settled after fleeing Earth and the Spanish Flu. Currently over two million Federation citizens lived in the large manmade habitats inside the massive asteroid.

"We have Luna Control on communications," Commander Breeman reported as the communications officer began speaking with her counterpart.

On the main viewscreen, the view switched to show a small crater on the Moon's surface. The crater floor was covered with buildings and a dome that allowed Earth normal atmosphere. On the edge of the crater, massive weapon emplacements were visible. This was the venerated Fleet Academy where all Federation officers were trained. It had a marvelous history and Admiral Johnson's own remote relative, Greg Johnson, was a part of that.

There were four shipyards on the sensor screen, three in orbit around Earth and another truly massive one above the Moon. This was the only shipyard in the Federation that came even close to being as large as the primary shipyard above New Tellus.

Even as she watched the sensor screen, two Fleet destroyers made rendezvous with the Victory to serve as her escort to one of the shipyards above Earth. Any ship entering Earth orbit was escorted in. Johnson knew the same thing was done to any ship approaching Ceres. Security in the home system was taken extremely seriously.

Looking over at the holographic imager above the plotting table, she gazed speculatively at the twelve large violet icons that were in orbit above the Earth. These were gigantic battle stations, nearly three thousand meters in diameter. Unlike the asteroid fortresses around New Tellus, these monstrosities were constructed of metal. Equipped with numerous power beams, lasers, and heavy missiles it was hoped that battle stations of this size would be able to stop an AI vessel. After all, Earth, with her six billion people, was the most heavily populated planet in the Federation.

"The Federation President and council have been called into session and will be awaiting your appearance," Commander Breeman reported as he listened to a message over his mini-com from the communications officer. "There is a lot of speculation going around on the news channels about what's going on. Numerous rumors are being reported that Hocklyn vessels have been spotted in Federation space. Several news stations have already confirmed that two Hocklyn escort cruisers were destroyed above Caden's World."

"Rumors will always circulate," Admiral Johnson replied with a sigh as the Victory continued her approach to Earth. "It's not surprising that the news has already gotten out. It will be up to the council and the president as to what the media stations are told about the actual battle."

Looking around the Command Center, Karla thought about her decision to activate the Ready Reserve Fleet and turn it over to Admiral Streth. She needed to buy some time to get the Federation ready for war. She hoped that Admiral Streth could buy her that time.

A few hours later, Admiral Johnson entered the massive Human Federation of Worlds capitol building on Earth. An honor guard of twelve marines escorted her to the innermost sanctum where the president and the twenty-eight senators of the Federation Council were waiting. Entering the spacious conference room, Admiral Johnson noticed that all eyes instantly focused on her. The marine escort did not enter but returned to their previous duties.

"Admiral Johnson," President Kincaid spoke with a warm and friendly smile as he stood up. "I hope your trip from New Tellus was uneventful."

"It was, Sir," replied Karla, respectfully. She had known Alvin Kincaid back when he was a senator from Mars. He was a very astute politician and extremely popular with the people of the Federation.

"Have a seat, Admiral," President Kincaid said, indicating a chair next to him. "We have a lot to discuss today."

For the next hour, Karla answered questions about the StarSearch's engagement with the Hocklyns. Some of the questions were very pointed, asking for additional details and explanations. It became obvious that many of the senators were frightened as they realized that the war they had been preparing for all these years might have finally arrived.

"One thing that bothers me is that we attacked first!" Senator Fulbright from the Federation world of Serenity in the Epsilon Eridani system spoke with narrowed eyes. "Why did we not try to establish communications with the Hocklyns first? It has been nearly four hundred years since they destroyed the original Human Federation of Worlds; they could have changed since then. Unprovoked attacks like these will not help us to establish peaceful relations with their empire in the future."

"An empire of slaves," Admiral Johnson reminded him in a cold voice, her eyes turning toward the senator. "Slaves that routinely die in their service to the Hocklyn Slave Empire. Is that what you want for us, Senator?"

"Of course not," Senator Fulbright stammered, sounding flustered. "I just meant that if the Hocklyns knew they were up against a powerful military force they might chose the path of peace instead of war."

"I know you mean well, Marcus," interrupted President Kincaid, keeping his voice calm. "We have discussed this many times before. From everything we know, the Hocklyns have never allowed a planet to live outside of their rule. If the Hocklyns find themselves up against a technologically advanced planet that they cannot handle, the AIs are called in. The AI ships wiped out the original Human Federation of Worlds without losing a single ship. Do you want to see AI ships above Serenity?"

"No, of course not," Senator Fulbright replied, his eyes looking down.

He knew he had overstepped himself. He just didn't want to see his planet destroyed in a war they might not be able to win. He felt that every effort possible should be made to negotiate with the Hocklyns. "I just wish there were some way we could avoid this war."

"So do I, Marcus," President Kincaid replied in a softer voice. "War is a horrible thing. We all would like to avoid it if possible."

"Do you believe war is inevitable, Admiral?" Senator Malle of Mars asked. "Is it coming soon?"

The room became very quiet. A chair squeaked as one of the senators leaned forward to hear Admiral Johnson's response.

"War is coming," she uttered as her eyes swept over the Federation senators. "We can't avoid it; all we can do is be prepared. Our best experts predict full scale war with the Hocklyns within eighteen months."

"Eighteen months!" Senator Fulbright moaned in shock. "We're all going to die!"

"Control yourself, Senator," admonished President Kincaid, his eyes focusing on the senator from Serenity. "We're not all going to die. The Fleet will protect us."

"Admiral, what are your plans to protect us from the Hocklyns?" asked Senator Anderson of Earth, shaking his head in disgust at Senator Fulbright's outburst. "Surely the Hocklyns will come searching for their missing ships, and when they do they will find the Federation."

"We believe that they will come," confirmed Karla, mentally preparing to try to sell her idea of activating the Ready Reserve Fleet to the council. "I have a plan that may give us some additional time. It's risky, but I believe it holds a great chance for success."

For the next two hours, she described in detail what she wanted to do and a general timeline. Many of the senators asked questions and requested additional information. Some of the information had to be sent for, but at the end of the meeting everyone seemed satisfied.

"It's a daring plan you have come up with," President Kincaid said at last as he took in a deep, steadying breath. "If we don't do as you suggest how soon before we see major engagements with the Hocklyn fleet in our own space?"

Federation space was considered to be all the space within thirty light years of Earth. Inside of that space were ten inhabited solar systems and over thirty additional systems with mining operations.

"As I mentioned earlier, our Intelligence analysts estimate we will see major engagement with Hocklyn forces within eighteen months if we wait and do nothing. If we do as I suggest we may be able to delay this for several years. That will give us the time we need to finish our war preparations."

This statement brought a look of worry, and even fear, to the faces of a number of the senators. Several took to talking to each other in subdued voices.

"Then we have no choice," commented President Kincaid, standing up and looking grimly around at the gathered senators. "I propose that we approve the activation of the Ready Reserve Fleet and turn it over to Admiral Streth. I propose we also place the Federation on a war footing in preparation for war with the Hocklyn Slave Empire."

Senator Anderson of Earth stood and was recognized by the president.

"Four hundred years ago the Federation warship Avenger crashed upon the moon of Earth and the Federation survivors settled inside Ceres. We have known for nearly two hundred and fifty years that this was in our future."

"The Hocklyns will show no mercy," Senator Barnes from Ceres reminded everyone. He looked slowly around the room. "We either fight or we die."

"Well spoken," Senator Anderson said, nodding at the senator. "The survivors from the original Federation of Worlds know full well what the danger is. I ask that we approve by acclamation the two motions put forth by Admiral Johnson and the president. This war has finally come to our doorstep, and we cannot avoid it. Let us take the appropriate actions to protect the new Federation and its citizens."

The vote was held and easily passed. Out of the twenty-eight senators, only two voted against it, both from Serenity.

President Kincaid nodded as the paperwork was prepared. The two resolutions would be signed by all the approving senators as well as by him.

Turning to Admiral Johnson, President Kincaid spoke. "Go to Ceres and awaken Admiral Streth and his people. You have the support of the Federation Council and myself to initiate a First Strike against the Hocklyn Slave Empire.

Chapter Three

In Hocklyn space, Fleet Commodore Resmunt gazed at the detailed map of the galaxy hanging on his office wall. Four colors dominated the map, each one representing one of the four races that controlled their particular section of the galaxy. In the center was an area nearly ten thousand light years across with no color that was controlled by the AIs. Commodore Resmunt did not let his thoughts dwell on the masters.

In recent years, the color representing the Hocklyn Slave Empire had slowed down its rapid expansion in this sector of space. Exploration escort cruisers had been vanishing in unusual numbers. A few times the destroyed remnants of the ships had been found, but nothing else. Several Hocklyn scientists had suggested defective self-destructs might be to blame, but an exhaustive inspection of countless Hocklyn ships had not indicated any type of problem with the nuclear charges.

Countless star systems had reported ghost sensor readings on their long-range sensors. Ships had been sent to investigate, but nothing had ever been found. Normally this would be discounted as mechanical errors, but the excessive number worried the Hocklyn High Council. Hence, Fleet Commodore Resmunt had been sent to the front of this sector where the mysterious sensor readings were the highest. He was known for being cautious as well as being one of the best, if not the best, Fleet Commodore the Hocklyns had. He had also ordered the construction of six new fleet bases to give him a powerful fleet asset to further explore this troublesome area.

Resmunt turned around and gazed coldly at the four War Leaders that were standing in the center of the room, waiting for his orders. "Progress in this sector has almost stopped," he grated out in a rasping voice, his large eyes narrowing dangerously. "Under my orders our exploration escort cruisers are now working in groups of two when they jump into unexplored systems. There are currently twenty groups out exploring the edge of this quadrant, which we believe may be near a large high tech civilization that has been destroying our escort cruisers for years."

"If it is a high tech civilization, then much honor could await us in combat," War Leader Bisth spoke in a hard voice. "We have had few opportunities for honor in recent years!"

"We have found many new civilizations, but all have been primitive or agricultural; only a few have advanced enough to fly to the stars. Those few were weak and easily conquered," War Leader Sangeth added. He craved for combat against an enemy that would allow him to increase his family's wealth and honor. He folded his powerful arms across the light armor that he wore.

Sangeth had been involved in conquering one of those space faring civilizations. It had only taken a few ships to conquer their foe, and the civilization's ships had been weak and easily destroyed in combat. Honor had been achieved in bringing new worlds to the Hocklyn Empire, but little personal honor had been found in battle.

Fleet Commodore Resmunt walked over to the window and gazed out at the massive spaceport below him. His office was in a high tower that looked out over the extensive works of concrete and steel. Thousands of slaves toiled upon the spaceport, expanding it and preparing it for what Resmunt thought was potentially in their future.

He had chosen a hospitable world to build his fleet base upon. Too often Hocklyn leaders chose hazardous worlds to build upon to help control their slaves. Resmunt had gone against that, it was troublesome to have to continuously replace dead or useless slaves because they couldn't survive the harsh conditions prevalent on some worlds.

This world was pleasant and reminded Resmunt of what the home worlds must once have been like. It was ninety percent water, and his fleet base was being built upon the largest land mass. The small continent was only six hundred kilometers across, but it would do for the base.

Up in orbit a shipyard was being prepared which would be capable of repairing any seriously damaged ships. The Hocklyn High Council had questioned this decision, but Resmunt had reminded them that if they did indeed face a serious threat he must be able to repair his warships. The High Council had reluctantly agreed.

"The exploration cruisers I have sent out will scout twenty systems each and then return," Resmunt informed the War Leaders as he gazed out at the base. "If any of the twenty groups fails to return, two of your fleets will be sent to investigate. The two fleets will stay separated by one jump in case the first falls into a trap. While achieving honor is important, getting word back as to what is out there is even more so. The High Council agrees, and no honor will be lost if a fleet returns in order to bring back information as to the enemy we are facing."

The four War Leaders looked uneasily at each other. None were pleased with this news. Achieving honor was the goal of every Hocklyn warrior.

"I have chosen you four War Leaders for a reason," Resmunt continued as he watched a shuttle come in for a landing at the spaceport. "You are known for your tactical abilities as well as for following orders. If we are indeed facing a dangerous enemy, I have no intention of losing ships needlessly."

"Then we are to retreat in the face of the enemy if they are more powerful," Bisth spoke as he thought this surprising concept over.

"I don't believe there is an enemy out there with ships more powerful than ours," War Leader Sangeth voiced in his rasping tone, his eyes holding back rage at the thought of retreating in the face of an inferior enemy. In normal times, this would result in a massive loss of honor.

Resmunt turned and gazed coldly at the four War Leaders, then spoke, "If anyone fails to do as I have just ordered, then you will indeed lose honor. The Hocklyn High Council feels there is a high tech civilization out there that may be a direct threat to us. Once it's detected, we will launch a full scale attack to bring it under our control." He paused and gazed back at one of the walls. On it was a horrendous and frightening ship. It was a sphere fifteen hundred meters in diameter with constructions all over its surface. It was an AI ship.

"If we fail to bring this civilization into the empire, then the AIs will destroy it, and there will be no honor for any of us. I will not have any of your throw your ships away pointlessly. The High Council has given me complete control over this sector of space. There will be no loss of honor unless I say so!"

"Then we will do as you order," Bisth replied in a neutral voice. He would decide on his own when the time came whether he should retreat in the face of the enemy. "There will be honor for all of us when we meet this new alien race in actual combat."

"Honor shall be ours," repeated the other three War Leaders.

Resmunt dismissed the four and then returned to stand in front of the map of the galaxy. Under his orders, five additional fleet bases were being built. While not as large as this one, they would allow him to launch a large and coordinated attack against any opponent. Each would have a full battle fleet assigned to it. He was confident he would be able to subdue this mysterious race that had been troubling them for so many years. His victory would bring much honor to him and limitless wealth to his family.

–

Later, up in orbit, War Leader Bisth entered the War Room of his dreadnought the WarCry. The 1,200-meter ship was ready for war, and he hoped that was what was in their future. He had come to this posting to gather honor and wealth for his family, not to spend his time orbiting this useless planet.

"Gresth," spoke Bisth, going over to his First Leader. "We may be seeing combat soon, and I want all ships of the fleet made ready. See that the latest equipment and weapons are installed, particularly the new shield update. We may soon face a very powerful enemy, and I want this fleet to bring honor home in victory."

"It will be done, War Leader," Gresth replied with a slight bow of his head. "I will have the engineers going over every component of the fleet. If it comes to battle, we will be ready. Honor has been long in coming."

Bisth nodded and went over to stand on the command pedestal. He looked up at the sensors that showed his fleet in orbit as well as the other three attack fleets. His flagship, the dreadnought WarCry, was a new ship built in the past year. In support, he had one other dreadnought, six war cruisers, and sixteen escort cruisers. Each of the other three fleets was made up similarly. It was a very powerful force that had been gathered a force capable of crushing any enemy.

–

Fleet Admiral Johnson was in a destroyer that was taking her to Ceres. The area around Ceres was surrounded with defensive satellites as well as numerous weapon emplacements imbedded on small asteroids. There were only a few safe zones a ship could travel to reach the massive home of the Federation survivors.

"Ceres is asking for our ship ID code," reported Commander Grayson, glancing over at Fleet Admiral Johnson. He felt nervous at having the Fleet Admiral aboard the Sydney. He had seen her before from a distance but had never actually spoken to the admiral.

"That's routine for Ceres since we have gone to a heightened state of alert," Admiral Johnson assured him with a slight smile. "At the moment, I imagine we have over one hundred weapons focused on us."

Captain Grayson turned pale, realizing how quickly his small destroyer could be destroyed. The Sydney had made numerous runs to Ceres before, but he had never known just how many weapons had been focused on his ship.

"Don't worry, Commander," replied Admiral Johnson, allowing a larger smile to show on her face. "They focus weapons on everyone."

"I guess I would be slightly paranoid too if all of my home worlds had been destroyed," Grayson spoke with a nod of his head.

"The Federation survivors have lived and worked for one thing only for the past four hundred years, and that's to defeat the Hocklyns and save the human race. That's taught in their schools and in their daily life," explained Admiral Johnson.

On the main viewscreen, the 950-kilometer asteroid was rapidly growing larger. Ceres was a dwarf planet with a human population of two million. The Federation survivors had carved out massive habitats inside the asteroid where Earth normal environments had been established. Some of these habitats were tens of kilometers in length and held large cities.

"I have four fighters closing on our position," the sensor operator reported. "They will be in range in forty seconds."

"Our welcoming committee," explained Admiral Johnson pleased with the rapid response of the fighters. "They will escort us in."

Commander Grayson nodded. This would be the first time his ship had been escorted in to Ceres. The Federation survivors were definitely taking this increased alert seriously.

Karla knew that there were over two thousand fighters based on Ceres as well as twelve hundred bombers. That didn't include the numerous warships that were being kept inside its massive ship bays. She also knew there were six light cruisers in orbit that could engage any enemy ship that got past the defenses. Karla doubted that anything could get past those massed weapon systems in one piece. Ceres itself was covered with numerous laser and power beam sites as well as hundreds of missile launching platforms.

"We're being instructed to land in ship bay seventeen," the communications officer reported with surprise on her face. Normally when they came to Ceres, they used shuttles to ferry supplies or people down to the asteroid.

"This is different," Commander Grayson murmured, looking over at Admiral Johnson. "We've never docked inside Ceres before."

"Just have your helm officer follow the beacon," Admiral Johnson suggested. "It will take you straight to a berthing dock. I think you will find this quite interesting."

As they neared Ceres, a large hatch slid open and blinking lights surrounding it came on. The helm officer turned control of the ship over to the navigation computer, which was now being controlled by Ceres Docking Control. The ship slowed down, entered the cavernous open hatch, and then proceeded down a long, brightly lit tunnel. Behind them, the hatch door slid shut, sealing them in. After a few minutes, they approached another hatch, which slid open and allowed the ship into the cavernous docking bay.

Commander Grayson's eyes grew wide as he looked at what was in the bay. There were two Conqueror class battle cruisers lying side by side in two massive berthing docks looking as if they had just rolled off the construction line. Next to the 1,200-meter battle cruisers, the 400-meter Sydney looked like a minnow.

"How many ships do they have in these docking bays?" asked Commander Grayson, looking with high interest at the main viewscreen and the large warships.

"That's classified," Admiral Johnson commented. "Even I am unsure of the exact total, and I'm the Fleet Admiral. I do know that they have forty- seven of these large docking bays inside Ceres."

The Sydney was maneuvered over to a small docking berth and settled down. Commander Grayson felt uneasy as this was the first time his ship had ever been out of space. Destroyers were built to be able to land on the surface of a planet, but he had never done so.

"There is a normal atmosphere out there as well as gravity," the sensor operator reported.

"Ceres Control says we can disembark at any time," the communications officer added.

"If you would like, Commander," spoke Karla, glancing over at Grayson, "I would be glad to arrange for you and your crew to be taken on a tour of the asteroid. I think you will find it highly enlightening."

"I would appreciate that, Admiral," Grayson replied with an excited nod.

He had never been inside Ceres before, and he thought it would be a great morale booster if he and his crew could take a tour, particularly of the habitats deep inside. He had been told that they were a remarkable sight and an incredible feat of engineering.

A few minutes later, Admiral Johnson walked down the long ramp that connected the Sydney to the floor of the bay where a group of Fleet officers were waiting.

"Fleet Admiral," Admiral Teleck spoke in greeting. "I am glad that you could come to Ceres for the awakening." Admiral Teleck was the highest-ranking fleet officer on Ceres and in command of the Ceres Fleet.

"Has it begun yet?" Karla asked with keen interest.

She wanted to be present when Admiral Streth woke up from his long sleep. He was a legend among the Federation survivors, and that legend had been passed on to the humans of Earth as they had expanded to the stars. This was a day that had long been looked forward to.

"Yes, Admiral Streth should be awake in the morning," Admiral Teleck responded, his voice expressing the excitement he felt at getting to speak and meet the legendary admiral. "Doctor Reynolds is supervising his awakening and several others personally. She doesn't expect there to be any problems."

"How soon before we can expect Admiral Streth to be able to perform his duties? Will there be any after affects from the long cryosleep?"

"Doctor Reynolds does not expect any," Admiral Teleck responded. "She thinks it will take one to two weeks before the sleepers are up and around. Within four weeks, they should be physically sound enough to return to active duty with some constraints."

"That's good to hear," responded Admiral Johnson, feeling relieved. "Is there somewhere we can talk? I have made a decision about Admiral Streth and what I would like him to do in the war. Since he is so close to the Federation survivors, I feel it's only right that you know the mission I have chosen for him."

"May I call in my staff?" asked Admiral Teleck, feeling curious about this mission.

He knew that the Federation survivors would be furious if Admiral Johnson had chosen a mission that was too dangerous; the life of Admiral Streth had to be protected. Many felt he was the best hope of defeating the Hocklyns. He had done it before, and many felt he could do it again.

"Yes, that would be fine," replied Admiral Johnson with a nod. "Also, would you mind arranging for the crew of the Sydney to be taken on a tour of Ceres? Most of them have never been here before."

"No problem," grinned Admiral Teleck. He always enjoyed being able to show off to the rest of the Federation what they had built inside the massive asteroid. "I will make arrangements for them to have accommodations at one of the resorts in the Aquarius habitat."

"That would be great," responded Admiral Johnson pleased with Teleck's response. Each one of the habitats inside of Ceres was named after one of the former Federation worlds the Hocklyns had destroyed. "We will be staying here for a number of days. There is a lot of planning that needs to be done."

A few hours later, they were deep inside Ceres in a secure conference room. Admiral Teleck had sent for his entire staff as well as the head of the civilian government. Governor Malleck was the current elected government leader of Ceres and a very astute politician.

Once everyone was seated and introduced, Admiral Johnson began going over her plan for a first strike against the Hocklyns. To say Admiral Teleck and his staff were surprised would be putting it mildly. When Karla was finished, she looked around at the group waiting for their response. She knew if she could not get the backing of the Federation survivors, the plan would have no chance of succeeding.

"That's a bold plan," commented Admiral Teleck, leaning back and drumming his right index finger on the conference table. He took a deep breath as he looked around the room at his staff and Governor Malleck. "It's one we have never discussed, taking the fight to the Hocklyns at this stage. I have always thought the plan was to lure them into attacking New Tellus and allowing the asteroid fortresses to annihilate their fleet."

"We still may," responded Karla, nodding her head. "It's just that they're so far ahead of their timeline, and we still have a lot to do in the Federation before we are ready to engage them here. This will set the Hocklyns back and put them on the defensive if it succeeds, at least for a while. It will give us the time we need to put the Federation on a war footing and finish our defenses. Later, when they mount a major attack, we can use New Tellus to cut them down to size."

"You say you will be turning over to Admiral Streth the entire Ready Reserve Fleet?" asked Admiral Kalen, looking curiously at a computer pad in front of him. "Just how many ships are we talking about?" Admiral Kalen was responsible for the upkeep of the fleet units based inside of Ceres.

"The life of Admiral Streth is very important to us," Governor Malleck added in a grave tone of voice. He looked directly at the Fleet Admiral and continued. "Admiral Streth may well be the best admiral we have for this type of daring operation, but we must be sure he has the assets to ensure its success. We won't risk his life needlessly."

Admiral Johnson nodded, activating her own computer pad and calling up the numbers of the Ready Reserve. She had updated this prior to leaving New Tellus Station. "It will be a massive fleet," replied Karla, allowing her eyes to look across the group. "This will be a general attack over a large area of space in an effort to drive the Hocklyns back hundreds of light years. We may even free a number of slave worlds they have conquered."

"Hundreds of light years?" Kalen spoke in surprise, his eyes growing very wide at the thought. To the best of his knowledge, no one had ever attacked the Hocklyn Empire like this before.

"That's all well and good, but the Hocklyns have a massive fleet as well," Colonel Grissim pointed out. She was in charge of Ceres's military intelligence division. "Even at the best estimates, we may still be outnumbered by a hundred or a thousand to one if they ever call in all of their forces, and that does not include the AIs."

Everyone was silent for a moment as they thought about the mysterious AIs that controlled the galaxy-spanning Slave Empire. They were still the wild card in all of their planning as no one knew exactly what type of weapons the AIs could bring to bear or the number of ships they had at their disposal.

"We will deal with the AIs when we encounter them," Karla replied in a firm voice. "We believe our new power beams and the new Devastator Three missiles may be able to take them out; we won't know until we have a chance to engage them. Our new strike cruisers have been designed just for that purpose."

"As you said, we will deal with the AIs when they make an appearance," Admiral Kalen said in agreement, focusing his attention on the Fleet Admiral. "Let's just hope that's not too soon. Now, how large is the Ready Reserve Fleet you're turning over to Admiral Streth?"

Karla pressed an icon on her computer pad and the numbers came up. "There are twenty-four Conqueror class battle cruisers, twenty-four Galaxy class battle carriers, forty-eight Monarch heavy cruisers, one hundred and twenty light cruisers, and one hundred and forty destroyers."

"That's a sizable fleet," Governor Malleck commented. Then his eyes narrowed. "But most of those ships are close to twenty years old! I don't know if I feel comfortable putting Admiral Streth in a Conqueror class battle cruiser with paint peeling off its hull."

"I agree," said Colonel Grissim, shaking her head disapprovingly. "I realize that a ten to twenty year old battle cruiser is a still powerful ship, but I would like Admiral Streth's flagship to be one of our newer models."

"We would be willing to provide a suitable flagship," Admiral Telleck volunteered. He thought that one of the newer Conqueror class battle cruisers would be more suitable; they had several that had been completed in the massive construction bays of Ceres in just the past year.

Admiral Johnson allowed a fleeting smile to cross her face. "I never said we weren't sending any new ships. Admiral Streth's flagship will be the new Vanquisher class battleship that is currently under construction at New Tellus Station. We will also be sending two new Conqueror class battle cruisers, two new Galaxy class battle carriers, four of the new Monarch heavy cruisers and eight of our new strike cruisers as support ships for the StarStrike."

"The StarStrike!" Admiral Teleck spoke in a stunned voice, his eyes widening at hearing the name of the ship.

"Yes, the StarStrike," repeated Karla, grinning. Then, with an even larger smile, "What other name could we choose for Admiral Streth's flagship?"

-

Admiral Streth opened his eyes and, for a moment, everything looked white, then his eyes began to focus and he started seeing colors. "Be patient, Admiral," a woman's gentle voice spoke close to his head. "Your eyesight should return shortly."

Gradually the room came into focus, and Hedon began to make out objects around him. "How long?" he managed to croak out, realizing that his throat felt parched. "Water."

"Here, drink this," the woman doctor next to him said, handing him a glass.

He reached up and had trouble holding it, so she helped him as he took a couple of swallows. Then, laying his head back down on the pillow, he looked at the doctor inquiringly.

"I am Doctor Evelyn Reynolds, and I am in charge of the cryosleep units here on Ceres."

"Why have I been awakened?" asked Hedon surprised at how weak he felt. Comparing this to the last time he had been awoken he realized that a very long time must have passed.

Doctor Reynolds looked at Admiral Streth and then replied in a calm and extremely respectful voice. "It's been nearly two hundred and seventy years since your last awakening, and it is time to fight the Hocklyns."

Admiral Streth gazed curiously at this new admiral who wore the rank of Fleet Admiral. Hedon wondered briefly how that was going to work as he also wore the same rank.

They were seated in a small conference room. Hedon had insisted the meeting be held somewhere else besides his hospital room. He also felt better being dressed in his fleet uniform; it made everything seem more familiar and easier to accept.

Two orderlies had helped him walk to the meeting room, which was inside the hospital. He still was aggravated at how weak he felt. He didn't like feeling helpless and having to depend so much on others to do simple tasks. He had even needed help just to put his uniform on! Doctor Reynolds had assured him that he would recover rapidly and had proceeded to describe the physical therapy he would be undergoing for the next few weeks.

"Hello, Fleet Admiral," began Karla, feeling awe at whom she was speaking to. "I am Fleet Admiral Karla Johnson, of Earth."

"Johnson," repeated Hedon, feeling curious and looking thoughtful as a memory tugged at the back of his mind. "Any relation to Greg Johnson of the New Beginning's mission?"

"Yes, Sir," replied Karla pleased that the admiral remembered Greg. "He was one of my ancestors."

"A good man," responded Hedon, recalling Greg and the time he had spent with him and his friend, Jason Strong.

They had traveled to New Tellus together. It was sad to realize they both had died long ago. So many friends and associates had decided not to go into cryosleep but had stayed awake instead to help build Ceres. This included his brother and his brother's wife Lendle. Hedon let out a long sigh, knowing that an important part of his life had been left forever in the past.

"Doctor Reynolds says it's time to fight the Hocklyns," Hedon finally spoke, his eyes looking over at the Fleet Admiral. "I assume you have a mission for me and that is why I have been awakened? Are any of the others being brought out of cryosleep?"

"Yes, Admiral, all of them," replied Karla as she began to explain the current situation and what had happened in the Gliese 667C system.

Hedon listened patiently as Admiral Johnson briefed him on the current status of the new Federation of Human Worlds and the task she had set for him. His eyes widened as she described the fleet she was placing under his command and what she wanted him to do with it.

"You may choose the admirals to command the separate task forces," she finally finished. "We need you to buy us the time we need to ramp up our fleet production and to finish our defenses."

"How much time are we talking about?" Hedon asked as he thought over what the Fleet Admiral was suggesting. He was already starting to feel tired and knew he would need to return to his room shortly.

"Two years," responded Admiral Johnson in a grave tone. She could see the weary and tired look in the admiral's eyes and knew she needed to allow him to return to his room to rest. Karla hoped she that Admiral Streth understood the importance of what she was asking him to do. "The Hocklyns are thirty years ahead of schedule, so some of our plans have to be rushed. We can do it; we just need a little more time."

Hedon was quiet for a moment. He knew he had a lot of questions he needed to ask, but those could wait until later after he had recovered more and his mind was sharper and not so full of drugs. "If you need two years, I will give them to you," replied Hedon confidently, his eyes widening in determination. "I agree with your plan to take the fight to the Hocklyns; I think it is a wise and good tactical decision." Hedon leaned back and knew it was time to return to his room. He just needed time to rest and figure out how to accomplish what the Fleet Admiral wanted.

-

Amanda opened her eyes and waited for her eyesight to return. She could sense someone else in the room with her. "Who's there?" she managed to ask. "Richard?"

"Relax, Colonel Sheen," a friendly woman's voice spoke. "I am Doctor Reynolds, and I am overseeing your awakening from cryosleep. Your husband, Major Richard Andrews, is also in the process of being awakened. You are both fine, and you should be able to see him later today."

Amanda's vision quickly returned, and she could see she was in some type of hospital room. "Is it time?" she asked, turning her head and looking directly at the woman doctor standing next to the bed."

Doctor Reynolds knew exactly what Colonel Sheen was referring to. "Yes, it's time. Admiral Streth and all the rest of you that have been in cryosleep are being awakened. It is time to fight the Hocklyns."

Amanda closed her eyes. She was glad to hear that Richard and the others were okay. It also pleased her greatly to hear that the time to finally confront the Hocklyns was at hand. She just hoped that Earth and Ceres were ready.

-

Jeremy opened his eyes and lay there quietly. He could hear noises around him as if someone was moving. Where am I, he thought? The last thing he remembered was going into cryosleep. Kelsey, Angela, Kevin, and he had all opted to go into cryosleep and fight the Hocklyns in the future. Jeremy had spent six years as an officer on a Federation light cruiser, rising to the position of executive officer before the four of them had volunteered for cryosleep. It had been a difficult decision for all of them to leave their families behind, but they had all felt it was what they needed to do.

During part of Jeremy's tour on the light cruiser, Kelsey had been on board as the lead Navigation Officer. The four had finally gotten together and decided on this course of action. The important thing was that they would be together and could bring justice to the Hocklyns for the forced destruction of the New Horizon. It was something that had haunted them throughout their careers.

"Is it time?" he asked in a dry voice.

"Yes, Major Strong," a woman's voice spoke from his side. "It's time."

-

Admiral Johnson left Major Strong's room, deeply moved by the things she had witnessed during the day. Almost every single sleeper had asked the same question. "Was it time to fight the Hocklyns?" They all seemed anxious to go into battle.

"What do you think?" Admiral Teleck asked as they sat back down in a small conference room to discuss the day's events.

"It's been an eye opening day," confessed Karla. "Meeting Admiral Streth and knowing some of the other sleepers and their ancestry was remarkable. I just spoke to Major Jeremy Strong, his father was Admiral Jason Strong who discovered the Avenger and built the Fleet Academy on the Moon. Jeremy and his three fellow officers that went into cryosleep together were the only survivors of the New Horizon mission, Earth's first FTL capable spaceship. It's the same with the other sleepers, Colonel Amanda Sheen, her husband Major Richard Andrews, and all the others. It's like reading a history book."

"They're all fine people, and they believe in our cause," spoke Admiral Teleck, softly. "They are the backbone of the Fleet."

Karla nodded in agreement. "With people like them, the Hocklyns had better be prepared. I have a feeling Admiral Streth and the others are getting ready to give the Hocklyns their first ever ass kicking."

"I agree," Admiral Teleck responded with a pleased smile. "History will long remember today as the true beginning of our war against the Hocklyn Slave Empire."

Chapter Four

It had been two weeks since Jeremy had awoken from cryosleep. For both of those weeks, he had gone through constant physical and mental therapy to help him adjust to his new surroundings. When he felt he was ready, he had put in a request to be allowed to return home. He was currently standing at the top of the high rim above the crater that contained the Fleet Academy on the Moon. From this location, his father had first set his eyes upon the crashed Federation light cruiser Avenger and set history in motion.

"It's hard to believe that's the Fleet Academy," Kelsey spoke from Jeremy's side, gazing down at the crater and the multitude of buildings. Some were truly massive, jutting up over thirty stories from the lunar surface.

"It's still even more amazing that we're standing out here without spacesuits," added Jeremy, turning to gaze around him.

An artificial dome covered the entire crater and the immediate area next to it. There was even a scattering of greenery around the Fleet Academy where grass and trees had been planted. From their high location above the crater, people could be seen out walking, going from building to building or just out for a casual afternoon stroll. Outside the dome, Jeremy could see weapon turrets and other emplacements on the dark, desolate surface, a stark reminder as to why the Fleet Academy was here.

"This memorial does great service to your father," spoke Kevin, respectfully.

He was standing in front of a large granite obelisk that towered nearly ten meters above him. On its face were depicted two men, Admiral Jason Strong and Greg Johnson.

A short inscription read, "From this site, men from the planet Earth first gazed upon the Avenger. This discovery sent the human race to the stars."

"The academy has grown so large," added Angela, feeling awe at all that had been done.

There was very little resemblance to the old academy she was so familiar with. From what they had been told, the academy now graduated nearly one thousand Fleet officers every year. Angela was dressed in a dark blue fleet uniform with the rank of lieutenant.

All four of them had found that they had a lot of adjusting to do; everyone they had known and grown up with were gone. It was a new day and age, and the war with the Hocklyns was nearing. They had been allowed to leave Ceres as part of their mental therapy that Doctor Reynolds was closely monitoring. She had thought it would be good for all four of them to make this trip.

"My father and mother left a number of recordings for me," Kelsey said quietly, feeling a tear form in her eye. "It's strange to hear their voices after all of this time and know I will never see them again."

"We were all left messages," Jeremy replied in understanding, knowing how she was feeling.

He had listened to several from his mother and father. He had been immensely pleased to learn that his younger brother had gone on to serve in the Fleet and had done quite well. His parents had continued their mission to bring Earth up to Federation levels of living and science, and then finally they had introduced the Federation survivors to the world. He had watched a short video of that historic announcement.

"What now?" asked Kevin, turning to glance over at Jeremy.

"We're going to spend a few days down on Earth and then report back to Ceres," answered Jeremy, looking over at his close friend. "Perhaps we can find out what our assignments will be."

"I hope we can all stay together," Angela said with a brief sigh. "I don't know what I would do if they were to split us up." She was also ready to go down and visit Earth.

They were going to visit the sites where Kevin and Angela's parents were buried. Doctor Reynolds had felt this would be a good form of closure. Jeremy's own father and mother were interned on the far side of the obelisk, as well as a few others who had been important during those early days.

Jeremy took one last look at the headstone that marked his parent's final resting place and then started down the slope toward the Fleet Academy. A set of wide stairs had been cut into the slope to make access to the obelisk easy. Every student at the academy was required to make the trip to the obelisk at least once since it was an important part of their history.

-

On Ceres, Admiral Streth was meeting with a group of officers to discuss the command makeup of his attack force. He understood from talking to Fleet Admiral Johnson that the entire Ready Reserve was in the process of being updated and fully modernized and should be ready for combat in less than six months. That was when he would launch his attack.

"A first strike against the Hocklyns," Colonel Sheen spoke, her eyes looking thoughtful. "Can it succeed?" She had never considered such a possibility.

"They are giving us over three hundred and seventy warships to mount the attack," Admiral Streth pointed out. "That's more ships than our Federation had when the Hocklyns originally found us. Not only that but these ships are much more powerful with stronger weapons and greatly enhanced energy screens."

Hedon had spent some time reviewing the specs of the ships in the Ready Reserve and had been a little surprised to see that the Federation had gone back to using railguns. Granted, they were much more powerful and cycled faster than the old ones, but they were still railguns. Admiral Teleck had explained that they had experimented with other weapon systems in the past, but railguns were unbelievably reliable and still capable of causing a lot of damage.

"It sounds like a lot," Major Andrews commented from where he was sitting next to his wife. "But we know the Hocklyns possess a massive fleet of their own; a fleet that numbers in the thousands. At some point in time, we will be facing them as well as the AIs."

"I like the idea of us attacking them," spoke Commander Adler, leaning forward in thought. "It is something they won't be expecting and may give us a significant tactical advantage, at least for a while."

Commander Adler and his executive officer Major Timmons, formerly of the battle carrier Victory and First Fleet, had gone into cryosleep to be part of the future war with the Hocklyns. They had both been surprised and then excited at the idea of Operation First Strike.

"We will have the element of surprise," agreed Hedon, nodding at Adler with a vengeful smile on his face. It was good to see some familiar faces in the room. "If we time our attacks properly, we can drive them back hundreds of light years and free some of their slave worlds in the process."

"Military Intelligence agrees," Colonel Grissim added with a nod of her head. "The Hocklyns have almost always had the upper hand in their conquests, and to the best of our knowledge no one has ever attacked them first. They won't be expecting it."

"What about allies?" asked Amanda, looking over at Admiral Kalen who was also in the meeting. "Surely, in all of these years, you have found a few?"

"You would be surprised," commented Kalen, shaking his head sadly. "There are a number of civilizations within four hundred light years of us, but most are not highly developed. It seems that a lot of civilizations stagnate in the late agricultural age. Their development seems to slow and most of their progress surrounds agriculture and making their lives more bearable. There is no desire or drive to go out and explore beyond their planet."

"So we have no allies?" stated Admiral Streth, feeling disappointed. He would have thought after all of this time there would be at least a few.

Admiral Kalen looked at the group and then continued. "We do have four races we have encountered in our explorations that are highly developed. Three agreed to aid us in the war against the Hocklyns once we showed them what the Hocklyns would do to their worlds. They have built up sizable war fleets and have been tasked with securing their sectors of space against Hocklyn aggression. This will help to defend our flanks as well as force the Hocklyns to spread their forces."

"You said there were four advanced races," Richard pointed out, his eyes focusing on Admiral Kalen. "What about the fourth one?"

"The Albanians," muttered Kalen with a heavy frown creasing his forehead. He let out a deep frustrated sigh. "They are a mystery to us. The race is highly developed, and in many areas their science is far ahead of ours, but they are refusing to get involved. They will not aid us in the war."

"Why not?" asked Admiral Streth, arching his eyebrows. "Don't they understand the threat the Hocklyns represent?"

"They understand, but they believe they can talk to the Hocklyns and avoid bloodshed. They don't believe in war."

"Then they are fools!" Commander Adler spoke, his eyes growing wide. "The Hocklyns will either conquer them or destroy them."

"How many systems do they control?" asked Amanda, shaking her head in disbelief and agreeing with Commander Adler. The Hocklyns would show no mercy to this strange race.

"They have sixteen large colonies in addition to a heavily populated home system. They have research installations and mining operations in at least fifty other star systems," replied Kalen, recalling the latest security report on the Albanians. "They have also refused to share any of their advanced technology with us even though we do have a trade agreement on non technological items."

"We have stressed how important some of their technology could be to us in the war," Colonel Grissim added with a heavy frown. "But they don't want to share anything with us that could be used for military purposes. They have been very clear about that in our negotiations with them."

"They're bigger than the Federation," said Amanda, letting out a deep breath as she thought about how powerful an ally the Albanians could be. "They could be a huge asset to the war effort."

"They have no armed ships at all?" asked Richard not believing that a race that advanced could be completely defenseless.

"That is unknown," Admiral Kalen said, leaning forward. "Our military intelligence people believe they must have a small fleet of armed ships to protect their space from potential invaders even though we have never seen one. We still have negotiators speaking with them, and we do have an embassy on their home world, but we have been told not to expect any help. They are willing to trade with us, but that is all for now."

"We have watched them from outside their space and have even followed a few of their exploration vessels," Colonel Grissim admitted as she looked around the group. "But we have not been able to spot any signs of weapons on board their ships. As near as we can tell, their exploration ships are completely unarmed."

"We have also been extremely careful not to intrude upon their explorations," added Kalen, hastily. "We believe they expect us to watch them, but we have ordered all of our ships to maintain a respectful distance."

"That's probably wise for now," Commander Adler agreed. There was no point in agitating a potential future ally. "They may have a change of heart later and join us."

"Perhaps," replied Colonel Grissim, doubtfully.

"At least we have three allies," spoke Admiral Streth, feeling satisfied that the Federation was not alone in this war. "We may find others in the worlds that we set free."

"How will you be setting up your staff and fleet command structure?" asked Admiral Kalen. Fleet Admiral Johnson and Admiral Teleck had both impressed upon Kalen that he was to give Admiral Streth anything he needed.

Admiral Streth smiled as he looked over at Colonel Sheen; this was something he had been looking forward to for several days. Reaching into his pocket, he took out a set of rear admiral collar pins and slid them across the table. "Congratulations, Rear Admiral Sheen. You will be in charge of Second Fleet."

Amanda felt her heart hammering in her chest as she gazed at the coveted insignia; she had not been expecting this.

Richard reached out and picked up the gold pins. He carefully attached the rear admiral stars to the collar on his wife's uniform. "Congratulations," he said, feeling proud. He knew in his heart that she would make a great admiral.

"I don't know what to say," stammered Amanda still feeling in shock. "I will do my best Admiral, and I promise not to let you down."

"I know you won't, Admiral Sheen," replied Hedon with a smile.

"Major Andrews," continued Admiral Kalen. "We have studied your battle at the shipyard above New Providence and would like to assign you temporarily to the New Tellus System to help with the defenses there. Your knowledge of Hocklyn tactics could prove invaluable in the system's defense." Reaching into his pocket, he smiled as he slid a second set of rear admiral gold pins across the table.

Amanda's face broke out into a big smile as she picked up the pins and carefully attached them to Richard's collar. "At least now I don't outrank you," she commented with a twinkle in her eyes.

"There is one more promotion," Admiral Streth continued. He took out a set of pins for a full admiral and handed them to Commander Adler. "Admiral Adler, you will be in charge of third fleet, which will have a heavy battle carrier component. You will also be my second in command for this campaign."

"Thank you, Sir," spoke Adler, taking the pins and allowing Amanda to attach them to his collar. He had never thought he would receive this high honor.

He could hardly wait to see his new command. He had some ideas about battle carrier tactics he wanted to discuss with the people in military intelligence as well as several strategists. If things worked out as he hoped, the carriers would be taking on a much larger role in the coming war.

Hedon looked around the room before continuing. "Colonel Grissim, I have asked that you be temporarily assigned to the Ready Reserve Fleet as my Intelligence officer."

"I would be honored, Sir," replied Grissim, knowing the position would carry a lot of responsibility.

"Let's get back to planning this mission," suggested Admiral Streth now that the pleasantries were out of the way. "Rear Admiral Stillson of New Tellus has over three hundred stealth scouts currently surveying the space between us and the Hocklyn Slave Empire."

"That's a lot of scouts," commented Richard surprised at the number. Three hundred scouts should be able to cover a lot of territory.

"We have tried to keep track of the advancement of the Hocklyn Slave Empire for years now," Colonel Grissom informed them. She looked around the group and continued. "We didn't want the Hocklyns to stumble across us before we were ready. The stealth scouts are the only way we have of keeping an eye on the Hocklyns without their knowledge."

"We're fortunate to have them," Hedon continued, nodding his head. "They are searching for any Hocklyn controlled worlds as well as their fleet bases, which will be the first priority in our attack. We know where some of them are, and we are currently conducting a thorough exploration of all nearby Hocklyn controlled space."

"The closest part of the Hocklyn Slave Empire is less than 600 light years distant," Colonel Grissim reported as she stood up and activated a large viewscreen on the front wall.

A map of that section of the galaxy was displayed, showing the section the Hocklyns controlled nearest to the Federation. There were also six flashing red icons that represented new fleet bases that were either complete or under construction.

"From what we know of current Hocklyn jump drive technology, that puts us only six days away in hyperspace from contact," she informed them.

"Their jump drives are still slightly better than ours," Admiral Kalen admitted. "We suspect it's because of the AI's. We know that a normal jump for a Hocklyn ship is approximately twenty-five light years with a cool down time of about two hours."

Hedon knew that the newer Federation ships could almost match that but not quite. "From experience, the Hocklyns don't keep a lot of ships in occupied systems," he said. "If we can locate all of their fleet bases and knock them out, we can force them back away from human space. We are fortunate that our lines of supply will probably be much shorter than the Hocklyns. If we can succeed in this initial attack, we can probably postpone any retaliatory strike for several years."

"We shouldn't be facing any AI ships," Amanda commented as she leaned back and thought about the attack Admiral Streth was proposing. "They only put in an appearance when an advanced adversary has been detected that the Hocklyns may have trouble with."

"That's correct," responded Admiral Streth in agreement, his eyes meeting hers. "However, due to the fact the Hocklyns may suspect that something is out here, there may be a few AI ships in nearby Hocklyn space."

"What happens if we encounter an AI ship?" asked Amanda, recalling how only two had wiped out the entire Federation fleet back in the old Human Federation of Worlds.

"We leave them to the heavy attack cruisers," responded Hedon, looking over at Admiral Kalen.

"The heavy attack cruisers have been developed for the primary purpose of engaging an AI ship," he explained. "We don't know if we can take one out, but our best shot will be with the Devastator Three missiles they are equipped with."

"Devastator Threes," commented Amanda, curiously. "Are those similar to the old Devastator Two missiles with sublight drives and an inertial dampening system?"

"Yes," replied Kalen, nodding his head. "Only these are more deadly and cost efficient. While still expensive to produce, we do have enough to arm the Fleet."

"The heavy attack cruisers are capable of launching multiple Devastator Three missiles simultaneously as well as being equipped with our new power beams. We believe a combination of the two should allow our weapons to penetrate the AI's energy shield."

"I am glad to hear about the new power beams," Admiral Adler commented. "From what I have read on their specs, they are more powerful than the Hocklyn's energy beams."

"That's why we need to attack first," emphasized Hedon, wanting to take advantage of the situation. "We have superior weapons for now, and we need to use them against the Hocklyns. I strongly suspect at some point in time the AIs will upgrade the Hocklyn's weapons if this war is going against them."

"We consider that a very real possibility," spoke Colonel Grissom, agreeing with Admiral Streth. She was impressed by how well he had thought everything out. "We have no idea of the actual ship strength of the AIs since they depend on their four warrior races to expand their empire. However, against a superior enemy as we will be, our war strategists feel the AIs will not only upgrade the Hocklyn's weapons but also commit a major portion of their fleet to defeating us."

"What are the odds of that?" asked Amanda, not wanting to think about facing large numbers of the giant 1,500-meter AI ships. She didn't see how anything the Federation had could stand up to a force like that. It would be suicide! "I mean, what if we encounter entire fleets composed of AI ships?"

The room was quiet for a few heart-stopping seconds, and then Admiral Streth spoke up. "Because of the distance involved it will take a while for any major commitment of AI ships. If we can knock out a few of them, it might give the AIs pause about committing their warships."

"Our Intelligence department concurs," added Colonel Grissim, her eyes gazing at Admiral Streth. The longer she was around the Fleet Admiral the more impressed she became. "We believe it will take the AIs nearly two hundred days to get a sizable fleet here from the galactic center."

Admiral Streth nodded. "That's what I was expecting. By the time they can send a sizable force, we should have already encountered smaller groups of their ships and learned how to destroy them. The AIs will be operating far from home, and hopefully that will give us an advantage."

"So far, none of the scouts have reported spotting an AI ship," Colonel Grissim informed them. "It might be a while before we have to face one."

"Rear Admiral Sheen, as soon as we have enough ships updated to form Second Fleet, you will proceed to the New Tellus System and begin fleet maneuvers. I want a highly trained force when the time comes to launch our attack."

"Yes, Sir," replied Amanda, thinking about what all would have to be done. At least Richard and she would both be stationed in the same system for a while. "We will be ready."

"Admiral Adler, I want you to get with the war strategists here on Ceres and discuss battle carrier tactics and see what we can come up with that may be effective against the Hocklyns. From our previous engagements, the Hocklyn ships are only equipped with fighters and no bombers. Perhaps we can use our own bombers more effectively against them."

"I was thinking along the same lines," responded Adler, nodding his head in agreement. "I will get on that immediately."

The small group spent a few more hours making plans and then broke up. They had a lot to think about as well as preparations to begin.

-

Admiral Johnson was back aboard New Tellus Station sitting in her office. She was watching several large viewscreens, which showed ships being towed carefully into the shipyard's repair bays. As she examined the ships on the screens, she noted that there were two battle carriers and four Monarch cruisers. All would be updated with new systems and modern weapons.

"We are working on what Admiral Streth is calling Second Fleet," Rear Admiral Bennett commented from the chair in front of the admiral's large wooden desk. "He wants it up and operational as soon as possible so Admiral Sheen can begin whipping it into shape."

"How long will that be?" asked Karla, turning her gaze away from the viewscreens and back to Rear Admiral Bennett. It had been amazing to meet Admiral Streth and the others. Some of those people she had read about in the history books, especially the survivors from the New Horizon incident!

"We are talking about four battle cruisers, six battle carriers, twelve Monarch cruisers, four strike cruisers, forty light cruisers and twenty destroyers," Admiral Bennett replied as he thought over the logistics of what needed to be done. "Fortunately, the strike cruisers are new and ready, so we just need to update the others."

"I want those ships to have first priority over everything else," Karla stressed, her eyes focusing intently on Admiral Bennett. "This fleet sounds like it may be Admiral Streth's Sunday punch with the way he has composed its elements and placed Rear Admiral Sheen in command. I suspect Second Fleet will be used to crack any heavy Hocklyn fleet concentrations or defenses."

"We have forty-two repair bays available in our six shipyards around New Tellus," Bennett responded. "Second Fleet is composed of eighty-six ships. The destroyers and light cruisers can be updated quickly. The ships are in rather good condition since they were part of the Ready Reserve. We are already well under way in updating a number of the units. I would estimate I can have all of Second Fleet fully operational in six weeks."

"What about the other shipyards in the Federation?" Karla asked. The Federation Council had agreed to make all of them available for updating the Ready Reserve Fleet. "How are they doing?"

"Only Earth has shipyards comparable to ours. Admiral Freeman is concentrating on the heavier ships being updated in Earth's shipyards and is using the other Federation shipyards to update the lighter units. If everything goes as planned, we will make your six month deadline, but just barely."

"We need to speak to Admiral Streth I'm afraid," commented Karla, knowing she was about to throw a wrench into Admiral Bennett and Freeman's plans. "He has given command of Third Fleet to Admiral Adler, a battle carrier commander. I suspect it will have a powerful battle carrier contingent."

Bennett was quiet for a moment as he mulled this information over. "I will talk to Admiral Freeman; we could move more of the battle carriers ahead of some of the Monarch cruisers if we need to."

"I think we should do that," Karla suggested. "Please work out the details with Admiral Freeman and get back with me."

"Once we get the Ready Reserve updated what will be next?"

"Then we will start on the Inactive Reserve," Admiral Johnson informed Bennett with a smile.

"I was afraid you were going to say that," replied Admiral Bennett with a groan and shaking his head, knowing that would be a big job. "Those ships have been inactive for twenty to forty years; it will take much longer to update them than the Ready Reserve. Some of them are in pretty bad shape."

"But we can update them much faster than building a completely new ship," Karla pointed out. "And we may need those numbers even though they are older ships."

"Yes," agreed Bennett, nodding his head slowly in agreement. "We can update one of those ships in half the time it takes to build a new one. They won't be quite as powerful as our newer ships, but they will still pack a solid punch."

"We're going to need them, Arnold," Karla said, leaning forward. "The Hocklyns have one hell of a fleet out there. There is no way for us to know how this war is going to turn out. Our major advantage is that our worlds are all within twenty light years of Earth, except for

New Tellus, and we have three allies on our flanks to take some of the pressure off. The Hocklyn Slave Empire is scattered over a quarter of the galaxy, and it will take them time to mount a major attack against us."

"The Federation Council has at least agreed to go on a war preparation footing for ship construction," Bennett added with satisfaction in his voice. "Admiral Freeman has already issued the orders for every shipyard in the Federation to begin constructing new warships."

"I know," replied the Fleet Admiral, letting out a deep breath. We can only hope that it's enough."

-

Jeremy, Kelsey, Angela, and Kevin had all been ordered to report to the heavy strike cruiser Avenger. It was berthed in bay twenty-one on Ceres, along with two other modern strike cruisers.

"Now those are ships!" Kevin said excitedly as he looked at the 1,000-meter ships in awe.

"The Avenger," Kelsey spoke affectionately, her deep blue eyes focusing on the strike cruiser closest to them. Her eyes took on a thoughtful look. "I wonder if that ship was named after the light cruiser Avenger that crashed on the Moon?"

"We can ask her commanding officer when we report in," responded Jeremy anxious to go aboard the ship.

He was very familiar with the old Avenger as he had been raised on board her. He had been very disappointed to learn while they were on the Moon, that the Avenger was now used only as a museum. Jeremy had come to know Ariel very well after they had returned from the New Horizon mission. He had been very sad to learn that the AI was no longer functioning. It was like losing a good friend.

Jeremy gazed thoughtfully at the heavy strike cruiser, wondering what awaited them. He had served six years aboard several light cruisers after the New Horizon incident and had been promoted to the rank of executive officer on his final posting. A light cruiser was not nearly as large or as powerful as this warship.

"Let's report in," suggested Kevin, pointing toward the ramp that led into the large open hatch on the side of the ship. "I'm getting hungry!"

"You're always hungry," admonished Angela with a chuckle, shaking her head. "I don't see how you stay so lean with as much as you eat."

"High metabolism," responded Kevin, patting his stomach. "I hope they serve good hamburgers on this ship."

The others all laughed and headed toward the ramp. At least they were all four still together.

A few minutes later, the four of them had made their way into the ship and reported to the officer on duty. They were told to report to the Command Center for their assignments. As they turned to leave, they failed to notice the slight smile that appeared on the officer's face.

"Why the Command Center?" asked Kelsey, feeling confused. Normally the ship's commanding officer would meet new crewmembers in his on board office, if at all. The executive officer or another ship officer handled most of the crew assignments.

"I guess we'll find out when we get there," Jeremy answered. He too wondered why they were reporting to the Command Center.

Nearly thirty minutes later, they made it to the ship's Command Center. They had heard these new ships had rapid transit tubes inside so the crew could get to their stations much quicker. However, they were hesitant to try the new tubes without some additional explanation about their function.

"Major Jeremy Strong, reporting for duty," Jeremy informed the two marines standing at the open hatch.

"Allow them to enter," a strangely familiar woman's voice spoke from inside.

The four looked at each other and then stepped inside the Command Center, pausing in astonishment. The Command Center was twice the size as the ones Jeremy had served in aboard the light cruisers. Crewmembers were busily going about their jobs, and all the stations were manned. But what drew Jeremy and the other's attention was what was on the main viewscreen.

"Ariel!" Jeremy blurted out in incredulity, staring at the dark headed AI that was watching them with a pleased smile. "What are you doing here?" He had never expected to see the AI again. For a moment, he almost felt as if he was back home in the old Avenger.

"She's the AI for this ship," another strangely and almost haunting voice spoke from behind Jeremy. Turning slowly, Jeremy saw a strikingly beautiful young blonde with green eyes stand up from where she had been working on the main computer console.

"Katie?" Jeremy spoke in a stunned voice, his eyes growing wide in shock.

"It can't be," added Kelsey, looking intently at the young blonde lieutenant who was coming toward them. "Katie was only twenty-one when we went into cryosleep and still attending the university here on Ceres."

"True," the young woman replied, smiling. "But I waited and went into cryosleep six years after you four did. I am now twenty-seven."

"Why haven't we seen you before this?" Angela asked curiously, finding it hard to believe she was actually talking to Katie. "We have been awake for nearly four weeks." Katie and she had become quite close after the New Horizon incident.

"After you four went into cryosleep, I continued my work with computers on Ceres. I discovered that Ariel and Clarissa's programs were beginning to fail. They had not been designed to function for such an extended period of time."

"What did you do?" asked Kevin, suspiciously. When it came to computers, Katie was capable of almost anything.

"I developed a computer memory crystal which could handle an AI's memories. We transferred Ariel and Clarissa's memories, or consciousness, to the new crystals, and they went into cryosleep with me."

"With you! Why?" asked Kelsey not understanding. Why not just install them in another ship?

"Ariel wanted to be back in a warship to fight the Hocklyns, and Clarissa didn't want to be left behind," explained Katie, recalling all the hard work and long hours she had put in trying to save the two AIs. "They were and still are the only two working AIs the Federation has."

"Why haven't they built more?" Angela asked, her eyes going back and forth between Katie and the AI on the viewscreen. "Surely Federation science is now at the point they could easily do so."

"Because of the AIs," Katie replied in a concerned voice. "No one knows how a Federation AI will respond when it comes into contact with the AI's from the center of our galaxy. There is some concern that the AI's from the galactic center could override the programming in our AIs and turn them against us. For that reason, the Federation has focused on better and more powerful computers. Some of the computers almost seem like AIs, but they are not."

"If Ariel is the AI on board this Avenger, then where is Clarissa?" Jeremy asked. He glanced at the main viewscreen and saw that Ariel was watching them very intently. It was strangely comforting to see her there.

"She's aboard the new StarStrike," answered Katie pleased that they had elected to put Clarissa on Admiral Streth's new flagship. It showed that the Fleet Admiral still had confidence in the AIs. "Clarissa and Ariel have worked with humans for such a long time that I don't believe their programming can be corrupted, but just in case I have installed some special firewalls that should be able to protect them."

"Where is the commanding officer?" Jeremy asked Katie. He looked around not seeing anyone ranked higher than a lieutenant to report to.

Katie only smiled and nodded toward someone standing behind Jeremy.

Jeremy turned and instantly came to attention. "Admiral in the Command Center!" he called out. Instantly everyone stood and snapped to attention.

"At ease, and continue," responded Admiral Karla Johnson pleased with Major Strong's quick response.

"Major Strong, we seem to have a slight problem with this ship," she began with a mystifying smile as she walked over to stand in front of the five.

"A problem?" spoke Jeremy, hesitantly. "What type of problem?"

"This ship is going to be assigned to Admiral Streth's fleet in the coming campaign. It doesn't seem to have a commanding officer, and our friendly AI here is insisting that she will only accept one individual as her commander."

Jeremy felt his heart start to beat faster. He had become good friends with Ariel after the New Horizon incident and had spent a lot of time in her presence. He had a suspicion what the admiral was about to say. He recalled how Ariel had named his father as her commander.

"Major Strong, effective as of today you have been promoted to the position of Commanding Officer of the heavy strike cruiser Avenger."

Kelsey, Angela, and Kevin could only stare and listen in amazement. None of them had expected something like this when they came aboard. Katie just smiled, knowing already who Ariel had wanted as her commanding officer. There was no doubt in Katie's mind that the AI had made a good decision, and it would be great for all of them to be back together again.

"I'm not qualified," stuttered Jeremy, finding it difficult to accept what the admiral was offering him. He wanted the command, but he knew it shouldn't be his. There were bound to be officers on the ship that were more qualified.

"Nonsense," replied Admiral Johnson with a smile. "My great ancestor and your father discovered the Avenger on the Moon over three hundred years ago. How could you be anything but a commander in the coming war? After all, Admiral Streth has been in cryosleep even longer and I gave him an entire war fleet."

"Yes, Admiral," spoke Jeremy not sure what else to say.

"You've served as an executive officer on a light cruiser for several years," Admiral Johnson continued. She had read the files of all five of these young officers carefully. "Colonel Maylen, who will be reporting for duty tomorrow, will serve as your executive officer. She is extremely familiar with the specifications and capabilities of a heavy strike cruiser. If you have any questions, she will answer them."

"I look forward to meeting the colonel," Jeremy replied, his eyes focusing on the admiral. He could feel his heart beating faster as he realized he was going to be the Avenger's commander.

"As for you other three, including Lieutenant Katie Johnson, you will be assigned to the Command Center as First Watch officers."

"Yes, Admiral!" they all spoke in unison.

The admiral's eyes softened as she looked at them. "All five of you represent a lot of Federation history. You were all on the New Horizon, and some of your parents were very important in creating the new Federation as we know it today. There is no doubt in my mind that you will continue that tradition on this ship. Make us proud."

"Yes, Admiral," all five responded.

"The ship is yours, Commander," spoke Admiral Johnson, saluting Jeremy.

Karla turned and left the Command Center, heading toward a transit tube. She prayed that nothing happened to those five, or six if you counted Ariel. Losing them and the history they represented would be almost as bad as losing Admiral Streth; it would be a hard blow to the Federation.

Jeremy watched the admiral leave and then slowly made his way over to the command console. It was nearly twice the size as the one in a light cruiser. He looked at it for a moment, noticing there were two chairs instead of one. He sat down and saw a mini-com lying on top of the console. Picking it up, he inserted it into his right ear.

"Don't worry, Jeremy," Ariel spoke in a pleasant and soft voice. "I will help you with everything; no one else can hear what I am saying to you. Tell the others to go to their stations and insert their mini-coms, and I will help them also. All but Katie, she has already been working on the Avenger's computer systems for over a week and knows what to do."

Jeremy passed on the order to the other three and watched as they went to their stations. In just a few short minutes, everyone was busy learning the differences that three hundred years can make in a warship and its intricate systems. Fortunately, they had Ariel, and she could work and speak to all of them simultaneously. After an hour, Jeremy began to feel his confidence returning. Then the reality set in. He was aboard a Federation heavy strike cruiser, and he was in command. Letting out a deep breath, he looked back at the computer console where Katie was sitting. So much had changed and Katie had certainly changed. Jeremy wondered just what that might mean for the future.

Katie was working on the computer system and thinking about what Admiral Johnson had said. When the admiral had commented that her remote ancestor had been with Jeremy's father when the Avenger had been discovered, a shock had passed through her. It had never occurred to her that she and Admiral Johnson might be related. She allowed a smile to cover her face; it felt good to know she had other family still around. She wondered how closely she and the admiral were related. Perhaps someday she would ask her.

-

In Hocklyn space, Commodore Resmunt looked at the latest reports from the escort cruisers that were out on exploration missions. His large, dark eyes grew wider when he saw that two of them were missing. Getting up, he made his way over to the large star map hanging on the wall, which depicted this section of the galaxy. It took him only a few moments to plot the general area where the two ships had vanished. He stepped back and thought for a moment. The two escort cruisers had disappeared in an area that had not been previously explored.

Activating his com system, he sent out orders for War Leaders Bisth and Sangeth to report to his office. Walking over to the large window, he looked out over the busy spaceport. Shuttles and small ships were coming and going constantly. From the last report, there were over ten thousand slaves working on the spaceport and the surrounding support facilities. In another six weeks, his forward fleet bases would be completed.

Looking upward toward space, he wondered if he should set up some type of orbital defenses. Only the home worlds had them, but he was facing a new and possibly dangerous situation. He was also a long way from major military support if he were to need it. The decision wasn't hard to make; once the shipyard was completed, he would begin building some basic defense satellites.

-

A few hours later, War Leaders Bisth and Sangeth reported to Resmunt's office. Both were curious about what the Fleet Commodore wanted and were hoping it meant action would be forthcoming. Hocklyns were meant for combat, not routine shipboard duties. It was time to go and find honor.

Resmunt watched impassively as the two entered. Letting out a deep breath, he gazed down at the six digits on his right hand. His hand was a light green in color, and his fingers ended in very sharp and thick nails, almost like talons.

"Two of our exploration cruisers are missing," he began in a cold and detached voice.

"This mysterious race you believe is out there; do you think they are responsible?" Sangeth asked in his rasping voice.

"Over the past month the amount of ghost sensor readings has increased dramatically," he spoke in a calm calculating voice. "If I didn't know better, I would think our defenses are being probed all along this sector."

"Then we could indeed be facing a well prepared enemy," commented Bisth already relishing the thought of combat. Honor could be coming in the very near future. Very seldom did the Hocklyns ever encounter an enemy that was worthy of combat.

Resmunt walked back over to the large map on the wall. "Based on when the increased sensor ghosts began to be reported and the two cruisers planned exploration path, I believe they were destroyed in one of these two star systems." Resmunt pointed to the two indicated systems on the map.

"That's less than seven hundred light years from our outer borders," commented Sangeth, realizing that the enemy could be much closer than he had thought possible. "What are our orders?"

Resmunt turned toward the two and spoke with authority in his voice. "You will take your two fleets to this sector of space and investigate both systems. If an enemy is there and you can destroy him, you are authorized to do so. If his forces are too great, you are to withdraw and report back here."

"Withdraw!" Sangeth uttered, his large eyes almost turning yellow with rage. "Hocklyns do not retreat in the face of an enemy!"

"In this case, you will," Resmunt spoke in a cold and deadly voice. He stepped over to stand directly in front of the War Leader. "If you do not, I will see to it that your entire family is stripped of their honor."

"We will withdraw," responded Bisth, knowing it was the wisest choice. "Honor will be served by bringing word of this potential threat back to the empire."

"War Leader Bisth, you will be in command of the two fleets," Resmunt added, stepping back. "Find out what's out there. Go and bring honor to the empire."

With that, Resmunt dismissed the two War Leaders. There was no doubt they would follow his commands. He knew that Sangeth was the more rash and excitable of the two, while Bisth was more calculating and might someday rise to the rank of Fleet Commodore. Walking back to the window, Resmunt gazed out, wondering whether Sangeth and Bisth would find a dangerous threat to the empire, or nothing at all?

Chapter Five

Admiral Tolsen gazed with deep concern at the main viewscreen. His fleet was stationed 2.7 light years from Gliese 667C, which contained Caden's World. In addition to his flagship, WarHawk, the battle carriers Liberty and Independence were slightly behind and above the powerful battle cruiser, as well as four Monarch heavy cruisers. A strong light cruiser contingent consisting of eight ships were intermingled amongst the seven powerful warships. On the periphery of the fleet, six fleet destroyers hovered in screening positions.

"I hate this waiting," complained Colonel Beck, letting out a long sigh. "It's been nearly fourteen weeks since the two Hocklyn cruisers were destroyed. I would have thought the Hocklyns would have responded by now."

"Be patient, Peter," replied Admiral Tolsen, looking over at his second in command standing next to him. "The Hocklyns will be here soon enough. Have you read the latest reports from military intelligence?"

"Yes, they're almost frightening. They've found six major Hocklyn bases less than seven hundred light years away from our borders. Major Ackerman believes they may find more before the survey is complete."

"They suspect something," Tolsen put forth, leaning back in his command chair and arching his eyebrows. "The escort cruisers we have destroyed over the years and the stealth scout spying has made them suspicious. They know something is out here and are preparing for it."

"I suspect Admiral Streth will make short work of those bases when he launches his attack," smirked Colonel Beck. "I would like to be there when he levels them."

"It will be the start of a long war," Tolsen said somberly, his eyes taking on a distant and sad look. "A war with the Hocklyns may go on for generations. Even our children may not see the end of it."

"It's better than being slaves in their empire," Peter replied with a nod of understanding. "We have allies and a powerful fleet; this won't be like when the Hocklyns attacked the original Federation."

It was at that moment that a warning alarm sounded, drawing their attention to the sensors.

"We have unauthorized FTL signatures in the Gliese 667C system," reported Lieutenant Anders as a flashing red light began blinking on his sensor panel.

Tolsen looked back over at Colonel Beck. "Bring the fleet to readiness, Peter. This may be it!"

On Caden's World, Captain Krandle gazed at the long-range sensors, which were now showing glaring red threat icons appearing in the system. She had been promoted since the original battle due to the fact that additional marines had been stationed upon the planet.

"Bring us to Condition One, Lieutenant Simmons," Krandle ordered as additional red threat icons continued to appear. Simmons had also been promoted. Then turning to Adam Severson, she continued. "Put your people in the deep bunkers, this may be the Hocklyn attack we have been expecting. I don't think those are freighters off course."

Severson turned and began passing on the orders. At least this time they had an additional two hundred marines to help provide security. There were even two heavily armed marines standing at the doorway to the operations center, which had been substantially reinforced. He knew it would take about two hours for the twenty thousand inhabitants of the planet to reach the underground bunkers. They had considered evacuating Caden's World, but this was their home and the people had wanted to stay.

"Fleet units are withdrawing to just beneath the defensive satellites," the corporal sitting at the sensor console reported. The young woman continued to monitor the sensors closely.

Captain Krandle nodded as she studied the sensor screen. There were currently two light cruisers and four destroyers in orbit. In addition, there were now eighty defensive satellites as well as ten missile-launching platforms. If this was a Hocklyn fleet, they might find Caden's World a hard nut to crack.

"We're at Condition One, and our marines are reporting to their assigned security positions," Lieutenant Simmons reported as he listened to numerous conversations over his mini-com. "Surface missile batteries are being activated and readied to shoot down any inbound Hocklyn shuttle or missile."

Krandle nodded her head in acknowledgment. They had two defensive missile platforms at each mining site. From the number of red threat icons on her screens, she wished she had more! Now it begins, she thought as she watched the red icons apprehensively. She knew that Admiral Tolsen and his fleet were nearby. She just hoped it was enough.

War Leader Sangeth gazed with cold eyes at the sensor screen. The fourth planet of the system was showing energy readings. There were also numerous satellites in orbit as well as a small number of ships.

"Send a message back to War Leader Bisth that we have found an inhabited planet and are closing to investigate."

First Leader Rahn quickly passed on the orders and then returned to studying the information from the long-range sensors.

As a safety precaution, the two Hocklyn fleets were not jumping together; they were staying separated by one jump. This had been War Leader Bisth's decision. If they encountered a weak enemy, Bisth's fleet would jump forward and help eliminate it. If the enemy were powerful, then his fleet could jump forward, help extricate Sangeth's fleet, and then both fleets would return to Commodore Resmunt's base with data on their new enemy.

What irked War Leader Sangeth was that Bisth had demanded that Sangeth leave over half of his fleet at Bisth's location. He claimed it was so the enemy wouldn't know their true strength until it was needed, but Sangeth did not agree that his fleet should be split; he preferred to have his entire fleet with him. When they returned to Fleet Commodore Resmunt's base, he intended to lodge a formal complaint against the other War Leader. Perhaps it would be necessary to fight an honor duel with War Leader Bisth to prove his point.

"Plot a jump to just outside of the planet's gravity well," ordered Sangeth, feeling energized at the thought of battle. "Let's see what is truly on the planet."

From what he was seeing on the sensor screens, this planet would not be able to withstand the power of his current fleet. The ships that had been left behind with Bisth would not be needed. Honor was a few short hours away. He smirked, knowing that this would be over before Bisth could jump in. He would miss out on this honor opportunity, which was just fine with Sangeth.

War Leader Sangeth was confident of an easy victory; he had his dreadnought the Crimson Oblivion, two war cruisers, and eight escort cruisers. With satisfaction, he saw a white spatial vortex form in front of his flagship, and the Oblivion moved into it. Honor was about to fall his way.

Moments later, the Hocklyn fleet appeared just two million kilometers from the inhabited planet. Instantly, small ships shot out of the two war cruisers as six small fighters took up defensive positions around the fleet. The Oblivion's sensors and scanners focused on the planet to see what lay ahead. Weapon ports opened and targeting systems were activated; it was the same on all of the Hocklyn ships as they prepared for battle.

"It is a mining operation," First Leader Rahn reported as he finished studying the data on the scans. "There are two quite large mining operations on the surface of the planet."

"What about those ships in orbit?" Sangeth demanded as his fleet edged into the planet's gravity well.

"Two are of cruiser size and the other four are lights. They are being run through the data files now for possible identification. We will be in combat range in twenty minutes. Should we send a message to War Leader Bisth to join us?"

"Against six ships?" Sangeth spoke in a harsh voice. "No! This victory will be ours."

"Very well," Rahn replied with a nod. He was actually pleased with Sangeth's response. Honor had been hard to achieve in recent years, and now here it was in front of them. More honor would be received if there were fewer to collect it.

"What about those satellites in orbit, there seem to be a large number of them? Surely a mining colony wouldn't need that many weather and communication satellites?"

First Leader Rahn was quiet for a moment as he studied more data. "We are getting high power readings from those satellites; they may be some type of defensive system."

"Task our long-range missiles with taking those satellites out first," Sangeth ordered as a precaution. He wanted honor out of this battle, but he was no fool. The satellites, along with those six ships, could damage his fleet. He would destroy the defensive satellites with his long-range missiles and then attack the six warships, if they were warships. They could just be harmless freighters waiting in orbit for cargo.

First Leader Rahn suddenly turned toward War Leader Sangeth with shock on his face. His large eyes seemed to grow even wider. "We have an identity on those ships," he reported in his rasping voice.

"Those are Human Federation of World's ships! The larger two are light cruisers and the four smaller ones are destroyers. We can expect weapons very similar to ours, including powerful lasers from the cruisers."

"Human Federation of Worlds?" spat War Leader Sangeth disbelievingly, his cold eyes focusing on Rahn. "That's impossible; the humans were wiped out centuries ago!"

"Nevertheless, that's what the computer is saying," responded Rahn. "Some of the humans must have escaped."

"Get a message out to War Leader Bisth and report these findings immediately," ordered Sangeth. "At least now we know who has been behind our recent exploration cruiser losses."

Rahn turned to the communications operator and after a moment, turned back to Bisth with concern in his eyes. "Our FTL communications are being jammed."

"Send one of our escorts back," ordered Sangeth angrily, wondering if he had walked into a trap. "We must get word back to Bisth of what we have discovered. Honor must be served!" He wished now he had the rest of his fleet.

"It will take a few minutes for the escort cruiser to move back out of the planet's gravity well."

Bisth nodded and turned his attention back to the sensors. They were still closing on the planet and would be within combat range shortly.

"Have all ships tighten our formation and prepare to attack."

-

Captain Krandle swore as she saw one of the Hocklyn escort cruisers suddenly vanish. She knew it had jumped out of the system, probably to report on what their fleet had discovered. There were four stealth scouts currently in the system that had initiated jamming as soon as the Hocklyn fleet had jumped near Caden's World.

"The Hocklyns will know about us now," she murmured quietly.

Simmons only nodded in agreement. It had always been a danger that the Hocklyns would send a ship back before their fleet could be destroyed. "The Hocklyns are nearly in range of the missile platforms, shall we launch?"

"Standby," Captain Krandle ordered. She wanted to use her missiles before the Hocklyns could destroy them. "Make sure our launch is coordinated with the orbiting Federation ships."

A few minutes later, she gave the order and ten missile platforms hidden amongst the other defensive satellites belched forth two hundred and forty Klave heavy missiles at the inbound Hocklyn fleet. The two light cruisers launched a dozen Devastator missiles tipped with nuclear warheads. It was hoped that these missiles would blend in with the Klave missiles and strike the Hocklyns a deadly blow.

Threat alarms began sounding in the War Room of the Crimson Oblivion. The Hocklyn command crew quickly went about assessing the inbound threat and activating their ship's defenses.

"Launch our war wing!" Sangeth spoke as he studied the inbound missiles on the sensor screen. He knew his defenses would not be able to stop them all. There were just too many. "All ships are to launch their fighters; they are to target those satellites."

"Some of those satellites are missile platforms," Rahn hissed in anger. "They launched at extreme range."

At that moment, additional red threat icons began to appear behind the Hocklyn fleet. With sudden dread, Sangeth knew that he had fallen into a well orchestrated trap. Those new icons were additional human warships and he was outnumbered as well as pinned inside the planet's gravity well! He needed Bisth, but there was no way to summon him.

"Close on the Hocklyn fleet and stand by to engage," Admiral Tolsen ordered as the WarHawk's sensors cleared. He had already sent a message back to Fleet Command and knew that additional ships were being rushed to support him.

Tolsen noticed with worry that at least one of the red threat icons was very large, possibly a Hocklyn dreadnought. "What are we facing?"

"Sensors show one Hocklyn dreadnought, two war cruisers, and seven escort cruisers," the sensor operator responded.

"Eight minutes until we reach extreme weapons range," Colonel Beck reported from his plotting table. He was studying the holographic image floating above the table showing the Hocklyn fleet as well as all Federation ships.

"Order the defensive fleet above Caden's World to maintain their position. They are tasked with taking out any missiles or fighters that approach the planet." Tolsen didn't want to risk any nukes striking one of the two mining settlements.

"Order the Liberty and Independence to launch their bomber strike. I want those energy weapons on the Hocklyn ships silenced before they can fire," Tolsen ordered. He had discussed this strategy with Admiral Adler back on Ceres. "Also, order the destroyers to fall back to the carriers and given them additional support. Their primary job in this engagement is to protect those two battle carriers."

Even as the destroyers were falling back, the carriers started launching. From the two battle carriers, 120 Anlon Space Superiority two-man bombers erupted from the large flight bays. Another 80 Talon fighters flew alongside them to protect the bombers from Hocklyn fighters.

"Knock those missiles down!" roared War Leader Sangeth. "I don't want a single one to strike this ship!"

He looked with anger at the red threat icons rapidly closing with his fleet. His own interceptor missiles were launching and the defensive systems coming online.

"Interceptors launched, defensive systems locking on targets," First Leader Rahn reported as missile after missile blasted out of the missile tubes of the Oblivion. "War wing has launched."

Defensive railguns tracked the inbound missiles and began firing nonstop; the rest of the ships in the Hocklyn formation were doing the same thing. Space instantly became filled with exploding ordnance and missiles.

Around the Hocklyn fleet, space was suddenly full of bright explosions as Captain Krandle's missile strike slammed home. Hocklyn interceptor missiles and defensive fire managed to take out 192 of the inbound Klave missiles. The other missiles and eight of the tactical nukes slammed home against the Hocklyn shields in bright, fiery explosions. On several ships, the shields failed and missiles struck the unshielded hulls, blasting jagged rents and causing massive damage to the interior of the ships.

"Target those missile platforms and destroy them," Sangeth ordered, trying to keep his anger under control as missiles ravaged his fleet. "Once we have launched, turn the fleet to face the incoming human ships. Order the war wing to break off their attack on the satellites and attack the human fighters instead."

The Hocklyns fired off a barrage of missiles at the defensive satellites and missile platforms as their fleet began to turn. It was still immersed in explosions from exploding missiles. The war wing swept by as it raced to engage the inbound human fighters and bombers.

War Leader Sangeth felt the Oblivion shudder as two nuclear-tipped missiles hit the shields. Fortunately, the shields held, and there was minimal damage to the ship.

"Report!" he roared, knowing his fleet had been hurt. He had not expected such a massive missile barrage from the satellites.

"The cruiser Thunder has lost her shields and is reporting heavy damage, several other ships are reporting lighter damage but are still fully combat capable. There has been no damage to the war cruisers."

It was at that moment that a brilliant flash covered the main viewscreen, attracting Sangeth's attention. "What was that?"

"The Thunder activated her self-destructs," explained Rahn, stone-faced. "They died with honor."

"As it should be," Sangeth replied, his eyes focusing on the sensor screens and the tactical situation. "Engage the humans!" His fleet was still inside the planet's gravity well. The only way to safety was through the human fleet. While he was willing to die in battle to bring honor to his family, his orders were to preserve his fleet and return, But he just didn't know if that was going to be possible. "All ships are to stay in fleet formation. We will try to blow throw them and get outside the planet's gravity well, then jump back to War Leader Bisth's fleet."

"Honor is before us," First Leader Rahn spoke as he moved to carry out the orders.

"Honor is before us," agreed War Leader Sangeth, wishing he had his other ships.

The Crimson Oblivion accelerated toward the inbound human ships. All of its weapon's ports were open and targeting systems were active. The two war cruisers took up positions on each side to add their heavy firepower to the flagship as the remaining escort cruisers moved into screening positions. Their orders were simple, blast their way through and jump out. Damaged ships would be left behind to self-destruct.

Behind them, explosive flashes began going off where the human defensive satellites waited. The Hocklyn missile barrage had slammed home, eliminating some of the satellites, particularly the ones the original missile strike had come from.

-

Captain Krandle watched with anguish as most of her missile platforms vanished from the sensor screens. She had hoped to save a few of the remaining missiles to hit the Hocklyns if they came any nearer to the planet and now that option was gone. Not only that, but over a dozen of the defensive laser satellites had also been destroyed.

"They hurt us," Lieutenant Simmons spoke as he watched the screens.

"Yes, but the Fleet is here now. Admiral Tolsen will finish off these Hocklyns," Krandle replied confidently, her eyes were glued to the sensor screen, which showed the friendly green icons of inbound Federation warships.

-

Admiral Tolsen watched tensely as his fleet's fighters and the Hocklyn fighters made contact. Above the plotting table, he could see ship icons and missile trails depicted on the holographic display. Occasionally a missile would strike its target and an icon would vanish.

In space, the fighters were in a fierce dogfight. The Hocklyn ships had launched sixty-eight fighters against the eighty human ones. They swirled in a lethal dance of death. Missiles and cannon fire filled space as the two groups tried to kill each other. Fighters exploded in deadly balls of orange-red fire as their heavily shielded fuel tanks detonated from the impact of the deadly ordnance.

While the fighter battle raged, the Anlon bombers continued their attack run. Each one carried two small missiles to be used against the target as well as two larger Shrike missiles tipped with tactical nukes.

"Target range in thirty seconds," the strike leader spoke to the attacking squadrons. "Begin evasive maneuvers and good luck. Once you have released your missiles, get back to the barn."

-

War Leader Sangeth watched the attacking bombers with deep concern. From the records he had called up, he knew that these were a larger human attack craft that carried missiles. He couldn't allow them to get close to his already damaged fleet. "Target those small craft and destroy them!" he ordered tersely. "I don't want any of them to launch their missile payloads!"

"Coming into attack range now," First Leader Rahn replied as he passed on the orders.

From the Hocklyn ships, numerous interceptor missiles blasted forth from their tubes, their targeting systems actively searching for and locking onto the inbound bombers. Energy beams also locked on and began firing. The bright blue energy beams struck first and when one struck a bomber, the craft simply disintegrated. The missile strike came next and more human bombers vanished in bright fiery explosions as they failed to outmaneuver the deadly Hocklyn missiles.

-

"Our bombers are having a bad time," spoke Colonel Beck, wincing as several more Anlons vanished from the holographic display.

"But they are in range now," Admiral Tolsen responded, trying to put the losses out of his mind. "See! They're launching their missiles."

On the main sensor screen as well as in the holographic image, over two hundred and twenty missile icons suddenly appeared rocketing rapidly toward their intended Hocklyn targets.

-

Major Archer was third in command of the bomber strike. The two senior officers had both been killed by Hocklyn missile fire and energy beams. It was extremely hard to focus with all the death and destruction surrounding them.

"Weapons released," he spoke over the com to all of the remaining Anlon bombers in the squadrons. He took a deep breath. "Let's get the hell out of here!"

His bomber swerved to avoid an inbound missile and his copilot launched additional counter measures. Archer knew they had made some major mistakes and taken some unnecessary losses on their attack run. Adjustments could be made in strategy for future battles but for now, he had to survive this one. He looked down at his sensor screen, seeing the Hocklyns had switched from attacking his bombers to trying to knock down the inbound missile strike. At least that should help allow the remaining bombers to get away.

-

War Leader Sangeth watched with consternation the inbound missiles nearing his ships. The human bombers had launched them from point blank range. Large numbers were being intercepted as bright flashes of light erupted near his fleet on the main viewscreen. Then nuclear fire washed over his ship's screens as missile after missile slammed home. Some of the screens wavered, and missiles began to strike the armored hulls of the Hocklyn ships.

The Crimson Oblivion shook and her screens wavered as several powerful blasts rattled the ship. A few red lights appeared on the damage control board, but for the most part the powerful dreadnought had come through the missile attack relatively unharmed.

"Escort cruiser Brantif has lost her FTL drive, it is not repairable," First Leader Rahn reported as the damage reports started to come in. "Most of the human weapons are targeting our weapon systems. The War Cruiser Delpin has lost her energy cannons, a human nuclear missile took them out. About ten percent of their missiles are making it through our screens, and they are all targeting weapon systems or the FTL drives of our ships."

"Clever strategy," spoke Sangeth, grudgingly. "They are trying to cripple us." These humans were deadly adversaries, they were worthy of honor. Even as he watched the sensor screens, he saw that his fleet's weapons were now in range of the inbound human fleet. "Lock onto their ships, and fire!"

Admiral Tolsen felt the WarHawk shudder violently as a Hocklyn missile managed to penetrate the energy screen. Half a dozen red lights sudden glared on the damage control board.

"We have fires in sections thirty-two and forty-one," Colonel Beck reported as he dispatched damage control teams. "A Hocklyn nuke blasted a hole in our energy screen, and we took a hit from one of their heavy missiles. We're lucky it wasn't a nuke or the damage would be worse."

"Hit them with our power beams," Tolsen ordered firmly as he watched the developing situation on the holographic tactical image. "They are trying to blast their way through our formation and escape." This was a surprise. From what Tolsen had studied of the first war, Hocklyn ships normally fought to the death.

Dark violet beams of energy erupted from the WarHawk, striking one of the war cruisers. Its screens wavered and then went down. The powerful beams struck the unprotected armor of the hull, vaporizing it as the beam cut deeply into the ship setting off secondary explosions. Then the war cruiser's energy screen stabilized, stopping the beam.

The Hocklyns own energy beams were not idle. Blue beam after blue beam shot out to strike the human ships. Missiles and heavy railgun fire raked the screens with fierce explosions. Occasionally a nuke would go off causing a screen to waver, allowing missiles or railgun rounds to penetrate.

"Light cruiser Crucible is down," Lieutenant Jarvis Anders reported from his sensor console. "She took a number of heavy nukes to her shields, causing them to collapse."

"Monarch cruiser Minotaur is reporting heavy damage," Colonel Beck added worriedly. "She is engaging one of the war cruisers."

Admiral Tolsen noticed that the Hocklyns ships were now becoming intermixed with his own fleet. Even the battle carriers would soon be involved. It might be wise in future battles to keep the battle carriers farther back with their destroyer escorts. That would give them enough time to land their bombers and rearm them for a second strike.

-

War Leader Sangeth felt growing anger as the War Cruiser Veldin vanished from the screens. The ship had been heavily damaged and rammed a human light cruiser. Both ships had vanished in a massive series of explosions. The Veldin's self-destructs going off had finished the job.

"Helm, turn us 80 degrees starboard, flank speed," grated out Sangeth, seeing his path was blocked by the human's two battle carriers. He knew both were heavily armed. "Get me a status report. All batteries, continuous fire!"

More human rounds and missiles were penetrating the shields, rattling the ship with each hit. More lights on the damage control console turned a glaring red. The ship seemed to roll as a human energy beam struck the Oblivion. Glancing at the sensor screen, he saw that only the War Cruiser Delphin and two escort cruisers were still with his flagship. Looking up at the viewscreen, he could see several ships burning in the human formation. His turn had not been soon enough. The two battle carriers were now pounding his remaining ships with missile fire and their energy beams.

"We can jump in two more minutes," First Leader Rahn grated out in pain from being thrown to the deck. His left arm now hung limply at his side. A jagged gash with blood running from it ran across his forehead.

"All ships are to jump as soon as we reach the threshold," Sangeth ordered as another of his escort cruisers blew up from being struck by the human's new energy weapon. Whatever it was, the beam was much more powerful than the energy beams on the Oblivion. This was vital information that needed to get back to Hocklyn space.

"The Delphin and the escort cruiser are too heavily damaged to jump," Rahn reported.

Sangeth only nodded. The two First Leaders on those ships knew their duty.

–

"Their flagship is nearly out of the gravity well," warned Colonel Beck. "We are focusing our weapons fire on it and the war cruiser."

"Sir, the war cruiser and the remaining escort cruiser are turning toward the battle carriers!" the sensor operator suddenly reported in consternation.

"They are what?" demanded Colonel Beck, looking sharply at the holographic display. Sure enough, the two indicated Hocklyn ships were changing course. "What are they doing? That's suicide! The carriers and the destroyers will destroy them!"

"Damn!" cried Tolsen in frustration, realizing the Hocklyn's intent. He quickly activated his mini-com, giving him instant contact with the two battle carriers and their destroyer escorts. He ordered the two battle carriers and the six destroyers to focus their fire on the two Hocklyn warships and forget the enemy flagship. "They're going to ram!"

He passed on more orders instructing all of his remaining ships to target the two Hocklyn ships. His gaze switched to the main viewscreen, which showed the Hocklyn war cruiser now glowing with intense weapons fire; its shields covered in massive explosions. The ship literally seemed to be on fire. Its own weapons were now firing only in self-defense.

"They've switched nearly all of their power to their shields," Colonel Beck spoke, his eyes growing wide. "We're not going to stop that war cruiser in time."

On the holographic image, the icon representing the Hocklyn escort cruiser suddenly expanded and then vanished as it was destroyed by the intense fire from the human fleet.

Admiral Tolsen could only watch the main viewscreen helplessly as the Hocklyn War Cruiser rammed the battle carrier Liberty. Moments later, the Hocklyn's self-destructs went off, destroying both ships in a series of massive nuclear explosions.

On the sensor screen, the red icon representing the Hocklyn flagship vanished as it escaped the gravity well and jumped safely into hyperspace. The battle was over.

Admiral Tolsen leaned back in his command chair, still gazing at the viewscreen, which showed the glowing wreckage of the battle carrier Liberty and the Hocklyn war cruiser. The entire command crew was in shock at the unexpected loss of the carrier. There had been 2,700 men and women on board that ship.

"Get me a fleet status report," Admiral Tolsen finally spoke into the silence, feeling an emptiness inside of him. He had screwed up, and he knew it. "How badly did they hurt us?"

Colonel Beck nodded and turned toward communications. He spent some time talking to the different ship commanders getting damage reports. He finally turned back to the admiral. "We destroyed seven Hocklyn escort cruisers and their two war cruisers, only their flagship managed to escape. In return, we lost the Battle Carrier Liberty, the Monarch cruiser Minotaur, and three light cruisers. Most of our other ships are damaged to some extent, but they can all jump if needed."

"Take us in and put us into orbit around Caden's World," ordered Tolsen, knowing his entire fleet was going to need some yard time. They may have won the battle, but this was one report he was not going to enjoy sending back to Fleet Command.

With the two light cruisers and the four destroyers that were still in orbit around Caden's World, they would help to augment his fleet strength until reinforcements arrived. In addition, most of the defensive satellites were still intact. He didn't know if more Hocklyn ships were around; the fact that sensors on Caden's World had indicated that the Hocklyn flagship had attempted to send out an FTL message indicated there might be.

Federation reinforcements should be arriving shortly. Once they were in the system, he would take his damaged fleet back to New Tellus for repairs and to report in. He knew there would be a lot of discussions about this battle and how it had been fought. He just hoped he was still an admiral when the debriefing was over. In his own mind, he wasn't sure he should be. The Hocklyn flagship had escaped to spread work back to the Hocklyn Empire that humans had survived.

-

Commander Bisth gazed in anger at the dreadnought Oblivion. He found it hard to believe that War Leader Sangeth had managed to escape this obvious human trap with only his flagship. Repair crews were currently working to repair the Oblivion so they could make the trip back to Resmunt's base. Every square inch of the ship's hull looked to be damaged. Massive burn marks, jagged holes, and destroyed weapon systems were hideously evident. Sangeth had been lucky to even escape. Bisth knew that the inside of the Oblivion was also heavily damaged.

His own fleet and Sangeth's flagship were in orbit around a small nebula where he didn't think the human ships would search for them. He had tried to stay away from star systems, knowing they might contain pickets watching for Hocklyn ships. He had been shocked, to say the least, when the escort cruiser had returned to inform him as to who their enemies were. More worrisome were the strength of their weapons. Even with the new energy shielding, Sangeth's fleet had been ravaged.

They would return and make their report to Commodore Resmunt, who in return would pass it on to the Hocklyn High Council. From there it would obviously go to the AIs. There was no way as of yet to know the size of human controlled space, but the fact they had placed a fleet of this strength in a system that contained only a mining colony did not bode well for the empire.

Bisth stood upon the command pedestal in the War Room of the dreadnought WarCry, deep in thought. He suspected that much honor was in store for the Hocklyn race in the coming years. The humans had escaped centuries ago from destruction. Now they were back, and Bisth strongly suspected they were ready for war!

Chapter Six

Admiral Tolsen was at New Tellus for a debriefing with Fleet Admirals Streth and Johnson. As he walked down the wide, immaculate corridors of New Tellus Station under a marine escort, he wondered briefly if he was going to be court martialed. He'd lost more ships than he should have against the Hocklyns. He still felt a numbing pain at the loss of so many good men and women. There had been several tactical errors he'd made, the worst of which had resulted in the loss of the battle carrier Liberty. Not only that, the enemy flagship had escaped! As commanding officer, it had been his responsibility to defeat the Hocklyns with minimal casualties and in that he had failed.

His marine escort stopped in front of a heavily armored hatch where two more armed marines were standing guard.

"You are expected, Admiral," one of the marines spoke as he stepped over and opened the hatch.

Tolsen nodded curtly and stepped inside. He felt some relief when his marine escort didn't follow.

Admiral Streth gazed thoughtfully at the young admiral who had just entered the room. He knew that Rear Admiral Tolsen was only thirty-eight-years-old and from Ceres. He was not married, and both of his parents were still alive. The rear admiral also had a sister that was in the Fleet and was currently serving as the executive officer on the battle carrier Scorpion.

"Have a seat," spoke Admiral Johnson, indicating a chair across from them.

Tolsen took his place at the highly polished conference table and waited expectantly. Whatever punishment he was about to receive he was willing to accept.

"You are not here to be disciplined," Admiral Karla Johnson began, her hazel eyes gazing thoughtfully at Tolsen. "Your fleet is the first one to actively engage the Hocklyns in over four hundred years and, all things considered, we feel you did surprising well in the battle."

"But the enemy flagship escaped," pointed out Tolsen, knowing this could spell trouble for the Federation. "They will shortly return in even greater numbers."

"And we will be ready for them," Admiral Streth assured him, his eyes looking deadly serious. "What you are not aware of Admiral

Tolsen is that we believe the Hocklyns had a second fleet also deployed close to Gliese 667C. From the readings we detected from our hyper sensor buoys, a Hocklyn escort cruiser jumped out of Gliese 667C as soon as they detected the mining colony and the ships around it. There was no way you could have prevented them from taking word back to their base about their discovery."

"This was obviously a survey in force to find out what happened to their two escort cruisers destroyed by Commander Thomas," Admiral Johnson continued. She leaned back and gazed thoughtfully at Rear Admiral Tolsen. "We are in the process of studying and analyzing your engagement with the Hocklyn fleet. Once we are finished, we will be sending out engagement recommendations to all of our fleet and ship commanders."

"How soon do you think it will be before they return?" Tolsen asked. He knew with a sinking feeling in his heart that the Federation was just a few months away from all out war with the Hocklyn Slave Empire.

Admiral Johnson looked over at Admiral Streth. He had fought the Hocklyns in the old Federation and knew more about them and their tactics than anyone else. It was the reason he had gone into cryosleep so that experience could be brought to the future.

"Less than two months," he replied with a frown spreading across his face. "They have six fleet bases within seven hundred light years of us that we have found so far. If I had to make a guess, they will assemble all of their available forces at those bases and throw them at us to see what we are up against. They have this crazy honor system where their warriors raise up in stature and authority based on the amount of honor they can accrue. From what our intelligence has gathered, they receive honor from discovering inhabited worlds to be added to their empire, but their greatest honor is achieved in combat."

"A warrior system based on honor," said Tolsen, shaking his head sadly. "It's a shame that so many good and valiant people have to die to appease this honor of theirs."

"It's what they have used to grow their empire," explained Hedon. He didn't like it, but this method seemed to work well for the Hocklyns.

"They will attack us immediately while they call in other forces from across their empire to reinforce their bases," continued Admiral Johnson, pursing her lips as she thought about what could be done.

"The good thing is we have detected no presence of any AI ships in our recent survey of their space."

"But the AIs will come eventually," Admiral Tolsen responded with a hint of worry on his face. "Then what? Can we destroy one of their ships without suffering catastrophic losses ourselves?"

"We are already working on tactics for that, Admiral," Hedon replied. It was a question he had pondered on himself. If they couldn't destroy an AI ship, then they wouldn't be able to win the war. He recalled briefly the traumatic videos he had watched of the two AIs ships that had attacked his home planets. They had nearly wiped out the entire Human Federation of World's fleet in just a few brief hours. "When they come this time, we will be ready for them."

Tolsen nodded. He could only have faith in Admiral Streth. The entire Federation was depending on him to guide them through this crisis and preserve the Federation.

"For the time being, your ships are to be repaired and then your fleet will be sent back to Gliese 667C," Admiral Johnson informed him. "We will be reinforcing your fleet as well as sending a second fleet for additional support if needed."

"This second fleet will be under the command of Admiral Adler on board the battle carrier Wasp," Admiral Streth informed Tolsen. "When the Hocklyns return, we have some new carrier tactics we want to try."

"Will that be enough ships to stop them?" asked Tolsen, looking doubtfully at the two Fleet Admirals. He wasn't sure two fleets would do it. "If they bring ships from six bases, we will be severely outnumbered."

Admiral Johnson looked shrewdly over at Admiral Streth and smiled. They had talked about this already. "We will be markedly increasing the defensive grid and fleet above Caden's World. We will also have several other fleets positioned to jump in when we need them. The Hocklyns may believe they can take the system. As a matter of fact, we want them to think that."

"You're setting a trap," Tolsen said in sudden realization, arching his eyebrows. He leaned back and gazed at the two admirals. "You want the Hocklyns to attack in overwhelming force!"

"Precisely," responded Admiral Johnson, nodding her head vehemently. "We are going to be fighting a war where our forces will almost always be outnumbered. We have to use superior tactics and methods to survive. The coming battle in Gliese 667C will help us to perfect those tactics, or at least we hope they will. It will also help to substantially reduce the number of Hocklyns ships in our sector of the galaxy."

"The Hocklyns are not used to fighting a superior enemy," added Hedon, leaning forward wanting to stress that point. He looked intently at Admiral Tolsen. "They encounter very few civilizations that can mount a successful defense against their warships. We will use that overconfidence against them."

Tolsen nodded his head in understanding. "We will be ready. What are my orders?"

"Go get your ships repaired for now, Admiral," Karla ordered. "Once we have finished analyzing your recent battle, we will call you back for a more thorough debriefing and give you some recommendations for your next engagement."

Tolsen left the room feeling relieved that he still had command of his fleet. He was determined that the next battle would be different. He already had some ideas of his own about how he would do things differently.

"What to you think, Hedon?" asked Admiral Johnson, turning her attention to the other Fleet Admiral.

"I think that young admiral of yours has a lot of potential. He just needs a little help with his tactics and the Hocklyns will not enjoy what they run into."

"My thoughts exactly," replied Karla, nodding her head slowly. "We need to decide which other fleet units will take place in this engagement. We need more of our admirals and commanders versed in fighting the Hocklyns."

Hedon nodded his head in agreement. Since his awakening, he had spent a lot of time with Fleet Admiral Johnson talking tactics and possible strategies to use against the Hocklyns in the coming war. Hedon closed his eyes briefly. There had been so much to do in the last few months in getting the Ready Reserve Fleet activated, and setting up First, Second, and Third Fleets so they would be operational.

Hedon had scarcely had time to think of those he had left behind. Particularly his brother Taylor and Lendle. Both had declined the offer to go into cryosleep. Instead, they had stayed awake and helped to build the Ceres colony and raise their family. He really missed not being able to talk things over with his brother. When he had time, he fully intended to look up their descendants. From what he had been able to learn, there were a number living on Ceres as well as serving in the Fleet.

"Helm, port hard forty degrees turn and down fifteen degrees, Tactical, fire upon completion of the turn. Navigation, plot a micro-jump to coordinates 280-47E and be prepared to jump on my command," Jeremy ordered calmly as he gazed at the holographic tactical display being projected above the plotting table.

"In range of primary target in fifteen seconds," Lieutenant Walters reported tensely, his fiery red hair in disarray.

"All weapons to fire on completion of the turn. Power beams are to fire ten seconds after lasers and railguns," ordered Colonel Malen, keeping her eyes on the tactical display and listening carefully to Commander Strong's orders.

Jeremy watched the tactical display intently. They were involved in a complicated war game. The Avenger was currently matched up against a Monarch heavy cruiser and two light cruisers while Jeremy's own escorts consisted of only two destroyers. He was about to attempt a daring maneuver to disable his opponent, one he had never tried before.

"Destroyers," Jeremy spoke over his mini-com to the two other ships in his command. "Maintain maximum range from those two light cruisers. Continue to hit them with long-range weapons fire; you just need to keep them occupied a little while longer."

The Avenger darted forward and made her sudden downward turn, bringing her eighteen railgun batteries in line with the intended target. On completion of the turn they opened up, joined by five of the heavy dual laser turrets.

The commander of the opposing Monarch cruiser swore in frustration as he realized what Commander Strong had done. He had been caught out of position, and the computer was now reporting major damage to his ship. Nevertheless, his own weapons were now locking onto the heavy strike cruiser. It was his turn to cause some damage.

"Fire power beams," Jeremy ordered, his eyes narrowing. "Stand by to micro-jump!"

"Inbound weapons fire," Kevin reported as his sensors detected the inbound ordinance. He knew all of this was generated by computer, but it damn sure looked and seemed real on his screens.

"Power beams firing," Lieutenant Preston at Tactical reported.

"Solid hits," Colonel Malen informed Jeremy as she saw the dark violet beams reach out and tap their target on the holographic display.

Jeremy nodded and counted to five. On the damage control board, a few lights were turning red. "Jump!" he ordered.

Instantly, a blue-white vortex of swirling light appeared directly in front of the Avenger. The Avenger's weapons fire stopped as she accelerated rapidly into the heart of the vortex.

"What the hell?" spoke the Monarch cruiser's executive officer as the Avenger vanished from the sensor screens.

"Where have they gone?" the ship's commander demanded frantically. "Find them, and find them now!" He knew that Commander Strong hadn't fled; he was up to some kind of trickery.

But it was too late. Kelsey was the best navigator in the Fleet, and she had plotted a quick micro-jump that took the Avenger to a position just behind the Monarch cruiser. A blue-white vortex formed, and the Avenger popped out. Instantly, she opened up with her power beams, nailing both the FTL and sublight drive of the Monarch cruiser. A moment later, the computer simulation indicated that the Monarch was destroyed.

On the Monarch, the commander watched helplessly as his ship powered down. He was left with life support and a few other systems until the computer operator restored full power back to the rest of the ship. His sensor screen was still working, and he watched helplessly as the strike cruiser, now joined by the two destroyers, turned on his light cruisers. Five minutes later, it was over. Commander Jeremy Strong had won again!

"That was a clever maneuver, Commander," Colonel Kyla Malen commented as she looked smugly at the screen that showed all three enemy ships had been destroyed. "Our own ships took only minor damage."

"They never expected us to use a micro-jump to catch them out of position," Jeremy replied with a satisfied smile. "They shouldn't have followed us out of the planet's gravity well; that's what allowed us to perform that jump."

"I couldn't have done better myself," Ariel said. She had watched the entire war game closely, monitoring everything.

She was very proud of Jeremy and the others. She wished that his father were alive to see how good a commander his son was becoming. Jason had been dead for hundreds of years, but his legacy was living on.

Katie was listening to the exchange and allowed a knowing smile to cross her face. She doubted that anyone could beat Ariel when it came to tactics. The AI was constantly running computer simulations of different battle scenarios. This was the sixth war game they had participated in, and the Avenger had as yet to receive any major damage.

What the crew wasn't aware of was that Ariel was doing everything in her power to make sure Jeremy's orders were carried out to the fullest. If he ordered a turn, she monitored the Avenger and even adjusted the ship's systems as needed to make sure the command was carried out. If the weapons were ordered to be fired, she made sure the maximum amount of ordnance possible arrived on target. Even with the jump that Kelsey had plotted, she had carried it out several more decimal points to make sure it was extremely accurate. Ariel also knew that even without her help, Jeremy would have still won all six of the war games. She had just made sure the wins were even more impressive.

"Take the ship back to Condition Five and secure from combat stations," Jeremy ordered as he activated the ship's interior com system. "Crew of the Avenger, congratulations on another victory. All three enemy ships have been destroyed, and we only received minor damage. Good job!"

"That's it for this series of battle drills," Colonel Malen commented.

She had been extremely surprised by Commander Strong's command ability. His tactical skills were remarkable. When she had been told about the group of five that were coming aboard the Avenger she had been apprehensive. But not anymore all five were exemplary officers and extremely talented. She knew she should have realized that, considering whom some of their parents had been. The crew was still a little bit in awe of all five, considering their history. They were already getting the attitude that they would soon be the best ship in the Fleet.

-

Later, all five of them were in the officer's mess eating a light meal. Jeremy enjoyed these rare opportunities where they could get together and talk privately.

"Wasn't that drill today great?" Kevin said as he chowed down on his normal meal of a hamburger and fries. "That Monarch never knew what hit them!"

"They never expected the micro-jump," Kelsey commented, her deep blue eyes looking over at Kevin. She grinned widely. "I put us right on their tail; there was nothing they could do."

"It was a perfect jump," admitted Jeremy pleased with the way everything had worked out. "It's a tactic that the Fleet should probably consider using against the Hocklyns."

"How can you eat so many hamburgers?" spoke Angela, shaking her head at Kevin. "You're going to turn into a hamburger one of these days."

"I just like hamburgers," Kevin answered defensively as he took another large bite.

"Ariel would like to participate in one of the war games," Katie mentioned, casually. She already suspected some of what the AI had been doing but had not mentioned it to anyone.

"I have been thinking about that," admitted Jeremy, leaning back and looking over at Katie. She was nothing like that crazy fifteen-year-old girl he had known so long ago. She was so much more mature and now a beautiful young woman. So far she had acted very properly, which was a relief to Jeremy considering how he felt about Kelsey.

"What's next on the agenda?" asked Kevin, putting his hamburger down, grabbing a couple of fries, and dipping them in ketchup. "More war games?"

"We are supposed to report back to Ceres for a briefing by Admiral Teleck tomorrow," responded Jeremy, looking over at his closest friend. "He's the one that's been receiving all of our battle efficiency reports from the war games. I haven't used Ariel yet, but I definitely intend to. She may be our ace in the hole if we ever get into a really bad situation. I just haven't found the right scenario to test her with."

Unseen by Jeremy, Ariel smiled to herself, feeling pleased. She could see and hear everything in the Avenger. She was always monitoring and watching the five. Unknown to any of them, it was something she had promised their parents long ago. She would always do whatever it took to keep all of them safe from harm.

Kelsey looked over at Jeremy, her dark blue eyes focusing on his. "I guess the war's coming soon. The crew is constantly talking about it. Some are pretty nervous about what we may be facing."

Jeremy nodded slowly. Years ago, Kelsey and he had decided to put off having a serious relationship or commitment until they were older. It was the only way they could serve on a ship together. They both still had deep feelings for each other, but they kept those out of sight unless they were on leave together.

"I've heard a few people talking," added Kevin, as he picked up his hamburger. "What do you think will happen, Jeremy?"

"I don't know," answered Jeremy, truthfully. He would never lie or mislead his friends. "We won't know until we face an AI ship. If we can destroy one, then we might be able to win this war."

"The AIs," Katie repeated, her green eyes showing some worry. "They're the big unknown in all of this; I wish we knew more about them."

It had been a big decision for her to go into cryosleep, but she just couldn't be left behind. She had known for years that her future was with Jeremy, Kelsey, Kevin, and Angela. They had gone through so much during the New Horizon incident that the five of them had formed a permanent bond of friendship.

She had spoken in length with her mom and dad about what she wanted to do. She could still recall her mother crying, knowing she would never speak to her daughter again, but they had supported her decision and Katie had gone into cryosleep.

"Don't forget about the other three races that control their parts of the galaxy for the AIs," Angela reminded them as she picked up her fork and took a bite of watermelon. "They could come and help the Hocklyns."

"We need more allies," Jeremy stated with a growing frown. "Particularly the Albanians."

"The mystery race," Kevin spoke his eyes glinting with curiosity. "What's up with them?"

"They control more worlds and are farther spread out then the Federation," Katie informed them. She had looked up everything she could find on the Albanians, but the more she investigated the more confused she got. Something just didn't add up.

"Perhaps when they are attacked by the Hocklyns they will agree to help us," responded Angela, laying down her fork and eyeing her now empty plate.

"At least we have three other alien races that are willing to help us," Kelsey added.

Jeremy nodded. He just wondered what was ahead of them. This could be a very long war.

-

The next day, Jeremy watched as his shuttle made rendezvous with a Federation battle cruiser in high orbit around Ceres. He was sitting in the copilot's seat, and Kelsey was piloting. She wanted to keep brushed up on her piloting skills since she claimed they could never know when they might come in handy.

"That's the WarHawk, Admiral Tolsen's flagship," Kelsey informed Jeremy as they neared the ship's brightly lit flight bay. "I heard some scuttlebutt that he will be the admiral in charge of the defense of Gliese 667C when the Hocklyns return."

"He's a good admiral," Jeremy responded as he watched Kelsey deftly maneuver the shuttle into the flight bay and onto the indicated landing pad. "If Fleet Admirals Streth and Johnson both trust the man, then so do I."

"I wonder what he wants with you?" asked Kelsey, looking over at Jeremy. When they were by themselves, they always used each other's first names. Only in the presence of others did they refer to each other by rank.

"He's assembling his fleet for the expected battle with the Hocklyns. Perhaps he wants the Avenger to be part of that."

Kelsey was silent for a moment as she depressed two buttons that opened the hatch and lowered the ramp. "This is why we went into cryosleep, Jeremy; we wanted to be part of this war."

Jeremy nodded as he unfastened his safety harness and stood up. "I don't know how long this will take."

"I'll be here," Kelsey promised with a smile. "I'm not going anywhere."

She watched as Jeremy went into the main shuttle cabin and down the ramp. She wondered if it would be possible for her and Jeremy to spend some alone time together before being deployed for combat. Over the years, they had become very attached to one another. They always had a great time together whenever they could manage to get away. Besides that, Jeremy was great in bed, and she really needed some of his loving attention.

Jeremy made his way to the Command Center of the WarHawk and, upon arriving, was admitted immediately by the two heavily armed marines standing guard at the entry hatch.

Stepping inside, he spotted Admiral Tolsen standing at the holographic plotting table talking to a colonel who was probably the ship's executive officer. The executive officer spotted Jeremy and spoke quietly to the admiral.

Admiral Tolsen turned. Jeremy instantly stopped, stood at attention, and saluted. "Commander Jeremy Strong reporting as ordered, Sir."

"At ease, Commander," replied Tolsen, returning Jeremy's salute. "Take a look at this tactical display and tell me what you think."

Jeremy took the last few steps to the large holographic display and studied it for a moment. "This is Gliese 667C, isn't it, Sir?"

"Yes," Tolsen replied with a slight nod. "If you were going to trap a Hocklyn fleet in this system, what would you recommend?"

Jeremy was silent as he studied the image, which depicted the planets and the defenses around Caden's World. "I assume we are adding additional satellite defenses to the planet?"

"Yes, we are creating a full defensive grid," Admiral Tolsen replied as he studied the young commander. "When we are finished, we will have two hundred laser satellites in orbit and twenty-six missile platforms. Beneath them will be twelve destroyers and two light cruisers in case anything gets through."

"Are we evacuating the planet?"

"We are in the process of doing that now. In place of the miners and their families, we are landing two thousand space marines. They will see to it that the mines are still operating, and everything will look normal when the Hocklyns arrive. A number of the mine supervisors will be staying on to make sure everything looks legit."

"I would seed the system with hyper detection buoys so we know exactly when the Hocklyns arrive and their exact location," Jeremy suggested. "If I were the Hocklyn commander, I would approach the system much more cautiously than the previous attack fleet. Particularly after the losses it took. I might send in a few light units to take some long distance scans before committing my forces."

"My thoughts exactly," spoke Tolsen, nodding his head. He had been told that Commander Strong had a good head for military tactics. "Then what?" He was curious to hear what else the young commander might suggest.

"I would jump into the system with my entire fleet right here," Jeremy said, pointing to a spot just outside of Caden's World's gravity well. The spot he had pointed to was between the sun and the planet but extremely close to the gravity well.

"Why there?" asked Tolsen, looking closely at the spot Commander Strong had indicated. That was awfully close to the planet's gravity well. It would also be a risky jump unless it was well plotted.

"For surprise," Jeremy replied, looking at the admiral. "They will be expecting us to be focusing our sensors outward away from the inner system. If I were them, I would jump in there, close to the planet, and then split my fleet. I would send in half of it to destroy the orbital defenses and the defense fleet. I would hold the other part back in case an enemy fleet is lurking nearby. That way, I could engage an enemy fleet while the rest of my forces subjugate the planet and grab whatever information they can find."

"Information?" spoke Colonel Beck, looking confused. "Do you think that's the purpose of this attack, information?"

"Yes, I do," responded Jeremy, looking over at the colonel. "Caden's World is the only Federation world they currently know about. They could spend time searching the surrounding stars for more of our worlds, but why bother? All the information they need is right here." Jeremy pointed directly at Caden's World.

Admiral Tolsen was quiet as he thought about what Strong had just said. It made a lot of sense. Admiral Teleck and he had already spent considerable time discussing this young commander. Commander Strong had won every war game he had been involved in with ease. It was time to give this young man more authority.

"Commander Strong, effective immediately you are being placed in charge of a special task force," Tolsen spoke in his commanding voice. "You will be assigned additional ships, including another heavy strike cruiser, two Monarch class cruisers, six light cruisers, six destroyers, and one battle carrier. All of these ships will come from the Ceres defense fleet."

Colonel Beck looked at Admiral Tolsen in surprise. "Admiral, I need to remind you that there might be a problem giving Commander Strong command of all of those ships with him being only a commander."

"It won't be a problem," answered Tolsen, looking gravely at Jeremy. "We will be giving Commander Strong the temporary rank of Rear Admiral. If he performs well, the rank will become permanent. We have also carefully chosen the commanding officers of all of these ships, and they are all younger than Commander Strong except the commander of the battle carrier. I have spoken to them myself, and they will do as he orders without hesitation.

"Rear Admiral?" Jeremy stuttered in surprise, his eyes growing wide in shock. This was the last thing he had expected when he had stepped into the Command Center of the WarHawk.

"You deserve it," responded Admiral Tolsen, handing over the rank insignia that he had been holding in his left hand. "We are in a time of war, or shortly will be, and rapid promotion will be the norm for well qualified officers. You have demonstrated through the war games that you have the potential for higher command. Now return to your ship; it will take us a few days to finish getting your fleet prepared."

Jeremy walked back to the shuttle in a daze, scarcely believing what had just happened. As he stepped inside, he was met by Kelsey, who looked questionably at him.

"What happened, Jeremy?"

Jeremy opened his right hand and showed her the new rank insignias.

"Rear Admiral!" she screamed in excitement, grabbing Jeremy and hugging him tightly. "Your father would be so proud!"

Jeremy held Kelsey for a moment enjoying the feel of her body up next to his, and then he stepped back and looked seriously at her. "They're giving me a fleet! Kelsey, I don't know if I am ready for this."

Kelsey was silent for just a moment. "It's just because of that doubt that you are," she replied with a knowing smile. "You will make a good admiral. I can't wait to get back to the Avenger and tell everyone. This is great!"

A few minutes later, Jeremy was in the copilot's seat watching as Kelsey maneuvered the shuttle out of the WarHawk's flight bay and back toward the Avenger. He had just been handed a boatload of responsibility. He hoped he was ready for it and that he didn't disappoint his friends, particularly Kelsey.

Chapter Seven

Commodore Resmunt frowned at the latest report he had just received. He was uncertain just what the latest message from the High Council meant. It was demanding to know how many worlds these new humans controlled and how soon they could be brought into the empire. Strangely, there was no mention of the AIs. Resmunt wondered if the High Council had neglected to mention to their masters that more humans had been found. If so, what did that mean for him? He let out a long, frustrated breath. It was very difficult dealing with the High Council.

War Leader Bisth was currently in Resmunt's office. They had been discussing the humans and what needed to be done when his aide had brought in the message.

"There can't be more than one or two human worlds," spoke Bisth forcefully, his cold, dark eyes focusing on the Fleet Commodore. "From the design of their ships, it is obvious that these are refugees from the Human Federation of Worlds that we destroyed over four centuries ago. Even if a few thousand escaped, they couldn't have increased in sufficient numbers to be a viable threat to the empire."

"They destroyed Sangeth's fleet easily enough," Resmunt reminded Bisth coldly, his large dark eyes focusing on the War Leader. "I have done much research into these humans. They were a very formidable enemy when we first encountered them, and our ship losses were staggering in the final few battles. We lost numerous dreadnoughts, more dreadnoughts against the humans than any alien race we've ever fought before. Don't underestimate them, Bisth!"

"Their weapons and shields are superior," admitted Bisth, gazing at Resmunt. "We were fortunate that our own ships had recently updated shields. However, we will have superior numbers in all future battles. Even their advanced technology will not be able to stand up to the number of ships we can bring to bear against them."

Resmunt walked over to the large window, looked out at the bustling spaceport below, and watched as several large shuttles took off, probably taking supplies to the orbiting warships above.

"I have studied the last battle in the human's home system," he spoke in his deep, rasping voice. "From the sensor scans, it looked as if the humans were trying to protect two very large civilian ships from being destroyed. I would guess those ships were some type of colony ships. In his later reports, War Leader Sigeth claimed that all human ships had been hunted down and destroyed. I am beginning to doubt the veracity of his claims."

"You think he fabricated those reports and filled them with falsehoods?" spoke Bisth in disbelief.

Surely, no Hocklyn would do such a thing! No Hocklyn would lie; it was against their honor system and everything they believed in. If a Hocklyn was caught in a lie, he could lose everything.

"Yes," Resmunt replied softly, turning and walking back to gaze at the large map of this section of the galaxy on his wall. "I believe those two colony ships escaped, as well as a number of warships. In order to preserve his honor, War Leader Sigeth fabricated the reports which told of their later destruction."

"Then more than several thousand humans could have escaped," hissed Bisth in anger. He couldn't imagine the audacity of a War Leader doing such a thing.

"Even if a hundred thousand of them escaped, that's still not enough to be a threat," Resmunt responded as his eyes focused on the star map and a system that was circled in red. "They may control one or two worlds at the most, and perhaps a few mining colonies like the one that Sangeth attacked. They will not have the numbers to seriously oppose us."

"What about the fleet that destroyed Sangeth's forces? It was a powerful one," Bisth pointed out.

He wondered if there was any way possible to further strengthen the energy shields of their ships. Losses were expected in combat, but losses due to the weakness of some Hocklyn weapon systems were aggravating, particularly since the AIs banned advanced weapon's research. Bisth had been surprised when the AIs had given them the new advanced shields and ordered them installed in all Hocklyn warships.

Bisth was anxious for combat. These humans could be a source of honor for himself and other Hocklyns. If they could destroy the human's warships, find their new home world, and bring it into the empire, honor would be forthcoming.

"I have studied this carefully," Resmunt spoke in a decisive voice. "We must subjugate these humans before our AI masters become involved. They ordered the destruction of the first human worlds and even participated in the battles; two of their warships were sent to destroy the human fleets that defended their systems. It was only after the AI ships left that the humans were able to launch a successful counterattack and escape with those two colony ships."

"We must strike quickly, then," Bisth replied, his dark eyes widening at the thought of how much honor could be awarded for defeating the humans.

"I agree," responded Resmunt, nodding his head. "I am giving you four fleets with which to conquer this system. I am also sending several vessels full of our Protectors to land upon their mining world. We must find out where their home world is. If not, we will be forced to survey the entire sector around that mining planet. We may not have time to do that before the AIs intervene."

"Four fleets should be sufficient," responded Bisth pleased at being given the command. "Victory will be ours!" With four fleets, he would have sufficient firepower to easily overwhelm the human's advanced technology.

"You have two weeks to prepare, then we launch our strike," ordered Resmunt, looking at Bisth with unblinking eyes. "Do not fail, for honor is at risk."

Bisth nodded and left the Commodore's office. He had much to do to prepare if they were to depart in two weeks time. Sangeth's flagship, the Crimson Oblivion, would have to finish being repaired and his fleet brought back up to full strength. He would also have to coordinate with the other three War Leaders on their method of attack.

Commodore Resmunt returned to the large window to gaze out over the spaceport. He had already put in a request for more ships. He had one fleet stationed at each of his new bases as well as three fleets above in orbit. Ships from the other bases would be used to reinforce Sangeth's losses. He'd also requested six additional full fleets to be used against the humans once their home world was discovered. He would not make the same mistake that Sigeth had in underestimating these humans.

-

Farther in toward the center of the galaxy a special meeting was being held on the Hocklyn home world of Calzen. All ten High Councilors were present, and there was much concern being expressed in the meeting.

"We must tell the AIs about the humans," argued Councilor Ruthan, vehemently. "To not do so is to invite disaster!"

"These humans will be few in numbers and not a serious threat to our empire," countered Councilor Nartel in a loud and argumentative voice. "They will have one or two worlds at the most to draw resources from. Their fleet, while it does possess powerful weapons, will not be large. It will be good to add their worlds to our empire."

Others voiced their feelings as the meeting dragged on. Finally, the High Leader of the Hocklyn High Council called for order. "We are obviously in disagreement as to how these new human worlds should be dealt with. Fleet Commodore Resmunt is even now preparing a powerful fleet strike against this recently discovered mining world. I propose we allow this strike to go forward; it will give us the information we need about the actual number of worlds these humans control as well as the size of their fleet. I fully expect that Fleet Commodore Resmunt can conquer these human worlds with his current forces."

"Then we are not going to notify the AIs?" Ruthan asked, his dark eyes showing deep concern. "If they find out, it could be extremely dangerous for us."

"The humans are not yet a threat," High Leader Ankler insisted, his large eyes focusing on Ruthan. "We do not as of yet know their actual strength. If they are more powerful than Resmunt believes, then we will notify the AIs, not before."

"What about these reinforcements he is asking for?" Ruthan demanded. "There must be a reason why he is asking for six additional fleets!"

"We will send him two," the High Leader replied. "Two fleets should be sufficient to replenish his losses in the coming battle. Once the human worlds are conquered, they can be used to garrison the human system and pacify the populace. They should make excellent slaves for our empire. Once that is done, we will notify the AIs. I believe they will be quite pleased with us in bringing these new human worlds into our domain."

Ruthan looked at High Leader Ankler with doubt in his large, dark eyes. This was a dangerous path the High Leader was embarking on. The AIs had considered the humans a dangerous threat in the past; there was no reason to think that opinion had changed. Looking around at the other council members, it was obvious they all supported the High Leader's decision.

"Very well," rasped Ruthan, finally. "We will conquer the human worlds first and then notify the AIs. But the sooner this is over with, the better."

A short time later, High Leader Ankler was standing on a balcony high up on the massive building that contained the High Council chambers. It was night outside, but darkness on Calzen was hard to find. Looking upward, he could see dozens of artificial habitats and a number of shipyards in orbit. From them, enough reflected sunlight shined down to change darkness into perpetual twilight.

There were ten star systems in the Hocklyn home systems. Every habitable world was packed with Hocklyns; there was very little green space remaining anywhere upon their worlds. Even the atmosphere on the inhabited planets was recycled through massive air machines that were located in every city. On the other planets and moons in each of the ten systems, massive domes covered even more cities packed with Hocklyns. Hundreds of ships arrived daily, bringing raw and fabricated materials that were used to construct even more habitats. All their food was brought in from the numerous slave worlds. Even the open space between the planets was now being used to place new space habitats.

Over two trillion Hocklyns were packed inside the ten star systems that the AIs allowed them to inhabit. Already, stringent population controls were being enacted. Ankler knew that the population situation was reaching the boiling point, and another meeting had been set up with the AIs to ask for additional worlds to colonize. Eight nearby star systems had been chosen. If the AIs turned them down again, Ankler was not sure how the civilian population would react.

Several of the other High Councilors had proposed that the military be used to reduce the civilian population to a more manageable level. This would be a drastic measure and would surely lead to a massive loss of honor for all involved. If the AIs refused them the right to colonize the new systems, they might have no other choice other than to eliminate their lower class citizens. The citizens with the lowest amount of honor would be chosen to die for the good of the empire.

Ankler became lost in thought; he was concerned about these new humans. What he had managed to conceal thus far was that the Hocklyn responsible for allowing these humans to escape, War Leader Sigeth, was one of his own ancestors. If the truth came out before the human worlds were conquered, he could lose his position as well as his honor. The human worlds must be brought into the empire before the AIs learned of them.

-

Jeremy looked carefully at the tactical display above the plotting table. "I want our ships ready for a quick strike," he informed Colonel Malen. On the tactical display, the seventeen ships of his new task force were displayed, including the Avenger, which sat at the center.

For days, the ships had been doing simple battle drills as the ship commanders became accustomed to one another.

"When we come out of hyperspace, I want our ships in combat formation and ready to fire their weapons."

"It takes a few seconds for our systems to come up after a jump," Colonel Malen reminded Jeremy. "To be at 100 percent battle readiness will take six to ten seconds."

"Seven point two seconds to be exact," Ariel chimed in. "However, I may have a way to reduce that time to three point six seconds if that will help. I assume the primary systems needed after the exit from hyperspace would be weapons, targeting sensors, and shields?"

"Yes," replied Jeremy, looking over at the main viewscreen where Ariel was watching them. Her dark eyes and black shoulder length hair were the same as Jeremy remembered them. He often wondered why she never changed her appearance.

"We can set a priority as to which systems are powered up first after a jump. Life support, communications, some sensors, and other systems could be put on hold until the shields, targeting systems, and weapons are fully online."

"You say we could do this on all of our ships in three point two seconds?" Jeremy demanded as he thought of the tactical possibilities.

"It should be simple enough," Ariel replied with a slight nod of her head. "I would need Lieutenant Johnson to help write a new computer program, but it shouldn't be that difficult." What Ariel wasn't mentioning was that it would be extremely difficult for anyone else but Katie.

"Do it," Jeremy ordered. "I want every possible advantage when we engage the Hocklyns."

-

Later, Jeremy, Colonel Malen, Lieutenant Charles Preston the tactical officer, Katie, and Kelsey were all in Jeremy's office discussing the current situation.

Jeremy leaned back in the large cushioned chair behind his desk and looked over at the far wall. On it was a painting of the lost ship New Horizon, Earth's first interstellar ship as she left the spacedock above the Moon. It held many painful memories for Jeremy. It was a stark reminder for Jeremy never to take anything for granted.

The majority of the crew of the New Horizon had died when Lieutenant Nelson had set off the ship's self-destruct to keep the Hocklyns from capturing the ship. Jeremy and his four friends had been the only survivors. Rear Admiral Sheen, in command of the WarStorm, had rescued them from certain death. In Jeremy's mind, it seemed as if it had happened only yesterday.

"I just received word from Admiral Johnson that we are to proceed to Gliese 667C to aid in its defense," Jeremy informed them, looking across his desk at the others. "Once we arrive, we will begin battle drills involving short micro-jumps to engage the enemy."

"Short micro-jumps," Kelsey uttered with a frown. "Those are very hard and complicated to calculate." She had a feeling that Jeremy was about to give her a headache.

"I know; have Ariel help you if necessary," Jeremy replied, his eyes meeting Kelsey's. "I also want to tighten up the fleet formation when we exit hyperspace. That means that all ships have to enter the spatial vortex at the exact same speed and angle."

"That will be difficult," responded Colonel Malen, shaking her head doubtfully. "With seventeen ships in our task force, there is bound to be some dispersion when the ships exit hyperspace."

"Not if we let Ariel control the jumps," suggested Lieutenant Johnson as an idea suddenly occurred to her. "If we give Ariel full control of our helm systems just prior to entering the vortexes, she can ensure that all ships are aligned properly and their speeds are dead on. I would have to write a new program for the helm control, but I could to it with Ariel's help."

"Is that possible, Ariel?" asked Jeremy, knowing the AI was watching.

"Yes, Admiral," Ariel responded. It was very seldom that Jeremy blocked her from viewing anything within the ship. "With the proper program the ships could be made to exit hyperspace in battle formation. Keep in mind though, that due to the math behind hyperspace travel, a ship can't exit too close to any object of appreciable mass. There would still be a minimum safe distance between ships we would have to maintain."

They continued to talk for another half hour, laying out tactics and discussing what needed to be done to make the task force ready for battle with the Hocklyns. When the meeting was over, Kelsey and Katie stayed behind.

"We'll be fighting the Hocklyns soon," Katie commented as she walked over and gazed at the painting of the New Horizon. It was hard to believe that all those events were over two hundred years in the past. She put out her hand and gently touched the painting.

Kelsey came to stand next to her and put her hand over Katie's. Her father, mother, and so many others were lost to the far distant past as a result of their cryosleep. Sometimes they all felt extremely lonely.

"It's what we wanted," she reminded Katie.

"I know," answered Katie with a weak smile. "I guess I'm just nervous about going into actual combat with the Hocklyns."

"We all are," commented Jeremy, standing up and walking over to the other two. "But I firmly believe that if we work hard enough, we will all come through this okay. That's why I want to perfect these new tactics."

The two women nodded, and they all went back and sat down. For the next hour, they talked about the old days back at the academy and how things had changed over the intervening years. So much had been left behind, but there was also so much more ahead of them.

-

Admiral Streth was on the surface of New Tellus eating a relaxing meal. Sitting across the table from him was Rear Admiral Sheen, to his left was Admiral Adler, and to his right was Rear Admiral Bennett.

They were in a small restaurant with a relaxing atmosphere, and the food was excellent. Admiral Streth took another bite of the medium well steak he was eating and closed his eyes as memories overtook him. It reminded him so much of the meals that Lendle used to cook back on Maken at the small cabin by the lake. Opening his eyes, he wondered if the cabin was still there and if he would ever be able to return to the Federation worlds. They were currently listening to Amanda describe her brief visit back to Aquaria.

"So there actually were survivors," Admiral Bennett commented with surprise. "I would have thought the Hocklyns would have eliminated all of them."

"A few survived," Amanda responded with a sad look in her blue eyes. Her brunette hair was still cut short in the current military style allowed for women. "On Krall Island there were fewer than twenty survivors at the time of our return. Many of them were quite old."

"That's a remarkable story," commented Admiral Adler. He had left family behind in the old Federation as well; they all had. After so much time, he doubted if there would be any way now to find out their fate.

"After all these years, I imagine there will be very little left of the old cities of the Federation," Admiral Bennett spoke, thinking about how the passage of time could quickly erase any signs of human habitation.

"You're probably right," responded Admiral Sheen, sadly. "Even when we returned, the cities were already being overrun by plant growth. All six of the old worlds of the Federation by now have returned to how they were before humanity set forth upon the planets."

"We have the new Federation now," Admiral Bennett stated. "Perhaps someday we can return to those worlds once again and claim them as ours."

"We can only hope," Admiral Adler responded in agreement. "It would be great if we could one day drive the Hocklyns out of our old systems."

Hedon reached forward and took a sip of the rich red wine in his glass. He had spent considerable time traveling around the worlds of the new Federation inspecting ships, bases, shipyards, and even the massive battle stations orbiting Earth. There were twenty-two billion humans living in the Federation; Hedon hoped that was enough and that they were ready for what was ahead.

"I spoke with Major Ackerman earlier today," commented Hedon, setting his glass down. "He believes the Hocklyns will be attacking Caden's World shortly."

"Admiral Johnson feels we're ready," Admiral Bennett added as he reached for a roll and began buttering it. "Admiral Tolsen's fleet has been heavily reinforced, and newly promoted Rear Admiral Strong will have his special task force on standby. In addition, the orbital defenses and defensive fleet have also been heavily augmented."

Amanda smiled and recalled the first time she had met Jeremy Strong; even then she had found him to be highly intriguing. Now he was an admiral. She shook here head as she thought about how quickly things could change.

"Perhaps so," Hedon responded in a grave and concerned voice. "But we need to annihilate this Hocklyn attack fleet while we have the opportunity. We may not have too many chances to destroy one of their large fleets in its entirety."

"What do you suggest?" asked Bennett, laying his roll down and focusing his full attention on Admiral Streth.

"We have discussed allowing Admiral Adler to try some of our new battle carrier tactics out in this battle."

"Yes, I recall Admiral Johnson mentioning that," Bennett responded. He still wasn't convinced how useful the Anlon bombers could be against Hocklyn ships. The survivability of a bomber going in close enough to release its missiles was very low. "But the main part of the battle will be fought by our main warships, not the battle carriers."

"That's the change I am recommending," Admiral Streth replied in a serious tone. He leaned back and pushed his plate away. "We have changed the makeup of the squadrons on the battle carriers. I think if handled properly, we can use this to our advantage and perhaps win a substantial victory in Caden's system over the Hocklyns."

"Why the battle carriers?" asked Bennett, feeling confused. "They ensure we can knock out the Hocklyn's fighters, and they are a good backup if we need heavier firepower. If I recall correctly, the bomber squadrons suffered nearly eighty percent casualties in Admiral Tolsen's engagement."

"It was our first major attempt since we left the old Federation to use our bomber squadrons in that way," explained Adler, taking a deep breath. He had spent a lot of time talking to some of the surviving Anlon pilots as well as reviewing battle video.

"In all of our engagements against the Hocklyns, they have never deployed any type of bomber or fighter capable of carrying a heavy missile," Hedon informed Admiral Bennett. "I intend to use Gliese 667C to test some new carrier tactics. Admiral Adler, will you please explain to Admiral Bennett what we have in mind."

Adler nodded and smiled wolfishly. "I have changed the squadron mix on my battle carriers," he began. "Each carrier will have two twenty-ship squadrons of Talon fighters and fourteen ten-ship squadrons of Anlon bombers. Each bomber is being equipped to handle four modified Shrike missiles with Klave class warheads. We can also use tactical nukes on the Shrikes if need be."

Bennett was silent as he mulled this over. "If your bombers go up against the Hocklyns, you're going to suffer heavy losses just as Admiral Tolsen did. While it's true they have no bombers, they do have powerful defensive systems to defend against fighters. To launch those missiles, you will have to be in range of those defenses. They will cut your bombers to pieces."

"We've managed to install a weak forward energy shield on the bombers," Hedon added with a grin. "It should allow the Anlons to take one or two hits. If the pilots are good, they should be able to get in, release their missiles, and then get the hell out."

Bennett nodded as he thought this over. "Even so, you're still going to lose a lot of your bombers."

Hedon was silent for a long moment. "I realize that. But I would rather lose the bombers with their two-man crews than a major warship where the losses would be in the thousands."

"What do the bomber crews think about that?" Bennett asked. He hated the idea of acceptable losses. He knew that if he were a pilot, he wouldn't want to be flying one of those bombers.

"They're all volunteers and have been told about the risks," Hedon answered. "We actually have more volunteers than we have bombers."

Bennett looked over at Admiral Adler. "What is the current makeup of Third Fleet for this battle? I understand there have been some changes."

Adler glanced over at Hedon, who nodded. "We have ten battle carriers, two Monarch heavy cruisers, four light cruisers, and twelve destroyers."

"You're risking a lot with this," commented Bennett, leaning back and looking at Admirals Streth and Adler. "That's almost half the carrier strength in the Ready Reserve."

"War is about taking risks," Hedon responded in a firm voice. "With the help of Admiral Tolsen, I intend to wipe out this Hocklyn fleet when it attacks."

"Then you will be there as well?" asked Bennett with arched eyebrows.

"With Second Fleet," answered Hedon, looking over at Amanda. "Second Fleet is fully ready, and we will be using it as a reserve force if the Hocklyns come in with a really powerful fleet. It will also give us the opportunity to give the commanders of our ships a taste of actual combat."

"Second Fleet is ready," Amanda responded. Hedon had already told her about his plans. "We have been conducting battle drills for the past ten days."

The four continued to talk for a while longer before Admirals Bennett and Adler had to leave. Once they were gone, Hedon looked across the table at Amanda.

"The war is here, Amanda," he said softly. "How is Richard taking his new assignment?"

Amanda took a small sip of her wine and then looked up at Hedon. "Admiral Johnson has placed him in charge of the asteroid fortresses in the New Tellus System. She feels that his experience in defending the shipyard above New Providence makes him perfect for the job."

"That's good," Hedon responded with a nod. "It's an excellent post for Richard."

He had been aboard several of those massive asteroid fortresses; they were unbelievably powerful. Each was capable of taking on a Hocklyn fleet on its own. He had been extremely impressed on his tour at all that had been accomplished since he had gone into cryosleep so long ago. The Federation had spent decades designing and building up their defenses to stand up to the Hocklyns. The human race was nearly ready for war. Hedon's only question was whether or not the Hocklyns could truly be stopped. While it was true that the human race had grown very powerful, the Hocklyns still outnumbered them hundreds or possibly thousands to one. Then, of course, there were the AIs.

"He likes it," Amanda spoke with a pleased smile. "He should be safe on the fortresses."

"What does he think about you being in charge of a fleet that will be going off to fight the Hocklyns?"

"He accepts it," answered Amanda, letting out a deep breath. "We both know this war is going to be long and dangerous and there will be risks involved, but we went into cryosleep so our descendants would be free of the Hocklyn threat. We both believe in that."

Hedon nodded in understanding. "I have faith in you, Amanda; there may be some extremely difficult things that I may ask of you in the coming years. This war will not be easy, and it might not be winnable, but we are going to do everything in our power to stop the Hocklyns and their AI masters."

The two spoke quietly for a few more minutes and then went their separate ways. Admiral Streth flew up to his new flagship, the

Vanquisher class battleship StarStrike. As his shuttle approached the new ship, he couldn't help but marvel at her 1,600-meter length. This new StarStrike was the most powerful ship ever built by the new Federation. It was fully capable of acting as a command ship for the entire Federation fleet.

A little while later, Hedon was in his quarters. He looked around, taking note of how new and immaculate everything was and let out a heavy sigh. It would take a while, but this was his new home. He reached into a bag he had brought aboard and took out several photographs. The first was of his brother Taylor and Lendle. It had been taken in front of the cabin on Maken down by the lake. The second was of his old flagship, the battle cruiser StarStrike. Hedon placed both pictures carefully on his desk and then sat down. He was quiet for quite some time as he thought about all the people and friends he had left behind.

Chapter Eight

War Leader Bisth stood on the command pedestal in the War Room of his flagship the Hocklyn dreadnought WarCry. He had just finished a briefing of his three subordinate War Leaders and they were in the process of returning to their respective commands. Tomorrow, they would be leaving to attack the human mining colony. It would take eight days to reach the targeted system by the route Bisth had chosen.

Bisth had wanted to make sure that the other three War Leaders understood their objectives in the coming conflict. The first was to eliminate any armed resistance in the system, which included all warships and orbital defenses. If any civilian freighters were located, they were to be disabled and boarded. Once that was done, they would form a cordon around the mining planet just outside of the planet's gravity well. Bisth did not intend to allow his fleets to be caught as Sangeth had.

They would then begin landing Protectors on the planet under the covering fire of several escort cruisers. The primary goal of the Protectors was to secure information; computers, star maps, and even captives were desirable.

In the two transports that Resmunt had furnished were 1,200 highly trained Protectors, all anxious to advance their honor in combat. Bisth allowed himself to bask in the thought that all of his mission objectives would be accomplished. His honor would be substantially increased as well as his standing as a War Leader. Fleet Commodore Resmunt had even requested that a number of human captives be returned to the fleet base. He was interested in seeing what type of slaves they would make.

Bisth turned his attention to the new orbiting shipyard that was nearing completion. Why Resmunt had demanded they spend so much time and labor building the monstrosity was beyond Bisth's understanding. The shipyard was six kilometers across and two wide. It contained four large repair bays as well as the facilities to make most of the parts to repair any ship of the Hocklyn fleet. The shipyard was also heavily armed. There were other larger shipyards deeper in the empire, where new ships were being built and others repaired, but he had never heard of one out on the outskirts of the empire such as this one.

Even more alarming were the defenses that Resmunt was putting up in orbit. Missile platforms and railgun satellites surrounded the planet. Much of the current construction capability of the completed sections of the shipyard were being dedicated to building these satellites. It made Bisth wonder if Resmunt knew something that he had not conveyed to the others in his command. Perhaps Resmunt had some other devious motive.

If Bisth didn't know better, it almost seemed as if Fleet Commodore Resmunt was preparing for an attack against his fleet base. He shook his head and had the view on the main viewscreen changed. The dreadnought Crimson Oblivion appeared. The ship had been completely repaired in one of the new repair bays on the station. It looked as new as the day it came out of its original construction bay. The Crimson Oblivion was 1,200 meters long and slightly wedge shaped, its hull covered with numerous weapon emplacements. Bisth knew that his own ship looked the same.

"All ships are ready for departure," First Leader Gresth reported from his position at the plotting table. "Supplies and munitions are on board, and the crews are anxious for battle."

"Excellent," Bisth replied, his large eyes turning toward his second in command. "We will be departing orbit in the morning. Hyperjumps will be twenty light years each, and we will be doing five per day."

"As you command," Gresth responded with a slight nod of his head.

His pale green skin was covered in gray colored body armor, which was customary among Hocklyn fleet officers. Gresth's six digit hands were a darker green, and the long, sharp nails on the tips of his fingers could be deadly in hand-to-hand combat. He also carried a sharp blade in a small scabbard attached to his armor at the waist. Gresth was renowned among the crew of the WarCry for his combat ability, and had personally been involved in four honor matches between Hocklyns that had substantially increased his honor.

Bisth had watched several of Gresth's matches. Hocklyns could challenge each other for honor points. The objective was to draw blood from your opponent. Normally in a match, each successful blow was awarded with ten honor points deducted from your opponent.

In a good match between skilled individuals, there would be much blood from numerous cuts as the battle waged back and forth. If an opponent appeared to be too severely injured to continue, the match was halted and the winner awarded the maximum amount of honor points allowed. The point of these matches was not to kill your opponent but to hone your combat abilities.

Bisth looked closely at the sensor screen, which showed his assembled fleet. He had eight dreadnoughts, twenty-four war cruisers, and sixty-four escort cruisers. It was an overwhelming force in normal times. In the previous battle, he had held most of his ships back, including over half of Sangeth's fleet. That would not be the case this time. He knew what he was up against, and he would use his superior numbers and firepower to annihilate any human ships that were in the target system. Even with their superior shields and weapons, the humans would be crushed by the massive amount of firepower the combined Hocklyn fleets would bring to bear.

Bisth spent several long minutes reviewing his strategy; there were still several questions he had about the ultimate objective of this mission. He also wanted to speak to Fleet Commodore Resmunt one more time. He changed the view on the main viewscreen and watched as a large shuttle left the shipyard and headed into orbit, doubtlessly to place more defensive satellites above the planet. He still felt as if he were missing something. Perhaps speaking to the commodore one more time would allow him to fill in the missing pieces.

-

Admiral Tolsen was sitting at the command console in the heavy battlecruiser WarHawk, gazing thoughtfully at the holographic display above the plotting table to his left. Colonel Beck was standing next to him as they discussed the tactical situation. His fleet was currently stationed twenty million kilometers outward from Caden's World.

"How much longer until they attack?" Peter asked as he studied the deployment of the laser satellites and missile platforms around the planet.

There were currently two hundred laser satellites as well as forty missile platforms in geostationary orbits. Beneath them were ten Federation destroyers and four light cruisers.

"Intelligence believes it will be shortly," replied Tolsen, letting out a deep breath. "Enough time has passed since our last engagement for the Hocklyns to have completed the plans for their next attack."

Tolsen's fleet had been heavily reinforced. He now had four battle cruisers, three battle carriers, six Monarch heavy cruisers, twelve light cruisers, and twenty destroyers. It was a massive fleet for a single Federation admiral to command.

"I think it might be wise if we divide our fleet," Tolsen said after a minute of thought. He had spent a lot of time thinking about how this battle needed to be fought.

Fleet Admirals Johnson and Streth wanted to make this system a trap. He was afraid that if the Hocklyns jumped in and found a fleet much larger than the one they had previously engaged, they might withdraw. However, Intelligence had pointed out that due to the Hocklyn's crazy honor system, withdrawal was not an option. But Tolsen was not so sure; after all, the flagship of the Hocklyn fleet he had engaged had fled.

"Divide the fleet?" Peter asked surprised, arching his eyebrows and shaking his head in confusion. "Why?"

"We want to set a trap," Tolsen explained. He then went on and told his executive officer his reasoning.

"You may be right," Peter agreed after a moment, folding his arms across his chest. "We can pull part of the fleet out to the comet ring, and they can jump back in when the Hocklyn fleet is committed."

"I think that will work," Tolsen nodded. "Rear Admiral Strong is also sitting out in the comet ring if we need him. If our ships jump back in after we have engaged the Hocklyns, then the trap will have been sprung. Hopefully we can hold them in Caden's World's gravity well between our fleet and the planet's defenses and finish them off."

"It would help if we had some advance warning of their coming," Peter continued, his eyes narrowing. "If we're lucky they will be detected on some of the hyper detection buoys before they arrive."

"Admiral Stillson has placed his stealth scouts along what Intelligence believes will be the Hocklyn's approach route," Tolsen informed Peter. "With some luck, we will have a day's warning before they hit us."

"Do we have enough ships to take them?" asked Peter, uneasily. There was a big question as to how large this attacking Hocklyn fleet would be.

"We have Admiral Strong's task group sitting nearby if we need them," Tolsen responded. "Admiral Streth will also be close by with the Ready Reserve's Second and Third Fleets."

"Admiral Streth seems to be taking this very seriously," Peter commented. He was also glad to hear that Admiral Streth was close by.

"He's fought the Hocklyns before and knows what they are capable of," Tolsen replied, hoping all the extra ships wouldn't be needed. "He wants this Hocklyn fleet not only defeated, but annihilated."

"What about other Federation fleets, how close will they be?"

"As soon as we detect the Hocklyns all Federation fleet units will go to Condition One. If we need additional forces we can call them in," answered Tolsen. He also knew that if that were necessary then the Hocklyns had attacked in overwhelming force and his fleet was probably in dire straits.

On Caden's World, Captain Krandle was standing behind the sensor operator watching the screens. She felt some anxiety since over two thousand marines were now on the planet and dug in. The mines were still in operation, but just barely. Everything had been made to look as if the civilian miners were still on the planet while in truth, less than one hundred were. Those were mainly supervisors and technicians that were necessary to ensure the equipment would stay running.

"Nervous, Captain?" General Abercrombie asked from her side.

Lucy nodded her head, not trusting her voice to speak.

"This will be a big battle," Abercrombie spoke in a steady voice. "We have our defensive satellites and the fleet above us in orbit as well as a lot of heavy weapons we brought with us. If the Hocklyns manage to get into orbit and land their Protectors, we'll be ready for them."

"I know," Lucy finally managed to say. "It's just the significance of what this battle means."

"The official start of the war," said Abercrombie, nodding his head in understanding. "Some say that already started with the previous battle with the Hocklyns in this system."

"But the Hocklyns didn't know what they were up against then, this time there will be no doubt."

Captain Krandle looked at several viewscreens on the wall next to the large sensor screen. She could see heavily armed marines on patrol in the two mining settlements as well as several missile batteries that were pointed upward. Caden's World had always been so peaceful. It wasn't the greatest world to live on in the Federation, but it had been home to over twenty thousand people. Now it was an armed military camp and one big trap for the Hocklyns.

Lieutenant Simmons was out inspecting the deployment of the marines around the operations center. He was carrying a heavy assault rifle with armor piercing rounds. Hocklyn Protectors wore heavy body armor and regular bullets would not penetrate. Much of the operations center was underground except for the top two levels. On the very top level numerous antennas, sensor dishes, and communications equipment was pointed upward.

He allowed his gaze to turn to the six marines in front of him; one was a corporal in charge of this particular squad. They were dug in with a wall of thick sandbags surrounding them, and all six marines were heavily armed. Inside sat a missile launcher capable of bringing down inbound troop shuttles as well as fighters. The missile launcher had six fire-and-forget missiles in its slim tubes. There were four of these emplacements around the operations center. Taking a deep breath, Lieutenant Simmons continued on his inspection tour.

On Ceres, Fleet Admiral Johnson was meeting with Admiral Teleck, Admiral Kalen, and Colonel Anne Grissom. Admiral Teleck had requested that the Fleet Admiral come to Ceres for the meeting.

"This is the beginning of the war, Admiral," commented Teleck, looking at several sheets of paper that were lying on the large wooden conference table at his fingertips. "Do you think it's wise to risk Admiral Streth this early in the conflict?"

"No, I don't," she confessed, wishing Admiral Streth wasn't taking this risk. "But he is a Fleet Admiral, and there is very little that I can do. He was adamant about being present for this battle."

"He wants this Hocklyn fleet annihilated to send a message to the Hocklyns," commented Anne, knowingly. "That's why he has moved Second and Third Fleet so close to Gliese 667C. He wants every ship in that fleet destroyed."

"I just wished he had taken the StarStrike," said Karla, shaking her head worriedly. If something happened to Admiral Streth, it would seriously shake the morale in the entire Federation, particularly the Fleet.

"He doesn't want the Hocklyns to see such a large ship," responded Anne, looking calmly around the small group. Her Intelligence group had discussed this very thoroughly. She would be returning to the StarStrike as soon as this meeting was over. "He is aboard Admiral Sheen's flagship, the WarStorm."

"So many names from history," commented Admiral Kalen, softly.

"People all across the Federation are familiar with the names StarStrike, WarStorm, and Avenger," Admiral Teleck responded.

"Those ships are part of our history, and now they well be a part of our future."

"I think there's another reason Admiral Streth is there," Anne stated, her eyes narrowing sharply. "Admiral Streth doesn't trust the Hocklyns; he is afraid they might show up with a truly large fleet and he wants to ensure that they are defeated."

"But why would they?" asked Admiral Kalen, shaking his head doubtfully. "By now they must know they are facing survivors from the original Human Federation of Worlds. They have only come across the one mining colony and won't believe there can be too many of us; there just hasn't been enough time. They may even believe that Admiral Tolsen's fleet is all that we have. They can know nothing of Earth."

"Perhaps," replied Admiral Johnson, thoughtfully. "But in this I think we need to trust Admiral Streth's judgment. He wants to land a telling blow against the Hocklyns and then launch his full scale attack against their empire with the Ready Reserve."

-

Later, Admiral Johnson and Admiral Teleck were walking down a heavily armored corridor that led to the capital city of Ceres. They passed through the last large armored hatch and stepped out into an artificial world. Karla paused as she took in the magnificent sight that spread out before her. Here, inside Ceres, the original Federation survivors had carved an amazing home out of the hard rock of the asteroid.

"It's beautiful," Karla spoke quietly as her hazel eyes took everything in. She had been here before, but each time it affected her the same way.

In front of her was a massive cavern over forty kilometers in length and twenty kilometers wide. At its center was the capital city of Providence, named after one of the original worlds of the Federation. Nearly four hundred thousand people called Providence their home. Around the city, the floor of the cavern was green and blue, with flowing rivers and streams as well as several large lakes. Even in the city itself, large areas of green could be seen.

"Its home," responded Admiral Teleck, proudly. "I don't know if I could live anywhere else."

"Ceres has been the home of the Federation survivors for over four hundred years," spoke Karla, taking in a deep breath. Even the air smelled unusually clean and fresh. It reminded her of the air on New

Tellus during a spring day immediately after a rain. "Your people have prepared for this moment in history ever since their arrival in the system; now it's finally here."

"The war with the Hocklyns," spoke Teleck in agreement, glancing over at Fleet Admiral Johnson. He wondered if she truly understood what this meant to his people. "Every waking moment of the people of Ceres has been aimed at being ready for this war."

"It's here," Karla stated with a long sigh. It was hard to believe that nearly three hundred years had passed since her distant ancestor Greg Johnson had set foot on the crashed light cruiser Avenger on Earth's moon.

Admiral Teleck turned and looked closely at Fleet Admiral Johnson. "Have you spoken to Katie and told her who you are?"

Karla laughed and shook her head. "I'm her great great niece many times removed. I don't think that will mean much to her."

"It might," Teleck replied. "All five of those young people on the Avenger have distant relatives still living. It might do them all some good to realize they are not alone."

"Perhaps you're right," Karla admitted as she gazed up at a few small white clouds drifting in the sky over Providence. She knew that the weather in the habitats inside of Ceres was controlled; they could make it rain or even snow.

"I know of a good restaurant in the city that has fabulous food," Teleck added with a friendly smile. "Why don't we grab a bite to eat before resuming our duties?"

"Sounds great," replied Karla. She was feeling a little bit hungry, and a little time off away from all the planning and war preparation would be nice.

-

Jeremy and Kelsey were eating in the officer's mess on the Avenger discussing the coming battle; both had been extremely busy the last few days. Jeremy had been working with the task force making sure that each commander understood the new tactics and what was expected of them. Kelsey and Ariel had been working on perfecting the hyperspace jumps so the fleet could emerge from the spatial vortexes in fleet formation ready for combat.

"Katie finished the last program we needed earlier today," Kelsey reported as she bit a large red strawberry in half. She loved strawberries; she always had.

"Then we're ready," said Jeremy as he watched Kelsey swallow the rest of the strawberry. He just hoped his tactics would work against the Hocklyns, if not his stint as an admiral would be very short.

"Angela says everyone is anxious for this battle to begin," Kelsey added as she reached for another strawberry. "The communication officers on the other ships report that this waiting is nerve wracking."

"Yes, I realize that," responded Jeremy, knowing how they felt since he was feeling anxious also. "I don't think we will have to wait much longer."

"Mind if I join you?" Colonel Malen asked. She was carrying a tray with a ham sandwich and a glass of tea.

"Have a seat," said Jeremy, motioning for her to sit down. "Lieutenant Grainger and I were just discussing the computer programs that Ariel and Lieutenant Johnson have finally finished."

"You know Admiral that if these micro-jump tactics you have come up with work, it will revolutionize how our ships fight."

"Perhaps," responded Jeremy, showing a little doubt in his eyes. "We won't know how well they will work until we try them."

"I had Ariel run some simulations based on past battles with the Hocklyns, and in every case the Hocklyns are taken by complete surprise," Colonel Malen reported confidently. "They have never seen anything like this."

Jeremy was silent as he listened to Colonel Malen continue to explain the results of the simulations in more detail. She was an excellent executive officer and the crew respected her, and she in turn respected them. Kelsey and the colonel began discussing the micro-jump calculations, and Jeremy continued to listen with interest.

-

On board the battle cruiser WarStorm, Rear Admiral Sheen was in the Command Center making sure all the units of her fleet were ready for instant deployment to Gliese 667C. Second Fleet was a very powerful and formidable force, consisting of four battle cruisers, six battle carriers, twelve Monarch cruisers, four strike cruisers, forty light cruisers, and twenty destroyers.

"It's a big fleet," spoke a familiar and friendly voice behind her.

Amanda turned and saw Admiral Streth standing there looking at the holographic display, which depicted her fleet. "You're the one that made it big, I just hope it's enough," she replied.

Hedon looked around the large Command Center, recognizing some familiar faces. Lieutenant Benjamin Stalls was sitting in front of the sensor control panel, Lieutenant Angela Trask was at Communications, and Lieutenant Ashton was sitting at Navigation. In some ways, it was comforting to see a few familiar faces from the old days.

"It will be," he replied, confidently. "The only problem will be if an AI ship shows up, and I don't expect that. None of our stealth scouts has ever detected one."

"Then I guess all we can do is wait and hope the scouts detect the Hocklyns on their way in so we'll know what we're up against."

"Don't worry, Amanda," Hedon replied in a quiet and calm voice. He smiled gently. "The new Federation is very powerful, plus we have three allies. We're not in this alone, this time it will be different. The Hocklyns have never faced or encountered anything like we're about to throw at them."

Amanda nodded as her eyes wandered to the ship's main viewscreen, which was focused on one of the new strike cruisers. With its 1,000-meter length, it was a very awe-inspiring sight and extremely powerful. Perhaps Admiral Streth was correct and this time things would be different.

-

War Leader Bisth smiled craftily to himself as his combined fleet completed its jump. He wasn't as confident as Fleet Commodore Resmunt was that the humans only controlled a few worlds with a small population. To him there were too many things that didn't add up such as the size of the fleet that had jumped Sangeth, plus their weapons. It suggested an advanced civilization with a large population. How this could be possible from a few thousand human survivors was unknown, but he had decided to err on the side of caution.

"Jump complete, War Leader," First Leader Gresth reported. "All ships report successful jumps."

Bisth nodded and gazed at the main viewscreen, which was showing the space around them. They had jumped close to a small nebula. He had decided to avoid jumping into any star systems as they neared the target world. If this was indeed a larger civilization than Resmunt believed, then the nearby star systems might have pickets in them. Bisth wanted no early warning of his strike; he would hit quickly and decisively.

His cold eyes slowly swept over the War Room seeing with satisfaction that everything was as it should be. Each Hocklyn was busy at their posts performing their assigned task with maximum efficiency. To do less could result in a loss of honor.

"Two more days and we will be at the human world," First Leader Gresth rasped, his cold gaze meeting the large dark ones of Bisth.

"Then we will earn our honor," Bisth spoke with satisfaction in his voice. "A quick victory over any opposing ships, and then we land our Protectors on their planet. After we have located the information we need, we will send a ship back to Fleet Commodore Resmunt. Once that has been completed, the rest of our ships well continue on to the human's home world and conquer it. We will achieve much honor in this campaign."

"Enough to rise in stature and wealth," Gresth added, his eyes showing fire. Gresth wanted to rise to the position of War Leader and this campaign might just allow him to do that.

"Enough for all of us," Bisth assured his Second Leader. Bisth's eyes returned to the viewscreen and the dark nebula. They were coming, and these new humans would soon know the wrath and power of the Hocklyn Slave Empire. After their worlds had been conquered and their military destroyed, the humans would become the newest slaves to serve.

Chapter Nine

Admiral Tolsen let out a deep breath. He could sense the growing apprehension in the crew of the Command Center as they waited for the expected Hocklyn attack. He knew part of the uneasiness was because he had split the fleet. Currently the WarHawk was waiting just outside of the gravity well of Caden's World with what remained.

Glancing over at the tactical image being projected above the plotting table, he could see his other battle cruiser, the Dawson and on the other side of her was the battle carrier Independence. The rest of the fleet was hovering in support positions awaiting orders. He still had two Monarch cruisers, four light cruisers, and eight destroyers that made up his decoy fleet. His fleet was acting as live bait to encourage the Hocklyns to launch their attack. It was a risky tactic, but he didn't feel he had any other choice.

In order for his plan to work, he needed to lure the Hocklyns in and then retreat into the gravity well of the planet, thus trapping them. If need be, he could call up the ten destroyers and four light cruisers in orbit around Caden's World to support his fleet. Once inside the gravity well, the Hocklyns wouldn't be able to escape into hyperspace using their jump drives. After that had been accomplished, he would then call in the rest of his fleet as well as the other waiting fleets from their hidden positions out around the system's comet ring.

"I hate this waiting," Colonel Beck grumbled as he checked the current status of the fleet units. He had been busy speaking to the other ship departments over his mini-com. Everyone was expressing nervousness over the long wait for the Hocklyns to attack.

He looked over at several young officers who were talking quietly to themselves. He let out a deep sigh, the crew was well trained, but there were a lot of young crewmembers, some just fresh out of the academy.

His eyes returned to the tactical display seeing that everything was the same as it was the last time he had checked. Commander Arie of the battle carrier Independence was also getting impatient. She had just put in a request to double the size of the fleet's CAP. She was finding it difficult to keep her aircrews at a high state of readiness. Currently, there were six Talon fighters on patrol around the fleet. She wanted to increase that to twelve as well as add a squadron of armed Anlon bombers. Giving her aircrews more flight time would help increase their morale until the Hocklyns showed up.

"Tell Commander Arie to maintain the current CAP," Tolsen replied after a moment, arching his eyebrows.

He was concerned that by increasing the size of the CAP and adding a squadron of Anlon bombers it would only add to the rising tension in the fleet. He also didn't want the Hocklyns to know that they were expected.

Colonel Beck nodded and quickly informed Commander Arie that her request was denied. However, Beck went on to tell Arie that she could keep a squadron of bombers at Condition Two in case they were needed. This seemed to satisfy the battle carrier commander for the moment.

"We're all getting on edge," Peter commented as he gazed around the Command Center. It was unusually quiet, with very little talking between crewmembers. Those that were talking to each other spoke in whispers.

"People seem to forget that in war, there is more waiting than fighting," Tolsen spoke with a long sigh. "Most of the crews in our fleet have never seen actual combat, and I suspect once they do they won't be quite so anxious for the next time."

-

At a small nebula four light years distant, War Leader Bisth was finally ready to launch his attack against the humans. He gazed intently at the large sensor screen in front of him, which was covered in friendly green icons. Overall, he had ninety-six Hocklyn warships under his command. He felt pride at knowing the honor this fleet would bring him.

It had been decades since the Hocklyn Slave Empire had assembled such a powerful fleet. Commodore Resmunt had made it extremely clear that the Hocklyn High Council wanted the humans dealt with quickly. If it dragged out, the AIs might become involved. If that happened, then the human home world would not be brought into the empire because the AIs would destroy it!

"Send in the four escort cruisers," Bisth ordered, looking over at First Leader Gresth. "I want detailed scans of that entire system! I want to know what defenses are around the mining planet as well as the human fleet strength. I don't want any hidden human ships that might cause us problems later."

First Leader Gresth nodded and activated the com system to pass on the necessary orders to the four chosen escort cruisers. Their First Leaders had already been briefed on their mission specifics to jump into the human mining system and take detailed scans of everything. Two of the cruisers would jump to just outside of the mining planet's gravity well to take scans of the planet's defenses; the other two would jump into the outer system to ensure there were no hidden fleets using the large gas giants to shield their energy emissions.

War Leader Bisth watched with satisfaction as his orders were efficiently carried out. He still felt a little uneasy about the coming engagement. His main concern was that these were humans they were dealing with, and highly advanced ones based on the weapons that had been used in the last engagement.

Bisth looked across the War Room; he could see excitement in the eyes of his crew, honor was at hand. Each crewmember knew their status and wealth in the empire would be substantially increased once they engaged the humans and destroyed their fleet. However, the biggest increase would come when they subjugated the human home world. If it was as advanced as Bisth believed, the honor and wealth to be had would be vast!

"Escort cruisers are away," Gresth reported as the four ships vanished from the sensor screen.

Bisth nodded. If everything went well, they would be launching their attack in a few more hours. War Leader Sangeth had requested that he be allowed to lead the first elements of the fleet into the human system. Bisth knew that Sangeth was still angry from his previous defeat. While no honor had been lost, it had galled Sangeth to retreat from battle. He felt his honor had been tarnished and only by leading this attack could he remove that stain from his reputation. Bisth had agreed, but not for the reasons Sangeth thought.

-

Captain Lucy Krandle fought to stifle a yawn. It was early morning on Caden's World and she had just made it to the operations center. Lieutenant Simmins was already there speaking to the young sensor operator who was just going off duty. Her replacement should be arriving shortly.

"Nothing to report, Sir" she was saying. "There have been no hyperjumps detected overnight. Admiral Tolsen has also reported that no unauthorized jumps have been recorded in any of the nearby systems."

Lieutenant Simmins turned toward Captain Krandle, seeing that she had made it to the operations center. "Still no sign of the Hocklyns."

"It can't be much longer," Lucy stated as she walked over to a small table with breakfast rolls and a steaming pot of coffee on it. She poured herself a cup and picked up one of the sweet rolls.

"We have a lot of fleet units tied down here," Simmins commented as Captain Krandle came over to stand in front of the sensor screen. It showed numerous friendly green icons that represented Federation ships.

"They will stay as long as necessary," Lucy replied as she took a sip of the hot coffee. She loved coffee in the mornings! It seemed to invigorate her. She knew it was only the caffeine, but it still tasted great and seemed to work miracles.

She had just taken a bite of her roll when a warning alarm sounded. Her eyes instantly snapped to the sensor screen, and she watched with apprehension as four red threat icons popped into being.

"What are those?" she demanded as the sensor operator sat back down and began looking at the new data that was coming across her computer screens.

"Information's coming through now," the sensor operator replied as her nimble fingers flew over the touch screen. Then her face turned pale as she looked at the data. "The sensors are showing that four Hocklyn escort cruisers have jumped into the system, two just outside of our gravity well and the other two out near the gas giants."

"This is it," Simmins spoke, his eyes widening. "The Hocklyns have finally arrived."

"Summon General Abercrombie and go to Condition One!" ordered Lucy, sharply. "Send a message to Fleet Command informing them of the Hocklyns arrival, then get me Admiral Tolsen on the com system."

Warning alarms began sounding in both of the two mining settlements. Instantly, heavily armed marines began pouring out of their barracks and proceeded hastily to their weapon emplacements. Missile batteries were activated and swiveled around to point upward toward the danger. Other marines took up positions in buildings that had been reinforced, offering them overlapping fields of fire down the main streets of the settlements. If the Hocklyns managed to land Protectors on the planet, they would be met with a heavy rain of defensive fire.

"Four Hocklyn escort cruisers detected," Lieutenant Anders reported from sensors. "Two near the sixth planet and the other two are just outside of Caden's World's gravity well. Distance to the nearest is two point six million kilometers."

Tolsen and Colonel Beck both shifted their gaze to the four blinking red threat icons that were now showing up on the tactical holographic display.

"Four!" Beck spoke with a heavy frown. "I don't like the looks of that. This could indicate a much larger attack force than we are expecting."

Tolsen thought over Beck's words and hoped the colonel wasn't right. They had been expecting an attack force approximately twice the size of the last one. Everyone except Admiral Streth, Tolsen reminded himself. Admiral Streth had mentioned that there was a real possibility the Hocklyns might attack in overwhelming force.

"Send a message to the rest of our fleet to prepare to jump back to our current location, also let Admiral Strong know what is going on and to place his fleet on standby."

"Yes, Sir," Beck replied as he turned to carry out the admiral's orders.

"Lieutenant Davis, send a message to Fleet Command that four Hocklyn escort cruisers have jumped into the system and are taking scans. We expect a full scale fleet battle shortly."

"The two escort cruisers around planet six have jumped again," Lieutenant Anders reported as they vanished from his sensor screen. A moment later, he spoke once more. "They have jumped to planet seven, the outer gas giant."

"What are they doing?" asked Beck, glancing over at Tolsen. "Why are they jumping to the gas giants?"

"Looking for other ships," Tolsen answered as he watched the tactical display closely. "They want to make sure no ships are hiding in the atmosphere or behind them where they couldn't be picked up by sensors. Whoever this Hocklyn commander is, he's being cautious."

"The attack should be imminent then," stated Beck, raising his eyebrows. "They won't wait too long after they finish their scans."

"Bring the fleet to Condition One and tighten our formation," ordered Tolsen, leaning forward and studying his fleet disposition on the tactical display.

Tolsen was expecting the Hocklyn fleet to jump into the outer system and then proceed slowly toward Caden's World. He would then gradually retreat, luring them down into the gravity well of the planet.

While Colonel Beck was carrying out his orders, Tolsen contacted Commander Arie and ordered her to begin arming her bombers with missiles. He also ordered her to bring the current CAP in and refuel the fighters. He had a sneaking suspicion they would shortly need every fighter and bomber at their disposal.

After studying the tactical display for another few moments, he dispatched two light cruisers and four destroyers toward the two nearer Hocklyn escort cruisers. If he did nothing, they might suspect something wasn't right.

"Hocklyn cruisers have jumped away," Lieutenant Anders reported as the two nearer red threat icons vanished from his sensors. A minute later, he passed on the information that the other two Hocklyn cruisers had also jumped away.

"We will stay at Condition One for awhile," instructed Tolsen, leaning back in his command chair as he allowed himself to relax for a moment. "If nothing happens in the next hour, we will drop down to Condition Two."

"Do you think we will have an hour?" asked Beck, walking over and standing next to the admiral."

"I doubt it, Peter," Tolsen replied with a slight shake of his head. "I expect the attack to be almost immediate. The Hocklyn commander won't want us to adjust our fleet formation."

-

Down on Caden's World, Lucy felt relieved when she saw all four of the red threat icons vanish.

"Don't get your hopes up," cautioned General Abercrombie, looking over at the young captain. "They came in, got their sensor readings, and have now jumped back to their main fleet. They will be back shortly."

"I know," she replied. Looking over at the reinforced door to the operations center, she noted that the two heavily armed marines had morphed into four. Marines surrounded the entire outside of the operations center. Little good it would do if the Hocklyns decided use a nuke.

Lieutenant Simmins had gone outside to check on security. For some reason, Lucy felt more secure when he was in the room.

Adam Severson walked over and looked at General Abercrombie. There were still a few civilians about that had been helping the marines keep this facade of an operating mining operation going. "Do you think the Fleet can prevent them from bombing the surface?"

"We can only hope," General Abercrombie responded. Then he went on. "Mr. Severson go ahead and order all of your remaining personnel to the deep bunkers. They should be safe there until this is over."

Severson nodded and then went to one of the communication consoles to pass on the order.

General Abercrombie had been impressed by Severson. The man had never complained about what was happening to his mining colony. He had done everything asked of him to keep up the pretense that this operation was still functioning normally so they could fool the Hocklyns.

-

Admiral Streth had been summoned to the Command Center of the WarStorm. He had already heard the orders to go to Condition Two and for the ship to standby for immediate combat operations. He knew that could mean only one thing, the Hocklyns had arrived.

Entering the Command Center, he saw Admiral Sheen and Commander Samantha Evans at the tactical display discussing the situation. He quickly walked over to them.

"What do we have?" he asked, looking over at Admiral Sheen. He could feel his heart beating a little faster knowing what was ahead.

"Four Hocklyn escort cruisers have jumped into Gliese 667C. We believe they took full scans of the system, particularly the space around Caden's World, and then jumped back out. They even searched the outer two gas giants for hidden ships."

Admiral Streth was silent for a moment as he mulled this over. From past experience with the Hocklyns, they normally just bulled their way in blasting everything out of their way. This sounded as if a more cautious War Leader or Commodore was in charge of this fleet. He knew the rankings of the Hocklyns from information they had learned when First Fleet had taken a Hocklyn space station and escort cruiser. There was also the tons of information the Clarions had sent them.

Second Fleet was on the far side of the comet ring with Third Fleet, under Admiral Adler, a few million kilometers away. Admiral

Strong was just inside the comet ring with his ships powered down to reduce the possibility of detection. The rest of Admiral Tolsen's ships were only a short distance away from Strong's and were also powered down. The trap was set, and now it just needed to be sprung.

"Admiral Strong and Admiral Tolsen's other ships are powering back up," Lieutenant Stalls reported from his sensor station as the green icons representing their ships began flaring up.

Admiral Streth nodded his head in acknowledgement. He gazed pensively at the tactical display, confirming the positioning of the fleets. Everything was as ready as it could be. "Now we wait for the Hocklyns and see what kind of playing cards they have brought to the table."

"You still believe this will be a large fleet they attack with?" inquired Amanda, looking over at the older admiral. Over the years, she had come to trust the admiral's intuition. He had a knack for strategy and sometimes doing the unexpected.

"Yes, I do" Hedon replied, his eyes focusing on Amanda. "I think this War Leader or Commodore is playing it cautious."

"I wonder why?" she asked, her blue eyes watching the admiral.

"Because they have found humans again," he replied in a calm and steady voice. "I suspect some heads will be lost in the Hocklyn Empire when word of this gets back to their ruling council. We were supposed to have been exterminated. Their AI masters will not be pleased."

Amanda nodded as she turned her attention back to the tactical display and the eighty-six ships that represented her command. She had never dreamed she would command such a powerful fleet. The humans from Earth and the Federation survivors had certainly outdone themselves preparing for this war, but they had also had four hundred years to do so.

-

War Leader Bisth looked carefully over the sensor data from the four scouts with interest and growing concern. The human mining world had certainly been reinforced. The space above it was flush with red threat icons, which indicated dangerous defensive satellites. There were over two hundred of the deadly little symbols. What also worried Bisth was that there were now four human light cruisers and ten of their destroyers just below the defensive satellites. There was also a fleet of seventeen more warships hovering just outside of the planet's gravity well.

To him, it indicated a much larger human population than Fleet Commodore Resmunt had suggested. He wondered if it were possible that they had missed a sizable human colony in the Human Federation of Worlds all those long years ago. Perhaps that colony had been evacuated out to this distant section of space. That was the only answer Bisth could come up with to explain the obvious size of their fleet as well as their technology.

"They have certainly been reinforced," Gresth hissed as he gazed at the sensor data. "They have more ships in the system than they did when War Leader Sangeth attacked last time. There will be much honor in this battle."

Bisth nodded and his cold, dark eyes turned toward his second in command. "We will send War Leader Sangeth in as well as War Leader Tantil. That will give us a decisive fleet advantage in numbers as well as in firepower."

"Forty-eight ships to the human's thirty-one," Gresth nodded in agreement.

"They only have five first line ships in their fleet," Bisth pointed out. "Sangeth will have sixteen."

"It will be a short battle," replied Gresth, wishing the WarCry could be there. However, he dared not make that suggestion; it would not go well with War Leader Bisth.

"Have the two Protector ships go in with Sangeth," Bisth commanded as he thought about what needed to be done. "They can begin their landings as soon as the orbital defenses and human ships have been annihilated."

Gresth quickly passed on the orders. He wished he were aboard one of the Protector ships. There would be much honor for the Protectors if the humans had military forces on the ground. His hand went tentatively to the knife at his waist. He would love to sink the blade into the flesh of a human warrior. Honor came swiftly in personal combat.

War Leader Bisth returned to his command pedestal and gazed around the War Room. It was a beehive of intense activity as everything was made ready for the attack. He would send War Leader Sangeth in first with War Leader Tantil's fleet to assist, then he would bring in his fleet as well as War Leader Canneth's. He would not allow Sangeth to claim all of the honor in this conquest.

Two long hours had passed and still there was no sign of the expected Hocklyn attack fleet. Admiral Tolsen had allowed his fleet to go back to Condition Two.

"Why don't they attack?" asked Peter, feeling frustrated at having to wait for a battle he knew was coming. "Surely they have had time to analyze the data by now. You don't think they detected the ships out around the comet ring, do you?"

"I doubt it," Tolsen replied, taking a deep breath. He too was feeling impatient. "It will take awhile for them to analyze the data and decide on the best way to eliminate our fleet and the defenses around Caden's World. Once they have formed a plan, they will be here."

"I just hope they don't come up with too good of a plan," responded Colonel Beck, trying his best not to sound irritated at the wait.

Captain Krandle was standing outside of the operations center looking around the large mining settlement. Normally the streets would be full of people going about their business, but now everything was quiet. It was late morning, and there wasn't even a breeze. The leaves on the trees were still, and not a single bird was in the air. All the shops were closed with their doors and windows tightly shuttered. The mining settlement had become a ghost town.

Only occasionally did she see movement where a marine was standing guard or on patrol. She had been posted on Caden's World for six months when the two Hocklyn scout cruisers had appeared. Now she was beginning to realize how much she missed those times before the Hocklyns showed up. She wondered idly if Caden's World would ever be the same again.

"You should probably go back inside, Captain," Lieutenant Simmins suggested as he walked up with four other heavily armed marines. General Abercrombie had placed him in command of the marines guarding the operations center.

"Shortly," replied Lucy, knowing Simmins was right. Her place was in the operations center, and she needed to get back.

"Captain," a voice spoke from the open doorway.

Turning around, Lucy saw Corporal Richard, who was in charge of the marine guards inside.

"General Abercrombie sent me to get you, the Hocklyn fleet is here!"

Lucy looked quickly at Lieutenant Simmins, their eyes meeting. "Be careful, Lieutenant," she spoke, softly. Then turning, she hurried back inside.

-

War Leader Sangeth felt the transition from hyperspace to normal space knowing that honor would be his shortly. If he could subjugate the human planet before Bisth arrived, then the majority of that honor would fall upon his shoulders. Ever since his flagship, the Crimson Oblivion, had escaped from this system, he had felt as if he had left his soul behind. Honor meant everything to a Hocklyn and running from an enemy had placed a dark cloud over Sangeth as well as his flagship. Now he would change that.

"All ships report successful jumps," First Leader Rahn reported. "Systems are coming online."

Sangeth gazed expectantly at the main sensor screen as it cleared up and he saw that the human fleet was already beginning to maneuver. They were starting to turn, obviously hoping to pin his two fleets between the planet and them. Well, that was not going to happen. He had the numbers and the firepower to do as he wanted. He would command this battle not these upstart humans.

Sangeth quickly activated the com channel, which placed him in instant communication with War Leader Tantil on the dreadnought DeadlyDawn. "War Leader Tantil, there is an enemy fleet closing on our position. You are to move forward and engage that fleet while my fleet moves into the planet's gravity well. I will destroy the planet's orbital defenses and the small fleet that protects it while you eliminate this other fleet."

"May honor be yours," War Leader Tantil replied over the com.

With satisfaction, Sangeth saw that War Leader Tantil was already beginning to follow his command as his twenty-four ships began to separate from the mass of green dots that represented the two Hocklyn fleets.

Turning toward First Leader Rahn, he passed on his next orders. "Take us into the gravity well; we will engage and destroy the human's defensive satellites and annihilate their fleet units. Honor will be ours!"

-

"Damn! They've split their fleet," Colonel Beck voiced in alarm as he studied the tactical image. "It looks as if half of their fleet is heading into the gravity well to attack Caden's World and the other half

125

is headed toward us." This was exactly what Admiral Strong had warned against.

"Total Hocklyn ship count is forty-eight vessels," Lieutenant Anders informed them. "Make up of the fleet is as follows; four dreadnoughts, twelve war cruisers, and thirty-two escort cruisers."

"How soon before they are in combat range?" Tolsen demanded as he gazed intently at the tactical display above the plotting table.

That was a powerful force to deal with and he was badly outnumbered in capital ships. Not only that, but the Hocklyns had surprised him by jumping almost into Caden's Worlds gravity well. His plan to lure them in would now have to be changed.

"Twelve minutes," Anders replied as he ran the calculations.

"Lieutenant Davis, contact the rest of our fleet and inform them to return in exactly fourteen minutes, also tell Admiral Strong his fleet is to stay at the comet ring until summoned."

The communications operator hurriedly complied, knowing how important those orders were.

"Fourteen minutes?" commented Beck, raising his eyebrow quizzically. "That's cutting it pretty close."

"That will trap the other fleet inside Caden's World's gravity well," Tolsen explained.

He knew he was taking a risk, but he needed that other Hocklyn fleet to be deep inside the gravity well before the rest of his fleet put in an appearance. That reduced the chance of the fleet he was about to engage jumping away. But being Hocklyns with their weird code of honor, he didn't see them jumping away from this battle no matter what the odds.

-

Admiral Strong was looking intently at the tactical display above the Avenger's plotting table. It currently showed the forty-eight red threat icons in the Gliese 667C system. He felt a nervousness in the pit of his stomach at knowing what was ahead. In the back of his mind, he could hear his father's steady voice telling him to stay calm and do as he had been trained.

"What are your orders, Sir?" Colonel Malen asked. She was standing next to him as they assessed the situation.

"They jumped in almost exactly where you suspected," Ariel commented as she examined the tactical data. It pleased her immensely that Jeremy had been so accurate in his assessment of what the Hocklyns would do.

The dark eyed, black haired AI was plainly visible on the main viewscreen. She had been following the recent developments with keen interest. The viewscreen showed Ariel from the waist up and to the casual observer she looked quite stunning.

She and Kelsey were already running micro-jump simulations to see where the most effective place would be to jump the fleet. Ariel was excited to try the new micro-jump maneuver that Jeremy had come up with. She also hoped that, at some point in the battle, Jeremy would allow her control of the Avenger to engage the Hocklyns. She knew that he would be very impressed by what she could do; she had an affinity for space combat.

"They are doing just what I thought they would," commented Jeremy, watching as one of the Hocklyn fleets began to enter the gravity well of Caden's World. "I tried to warn Admiral Tolsen they might do this."

Now would be the opportune time to jump in behind the second fleet and launch their attack, he could then turn and engage the Hocklyn fleet going into the gravity well while Admiral Tolsen finished off the other Hocklyn fleet. But he had been ordered to wait. He was feeling impatient, but he had to follow orders. His father had always stressed that one thing.

"Ariel, I want you and Lieutenant Grainger to plot a micro-jump to these coordinates," he ordered, using a laser pointer to indicate exactly where he wanted the fleet to go.

"You don't think these are all of the Hocklyn ships, do you?" Colonel Malen spoke in surprise, her eyes growing wide as she looked over at Admiral Stone. "You think there are more."

"Yes," Jeremy answered with a nod of his head. His eyes turned back to the tactical display as he thought about the Hocklyn tactics. "They are risking unnecessary losses by splitting their fleet this way. I actually thought the first attack would be with a larger fleet. I don't believe even the Hocklyns would accept these losses unless they had another fleet nearby."

-

War Leader Tantil swore in anger as his ship shook from the massive amounts of ordnance that were striking its energy shield. The two opposing fleets had just entered weapons range and already the first powerful salvos were landing. He knew from studying the data from Sangeth's battle with the humans that the human's weapons were more powerful.

"War Cruisers are to focus on those two Monarchs," he ordered as he studied the tactical data. "Don't worry about the destroyers for now. I want the DeadlyDawn and our other dreadnought to concentrate on the two human battle cruisers. Once they are eliminated, then we can concentrate on their lighter units." Even as he spoke, he felt his ship shake again, and several warning alarms began sounding as red lights began flashing on the damage control board.

"Fire our energy beams," he ordered heatedly, his eyes flashing anger, realizing his ship was taking damage. "Honor will be ours today!"

-

Admiral Tolsen felt the WarHawk shudder violently as a nuke went off against her energy screen. On the viewscreens, bright explosions seemed to be occurring everywhere. All the ships in both fleets were now heavily engaged except for the Independence, which was hanging slightly back.

"Light Cruiser Sundowner is reporting heavy damage," Lieutenant Anders reported. A sudden bright flash lit up the main viewscreen. "Sundowner is down," Anders continued his face turning ashen as he realized that close to five hundred men and women had just died.

Tolsen activated his mini-com, which placed him in immediate communication with Commander Arie. "Launch your Anlon strike."

From the Independence, sixty Anlon bombers erupted carrying shrike missiles tipped with tactical nukes. Their targets were the Hocklyn war cruisers. Forty Talon fighters formed up around them for protection. Other Talons were launching from the battle carrier as well as the other human ships to engage the numerous Hocklyn fighters that were present.

In less than a minute, a massive dogfight opened up as space became littered with tracer fire and the fighter duel began.

The space around and in between the two fleets was full of exploding ordnance and missile trails. Energy screens lit up briefly as weapons fire smashed into them. Missiles crashed into the screens trying to knock them down, detonating in brilliant flashes of light. Occasionally a screen would fail, and the unlucky ship would quickly die. Defensive lasers flashed destroying inbound missiles.

"Hammer and Justice are down," Lieutenant Anders reported, as the two human destroyers were annihilated when heavy nukes struck their hulls, blowing the ships apart.

Tolsen flinched as he listened to the damage that was being done to his fleet. Looking at the tactical display, he saw the other Hocklyn fleet was now far into the gravity well. He felt his heart pounding, knowing good people under his command were dying. He grabbed the edge of his command console as the WarHawk took a hit from a powerful missile. A console in the Command Center blew out, sending a shower of sparks across the room. Several damage control personnel rushed over and began putting the small fire out. Glancing over at the damage control board, he saw several red lights glowing ominously.

In space, the dogfight was raging furiously. Hocklyn and human fighters were locked in an intricate but deadly dance of death that ended occasionally in a bright explosion as a fighter was destroyed. For every two Hocklyn fighters that were blown out of space, a human one died also.

Nuclear fire blossomed across the wavering shields of ships of both fleets. Heavy missiles and railgun rounds struck the energy shields and occasionally, when a nuke went off, managed to penetrate causing major damage. Deep holes were blasted in ship's hulls, hammering at the delicate insides of the warships.

Orange-red laser beams and dark violet power beams flicked out at the Hocklyn ships, only to be answered back by the Hocklyns own heavy blue energy beams. The deadly carnage grew worse as the fighting intensified and the two fleets continued to close with one another.

Admiral Tolsen watched worriedly as the final seconds ticked by and the ship damage mounted up. Suddenly space was full of more friendly green icons behind his fleet. The other twenty-eight warships of his fleet had arrived!

-

"A trap!" roared War Leader Tantil in anger as he saw his numerical advantage suddenly vanish. He had been within mere minutes of wiping the human fleet in front of him off his sensor screen.

"The new human warships are eight minutes from extreme weapons range," First Leader Klessen reported as he studied the data. "We can still destroy these first human ships before their reinforcements can get here."

"Honor will be ours," Tantil hissed loudly in agreement. "Press the attack."

-

Jeremy saw with deep concern that the rest of Admiral Tolsen's ships had miscalculated their jump and jumped in too far away from the battle. By the time they reached combat range, Admiral Tolsen's ships might be wiped out. The second part of Tolsen's fleet had been too cautious in their jump.

"Prepare to jump," ordered Jeremy, reaching a quick decision. "Ariel, Lieutenant Grainger, prepare to activate our new program."

"We haven't been ordered in yet, Admiral," Colonel Malen reminded Jeremy, her eyes focusing on him.

"We don't have time to wait, Colonel," he replied, firmly. "Ariel, you have control of the fleet take us to Caden's World."

Colonel Malen nodded. She knew it was the right decision.

Instantly, swirling blue-white spatial vortexes formed in front of the seventeen ships of Jeremy's fleet. Ariel quickly guided the fleet ships into the individual vortexes with the Avenger being last, but only by a microsecond.

Above Caden's World and just outside of the gravity well, seventeen blue-white vortexes formed directly behind the attacking Hocklyn fleet. Out of the vortexes stormed Jeremy's fleet. In less than four seconds, the sensors, screens, and weapons were online.

"We're in combat range," Lieutenant Preston from Tactical reported. "Weapons are locking on."

"Fire!" Jeremy ordered, his gaze focusing on the main viewscreen, which was now focused on a massive Hocklyn dreadnought. "All ships continuous fire, don't let those Hocklyns escape. We need to make these first shots count!"

From the seventeen ships of Jeremy's fleet, massive weapons fire erupted. Orange-red laser beams snapped out to strike the shields of the Hocklyn ships. Dark violet power beams clawed at Hocklyn energy shields, knocking them down and cutting deep into the hulls. Missiles and railgun rounds filled space as an onslaught of heavy fire rained down from behind on the now trapped Hocklyn fleet. Two Hocklyn war cruisers exploded as they were ravaged by this sudden and unexpected attack.

Admiral Tolsen breathed a deep sigh of relief as he saw Admiral Strong's fleet jump in nearly on top of the Hocklyns. He wasn't sure how Strong had managed it, but it had saved his fleet. Even as he watched, another Hocklyn war cruiser exploded followed rapidly by two of the escort cruisers. Commander Strong had taken the Hocklyns by complete surprise and was making mincemeat out of their fleet.

"Move us in," he ordered calmly, glancing at Colonel Beck. "We don't need to let Admiral Strong to do all of the work for us."

-

War Leader Tantil blanched as he saw the new human fleet appear impossibly close to his ships. It was impossible to plot that type of micro-jump, but the humans had done it! He was trapped between two fleets with a third closing. A bright white light flashed across one of the viewscreens as another escort cruiser exploded from the withering fire of the humans. Death and destruction marched across the energy screens of his fleet, knocking many of them down. His fleet was doomed unless War Leader Bisth arrived soon.

-

War Leader Sangeth gazed at the sensor screens in frustration as he saw his plan starting to come apart. If this continued, War Leader Tantil's fleet would be destroyed. Once again, it seemed as if they had underestimated the humans.

"We're at extreme weapons range of the human defense satellites," First Leader Rahn reported.

Sangeth turned his gaze back to the First Leader. They could still accomplish the mission if he could knock out the planet's defenses and send the Protectors down to search for the information on the human home world. Yes, victory could still be his! When Bisth arrived he could deal with these new human ships, but Sangeth would have the necessary information that would lead to the human home world. Honor was still within easy reach.

"Fire missiles!" Sangeth ordered determinedly in a cold and deadly voice. He had learned his lesson the last time. He would destroy the human's defensive satellites from long-range.

From his twenty-four ships, two hundred missiles belched forth on pillars of fire from his missile tubes. Twenty seconds later another two hundred missiles followed. The humans might be able to stop some of them, but they couldn't stop them all. Behind the two missile barrages, his fleet followed.

-

"They launched from extreme range," Lucy cried as she saw a rain of destruction headed for the orbital defensive satellites.

"Launch our missiles," General Abercrombie ordered with determination in his voice. He turned to face Lucy. "It's either use them or lose them. At least this way we may be able to take a few of them out."

"We're not going to be able to stop them from going into orbit, are we?" asked Lucy nervously, knowing that soon Hocklyn Protectors would be coming down to the two mining settlements. There was going to be a battle for control of the surface; she hoped Lieutenant Simmins was ready.

"No, we're not," admitted General Abercrombie in a grave tone, his dark eyes gazing at Captain Krandle. "We can take out some of them, but not all."

In space, Hocklyn missiles began to explode as laser beams from the defensive satellites locked on and took them out. But the lasers had to stay focused for several long seconds on a target to destroy it. The lasers managed to take out one hundred and forty of the Hocklyn missiles in the first wave, but the other sixty took out forty of the defensive satellites.

Unfortunately, the defending human ships beneath the satellites were too far out of range to intercept the incoming missiles. Their job was to destroy any missiles that might get past the satellites and strike the planet. Seeing the danger, the commander of the defending task force immediately ordered his ships to move closer to the satellites so he could add his defensive fire to theirs. But it was already too late as the next wave of missiles arrived and forty-eight more satellites ceased to be.

Jeremy was feeling elated as another Hocklyn escort cruiser fell to the Avenger's weapons. The viewscreens were full of damaged and exploding ships, most of them Hocklyn. The rest of Admiral Tolsen's fleet was nearly in weapons range. They would quickly annihilate the rest of this Hocklyn fleet and then proceed to engage the Hocklyn fleet attacking the planet. Just as he thought nothing could go wrong, red warning alarms began sounding.

In shock, Jeremy gazed at the tactical display as more deadly red threat icons suddenly appeared.

"Forty-eight additional Hocklyn warships have just jumped in," Lieutenant Walters reported from his sensor console in a grave voice. "I am detecting four more dreadnoughts, twelve war cruisers, and thirty-two escort cruisers."

"Get us turned!" Jeremy ordered heatedly as he quickly adjusted to the sudden change in the tactical situation.

His fleet was the only one that could turn quickly enough to engage this new fleet. Admiral Tolsen would have to deal with the other Hocklyn fleet for now. Looking across the Command Center, he could see a look of fear on a number of faces. He couldn't blame them since he was feeling the same.

-

War Leader Bisth gazed at the sensor screen with deep satisfaction. The human fleets were out of position, and he would be within weapons range within twelve minutes. They couldn't break off engagement with War Leader Tantil without risking grave damage to their ships, and they had to finish Tantil off before engaging him. As he gazed at the sensor screen, he knew much honor was about to come his way. This would be a great Hocklyn victory!

Chapter Ten

Admiral Tolsen stared in dismay at the new group of Hocklyn Warships that had just jumped into the system. He had never expected the Hocklyns to commit so many of their warships to this battle. Even as he watched the tactical display, he saw that Admiral Strong was quickly disengaging and turning his ships to face this new incoming threat.

"Admiral Strong's disengaging," reported Colonel Beck, looking over at Tolsen with deep concern in his eyes. "He won't last long against that fleet. There are four dreadnoughts and twelve war cruisers bearing down on him."

"I know," replied Tolsen, reaching a quick decision. He took a deep breath. "Communications contact Admiral Adler and tell him to jump here immediately. His target is that new Hocklyn fleet."

"Destroyer Olivia is down," Lieutenant Anders reported as another friendly green icon expanded and then vanished from the sensor screen.

In space, the small destroyer had blown apart from multiple missile strikes. All that remained was a glowing mass of wreckage.

"What are we still facing?" demanded Tolsen, starting to feel desperate as he tried to make sense of the tactical situation.

Colonel Beck glanced at his tactical computer screen before answering. "We still have two Hocklyn dreadnoughts, three war cruisers, and ten escort cruisers engaging us. Our other ships will be within range in another two minutes."

"What about our losses?"

We've lost two light cruisers and five destroyers," Beck answered. "However, both of our Monarchs are reporting heavy damage and are under attack from the remaining three Hocklyn war cruisers. They won't last much longer, Admiral."

Admiral Tolsen felt the WarHawk take another hard jolt, and the lights in the Command Center flickered briefly. On the damage control board, he saw a large number of lights suddenly turn a glaring red. Then the ship seemed to be kicked solidly in the side.

"A nuke's made it through our shields!" screamed Beck, grabbing for the edge of the plotting table only to be thrown violently to the floor.

Several consoles exploded, sending showers of bright sparks across the Command Center. Admiral Tolsen could hear people screaming. The ship shuddered again as more Hocklyn ordnance pounded her hull. The Command Center began to fill with smoke. He knew the WarHawk was taking heavy, if not fatal damage.

"Shields are down," Tactical reported frantically as the WarHawk continued to fire every weapon she could bring to bear.

Tolsen knew that, without shields, his flagship wouldn't last long. With great sadness, he knew the WarHawk was dying around him.

The shuddering lessened and seemed to stop. "What's going on?" he demanded, looking over at Lieutenant Anders. Colonel Beck was getting back up with a wicked looking cut across his cheek bleeding profusely.

"The Monarch cruiser Caledonia has taken up position in front of us," Anders responded. "The Hocklyns have shifted their fire to her."

"Get our shields back up," Tolsen ordered with a grim look upon his face. He knew as badly damaged as the Caledonia was she wouldn't last long under bombardment from a dreadnought.

"Working on it," Colonel Beck replied as he talked frantically to Engineering.

"Get crews working on the damage!" Tolsen ordered the officer at damage control. "Concentrate on the fires and get all the protective bulkheads closed. We're bleeding too much damn air!"

"Crews are being dispatched," the officer reported as he passed on his orders over his mini-com. Then he turned and looked gravely at the admiral. "We have numerous fires that are being reported out of control and many compartments that are in a vacuum, some we can do nothing about. We just don't have the people."

Tolsen nodded his understanding, his face turning grim. He feared that his flagship was mortally wounded. He gazed around the Command Center and noted the worried and frightened looks on the crew.

"Fight the ship, people," he ordered, trying to sound as calm as possible. "Admiral Adler and Third Fleet will be here shortly."

"Admiral, Engineering is reporting that they have several fires that are out of control in the engineering spaces," Colonel Beck reported bleakly, and then he passed on more bad news. "The main fusion reactor is down, and we are running on the auxiliaries. They say it will take at least an hour to knock out the fires and to repair the main reactor."

"We don't have an hour, Peter," Tolsen spoke quietly to his executive officer, his eyes showing his deep concern.

"I know," Beck replied with a slight nod of acknowledgement of what was in store for them if Admiral Adler didn't arrive shortly.

On the main viewscreen, someone had switched it to show the Caledonia. The valiant Monarch cruiser's screens were covered with exploding ordnance. Bright flashes of light blasted at the energy screen, trying to knock it down. Occasionally it would weaken in a spot and a railgun round or missile would penetrate, smashing into the hull and causing damage to the valiant cruiser. Its hull was already pockmarked with heavy damage, and fires could be seen burning where escaping air was bleeding from the ship. Its hull was glowing cherry-red in numerous places.

"What about our bomber strike?" asked Tolsen, looking at the tactical display. "What happened with it?"

"Not good," Beck responded as he studied the information on the tactical computer screen. A medic was applying a bandage to his cheek to help stop the bleeding from his wound. "Most of it was wiped out by Hocklyn defensive fire and the few that got through caused some damage but not enough to make a difference."

Admiral Tolsen let out a deep breath. So many good people were dying, and there was nothing he could do to stop it. He clenched his fist in anger as he watched the Caledonia on the viewscreen.

On the main viewscreen, half a dozen blue Hocklyn energy beams suddenly stuck the Caledonia simultaneously. The ship's screen wavered and then failed completely. Missiles and railgun rounds ravaged the hull, causing massive explosions. Even as Admiral Tolsen watched, the ship started to break apart, at which point her self-destructs initiated, blasting the heavy Monarch cruiser to oblivion.

"It will be our turn again now," Colonel Beck said calmly, knowing the end for the WarHawk was close.

"Our energy screen?" asked Tolsen his eyes focusing on Peter, knowing that, without it, they were doomed.

"No, Sir," Beck responded in a lower voice. "Too many power conduits have been destroyed. We're trying to reroute power, but it will take time."

On the main viewscreen, a blue energy beam seemed to lash out at the WarHawk, and the screen became covered with static. The ship began shaking violently, and Tolsen could actually hear distant explosions. People were screaming, and frantic cries for help could be heard over his mini-com.

"The rest of our fleet's arrived," Lieutenant Anders called out jubilantly as a massive explosion rocked the WarHawk.

The entire Command Center seemed to be hurled upward. The last thing Admiral Tolsen saw before he lost consciousness was a massive metal beam falling and crushing Colonel Beck. Then everything went black.

-

War Leader Tantil cursed as the rest of the reinforcing human fleet stormed into combat range. He was now outnumbered and in an untenable position. The human flagship was out of action and burning. On the main viewscreen, he could see numerous fires burning inside the ravaged ship where there was still oxygen. Occasionally an explosion would rattle the human ship, throwing more debris into space. He doubted if any humans were still alive on it. There was only one thing left for him to do.

"First Leader Klessen, prepare to advance and engage the enemy. We are outnumbered, and our ships are heavily damaged. In death, there will be honor."

First Leader Klessen heard the words and knew what the War Leader was expecting. They were cut off from War Leader Bisth with a numerically superior enemy bearing down on them; there was only one clear choice.

Seeking to enhance their honor, twelve Hocklyn ships hurled themselves at the approaching enemy in a mad rush. The human ships opened up a horrendous fire of power beams, lasers, missiles, and railguns. The screens on the charging Hocklyn ships were covered in bright explosions from detonating ordnance. Several screens wavered and went down, allowing the weapons fire to impact the now unprotected hulls. Two more escort cruisers exploded in bright fury just short of the human fleet. Then the Hocklyns were amongst the human ships and still accelerating, but now their weapons fell silent as their ships became the weapons.

-

Jeremy watched stunned as ten human warships vanished in massive fireballs as the Hocklyn ships rammed the surprised human fleet.

"Oh my God!" Jeremy heard Kelsey scream as one of the viewscreens next to Ariel showed the extent of the destruction and fleet losses.

"Lieutenant DeSota," Jeremy spoke quickly to Angela. "Contact those surviving ships and Tolsen's survivors and have them join up with us."

"Helm, bring us to a dead stop until the other ships can reach us. Lieutenant Walters, how soon before that new Hocklyn fleet reaches extreme weapons range?"

"Ten minutes," Kevin responded with a grim look. "It will take Tolsen's survivors six to eight minutes to reach us.

"Very well," Jeremy replied as he weighed his options. Looking across the Command Center, he knew his people were depending on him to make the right decision.

"We're still going to be outnumbered," Colonel Malen spoke as she looked at the opposing Hocklyn fleet that was steadily approaching. "We can't stand up to four dreadnoughts and twelve war cruisers. We need Admiral Adler's fleet!"

Jeremy leaned back and gazed at the tactical display. He had forty-eight Hocklyn warships bearing down on him. His fleet had to be maneuvering before the Hocklyns reached weapons range or his ships would make easy targets. Even with the survivors from Tolsen's fleet, he would be badly outnumbered. Looking at the main sensor screen, he wondered where Admiral Adler and Admiral Streth were. They had to be on their way by now.

Admiral Streth gazed unflinchingly at the WarStorm's tactical display. He had watched unsurprised as the surviving Hocklyn ships had crashed headlong into the incoming human fleet. A Hocklyn did not retreat from battle, it was better to die in combat than to return home without honor. It was a lesson they would have to remember in future engagements.

"Ten more ships gone," Amanda reported as she glanced worriedly at the data coming in. "Even when Tolsen's survivors get to Admiral Strong, the Hocklyns will still have a numerical advantage and far more firepower. They have too many capital ships, and he won't stand a chance."

"Any word on Admiral Tolsen?" Hedon asked as he weighed his options.

He had already countermanded Admiral Tolsen's orders to Admiral Adler. Hedon wanted to destroy this Hocklyn fleet and in order to do that it had to be heavily engaged with Admiral Strong's forces. If he jumped in too early, there was a chance some of the ships might escape and spread word back to the Hocklyn Empire.

"The WarHawk is heavily damaged," Commander Evans responded as she listened to the battle over her mini-com. "We're lucky her self-destructs didn't go off. The light cruiser StarFly has come alongside her and is sending rescue teams over to search for survivors. There is no communication with the ship."

Admiral Streth nodded. He hoped Admiral Tolsen survived, but he had come to know that, in war, there were no guarantees. He turned to face Amanda and Commander Evans. "Here is what I want to do. We have two Hocklyn forces to contend with, the one Admiral Strong is facing and the one attacking Caden's World." Hedon quickly outlined his plan. It was risky, but it should work.

-

Captain Krandle watched apprehensively as the approaching Hocklyn warships swept more of her defensive satellites away. Their missile strike had failed dismally as they had launched from extreme range, giving the Hocklyns plenty of time to intercept. Not only that, but the Hocklyns were now launching their own fighters and shooting down every missile launched and destroying more of the precious defense satellites.

"Our warships will be engaging soon," General Abercrombie commented as he watched the sensor screen and the Hocklyn fleet coming toward them. He had hoped to be able to damage them with the orbital missile platforms, but that had failed miserably.

"They won't be able to stop them," spoke Lucy worriedly, seeing how badly outnumbered they would be. "They don't have the firepower."

"No, they don't," General Abercrombie agreed in a solemn voice. "We never expected the Hocklyns to attack in these numbers. I suspect that Admiral Streth will be appearing shortly. His fleet can handle this, but until then we're going to be on our own. I hate to say this, but we need to evacuate to the auxiliary Command Center. This operations center will be the prime target."

Lucy nodded; she understood what needed to be done. She turned to a corporal standing behind her. "Corporal Higgins, set the self-destructs for thirty minutes." She then turned to a pale looking

Adam Severson. "We're evacuating; the Hocklyns are going to make orbit."

Severson nodded as he began giving instructions to his remaining people, making sure they had either were on the way to the deep underground bunkers or already there. It had taken him and his people years of backbreaking work to make Caden's World a good place to live for its 20,000 inhabitants. Now that was over, the population had been evacuated, and it was a warzone. He wondered dismally if there would be anything left to rebuild after the Hocklyns got through.

Jeremy watched tensely as the Hocklyn fleet maneuvered in front of his position. The survivors from Admiral Tolsen's force had finally made rendezvous, and he was hurriedly melding them into his fleet.

"Total fleet count, including ours, are two battle cruisers, two battle carriers, two strike cruisers, four Monarch cruisers, twelve light cruisers, and eighteen destroyers," Lieutenant Walters reported. "Sir, a number of Tolsen's ships are heavily damaged and are barely combat worthy."

"Keep the more heavily damaged ships to the back of our formation," ordered Jeremy, looking over at Colonel Malen. "What about the carrier?"

"The surviving carrier is the Independence, and most of her flight squadrons have been decimated," responded Colonel Malen, grimly. "Commander Arie is reporting that she has only one squadron of fighters and half a squadron of bombers left."

"Hocklyns are advancing, Sir," Lieutenant Walters reported suddenly, his eyes focused on his sensor screen.

"Let's go get them, Colonel," Jeremy ordered with resolve in his eyes. "Hold the two battle carriers back; we will need their fighters, and they can help cover the damaged ships."

"I wish we would hear something from Admiral Streth," Angela commented over her secure line to Kelsey. "Where is he?"

"Patience, Angela," replied Kelsey, trying her best to keep her voice calm. "Jeremy is here, and he will win this battle, he's too good not to."

Angela was silent as she looked over at Kevin. He was quiet, not trusting his voice to say anything. He only nodded and then turned back to his sensors.

Ariel had listened to the brief conversation and knew that her friends were scared. She couldn't blame them; they were in a bad situation. She needed to talk Jeremy into letting her have control of the ship.

–

War Leader Bisth felt great satisfaction as he watched the humans advance to meet his fleet. One thing about these humans, they were not cowards. They were worthy warriors and deserved respect as such. Much honor would be gained in defeating such an enemy.

"We're in extreme weapons range," reported First Leader Gresth, looking over at War Leader Bisth. "What are your orders?"

Gresth was pleased and excited. Honor was within easy reach, and he could already taste the victory. The Hocklyn fleet had superior numbers and firepower and too many of the human ships were damaged.

"Continue to close to optimum firing range, target their capital ships with our first salvos. I want all energy beams focused on their two surviving battle cruisers, that's where their commander will be," Bisth ordered from his command pedestal as he gazed out triumphantly over the War Room. Honor would soon be forthcoming now that his victory was assured.

"What about these two new ships?" Gresth asked as he put one of the strike cruisers up on the main viewscreen. "They are 1,000 meters in length and heavily armed."

"A new development of their Monarch cruiser," replied Bisth, dismissing the new ship as a major threat. "Once the battle cruisers are destroyed, switch our energy beams to deal with them."

–

Both fleets continued to close with neither firing. Jeremy watched impassively as the numerous red and green icons on the tactical display gradually grew nearer. "Stand by to fire," he finally ordered. "All power beams are to focus on their war cruisers. We will get the dreadnoughts later." Jeremy knew that by destroying the more numerous war cruisers it would take some of the pressure off his lighter units. With the powerful screens the dreadnoughts were equipped with, it would be a waste of time for his lighter units to fire upon them.

"Hocklyns are launching fighters," Lieutenant Walters reported as numerous red threat icons began leaving the Hocklyn ships.

"Fighter count is 328," Colonel Malen informed Jeremy as she read the data coming across the tactical computer. "That's a lot of fighters, Sir."

"How many do we have?" asked Jeremy, knowing his fighters would be badly outnumbered. The Independence had only one squadron to send while his carrier, the Retribution, had yet to commit her fighters.

"Only 212 to send against them," Malen replied with narrowed eyes. Then she asked her next question. "Do we send in the bombers?"

"Yes," replied Jeremy heavily, knowing he was probably sending them to their deaths. "Have them target the Hocklyn's escort cruisers only; the capital ships have too much defensive firepower."

"Hocklyns are firing!" Lieutenant Preston called out in warning from Tactical."

"Return fire, all batteries," Jeremy ordered, his eyes focusing on the tactical display. Then they took on a deadly glint of determination as he realized what had to be done. There was only one way they were going to survive this. "Contact the Nemesis and have them put Devastator Three missiles into six of their missile tubes and regular Devastator missiles in six more. I want our tubes loaded the same."

"Devastator Three's!" Malen responded her eyes widening in shock. "We don't have permission to use those in this battle!"

"It's a command decision," Jeremy replied, his eyes holding steady. "I want to target all four of their dreadnoughts. If Devastator Threes are supposed to knock down an AI shield, then they should smash the shields on a dreadnought. I want a follow up strike from our power beams and railguns; we need to destroy those four dreadnoughts. It's the only way we're going to win this."

Even as Jeremy finished speaking, he felt the Avenger shudder from weapons fire striking her shields. He looked up at the main viewscreen and Ariel. "Ariel, once the Devastator Three strike has been launched, I am turning control of the Avenger over to you. Can you take control of the Nemesis as well?"

Ariel smiled in anticipation. "Yes, Lieutenant Johnson and I have prepared a special program just for this; it has already been loaded in the Nemesis's mainframe."

Jeremy merely shook his head; even now it seemed that Ariel and Katie were one step ahead of him.

Around the Avenger, Hocklyn missile fire spread nuclear fury across the screens of the human fleet. Occasionally, a screen would fail and the ship's hull would suffer from the onslaught. The space between the two fleets was full of exploding weapons as missiles and missile interceptors collided, defensive fire destroyed inbound ordnance, and power beams, energy beams, and lasers leaped between the two fleets.

War Leader Sangeth watched his main sensor screen as the last human warship was destroyed above the mining planet. The battle had been swift and brutal, with all fourteen human ships being annihilated as well as the defensive satellites, but they had extracted a heavy cost to Sangeth's fleet. One war cruiser and six escort cruisers were gone.

"Begin landing our Protectors," ordered Sangeth, wanting to find the needed information about the human home world before War Leader Bisth arrived over the planet. Already much honor had been achieved. While it was true War Leader Bisth was also adding honor to his name, it would be Sangeth that would bring the information about the human home world back to Commodore Resmunt.

Examining the sensor screen, he noticed that Bisth was heavily engaged with the remaining human ships. The humans had been much more powerful than expected. There was no doubt in Sangeth's mind that a heavily populated human world lay somewhere close by. Its conquest would bring tremendous honor to his family as well as himself. He would soon be a Fleet Commodore after this victory and extremely wealthy.

Captain Krandle and General Abercrombie had made it to the underground Command Center. Unlike the operations center, this large room was staffed completely by military personnel and heavily shielded.

"Hocklyn shuttles are descending," a corporal reported from his sensor console as numerous small red threat icons left two of the orbiting ships and proceeded into the atmosphere.

"Surface batteries standby to fire," General Abercrombie ordered into his mini-com. He was in communication with all of his forces and planned to direct the battle from here. The Hocklyns would not be allowed to land unopposed.

A bank of large viewscreens on one wall showed scenes from across the two mining communities. Several were showing the space above both settlements, and already contrails could be seen from descending Hocklyn shuttles.

"Fire on target lock," Abercrombie ordered as his eyes focused on the screens. Every Hocklyn Protector killed in their shuttles was one less his marines would have to deal with on the ground.

Almost instantly, blazing interceptor missiles launched arrowing upward toward the descending shuttles. No sooner did they launch than horrendous explosions struck the launching sites. Railgun fire from the orbiting Hocklyn ships was targeting every missile firing location.

Lucy felt sick, knowing brave men and women were dying up above in the town. She hoped Lieutenant Simmins was still okay. Her eyes were glued to the screens as explosions continued to rock the settlement. Several buildings had already collapsed, and others were starting to burn. Out of the corner of her eyes, she could see the pained look on Adam Severson's face as the work of years was being systematically destroyed.

General Abercrombie was watching the screens intently. He saw several of his interceptor missiles strike the inbound shuttles. Fiery red explosions dotted the early afternoon sky, and then it was over.

"Hocklyn shuttles are down," the corporal reported. "Our defensive missile fire took out twelve of them, but the other twenty-eight managed to land."

"Now it's up to our marines," Abercrombie stated grimly as he passed on the warning to his people up above. He knew that shortly they would be facing a lot of heavily armed Hocklyn Protectors.

-

Jeremy felt the Avenger shudder again as a railgun round slipped through the battered energy screen. He was waiting for point blank range to hit the Hocklyns with the Devastator Threes. With their miniaturized sublight drive and inertial dampening system, the Hocklyns would never detect the launch. He glanced over at the damage control board, noticing a few more red lights were glowing. The Avenger was taking some damage, even with her powerful energy screen.

"Optimum range now," spoke Ariel, wanting Jeremy to launch. The Avenger was taking too much damage. Already, her weapons systems had been degraded by eight percent.

"Launch," Jeremy ordered softly. Around the Command Center, it became so quiet you could hear a pin drop. This would be the first time any of them had seen a Devastator Three used.

"Launching," replied Lieutenant Preston, as he pressed a series of buttons.

On the Avenger's outer hull, twelve hatches slid open on the ship's missile tubes. From six of them, there was a bright flash and then nothing. From the other six, Devastator missiles rose up on pillars of flame their targeting sensors reaching out and pinpointing the Hocklyn dreadnoughts.

-

War Leader Bisth was feeling the satisfaction of victory as his ships pounded the human fleet. Already several of their lighter units had fallen to Hocklyn weapons fire, and their heavier units were suffering significant damage.

Suddenly a series of bright flashes covered all the viewscreens and the WarCry shuddered violently, then the ship seemed to be struck by a massive object, which threatened to break the ship apart. Bisth could hear loud explosions and wrenching sounds from the ship's hull as he struggled to hold onto the command console, then he was thrown violently to the deck. All the lights went out and several consoles exploded, sending bright showers of sparks across the room. Several supporting metal beams broke loose and came crashing down. Cries of pain and shock filled the War Room.

"First Leader Gresth!" Bisth rasped loudly as he stood back up, feeling a sharp pain in one leg.

The emergency lights flashed on, and he saw the War Room was in shambles. It was rapidly filling with smoke and several small fires were burning. Looking over to his side, he saw Gresth with his head up against a console. From the angle, Bisth knew the First Leader was dead.

-

Jeremy closed his eyes briefly as brilliant explosions lit up the viewscreens on the front wall of the Command Center. Rolling nuclear fire covered the location of all four of the Hocklyn dreadnoughts. Even as he watched, the second wave of weaker Devastator missiles arrived and added to the maelstrom.

"Did we get them?" Jeremy asked intently, his eyes turning to Kevin.

"Sensors are off line," Lieutenant Walters reported. "There was too much of an EMP blast from those missiles and it will take a moment for the systems to recover."

Finally, the tactical image above the plotting table flickered and then came back on.

"Two dreadnoughts are down, and the other two are heavily damaged," Colonel Malen told Jeremy as she studied the data. "The two surviving dreadnoughts are finished; they're just floating wrecks."

Jeremy smiled viciously. "Ariel, the Avenger and Nemesis are yours. Let's go get those war cruisers; all other ships are to continue to pound the escorts. I want both battle carriers to move up into optimum combat range and add their firepower to the rest of the fleet."

"It's your turn now, Ariel," Katie spoke over their private channel. Let's go show Jeremy what you can do."

Ariel felt a flush of excitement at getting to show Jeremy what she was capable of. The Avenger and Nemesis suddenly accelerated sharply and closed on a Hocklyn war cruiser. Every weapon the two ships could bring to bear fired in unison, all impacting a target only a few meters across on the Hocklyn's energy screen. Its shields instantly collapsed, and Ariel sent through a Devastator missile. The war cruiser ceased to be as nuclear fire consumed the ship.

Jeremy was silent as he watched. He hadn't given Ariel permission to use Devastator missiles but after seeing the result, he wasn't going to argue.

-

Admiral Streth nodded in satisfaction as the WarStorm's long-range sensors detected the Devastator Three missiles going off.

"Take us in, Amanda," ordered Hedon, knowing the time had finally arrived. "Let's go help Admiral Strong finish off those Hocklyn ships. Those missiles should have knocked their FTL drives offline; they can't escape now. Tell Admiral Adler he has a go."

"You knew he would use those missiles, didn't you?" spoke Amanda gazing accusingly at the admiral in surprise.

"I suspected," replied Hedon with a satisfied smile. "From what I have learned of Admiral Strong, he doesn't believe in losing. The Devastator Threes were his only choice."

-

War Leader Bisth looked at the sensor screen, which had just been brought back online. Very little else was working in the War Room. Even the heavy metal hatch was jammed so they couldn't get out and help couldn't get in. Communications with most parts of the ship were down. From what little information he had been able to receive, he knew his ship was mortally wounded and all that was left was for it to finish dying. He wondered just what the humans had hit his ships with and why they hadn't used it before. The Hocklyns possessed no weapon comparable to what had just been used against him.

146

He felt utter shock when numerous red threat icons began appearing on the sensor screen behind his fleet. More human ships! Now he knew why the humans had waited to use this final weapon. From the scattered communications he had been able to receive from his other warships, all of their FTL drives were down from the EMP blasts. His fleet could not escape. With a heavy sigh, he knew it was over. Reaching down on the command console, he pressed two bright red buttons embedded in the panel. He would find honor in death. Moments later, the WarCry exploded as its self-destructs went off.

Admiral Adler looked grimly at the tactical display in the Command Center of the battle carrier Wasp. Admiral Strong's daring attack with Devastator Three missiles had stunned the Hocklyns. All four of their heavy dreadnoughts were either destroyed or out of action. Even as he watched, the last went up as its nuclear self-destruct charges detonated.

"Status," he barked as he looked over at his executive officer.

"All four of their dreadnoughts are gone, and Admiral Strong is pressing the attack," Commander Timmins responded. "The war cruisers seem to be recovering from the loss of their dreadnoughts and are renewing their assault on Admiral Strong's forces."

"Launch our bomber strike," Adler ordered with a fierce grin.

He wanted to take the pressure off Strong's ships, and right now he had the Hocklyns at a disadvantage. Following Strong's example, he had jumped in just behind the Hocklyn fleet. He planned on a long-range attack campaign using his Anlon bombers, but the bombers on his ten carriers were different. They had a weak forward shield and his carriers had many more of them than a normal battle carrier.

In the flight bay of the Wasp, Colonel Karl Arcles was the fleet's acting flight leader. He had gone into cryosleep along with his copilot Captain Lacy Sanders over four hundred years ago.

"Let's go get them," he spoke over his com to all of his squadrons. "Form up on me and let's kick some Hocklyn ass."

Arcles expertly guided his Anlon bomber out of the flight bay and quickly set course for the Hocklyn fleet. From his cockpit window, he could see numerous explosions occurring around both of the two battling fleets. His other squadrons quickly formed up around him. Each carrier group had an acting wing commander and Arcles would facilitate the attack through them.

"Target their remaining war cruisers first, then the escorts," he ordered in a calm and steady voice. "That's where their advantage is right now. If we can take them out, then Admiral Strong can handle the rest."

The other nine wing leaders confirmed his instructions as they zeroed in on their intended targets.

"Activate forward shields," he instructed Captain Sanders.

"Just like old times," quipped Lacy, trying not to sound nervous about going back into combat after so long. "I just hope these shields work."

"Just like back home," replied Arcles, recalling the last battle in the home system back in the old Federation. "Only this time, we're going to win!"

Arcles's squadron was slightly in the lead. Behind him, another 1,260 Anlon bombers were lined up each equipped with four Shrike missiles armed with a tactical nuclear warhead. It would be the most devastating bomber strike ever launched by a human fleet.

-

Aboard the war cruisers, the First Leaders looked in anger and fear at what was coming toward them. War Leader Bisth was dead and the command structure was in tatters; each First Leader was on his own. Some chose to continue the attack against the human ships; however, several others turned to face the incoming attack bombers of the humans.

-

Admiral Streth had jumped in as close to the gravity well of Caden's World as he dared. Even so, it would take nearly thirty minutes for his fleet to reach the planet.

"Admiral Sheen, I want half of the fleet to micro-jump to the other side of the planet's gravity well. Our drive cores are still cool enough to handle a short micro-jump. I don't want any of these Hocklyn ships to escape."

"Yes, Admiral," Sheen responded as she quickly passed on the orders to the necessary ships.

As soon as the ships had micro-jumped, Hedon ordered the remaining part of the fleet to head in toward Caden's World. It was time to extract some revenge for what the Hocklyns had done to his home worlds.

-

"Looks as if the cavalry's arrived," General Abercrombie commented with obvious relief in his voice as he watched the arrival of Second and Third Fleet. "The space battle will be over shortly, that will just leave the Hocklyn Protectors down here."

Lucy nodded. Looking at the viewscreens, she could see that heavy fighting was already erupting in the settlement above them. The Hocklyns had brought all of their shuttles down around the settlement with the operations center.

"If you notice, the Hocklyns have been careful not to target any weapons batteries close to the operations center," General Abercrombie pointed out as he studied the developing situation up above. "I believe they want to capture it intact."

"They want information," Lucy replied with a knowing nod. But the information was gone, destroyed by self-destruct charges set by the human marines. "They want to know where Earth is."

"Well, they won't find out from us," Abercrombie responded as he listened to his embattled marines over his mini-com.

Looking up at a screen, Lucy saw a squad of Protectors coming cautiously down a street. This was her first look at a live Hocklyn. The Protectors were nearly two meters tall, dark green in color and wore black body armor. Their arms were very muscular, and they were carrying some type of heavy assault rifle. A lighter color crest extended from their forehead to the back of their head. There was no body hair and their eyes were extremely large and set wider on the head than human eyes. Lucy shuddered involuntarily; she was glad she was down here in the Command Center and not up there facing those fearsome looking Hocklyn Protectors. She just hoped that Lieutenant Simmins was ready for what was coming toward him.

-

Lieutenant Simmins laid down the view scope he had been using to watch the advancing Hocklyn Protectors. Already, heavy weapons fire and occasional explosions could be heard throughout the settlement. The Hocklyns were advancing along three routes, and all were aimed at the operations center. More marines had already been pulled back from the outlying areas and were taking up defensive positions around it. Simmins knew the battle was only going to get more intense.

-

War Leader Sangeth was venting his growing rage at the deadly information being displayed on the main sensor screen. More human ships had jumped into the system. He knew now that they had fallen into a well planned trap. No Hocklyn ship would escape from this system to spread word of this human danger back to the empire. No matter which way he went with his fleet, he would face a numerically superior enemy who would trap him in the planet's gravity well. There was no doubt that this was what the humans had intended all along.

Sangeth looked over at First Leader Rahn, his dark eyes wide. "Honor will be ours today."

"Honor will be ours," agreed Rahn, knowing the only honorable decision to be made and hoping War Leader Sangeth would make it. "The enemy comes toward us, War Leader. What are your orders?"

Sangeth was no coward. He had fled from the enemy in this system once before, but not again. His cold eyes gazed unafraid at the approaching human ships. "Break orbit and proceed toward the nearer human fleet. The two Protector ships are to stay here and, if they recover the necessary information, try to escape."

Rahn nodded his head in respectful agreement, his cold, dark eyes gazing at War Leader Sangeth. He suspected this battle would be very short.

-

Colonel Arcles flinched as a railgun round impacted the forward screen of his bomber, covering it in light. Captain Sanders was continuously firing off countermeasures as Arcles weaved their craft through the intense defensive fire toward the war cruiser he had chosen as his group's target. A green light finally blinked on, indicating that the targeting computer had a positive lock on the Hocklyn ship.

"Missiles fired," he stated over the com. Moments later he heard other confirmations from other squadron leaders.

Arcles pulled the Anlon bomber up in a sharp turn, accelerating it to top speed to get away from the defensive weapons fire. Looking down at his sensor screen, it seemed to be full of missiles targeting the Hocklyn's eight remaining war cruisers. They had lost a few bombers going in, but not nearly as many as had been feared. The forward shields actually seemed to work!

-

"Get us out of here," Jeremy ordered Ariel when he saw the massed missile attack from the Anlon bombers. He had never seen so many missiles fired at once.

The Avenger and Nemesis instantly turned and accelerated away. Ariel had managed to take out two war cruisers while receiving only minor damage in return.

Jeremy and Malen watched the viewscreens as roaring atomic fire played across the Hocklyn's screens as the Shrike missiles struck. Their screens seemed to be covered in fiery nuclear energy.

"My God!" Malen spoke, aghast at the sheer destruction the Anlon bombers had released.

"If these are the new bomber tactics, I think I am going to like them," Jeremy responded as reports began coming in of Hocklyn energy shield failure.

Each time a shield failed, multiple Shrike missiles would strike the ship's unprotected hull. Hocklyn ship after Hocklyn ship died. Finally, the screens began to clear as the bombers finished their attack run and headed back to Third Fleet.

"What's left?" Jeremy demanded still seeing a few red threat icons on the main sensor screen.

"Not much," Kevin replied as he studied his sensors. "There are six Hocklyn escort cruisers still intact, but they are heavily damaged."

"Let's move in and finish them off," ordered Jeremy, knowing this part of the battle was almost over. He quickly activated his fleet com. "All ships, move in and finish off the remaining six Hocklyn escort cruisers and be wary of suicide runs."

A few minutes later it was done, and the Hocklyn fleet was destroyed.

War Leader Sangeth watched in dismay as another of his war cruisers exploded as its self-destructs went off. The humans had hit him with a large bomber attack from their three battle carriers and then moved in and blasted his fleet with their new beam weapon. He had managed to destroy several of their lighter units, but their superior shields and weapons were having a telling effect.

Sangeth looked wearily over at First Leader Rahn, knowing the battle was lost. "All ships are to accelerate and ram the enemy. Honor will be ours."

"Honor will be ours," Rahn replied as he passed on the order.

Instantly, the Crimson Oblivion and the other surviving Hocklyn ships accelerated toward Second Fleet. The weapons fire intensified, and most of the Hocklyn ships were destroyed short of their intended targets, but the Crimson Oblivion and the other Hocklyn dreadnought reached their targets. A Monarch cruiser and a battle cruiser died in a massive series of explosions as the nuclear self-destructs in all four ships went off.

-

Amanda felt stunned at the sudden turn of events. There had been only two battle cruisers in her section of Second Fleet, and one had been destroyed. She knew it could have just as easily have been the WarStorm. What would it have meant to the Federation if Fleet Admiral Streth had died in this battle? She didn't even want to think about the ramifications.

"Take us in to Caden's World," Hedon ordered as he looked at the swirling display of energy and gases that remained of the battle cruiser Olympia. He knew only the fact that the Olympia had been closer to the enemy dreadnought had saved the WarStorm.

-

Lieutenant Simmins was firing round after round from his heavy assault rifle into the advancing Hocklyns. Their combat armor was damn tough, but an armor piercing bullet could still penetrate it. The surviving marines had pulled back to an area just around the operations center and had already thrown back several heavy Hocklyn attacks.

"They're getting closer each time," spoke Corporal Blevens, breathing heavily as the fighting died down for a moment. "We might not be able to stop them next time."

Simmins looked over at the young corporal as he slid a new magazine into his rifle. Blevens looked to be in his early twenties. "The Fleet will be here soon, son, and then this will be over."

"Here they come!" Simmins heard over his mini-com. Looking up over the pile of sandbags they were behind, Simmins saw the Hocklyns charging forward. "It's time, Corporal." Simmins spoke as he raised his rifle and began firing in short controlled bursts.

With satisfaction, he saw a Hocklyn go down. But this attack was different; the Hocklyns acted as if they were desperate. The Fleet's won, Simmins thought as the Hocklyns began to overrun the marine's positions. He heard a loud scream from his side and, turning his head, saw Corporal Blevens fall. The young man was dead, shot through the head!

Simmins turned his attention back to the Hocklyn Protectors just as one leaped over the sandbags pointing his rifle. Lieutenant Simmins fired first and the Hocklyn dropped, then Simmins felt a sharp pain in his back. Looking down, he saw blood coming from his chest. Damn!

He thought as he fell. Falling to the ground Simmins rolled over, looking up into the sky. Human assault shuttles were coming down. He felt a wave of dizziness pass over him, and he realized he was dying. As he closed his eyes, he heard the heavy roar from an assault shuttle's engines as it landed near him. He knew the battle was won as darkness overcame him, and everything became peacefully quiet.

Chapter Eleven

Admiral Streth was walking down a street on Caden's World. General Abercrombie and his aide, a Captain Krandle, were with him as well as a squad of heavily armed marines. Everywhere around them was a scene of destruction.

"I never saw anyone fight like these Hocklyn Protectors," Abercrombie commented gravely as they halted where a long line of covered marine bodies lay.

Several officers were slowly going down the long row, making sure they could identify each fallen marine. They all had dog tags, and after each was checked, one of the officers would mark off a name on the list he was carrying.

"How many did we lose down here?" asked Hedon, looking over at General Abercrombie. He knew a lot of brave men and women had died today, up in space as well as down here on the planet.

"We had twelve hundred marines protecting this settlement and eight hundred in the other," replied the general, motioning for one of the officers to come over. "Unfortunately, the Hocklyn Protectors all landed in this settlement. We estimate there were nearly eight hundred of the enemy. Fighting toward the end was fierce; it even got down to hand to hand in some areas when the Hocklyns overran our defenses."

An officer walked up and handed General Abercrombie a list. He examined it briefly, taking note of several names, and then looked over at Admiral Streth. "We lost 412 marines KIA and another 262 are injured." He then gazed at Captain Krandle with a sad look in his eyes. "I'm sorry to say that Lieutenant Simmins is on the list; he was one of those killed as the Hocklyns overran the positions on the west side of the operations center."

Lucy felt stunned by the news. She felt a wave of dizziness sweep over her and then felt a steadying hand. Admiral Streth was holding her arm with a sympathizing and understanding look in his eyes.

"We lost a lot of good people today, Captain," he spoke softly. "I'm sorry to hear about Lieutenant Simmins. I'm sure he was a good marine."

"He was, Sir," replied Lucy, forcing her voice to remain steady. "He was one of the best."

"Captain Krandle, why don't you return to the Command Center." Abercrombie suggested. "The admiral and I can finish our tour."

"Thank you, Sir," replied Lucy, trying to hold back the tears.

At the moment, all she wanted was to find someplace where she could be alone. She had never been in combat before, and there was so much death surrounding her now. Lieutenant Simmins and she had grown very close since her posting here. It would be difficult to stay here without him.

Abercrombie watched her walk off. "She will be fine after a while; she's a good officer." Then turning back to Admiral Streth, he said. "We didn't capture a single Hocklyn Protector, they fought to the death. When they realized their fleet had been defeated, they did everything they could to take as many of us with them as possible."

"That crazy honor system of theirs," explained Hedon, shaking his head. "I don't think we will see many prisoners taken on either side in this war."

"What now?" Abercrombie asked as they continued on their tour of the settlement.

"Admiral Johnson is sending additional marines to replace those you lost," answered Hedon.

The air was still full of smoke and numerous buildings were still burning. Hedon knew it would take some time to rebuild the settlement if they chose to do so. He suspected, knowing that many of the miners and their families considered Caden's World to be their home that the settlement would be rebuilt. He couldn't blame them; it was good to have someplace you could call home.

"What about the defense satellites?" General Abercrombie asked. "What are we going to do about replacing them?"

Abercrombie felt as if they hadn't work well at all. The missile strike had failed from the platforms, and the only real use the laser satellites provided had been was shooting down stray missiles. They were just too vulnerable to Hocklyn weapons fire.

"They didn't work very well because of our fleet disposition," Hedon responded, his brow creasing in a frown. "I think in future battles some fleet units are going to have to be positioned in the same orbit as the satellites to ensure their survival. That may be a good use for our destroyers. This is war and we must learn from each battle."

"Do you think the Hocklyns will attack us here again?"

"We will be leaving a fleet in orbit until additional units are assigned to this system," Hedon replied as they stopped and watched some marines trying to put out a fire. The two-story building was burning so badly Hedon knew it was a losing effort. "It will be at least several months before the Hocklyns can respond to their failure to take this system. In the meantime, we are preparing a surprise for them. If it works, I don't think you need to worry about the Hocklyns attacking Caden's World anytime soon."

"That's good," General Abercrombie responded as he watched more marines coming up to fight the fire. "We will be bringing the miners and their families back soon, there's a lot of rebuilding that needs to be done. I'm sure the Federation will be helping with that. At least the second mining settlement is still intact."

"I will talk to Admiral Johnson," Hedon said, thinking about what he could do to help. "She can in turn talk to President Kincaid about making the necessary resources available for the people here to rebuild."

"Adam Severson will be glad to hear that," Abercrombie responded. He knew that Severson and several of his people were already surveying the settlement to see what would be needed.

-

A little later, Hedon was back in his shuttle returning to the WarStorm. He had wanted to go down to the planet to see the combat zone first hand to give him a better feel and perspective for the enemy. Settling back in his seat, he thought about how the battle had gone. They had lost a lot of ships, but the Hocklyns had lost more. The massed carrier attack had worked beyond expectations, and he would be talking to Admiral Adler about future tactics.

He gazed out of one of the viewports at the approaching WarStorm. He wished he could talk to Taylor about what he was planning to do. His brother had always been the more rational and cautious of the two. Closing his eyes, Hedon thought about what Taylor would be saying right now. He knew that he would be telling him to be careful and not to take this victory for granted that this was just the first of many major battles ahead.

Opening his eyes, Hedon let out a heavy sigh. Someday, he would return to Maken. There was a lake there where he intended to build a cabin. In some ways, he considered that to be home since it held so many important memories.

-

Colonel Arcles was sitting in the officer's mess of the battle carrier Wasp when Captain Sanders walked in. As their eyes met, Karl gestured for her to come over and join him.

"How are you doing, Lacy?" asked Karl, knowing she had been feeling nauseous after their combat mission.

"Better," she admitted as she sat down with her tray. She had a tuna fish sandwich and a glass of tea. "I was just so afraid we were going to die out there. Those bombers don't handle like a fighter."

"Not if I can help," Karl responded with a smile. "You and I both will see the end of this, I promise you. We will probably be back in our fighters after this. I just felt it was necessary to lead this first bombing mission."

"I hope so," Lacy replied as she took a small bite of her sandwich. "Sometimes I just wonder if we made the right choice going into cryosleep."

Karl was silent for a moment. It had been a tough decision, especially when his sister Teena and Jacen Barnes had decided not to go into cryosleep but instead to get married. They elected to stay behind and raise a family. It had been the hardest thing he had ever done, leaving Teena like that. She had always been his little sister, and he had watched over her. But he knew that Jacen would have taken good care of her as well. Teena had left Karl several recorded messages, and he knew that Teena and Jacen had raised several children and lived out good, productive lives on Ceres. Someday, when he had the time, he fully intended to look up their descendants. Family was important to him.

"I think so," Karl replied slowly. "We have a war to fight and you saw how all these newbies did. We lost a lot of pilots today. They need us to train them on how to fight the Hocklyns."

"Perhaps you're right," said Lacy with a sigh. She leaned back and gazed over at Karl and then she spoke in a soft voice. "I just hope we both make it through this."

"We will," Karl assured her. "Someday we will see the end of this war and be able to return home. I promise you that."

Lacy nodded feeling better after Karl's reassuring words. He had never let her down on one of his promises.

-

Jeremy and Colonel Malen were in his office reviewing the battle. The Avenger had taken some damage, but nothing severe. Even the Nemesis had come through relatively unscathed.

"Repairs should be completed in a few more hours," Malen reported as she looked at the computer pad she was holding in her right hand. "Engineering wants to fine tune the sublight drive since some of the maneuvers Ariel put the ship through were right at the maximum tolerance levels."

"I was watching the drive," interjected Ariel, defensively. "It's fine, but I understand the chief engineer wanting to double check."

"Just a precaution," responded Jeremy, calmly. "Ariel, you did fine in the battle, and your tactics against the Hocklyns were outstanding. Just understand we can't do that very often. We have a fleet to command and the Avenger can't go rushing off and leave them behind."

"I realize that, Admiral," Ariel replied. She had already sent off a message to Clarissa telling her what had happened. Clarissa would be thrilled at hearing what Ariel had done.

"What were our losses in the battle?" asked Jeremy, looking over at Colonel Malen.

"We lost the destroyers Fredrick, Kincaid, and Darwin," she replied as she studied the information on her computer screen. "We also lost the light cruiser Lightning."

Jeremy knew his fleet had gotten off lucky. Admiral Adler had launched his Anlon bomber strike at the most opportune moment. He was also relieved that Admiral Streth had said nothing to him about using the Devastator Three missiles. "What about damage, how did we come out on that?"

"The Monarch cruiser Vengeance will need some yard time," Malen answered, her eyes looking grim. "She took a heavy nuke to her port side. Commander Smith is reporting over two hundred casualties, but he says the Vengeance's FTL drive is still fully operational. The light cruisers Kallen and Malven will also need some extensive yard time. They were pretty well pummeled there toward the end by the war cruisers. The rest of the ships are reporting minor to moderate damage."

"Admiral Streth has ordered us to report to New Tellus for repairs," added Jeremy, recalling his short conversation with the Fleet Admiral. "We're going to get some leave time at the New Tellus resorts while our ships are in the shipyards. Then it will be time to launch Operation First Strike."

Malen was quiet for a moment as she weighed Admiral Strong's words. "I hope the admiral knows what he's doing, that's a significant part of the Fleet we're committing to this."

"He's Admiral Streth, of course he knows," Jeremy responded in a firm and confident voice. "If anyone can hurt the Hocklyns, it's him. Look at this battle, not a single Hocklyn ship escaped."

Malen nodded; of course Admiral Strong was right. She just wondered what was ahead for the Avenger. Once the operation was launched, they would be gone from the Federation for quite some time. She just hoped it was still there when they returned.

Katie was in her quarters with Angela. Katie's quarters were quite large as part of it was dedicated to computer research. An intervening bulkhead had been removed to allow her the extra space she needed for all of her equipment.

"What have you done now, Katie?" asked Angela, curiously. Since discovering that Katie had also gone into cryosleep, Angela and Katie had continued to grow their friendship.

"Ariel, are you watching?" asked Katie, looking over at one of the monitors in the room.

"Yes, Katie," Ariel answered. These last few months being with Katie again had been fabulous for the AI. She had long since forgiven Katie for tricking her into getting on board the New Horizon.

"I have something new for you, Ariel," replied Katie, feeling excited about what she was about to do. She wanted Angela to be here to see it also.

Katie stood up and, walking around her quarters and research area, turned on several pieces of equipment.

"What are you up to, Katie?" asked Angela, sitting down in a chair in front of some computer equipment on a large table.

Katie smiled mysteriously and, walking back over to a large computer console, pressed several icons on the screen. Instantly, a green haze seemed to appear throughout the room. After a moment, the haze faded as if it had never been there.

"What was that?" asked Angela, looking around suspiciously. With Katie, anything was possible.

"You know how the emitters work in the plotting table to generate a tactical image above it?" Katie asked as she turned around to face her friend.

"Yes," replied Angela, trying to figure out what Katie was up to. "They give us a three dimensional view of the space around us."

Smiling really big and with a twinkle in her green eyes, Katie turned and pressed another icon. Instantly, in the center of the room, a figure of a woman appeared. She was slightly taller than Angela was, with dark eyes, shoulder length black hair, and dressed in the full uniform of a fleet officer.

"Ariel!" Angela screamed excitedly as she realized what Katie was up to.

The figure turned to look at Angela with a look of confusion and then surprise as she gazed about.

"Katie, how are you doing this?" Ariel asked as she took several tentative steps in Katie's direction.

Katie turned toward Ariel with a big grin on her face. "I have installed holographic emitters throughout my quarters," she replied, reaching up and moving a wayward blonde curl from in front of her eyes. "I have written a new program that will allow you to see everything from the hologram's perspective, and I also set it up so you can turn it on and off at will."

Angela stood up and, walking over to Ariel, reached out and touched her shoulder. She jumped as her hand passed completely through it. "You look so real," Angela said, stepping back and gazing at the young woman in front of her.

"I really like this," Ariel said as she raised up her right hand and stared at it. "Thank you, Katie!"

"You're welcome, Ariel," responded Katie, feeling extremely pleased. "This is something I have always wanted to do, but the technology just wasn't there. In this new day and age, it is."

"Can we set these emitters up anywhere else?" asked Ariel, realizing how great this would be. She could interact with the crew much better this way.

"I'm going to talk to Jeremy, but I would like to install them in the Command Center and the officer's mess for now."

Ariel nodded as she walked slowly around Katie's quarters. She marveled at how real this all seemed. She knew now that she had been right so long ago when she had told Jason Strong that Katie was something special.

"Now let's all sit down and talk," suggested Katie, walking over and sitting down in a comfortable chair. "You need to get used to associating with people in this new way."

Ariel nodded and walked over to another chair. She hesitantly sat down and found it was no problem whatsoever. Then she looked down and noticed that her right hand had passed through the arm of the chair. She looked inquiringly at Katie.

"We may have to modify the program a little," Katie confessed as she watched Ariel. "It's bound to have a few bugs in it."

"I think it's wonderful," replied Ariel, looking over at Angela and Katie with a big smile. "This is the best gift ever, Katie. How can I thank you?"

"Just continue to watch over us," answered Katie, nodding at Angela. "You seem to be very good at that."

Ariel smiled. She would always watch over the Special Five. They were her connections to her past, and they would always be important to her.

Jeremy watched from the Command Center, a few hours later, as the Avenger entered a swirling blue-white vortex. He felt the momentary queasiness as the ship jumped into hyperspace, and then everything returned to normalcy.

Kelsey came to stand next to Jeremy and asked a simple question. "How soon do you think it will be before we launch First Strike?" The battle had made her nervous; all the friends she had left at this time were on the Avenger. Even the few new friends she had made on the ship would all be lost if something drastic happened.

Jeremy paused for a moment. This battle had brought a lot of questions to his mind. He thought about the personal messages his father and mother had left him. Perhaps it would be a good idea for all of them to do some research just to see what kind of family they still had living. It would give them a connection to home, something they might need when they left to fight the Hocklyns.

"Probably four to six weeks," Jeremy answered in a quiet voice, his eyes focused on the main viewscreen, which showed the swirling black and purple mass that was hyperspace.

He pressed a button on his command console and the image vanished, to be replaced by one of Ariel. Jeremy was surprised because Ariel looked as if she were preoccupied, something he had never noticed before. Glancing over at Katie's computer console, he noticed an ensign was operating it. Whatever Katie was up to, he was sure she was responsible for Ariel's lack of attention to what was happening in the Command Center. He had a sneaking suspicion he would eventually find out, he just hoped it was nothing mind shattering. Then again, this was Katie and mind shattering seemed to be the norm for her.

Then in a quieter voice, that no one could overhear, Kelsey added. "When we get to New Tellus and get everything sorted out, we're going to spend some time at one of the seaside resorts. I need a good tan and the beach will be perfect. It will also be the last alone time you and I will have for quite sometime."

"Sounds fine to me," Jeremy responded with a nod of his head.

It was hard to be on the ship with Kelsey and keep his feelings for her hidden. Even though he suspected that Colonel Malen knew what was going on. The colonel missed very little of what went on aboard the Avenger.

The next day, Admiral Streth was aboard New Tellus Station having a meeting with Fleet Admiral Johnson and Admiral Teleck. They were discussing the battle above Caden's World. Admiral Teleck had arrived in the battle cruiser Ceres, which was his flagship, so he could attend.

"I understand why you held your ship units out as long as you did," Admiral Teleck spoke. He was totally in agreement with the need to send the Hocklyns a message, to enter human space meant death!

"I know how you feel about the Hocklyns," Admiral Johnson spoke with a deep sigh. "But we lost a lot of ships, ships we might need later."

Hedon turned to face Admiral Johnson with a deadly serious look upon his face. "Admiral, I understand your concern. I hated sacrificing those ships as well, but you have to understand the enemy we face. They understand one thing and one thing only and that is brute force. From our latest count, we have eliminated four of their fleets that were guarding the new fleet bases they are building. I don't expect those bases to be reinforced until they realize the fleets are not returning. Even then, it will take them several months to receive new ships. By not allowing a single Hocklyn ship to escape, we have ensured that we can strike without warning and without having to worry about heavy Hocklyn fleet units arriving shortly afterward. We will have months to prepare for the eventual counterattack and that will occur at least six to eight hundred light years from the Federation. That will buy you the time you need to finish your war preparations here."

"Admiral Streth's right," added Admiral Teleck, leaning back and folding his arms across his chest. "I know it's hard to talk about acceptable losses, but this battle was necessary. The Hocklyns don't know about us or what is coming at them. That is absolutely necessary if we want Operation First Strike to succeed."

Admiral Johnson closed her eyes briefly and then opened them. She knew the two admirals were right; it was just difficult to accept. "What were our final ship losses from the battle?"

Rear Admiral Bennett looked at his computer screen setting on the conference table in front of him and called up the information.

"Our total ship losses were four battle cruisers, two battle carriers, five Monarch heavy cruisers, eleven light cruisers, and twenty destroyers."

"Hocklyn losses?" asked Admiral Johnson, grimacing at the loss of life on the destroyed ships.

"Ninety-six ships," Bennett responded. "Eight dreadnoughts, twenty-four war cruisers, and sixty-four escort cruisers."

Admiral Johnson nodded. She knew it was a decisive victory any way you looked at it.

She looked over at Major Ackerman, seeking additional information. "What does Intelligence have to say about all of this?"

Major Ackerman looked around the group. "We believe all four of the fleets that the Hocklyns used came from their primary base located 680 light years from here. We recommend launching Operation First Strike as soon as possible to take advantage of their ship losses."

Admiral Johnson looked over at Rear Admiral Stillson. "What have your scouts found, anything new?"

"We have been keeping about two hundred stealth scouts out at all times surveying Hocklyn controlled space," Stillson replied. Standing up, he walked over to a computer console and, activating it, a detailed tactical hologram appeared.

A large area of space six hundred light years from the Federation and extending back for about four hundred light years and a thousand light years across began flashing in a light yellow. Within that were a number of red and gold icons.

"The red icons represent Hocklyn bases," Stillson began. "There are twenty known Hocklyn bases in this area. Six are toward the front of their expansion and pose the most danger. One of these bases, this one here," he pressed a button and one of the red icons began flashing. "Is being heavily fortified. It was from this forward base that the recent

Hocklyn attack was launched. Whoever is in charge of this base is no fool. He has built a substantial shipyard above a Tellus type planet and is placing defensive satellites in orbit."

"Is he expecting an attack?" Admiral Teleck asked with a worried frown. "I have never heard of Hocklyns using defensive satellites before."

"We don't know," Major Ackerman broke in. "We believe this base commander is deeply concerned about what may be out past their controlled space. He's taking no chances."

Admiral Stillson nodded, gesturing at the hologram. "If we can take out these bases there are thirty-four slave worlds that we can free in this space." Pressing another button, all the gold icons began flashing.

Admiral Streth nodded as he gazed thoughtfully at the display. "Then that's what we will do. We take that entire area of space from the Hocklyns and free those worlds!"

Hedon stood up and walked over to the holographic display, gazing at it thoughtfully. "I want to capture those six forward fleet bases," he said after a moment.

"Capture them!" Major Ackerman blurted out, surprised. "Why?"

"For our own use," explained Hedon, turning back around to stare at the group of officers. "We fortify them and use those bases to control this area of space. We then let the Hocklyns come to us. We can harass them all the way across the conquered space until they reach the bases where we will have heavy defenses set up. We will try to bleed them as much as possible before leading them to New Tellus and their destruction."

"Good strategy," spoke Teleck approvingly, looking over at the holo image. "But you will need a lot of hyper detection buoys so you can spot the incoming. Even then, you might not be able to locate them. They managed to sneak up on Caden's World without us detecting them."

"I'm well aware of that," Hedon replied. It had taken them awhile to figure out how the Hocklyns had managed that. "Colonel Grissim believes the Hocklyns were using small nebulas and possibly dust clouds from which to jump their fleet."

"That's a dangerous maneuver," commented Admiral Teleck, arching his eyebrows. "One miscalculation could have destroyed their ships."

"Perhaps," Hedon said. "But keep in mind the Hocklyns have been navigating hyperspace like this for thousands of years."

"What are you going to need to do all of this with besides the Ready Reserve?" asked Admiral Johnson, suspecting she was about to get a new list from the Fleet Admiral.

She was already beginning to feel uneasy about everything she had committed to this operation, and now it sounded as if Admiral Streth wanted even more. She knew she had no choice she never had. This operation had to succeed! The Federation needed the extra time this operation would provide.

"Buoys, marines, defensive satellites, and missile platforms." replied Hedon, looking at Fleet Admiral Johnson. "We're going to need a lot of marines to take the bases and free those planets."

Admiral Johnson leaned back, and her eyes narrowed as she thought of her choices. "Would General Abercrombie do as commander for the marines?" she asked, looking at Hedon.

"I think General Abercrombie will do fine," Hedon responded. From talking to the general on Caden's World, Hedon had been impressed by the man's concerns for his people as well as his professionalism. He was just the type of officer Hedon enjoyed working with.

Admiral Johnson turned to look at Admiral Freeman. "How soon before the Ready Reserve is updated and ready to deploy?"

Freeman checked a computer screen, calling up several different sets of data. "We are ahead of schedule," he announced. "We will have to repair the damage to the ships in the battle at Caden's World but the fleet should be ready to deploy in three more weeks."

"How soon after that can we launch Operation First Strike?" Johnson asked Admiral Streth. This was a question that President Kincaid wanted an answer to as well. The entire Federation was on pins and needles after the battle with the Hocklyns above Caden's World.

"Three weeks after," replied Hedon, confidently. "I would like to have more time, but the sooner we strike, the better,"

"Very well then," said Admiral Johnson, standing up. "I will inform President Kincaid and the Federation Council that we launch the operation in six weeks. Are there any objections?"

Everyone was silent.

-

Amanda and Richard were on their way down to New Tellus, having reserved a room at one of the plush mountain resorts. Admiral Streth had informed her that she could give her crew a three-week leave before they had to report back for duty, and that included her. He had stressed the point that he expected her to take some time off.

She gazed out the viewport at the rapidly approaching planet below. She could see vast deep blue oceans and white puffy clouds covering some of the landmasses. Large areas of untouched forests covered the continents. This must be what home looks like now, she thought, recalling how Aquaria looked from an approaching shuttle.

"Thinking about home?" asked Richard, seeing the sad and faraway look on his wife's face.

"Yes," answered Amanda, turning back around to look at Richard. "It's hard not to at times. This new Federation is great, but it will never be home."

"I know," Richard replied in agreement. He knew that Amanda still missed her parents and those carefree wonderful times diving off Krall Island. "Perhaps when this is all over we can return there."

"You think so?" Amanda asked, her eyes widening at the thought.

"I think if Admiral Streth has his way that is his intention," Richard replied quietly so no one could overhear. There were a number of other people on the large passenger shuttle. "I think if there is any way he can pull it off, someday we're going back to our worlds."

Amanda was silent. She just hoped she lived long enough to see it happen.

-

Jeremy, Kelsey, Kevin, and Angela were at a fabulous seaside resort soaking up the sun. They had been there for nearly two weeks.

"I wish Katie could have stayed longer," commented Angela, missing the green-eyed blonde.

"Why did she leave?" asked Kelsey, curiously. She didn't think Katie still had a crush on Jeremy and had left because of that. Katie was well aware of the relationship that she and Jeremy had.

"She wanted to return to work with Ariel on the Avenger," responded Jeremy, leaning back in his lounge chair and stretching.

He reached over and picked up a fruit drink setting on the small white table next to him. Taking a long sip, he smiled. He had discovered this drink the first night they were here and fallen in love with it.

"You're going to turn into one of those drinks," Kelsey admonished with a teasing grin.

"So what are Katie and Ariel doing on the Avenger?" Kevin asked curious to know.

"They're working on Ariel's holo program," answered Jeremy, sitting up. He looked at the calm ocean water; there was barely a wave slapping the beach. It looked extremely inviting. "She wants to finish up with Ariel and then go over to the StarStrike and work with Clarissa."

"Let me guess," groaned Angela, rolling her eyes. "Clarissa heard about what Katie is doing for Ariel, and now she wants the same."

"That's right," answered Jeremy, standing up and setting his fruit drink back down on the small table. "Anyone for a swim?"

"Sure," the others responded.

"We'd better enjoy the water while we can," suggested Angela, gazing at the others. "It might be a long time before we get back."

Kevin looked at Angela and tried his best not to stare. She was wearing a dark blue two-piece that barely covered the essentials. When Angela walked down the beach, all the guys turned to watch her. Kevin sometimes thought that Angela liked all the attention. She didn't use to be that way, but times change.

Kelsey saw Kevin staring at Angela and smiled to herself. Kevin and Angela had never developed the relationship that Kelsey had always hoped for. She knew they did occasionally spend the night together, but both had agreed that there were just too many differences between the two to make a long-term relationship work.

The four made it into the water and were soon enjoying the feel of the warm ocean. Kevin had a snorkel mask and was continuously going underwater, watching the myriad of different colored fish. There were also sea turtles but the turtles on New Tellus, while similar to those of Earth, had shells that were more brightly colored.

As Kevin continued to take long breaths and dive beneath the water, he realized that he really missed Katie. The two of them had been having a great time while she was here. She was always wanting to do things, and she had chosen Kevin as her victim for exploration. They had gone sailing, diving, snorkeling, and about everything else you could think of that was available at the resort. Kevin wondered if he was starting to have feelings for her other than friendship. He hadn't slept with Katie or anything, not even a kiss, but she was definitely fun to be around and he enjoyed her company.

Amanda and Richard had just come in from the slopes; they had been skiing for several hours down some of the harder tracks. Richard was an expert and had been helping Amanda. At least today she hadn't tumbled down the slope. Yesterday she had been afraid from all the tumbling; she was going to end up being one giant snowball rolling down the steep slopes taking everybody out.

Richard gazed over at his wife and couldn't help noticing her deep blue eyes; they were the first thing he had noticed when they first met. He could get lost in their caring depths. "Ready for some hot tea?" he asked as they took off their heavy ski jackets and hung them up.

"Hot chocolate," Amanda responded with a happy grin. The hot chocolate here at the resort was to die for. She didn't know what blend they used, but she fully intended to bribe someone in the restaurant for the recipe before they left.

The two went inside the smaller of the two restaurants in the lodge. The other restaurant was much larger and there was less privacy. They chose a side booth with dim lighting and sat down.

"Another week and then back to the WarStorm," said Amanda, taking a deep breath. The restaurant was full of enticing smells from cooking food. Amanda heard her stomach growl quietly.

A waiter brought over a large steaming cup of hot chocolate and hot tea. He had served them several times previously and knew exactly what the couple wanted to drink.

"I wish I were going with you," spoke Richard, knowing they would be apart for months.

"We will be rotating some of the crews occasionally," replied Amanda, taking a small sip of the hot chocolate. God! This tasted great! "Perhaps I can come back a couple of times for a short leave."

"I hope so. How long will it take to get to Hocklyn space?" asked Richard, taking a long sip of his tea.

"A little over ten days," answered Amanda, recalling the calculations. "We will be making a total of thirty-three jumps." Admiral Streth plans on stopping several times to retune the drives or we could make it in eight."

"Three jumps a day," spoke Richard, thoughtfully. "That doesn't sound too bad."

"It won't be," Amanda assured him. "I don't know about you, but I can't sleep through a jump."

"Very few people that I know of can," Richard nodded in understanding.

"So how about these giant asteroid fortresses up in orbit?" Amanda asked with a teasing smile. "Any pretty executive officers floating around up there?"

"None that compare to you," replied Richard, grinning. "You really need to come aboard one of those big babies. When the Federation survivors decided they wanted something to hold back the Hocklyns, they knew what they were doing. The Command Fortress is twenty-two kilometers in diameter with the Command Center located at its heart. The asteroid is honeycombed with passages and power plants."

"Impressive," Amanda responded glad that at least Richard was somewhere the Hocklyns would have a difficult, if not impossible time destroying.

"Just the Command Fortress itself could have destroyed the entire Hocklyn fleet that attacked Caden's World."

"That's why they built it," Amanda reminded her husband in a darker tone of voice. "The entire New Tellus system is one giant mousetrap for the Hocklyns. When they finally drive us away from their space, the plan is to retreat to New Tellus and lure them here."

"If they come here, the trap will spring shut on them," said Richard, firmly. "They won't be leaving. Just make sure you return safely."

Amanda reached over and took Richard's hand. "I will. Why don't we get something light to eat and then go up to the room?" she suggested with a hint of a sexy glint in her eyes.

Richard knew what that look meant. "Waiter," he said, motioning. The sooner they ate the sooner he could be alone with his wife.

-

Admiral Streth was with Admiral Adler in the Command Center of the StarStrike. The 1,600-meter Fleet flagship was berthed inside New Tellus Station. It had gone out recently and conducted a two-week shakedown cruise, jumping to every inhabited system in the Federation. Admiral Streth had thought it would do the morale of the people some good to see the massive ship. In each system, he stayed just long enough to allow a few media people to come aboard and look around the non-sensitive areas. They were handed out packets of information and videos about the giant Federation flagship.

"This ship is impressive," Admiral Adler commented as he gazed around the massive Command Center. All other Command Centers had only one plotting table and this ship had four! Each was capable of producing any tactical display needed by the officers who operated them.

"I have a reason for wanting you to come over here, Jacob," explained Hedon, looking over at his long time friend. Jacob Adler had been with him from the very beginning. "I want to change the makeup of Third Fleet."

"I suspected that after Caden's World," replied Jacob, nodding. "If the Hocklyns could have pushed through to my ships we could have suffered a lot of damage to the carriers."

"My thoughts exactly," replied Hedon, nodding his head. "However, we did learn a lot from our engagement. Once we battered down the Hocklyn's defensive fire by damaging their ships, your bomber strike was devastating."

"So you think we should wait awhile before committing our bombers?"

"Yes, I do," admitted Hedon. "We may suffer more Fleet losses in the beginning, but once we have reduced the defensive fire to the point where a massed bomber attack can get in, then the battle is basically over. We just need to make sure the carriers are adequately protected until that moment."

"So what are we going to change?" asked Jacob, feeling curious.

Hedon grinned as he called up the information on his main computer screen at his large command console.

"The new Third Fleet will consist of the following. Ten battle carriers, two battle cruisers, two Monarch heavy cruisers, twelve light cruisers, and twelve destroyers."

Jacob nodded. "That greatly increases the firepower for the fleet, particularly by adding the battle cruisers and the extra light cruisers."

"You will be operating in conjunction with Second Fleet," Hedon continued. "If we find a tough nut to crack, I will be calling upon Admiral Sheen and you to crack it."

"We will do it, Sir," Jacob promised. "You tell us what to hit, and we will take it out."

"I will be sending a list of your new ships over to the Wasp shortly," Hedon added. "Just be careful when all of this starts, Jacob."

"I'm not going anywhere," Jacob promised with a friendly nod. "I want to see home someday too."

Katie was sitting at the StarStrike's main computer panel having an argument with Clarissa and Ariel. Clarissa wanted the ability to alter her appearance whenever she wanted, particularly her hair and uniform.

"What's wrong with a regular fleet uniform?" Ariel asked over the com system, which connected them to the Avenger.

"I just want to look different from time to time," repeated Clarissa, stubbornly. "Human women change their hairstyles, wear makeup, and different clothes all the time."

"But not on warships," Ariel reminded her.

"Please, Katie," Clarissa pleaded. "Do it for me."

Katie hesitated for a moment, she should really ask Admiral Streth before she gave this ability to Clarissa, but he seemed busy at the moment.

"All right," Katie finally agreed. "Just don't take advantage of it."

"Great!" spoke Clarissa, feeling pleased.

Ariel was silent for a moment, then chimed in. "If Clarissa has that ability, I want it too!"

Katie sighed deeply, as intelligent as these two AIs were, sometimes they still reminded her of children. "Very well," Katie responded. "You will both get the upgrade, but if I hear of either one of you misusing it I will remove it from the program."

"We won't," they both promised.

Katie nodded her head, knowing that both AIs were watching her. She was sure that Clarissa was supplying Ariel with a video feed of everything she was doing. It would take her another two days to finish installing all of the holo emitters and then, if she had time, it would be back to the resort for a few final days of leave. She wanted to go parasailing, but she wanted Kevin to go first. She smiled thinking about him; she had really enjoyed herself at the resort. Kevin was a lot of fun to be around, particularly when they were away from the ship.

Chapter Twelve

Fleet Commodore Resmunt's large eyes gazed impassively out the thick, reinforced window of his office down at the now finished spaceport. Around the edge of the spaceport massive weapon platforms were visible and more were being constructed. Energy beam installations, interceptor missiles, and even railguns for close in defense. His underlings had looked at him as if he were mad when he ordered the slaves to begin building the housings and platforms for the weapons.

"You still think something is wrong?" asked his aide, coming over to stand at his side and looking out to where a crew of slaves were constructing the solid base for a missile launching system.

"Yes, Jentil, I do," Resmunt responded in his cold rasping voice, glancing over at his long time aide. "It has been four weeks since War Leader Bisth left to attack the human mining world, and we should have heard back from him by now. I don't like this, something isn't right. These humans were extremely dangerous the first time we encountered them, they may have become dangerous again!"

"He had four full fleets," Jentil reminded the commodore. "The humans have to have been defeated. War Leader Bisth probably discovered where their home world is and has gone on to conquer it. When he returns, we will have added several new worlds to the empire and the High Council will be quite pleased. There will be much honor for everyone."

"The High Council," Resmunt spoke in a harsh tone. "I asked for six more fleets to reinforce this sector of space and they are only sending two. High Leader Ankler feels that I am exaggerating the danger from these new humans. He believes they must be weak and not a serious threat. There is also no explanation as to why the word of their escape from their original worlds was never reported. I don't like this at all."

"Strange," Jentil responded, his large eyes turning even darker. "Wasn't it High Leader Ankler that demanded we attack the humans as soon as possible?"

"Yes," Resmunt answered his eyes growing even wider as he thought about his orders. "He demanded we attack the humans immediately."

Resmunt stepped away from the window and gazed over at the large map of the galaxy, which showed the area of space he was responsible for. He knew he had been given this command because he had a reputation for unorthodox thinking. That type of thinking was heavily frowned upon in the empire, and most warriors that exhibited these tendencies were quickly demoted and assigned to menial duties. However, Resmunt had demonstrated repeatedly that a fleet under his command could defeat any other Hocklyn fleet in the few war games the empire allowed. For that reason, he had been assigned to this distant post and empire expansion sector.

"We have a number of small bases in this area here," he said, pointing to seven small fleet outposts far behind the current lines of expansion. I want all of their ships, except for two escort cruisers each to be reassigned to this base."

Jentil was silent for a moment as he contemplated the order. He knew the commodores of those bases would not be pleased with losing their fleets. While not large, they were still respectable.

"The commodores of those bases will demand explanations as to why their fleets are being reassigned," spoke Jentil, softly.

"I am in command of this sector," Resmunt hissed in a threatening voice. "Remind them of that and tell them their fleets will be returned as soon as War Leader Bisth appears. Their fleets are doing nothing anyway but setting in orbit around their bases."

"As you command, Commodore," Jentil responded as he turned to leave and carry out his orders.

Resmunt stood looking with growing concern at the map and then returned to stare out the window. He just felt something was wrong. Up in orbit he had his flagship, the dreadnought Liberator, two war cruisers, and four escort cruisers. In normal times he wouldn't be concerned, but he had an uneasy feeling that this time things were different. The humans were a big unknown in the equation.

The reinforcements from the seven support bases would give him two more full fleets. With the other two fleets set to arrive in less than ten more days, that would give him a sizable force to defend the planet with. He still felt something about these new humans wasn't right and that they presented a grave danger to the empire. He also wondered what High Leader Ankler knew and was not telling him.

-

Back on the Hocklyn's home world of Calzen, High Leader Ankler threw his knife against the far wall of his office, imbedding it almost to the hilt. The blade had been blooded numerous times in his earlier years during honor duels. He was frustrated by the latest report from Fleet Commodore Resmunt. At least he could communicate with the Fleet Commodore. As the empire had grown, the AIs had furnished the Hocklyns with a better form of FTL communication. The newer FTL transmitters were only allowed on the larger fleet bases where expansion was still occurring; they were too large to place upon a ship. Ankler was certain the AIs had designed them that way on purpose.

He sat back down at his desk and gazed in frustration at the latest message from the commodore. There was still no news from War Leader Bisth, and another High Council meeting was scheduled for the next day to discuss the human situation. High Councilor Ruthan had called it with the support of several other councilors. He was still demanding that they inform the AIs immediately of the discovery of these new humans. Ankler wadded up the message and thought worriedly about what he could do to get the High Council to agree to delay notifying the AIs.

Ankler had been so certain these new humans would not be a major threat. He wondered now if he should have sent Resmunt the six fleets he had requested from the beginning. If only his ancestor, War Leader Sigeth, had done his duty and upheld the family honor! With resignation, Ankler knew he might not be able to prevent the council from agreeing with Ruthan this time around if it came to a vote. He needed to find a way to buy more time! The council must not learn that War Leader Sigeth was his direct ancestor.

Striding over to the window, he gazed upward into the night sky. The sunlight reflecting off of the numerous shipyards and habitats was enough to make it seem almost like daylight on a heavily clouded day. Ankler knew he would have to play a secret he had been keeping now for several days if he were to avoid discovery.

He had met with a representative of the AIs just a few days back. They had agreed to allow the Hocklyns to settle four more nearby star systems. The AI representative had also warned Ankler that there would be no more concessions after that. There were very few things in the galaxy that had ever frightened Ankler, but meeting an AI was one of them. He shuddered at just recalling that meeting. It was hard to describe an AI since he had only actually seen one on four different occasions over the years. Each time the AI had looked drastically different from the one before.

Walking over to the wall, he pulled his knife free and placed it in the scabbard at his waist next to his body armor. He would tell his fellow council members of the AI offer. He would also mention that if the AIs discovered that the High Council had withheld information about the new humans the addition of four new star systems to colonize could be put in jeopardy. That should buy him at least a few more weeks. Surely, by then Bisth would be back and would be reporting that the new human worlds were now part of the empire.

Admiral Streth was having his final meeting with Fleet Admiral Johnson on New Tellus Station. "All the ships are ready, and we will be departing for fleet maneuvers tomorrow," he reported.

Karla looked over at the admiral, wondering what to say. "Hedon, I know I have placed a lot of responsibility on you. All of our shipyards are now working 24 hours a day on new construction. Training of new recruits has reached an all time high, and we are strengthening our defensive grids above all of our worlds, including the mining colonies. My experts say we are six months away from peak war production and nine from finishing the deployment of all the defenses we need to protect our civilized worlds. Buy me nine months and we will be ready to turn the full might of the Federation and our allies on the Hocklyns."

"Speaking of our allies, what are they doing?" Hedon asked. He had not, as of yet, had the opportunity to meet any representatives of the three alien races that were allied with the human race in this coming war.

"They are preparing also," answered Karla, recalling her latest conversation about that with President Kincaid. "We sent them videos of the battle at Caden's World and some of the Hocklyn bodies for them to examine. All three have switched their economies to war production. The Hocklyns will not like this part of the galaxy."

"And the Albanians?" continued Hedon, wishing they knew more about what was going on with the highly advanced aliens. "What about them?"

"We don't know," confessed Karla, allowing frustration to show in her voice. "Since Admiral Tolsen's first battle in Gliese 667C they have closed their borders to our ships. They still have an embassy on Earth, but they are saying very little."

Hedon nodded, understanding the Fleet Admiral's frustration. "I spoke with General Abercrombie. We are taking 20,000 marines in twenty marine transports along with us."

"As well as half a dozen fully equipped hospital ships, twenty ammunition colliers, and forty supply ships," the Fleet Admiral added, her eyes narrowing. "That's a lot of Federation ships we're putting at risk."

"This is war, Admiral," answered Hedon, thinking of the logistics involved. "We will need those supplies. It will take a resupply convoy ten to twelve days to reach us."

"Don't let me down, Hedon," Karla continued somberly, her eyes focusing intently on the admiral. "The Federation is depending on you. Don't do anything heroic. Come back alive, the Federation needs its heroes."

"I don't know about being a hero," Hedon responded with a frown. He had grown to dislike that term being used when people spoke about him. "I am just an admiral doing my job. Speaking of heroes, how is Admiral Tolsen doing?"

"He's still in the intensive care hospital in Ceres," Karla responded, her eyes looking sad. "He was badly injured. Only three people in the Command Center of his flagship were found alive. The doctors say it will be months before he is fully recovered."

"He's a good man," responded Hedon, recalling how Tolsen had fought in the battle at Caden's World. "We can't afford to lose officers of his caliber."

"We won't," Karla replied fully in agreement. "Once he has recovered and gone through rehab, I'm giving him another fleet."

"That's good," Hedon responded pleased to hear that. "I hope to see him when I return from First Strike."

After the meeting was over, Karla leaned back in her chair and crossed her arms over her chest. She wondered if Admiral Streth truly understood just what he meant to the Federation. Every Federation child was taught in school what Hedon had done to save the survivors from the original Human Federation of Worlds and that the great Fleet Admiral Hedon Streth would be awoken someday to destroy the Hocklyns. That time was here! Children believed that the great Fleet Admiral would save them, and so did Karla. Shifting her thinking, she had one more important meeting scheduled for today. This was a meeting she was going to enjoy.

-

Jeremy, Kelsey, Kevin, Angela, and Katie had been summoned to Fleet Admiral Johnson's office. They were all nervous, wondering if something had happened or if their group of five was going to be split up.

"What did you do now?" asked Kevin, glancing accusingly over at Katie. "Did you modify the entire defense mainframe for the system without telling anyone?"

Katie glared at Kevin and then realized he was only teasing. "No, at least not yet."

"I hope they're not going to split us up," Angela spoke with concern. "I don't know what I would do if the rest of you weren't on the same ship I am."

"I guess we will find out shortly," Jeremy said as they reached the Fleet Admiral's office.

One of the two marine guards stepped over and opened the heavy metal hatch, allowing them entrance. They stepped inside and were surprised to see Admiral Teleck and a large number of other strangers in the room. Some were dressed in standard fleet uniforms and others in civilian clothes.

"Ah, here they are now," Admiral Johnson spoke with an expectant look upon her face, which quickly grew into a friendly smile.

"Rear Admiral Strong, reporting as ordered," Jeremy spoke as the group of five came to attention.

"At ease, Admiral," the Fleet Admiral responded. "For this meeting we will be using first names only."

"First names?" Kevin blurted out in shock. How could he call the Fleet Admiral by her first name? It seemed like a very strange request.

"I'm sure all of you are curious as to why you have been called to this get together," Admiral Teleck spoke with a mystifying smile. "The reason is very simple; all five of you recently awoke from a cryosleep of over two centuries. Everyone you knew has long since passed away, even though from my understanding you were all left video and voice recordings from your families."

"Yes, Sir," Jeremy said, feeling confused. "We have all listened to those recordings, and they have helped tremendously."

"Then I have another surprise for all of you today," added Admiral Johnson, breaking out into a larger smile. "All of you still have relatives living in this day and age and that's who all of these people are. I will start first." Admiral Johnson walked over and stood in front of Katie. "Katie, I am your niece. I am a direct descendent of your brother Mathew. Mathew was my great great grandfather."

Katie stood there speechless, not sure what to do or say. She suddenly realized she was not alone; she had others besides her friends.

Admiral Johnson stepped forward and placed her arms around Katie. "I'm so proud of you, and there are others here to that are related to us as well."

Over the next hour, more introductions were made. Kelsey discovered she was related to Admiral Teleck, who was a distant cousin, and the others found out they had numerous relatives scattered throughout human occupied space. All five were deeply touched, and the girls had to continuously wipe tears from their eyes as they were introduced to more people. Even Jeremy and Kevin felt themselves tearing up at times as they realized they still had close family.

Jeremy found himself talking to a Colonel Don Strong who was a direct descendent of Jeremy's younger brother. Jeremy remembered how happy his parents had been when his brother had been born six months after the New Horizon incident.

"It's hard to believe I am actually standing here talking to you," Don said with an excited smile on his face. "All my life I have heard so much about you and our family in those early years."

"Do you have any sisters or brothers?" asked Jeremy, curiously.

"Yes," replied Don, nodding. "I have another younger brother and an older sister, but they couldn't make it today. David is a captain in the marines and is out on training maneuvers. Annette is nine months pregnant and due at any time. Her doctor didn't want her traveling. She was really disappointed she couldn't come and meet you."

After awhile, Karla announced that they would be eating in one of the station's cafeterias that had been set up for this special occasion. They all made it there to find that each table was set up so the five could sit with their newfound relatives.

Jeremy found it interesting to note that each of the five had at least six people sitting at their table with them. He also knew that it had to have been a monumental task to find and bring all of these people here at the same time. Someone had expended a lot of effort as well as money.

The meal was excellent; it was perhaps the best meal that Jeremy had eaten since he had awoke from cryosleep. As the meal progressed and they continued to talk, Jeremy became more relaxed and began to really enjoy himself. Don was sitting next to Jeremy and another young woman, who was a cousin, both were informing Jeremy about their family history and what had happened after he went into cryosleep. Jeremy listened intently as a lot of what they were describing was truly interesting. They described the continued growth of the Fleet Academy, the colonization of the new worlds, and finally the earthshaking revelation when the existence of the Federation survivors on Ceres was revealed.

Jeremy could only shake his head as he realized what they had all missed. But his parents and the Johnsons had been involved in all of it. They were considered to be the true pioneers and heroes of the modern space age.

Kelsey was sitting next to Admiral Teleck and several other cousins. She was fascinated to hear what had happened on Ceres after she had gone into cryosleep. Looking around the table, Kelsey was amazed that all of these people were her relatives. She had found her family or, to be more precise, they had found her.

Kevin and Angela were going through the same thing. Talking to people and meeting people who knew a lot about them and could fill in the holes in their family history since going into cryosleep. It was almost like returning home again.

At last the meal was over and Fleet Admiral Johnson stood up. The room grew quiet as everyone's attention focused on her. "I want to propose a toast," she said as several waiters suddenly appeared setting glasses of sparkling red wine down in front of each person. "To the survivors of the New Horizon and the current crew of the heavy strike cruiser Avenger. May their future history be as glorious as their past."

Later, the five were returning to the Avenger still in awe over what had just happened.

"All those people," spoke Katie, excitedly. "I can't believe I am related to Fleet Admiral Johnson."

"I think it was just what we needed," Kelsey added with a smile. "It makes us all feel we still have a home. Some of the people I met were really nice and fun to talk to."

"Same here," Kevin added. "I have a cousin whose sister is married to a Federation senator!"

"I think it was wonderful that Fleet Admiral Johnson and Admiral Teleck did this for us," Angela said with a big grin. "I have several cousins I would like to get to know better. Next time we have some leave, I'm going to spend some time with them."

Jeremy nodded his head in agreement. Don was coming over to the Avenger later, and Jeremy was going to show him around. It had truly been a remarkable day.

Several days later, Jeremy watched the main viewscreen carefully as the Avenger was undocked from New Tellus Station.

"We're on our way," Ariel said from where she was standing next to him.

Looking over at the AI, Jeremy noted that she was dressed in a standard dark blue fleet uniform without insignia. Her eyes were not quite as dark as they once were, and her hair was slightly shorter. It came to a stop just above her shoulders with just the barest hint of a curl.

"We're going to the outer system to join up with the rest of our fleet," Jeremy informed Ariel.

The AI had been a great help to Jeremy keeping everything organized. He was still trying to get used to the idea that she was now a hologram and could walk around in the Command Center. If one didn't know better, they would think she was a regular crewmember until she walked through someone. Katie had to remind her several times not to do that as it made people nervous.

"The new ships assigned to us will give us a very powerful fleet," Ariel responded. "In any battle with the Hocklyns we should be able to defeat them."

"I hope so," Jeremy responded. They were only a week or two away from launching First Strike, and Jeremy wanted a week to work with the new ships and their commanders. It was essential that they understood the tactics he would be using.

After clearing New Tellus's gravity well, the Avenger made a short micro-jump and exited the blue-white swirling spatial vortex close to a group of waiting ships.

"I have the fleet on sensors." Kevin reported as he transferred the information over to the holographic tactical image above the plotting table.

Jeremy gazed at his fleet and the new ships that he had been given. He strongly suspected that Admiral Teleck had been involved in getting Jeremy some of the ships, as they were brand new warships directly from Ceres and not part of the Ready Reserve. He now had two battle carriers, four heavy strike cruisers, four Monarch cruisers, eight light cruisers, and ten destroyers in his fleet.

Jeremy's fleet had been renamed Fourth Fleet and would be working directly with Fleet Admiral Streth and First Fleet. Jeremy now had twenty-eight warships under his command. He was particularly pleased with the extra battle carrier and the two strike cruisers. The two extra Monarchs would add considerably to the fleet's firepower, and Jeremy was already coming up with a plan for their use.

"What first, Jeremy?" asked Ariel, curiously. She very seldom called him admiral if no one else could hear. She would always consider the Special Five her family.

"I want to meet with all the commanders to discuss tactics, particularly using micro-jumps. The program Katie and you designed to allow precise entry into the spatial vortexes needs to be installed in all of the new ships."

"When would you like to meet with the commanders?"

"In two hours," responded Jeremy, looking at the main viewscreen, which was now focused on the new battle carrier Cygnus from the Ceres fleet. Jeremy knew it was the latest battle carrier out of the Ceres construction bays. He was anxious to tour the new ship to see what modifications it might have compared to the rest of the ships in the fleet.

Kelsey was also looking at the new battle carrier when she heard a familiar voice over her mini-com.

"Quite impressive, isn't she?" Kevin commented on the channel that Ariel provided so no one else could hear the five talking privately to one another.

"She's new out of Ceres," replied Kelsey, feeling pride knowing this ship was built by the Federation survivors as were all the ships that made up Fourth Fleet.

All of the heavy strike cruisers in the fleet were new construction as well as all of the new ships from Ceres. She suspected it was Admiral Teleck's way of ensuring all five of them stayed safe by giving them the best ships that Ceres had built recently. Someday, she would have to thank the admiral.

"I guess we will be leaving for Hocklyn space shortly," Angela added in a pensive voice. "I just hope we make it back."

"We will," Katie broke in, sounding unusually calm for her. "Jeremy and Ariel will keep us safe."

Ariel smiled to herself upon hearing Katie's words. She would do everything in her power to make sure the Special Five returned safely. That was why she was here.

-

Admiral Streth was having his final meeting with Rear Admiral Sheen before they departed for six days of war games. It would be Second Fleet against Third Fleet.

"This is the final makeup of Second Fleet," he commented as he slid a computer pad with the ships on it across his desk. "You're getting six battle cruisers, two battle carriers, twelve Monarch cruisers, four strike cruisers, thirty light cruisers, and twenty destroyers."

"I hate losing the extra battle carriers," commented Amanda, but she was pleased to see the increase in her light cruisers.

"You will be working in conjunction with Third Fleet most of the time," Hedon explained. "Your battle carriers will primarily carry the newer Talon fighters with two bomber squadrons, whereas Admiral Adler's carriers will primarily carry bombers with only two squadrons of the newer fighters."

That was one thing that had pleased Admiral Streth; the newest version of the Talon fighter had been given to his fleet. They were a little slimmer, faster, and more maneuverable than the older version. They were also very heavily armed with twin 30 mm cannons and hard points for two small interceptor missiles. He had spoken to Colonel Arcles earlier from the Wasp, and the colonel had been very impressed with the new version.

Amanda looked down at another computer pad she had brought with her and then looked back up at Hedon. "In these war games, they are primarily aimed at improving the bomber's efficiency in their attack runs?"

"Yes," answered Hedon, nodding his head and leaning forward, placing his right hand on the desk. "If we commit the bombers too early the survival rate for our pilots is very low. We learned from Caden's World that if we wait until the Hocklyn's fleet defenses have been hammered the survival rate goes way up, and the bomber attack can be devastating against the weakened Hocklyn energy shields and defenses."

Amanda understood the reasoning behind the war games and agreed with it. Successful bomber attacks could significantly reduce her ship losses.

"What about repairs to badly damaged ships?" she asked. She knew most ships could do a lot of repairs themselves, but severe damage was another matter. They were going to be far away from Federation space and a severely damaged ship could be a hindrance to other ships in the fleet.

"We have six repair ships that will be going along with us," answered Hedon, thinking about the massive ships. Each was nearly the size of a battle carrier and Admiral Johnson had thrown a fit when he demanded them. There were only ten of the large repair ships in the entire Federation. "Their main job will be to repair badly damaged ships so they can return safely to Federation space and enter a shipyard repair bay."

Amanda leaned back and gave Hedon a serious look. She took a deep breath before asking the next question. "What do you think our real chances are of winning this war?"

Hedon was silent for a long moment as he studied Amanda. They had been friends for a long time, and he very seldom kept secrets from her. Then with a heavy sigh, he answered. "I honestly don't know. The Hocklyns control a huge empire. They have thousands of ships to call upon and vast resources at their command. Then of course, there are the AIs. Our best defense right now is that we are far away from the Hocklyn home worlds as well as the center of the galaxy where the AIs reside. It will take time for them to martial a sufficient force against us to drive us back to the Federation. Then we have to hope our defenses and new fleet construction can hold them at bay."

"At least we have allies and a fighting chance," said Amanda, realizing that Hedon really didn't want to admit that this was a war they might not be able to win. There were also three other races that the AIs were using to conquer the rest of the galaxy. Even if by some miracle the Hocklyns could be defeated, they might very well have to face those as well.

"Did you get to say goodbye to Richard?" asked Hedon, hoping the two had managed to spend some quality time together over the last few days.

Amanda nodded her head. "We went down to New Tellus for a few days to relax. He still has a lot of work to do with organizing the asteroid fortresses and preparing them for a Hocklyn attack. Both of us just hope we get to see the end of this someday."

Hedon didn't reply because he knew the odds were deeply stacked against them.

"I can't believe you want to do this!" Fleet Admiral Johnson was saying loudly to Admiral Teleck. "The Federation Council will never approve it."

"The Federation Council doesn't play into this," Teleck replied in a calm and controlled voice. "The Ceres defense fleet is under direct control of myself and Governor Malleck. We turn over half of all the ships we construct every year to the Federation; in return we keep the rest for our own defense."

Admiral Johnson stood up and stepped around her desk to stand face to face with Teleck. "We could need those ships if the Hocklyns stop Operation First Strike. By doing this, you could be endangering the entire Federation!"

"The ships may never be needed," responded Teleck, not backing down. He gazed calmly at Admiral Johnson before continuing. "We still have a large fleet at Ceres, and more ships are under construction in our bays even as we speak."

"Admiral Streth's survival is that important to you?" Karla demanded, her eyes widening.

"Isn't he to you, also?" countered Teleck.

Karla stepped back, frowning. Teleck was right. It would be devastating to the Federation if Admiral Streth were to die in this campaign.

"How many ships are we talking about?" she finally asked, realizing that she wasn't going to change Teleck's mind.

Admiral Telleck paused before he spoke, knowing his words would shock the admiral. It had always been a highly guarded secret just how many ships were hidden inside Ceres's vast fleet bays.

"We are sending eight battle cruisers, six battle carriers, four strike cruisers, ten Monarch cruisers and twenty light cruisers," he stated, his eyes meeting the Fleet Admirals.

"Forty-eight ships," Karla breathed surprised at the number. She wondered just what else was hidden inside Ceres. She suspected but couldn't prove that this was only a small portion of the ships the Federation survivors inside of Ceres had at their disposal. After all, they had been building warships nonstop for several centuries.

"It is part of our agreement with the Federation that we be allowed to maintain our own defense fleet," Teleck reminded the Fleet Admiral. "Those ships can be committed as we see fit. At this time, these ships will act as an emergency support fleet if First Fleet becomes imperiled. The fleet will stay behind and hidden from the Hocklyns as well as Admiral Streth. He won't know they are there unless they're needed."

"How will he know?" Karla demanded, her eyes narrowing suspiciously.

"It's actually quite simple," Teleck replied with a knowing smile. "Clarissa will call for us. She will know if we're needed and she will also always know where we are."

"Clarissa?" Karla mumbled in realization. "She is the AI on the StarStrike."

"Yes," Teleck answered. "That's one of the reasons we put her there."

Then, in a more condescending voice, he added. "Karla, we must keep the admiral safe. He is our best chance for winning this war. Operation First Strike will succeed. More than likely he will never need our fleet and will never know it was there."

Karla nodded her head in defeat. She knew in her heart that Admiral Teleck was correct. She also knew that Operation First Strike had to succeed or the Federation's chances of survival would be very low.

Chapter Thirteen

High Leader Ankler had just dismissed the latest meeting of the Hocklyn High Council. Once again, High Counselor Ruthan had demanded to know when the AIs would be notified about the humans. The debate had become heated, and the council was obviously divided on the issue. The councilors were becoming highly worried about the absence of any word from War Leader Bisth and the four fleets he had left Fleet Commodore Resmunt's base with. Ankler had managed to put off notifying the AIs by the slimmest of margins in the final council vote.

It had been over a week since he had revealed that the AIs had agreed to allow them to settle the four new star systems. Already Hocklyn construction crews were descending on the four new inhabitable planets laying the groundwork for immediate colonization. That had kept the council pacified for the time being. Now several council members, led by Ruthan, were becoming even more worried about what would happen when the AIs found out about the humans.

"This is a dangerous game you're playing," High Councilor Nartel warned as he watched the others file out of the large ornate room where the council met. "A number of the councilors are coming to believe that you are hiding something from us. I warn you now, High Leader, the next vote will go against you unless we hear positive news from War Leader Bisth."

Ankler turned to gaze unblinking at Nartel. He was slightly larger in build than Ankler with a bulkier stature and thick sinewy arms. "I hide nothing," he spoke in a rasping voice. "Bisth is taking longer because he is subduing the human home world."

"Perhaps," Nartel replied in a steady voice, unafraid of the High Leader. "But it has been nearly six weeks since he left Resmunt's base. Some word should have been sent back by now. I am beginning to wonder if these humans might be a bigger threat than we originally believed. If by some chance the humans have defeated Bisth, the AIs will not be pleased with us. There could be some serious consequences, including taking the four new systems away from us. If that happens, you will not survive as High Leader of the council."

"Don't threaten me, Nartel!" snarled Ankler, letting his anger show. He reached down and tapped the blade at his waist. "I have fought honor duels with others for far less than what you have just said and won."

"It was no threat, High Leader," responded Nartel, taking a step back. He tapped his armor and touched his own blade. "I too have fought honor duels and won. A victory over me might not be as easy as you think. I was not challenging your honor. I was merely explaining what might happen if things don't change quickly."

Ankler was silent. He knew an honor duel between council members would be highly frowned upon and only further weaken his position.

"Very well," responded Ankler, moving his hand away from his blade. "If we have not heard from War Leader Bisth in another ten days, then I will agree to notify the AIs about these new humans."

Nartel nodded, pleased with this concession from the High Leader. It was not good for the council to argue any longer over this subject, they needed to begin expediting the work on the new colony worlds and moving some of their expanding population. The civilian population was becoming more disgruntled every day. If the colonization plan were to fall through, it would be necessary to bring the military in and reduce the Hocklyn overpopulation. Nartel did not even want to contemplate the difficulties involved if such a drastic move became necessary.

–

Fleet Commodore Resmunt was in orbit in his flagship, the powerful dreadnought Liberator. He was in the process of organizing a defense of this system. There still had been no word from War Leader Bisth, and Resmunt was starting to believe that Bisth had failed in his attempt to conquer the human mining world or had met his end in an effort to take their home world. It was very seldom the Hocklyns encountered a powerful enemy, but all the evidence was now pointing to that worrisome possibility.

"The two new fleets sent by the council have arrived in the system," First Leader Ganth reported as he gazed at the numerous green icons appearing on the long-range sensor screen.

"What are the make up of the fleets?" Resmunt demanded. The fleets came from a distant base, and he had no idea what he had been sent. He had requested additional information, but High Leader Ankler had not replied.

"Each fleet has two dreadnoughts, four war cruisers, and twelve escort cruisers," Second Leader Aanith reported from his position at a computer console.

"Honor is lacking in this," swore Resmunt, wondering if High Leader Ankler was out to destroy him. These were small fleets! "I was expecting more escort cruisers."

"We have our own two fleets we have pulled from the other bases," First Leader Ganth reminded Resmunt. "They have a large complement of escort cruisers."

"Weak in capital ships though," responded Resmunt, wishing he had more ships. The two fleets made up from the seven bases consisted of four war cruisers and fourteen escort cruisers each. With a heavy breath, he knew he needed more dreadnoughts. Unfortunately, there was only one way he could get them.

"Contact our other five forward bases," ordered Resmunt, coming to a quick decision. "I want each base to send us one of their dreadnoughts."

Ganth was silent for a long moment as he mulled over these new orders from the commodore. "The base commanders will not be pleased with that order. That will significantly reduce the firepower of their fleets."

"It still leaves them their command dreadnought," responded Resmunt, giving his second in command a hard look. "This is our primary base in this sector and must be protected at all costs."

Ganth nodded and moved toward the communications console to pass on the order.

Resmunt gazed about the massive War Room of his flagship. The ship had served him well and had brought honor to him and his crew, but his concern over these new humans was growing. He had asked himself what he would do if he were the humans and an alien race attacked his home world. The answer was simple, immediate and overwhelming retaliation.

Because no word had come back from Bisth, he had no idea what he might be facing. Perhaps nothing at all. The humans might have been weakened by Bisth's attack to the point where it might not be possible for them to retaliate. But in his gut, Resmunt knew that was wrong. All the years of sensor ghosts and missing escort ships that didn't return from long-range exploration missions warned otherwise. Now Bisth's fleets were failing to report in. Four powerful Hocklyn fleets had gone missing as well as four War Leaders. Resmunt knew something was not right. Either more humans than believed possible had escaped the destruction of the Human Federation of Worlds, or there was another human civilization in this sector of the galaxy.

Fleet Admiral Johnson was on Earth at the Federation Council Chambers meeting with President Kincaid.

"What do you think the odds are of Admiral Streth succeeding with Operation First Strike?" the president asked in a concerned voice with lines of worry showing around his eyes.

"I think the first part of the attack will be a success," Karla replied with confidence in her voice. "The Hocklyns will not be expecting an attack and should be taken by complete surprise. If he can eliminate the Hocklyn fleets at those six advance bases, then he should be able to push them back several hundred light years at least."

"When will he know when to stop his advance?" Kincaid asked, his eyes focusing on the Fleet Commander.

"When he begins running into heavy resistance from the Hocklyns," Karla answered. "It will take them a while to respond and we are not sure what type of FTL communications they have for the vast distances across their empire. Admiral Streth has over fifty stealth scouts on the various carriers in his fleets. He will use those to determine targets of opportunity once he reaches unknown sections of their empire."

President Kincaid was silent for a long moment. "I spoke with Governor Malleck yesterday," continued Kincaid, recalling his long conversation with the Governor of Ceres. "He told me about the fleet he has sent to support Admiral Streth if needed. It concerns me that we are committing so many ships to this operation, ones we might need later."

"I don't think we had a real choice," Karla confessed with a tired look crossing her face. "The Hocklyns found us sooner than we expected. We need the time Operation First Strike will give us. It also serves to bring home to the civilian population just what is at stake in this war."

"How strong are our defenses if the Hocklyns attack us here?" asked Kincaid, looking over at a large, detailed star map that showed the ten inhabited human systems and the thirty mining colonies. "Can we hold against them?"

"I believe New Tellus can," responded Karla, carefully. She had spent a lot of time studying the defenses of the various inhabited systems and what could be done to strengthen them. "Those asteroid fortresses are monstrosities in both firepower and defensive shielding, and I believe Earth and Ceres are the same. Our orbital battle stations should be able to stop the Hocklyns here in the Sol System. The other inhabited planets will have to depend on their defensive grids and our fleets until their defenses can be sufficiently upgraded."

"What about the AIs?" asked Kincaid in a quiet and worrisome voice. He could picture the new Human Federation falling under their onslaught; the first Human Federation had.

"We don't know," admitted Karla uneasily, her eyes shifting to the star map. "New Tellus is confident their asteroid fortresses can stop them, the same thing with our battle stations here above Earth. We don't have that capacity in the other systems, at least not yet."

"What about Admiral Streth and his fleets?" President Kinkaid continued, his eyes showing deep concern about what he was about to ask. "What if the AIs attack him?"

Karla didn't answer for a moment. The AIs were the big question and unknown in all of this. Admiral Streth had fourteen of the new heavy strike cruisers with him that had been designed specifically to take on an AI ship with their Devastator Three missiles and heavy energy shielding. "We won't know until he encounters them," she answered, her eyes meeting the president's. "He is laying a series of FTL communication booster buoys behind him. We should have reasonable communications with the admiral even when he reaches Hocklyn space."

"How reasonable?" Kincaid asked. This was a vast distance of over 600 light years. Most FTL communication in the Federation was less than thirty light years with New Tellus, the fartherest from Earth at twenty-seven light years. He knew at that vast a distance there would be some communication delay.

"Fifty-six hours at that distance."

President Kincaid nodded, knowing they could do no more. "If Admiral Streth succeeds in buying us the time we need to finish our defenses, it will be a miracle."

Fleet Commander Johnson stood up and smiled. "That's why we're sending Fleet Admiral Hedon Streth. He has performed miracles in the past, we're just asking for one more."

President Kincaid looked at the map depicting the new Human Federation of Worlds. He just prayed they were all still there a year from now.

Admiral Streth watched the main viewscreen as the StarStrike and the rest of First Fleet made the transition from hyperspace and exited the spatial vortexes. First Fleet comprised seventy-one powerful warships.

"Jump complete," Captain Jarvis Reynolds reported from the ship's main sensor console. Captain Reynolds was from Harmony in the Alpha Centauri star system

"All ships moving into standard defensive formation," Colonel Trist informed the admiral. He was standing at the main tactical holo display, watching intently as the ships moved into position. Trist had been third in command of the old StarStrike and had gone into cryosleep along with the admiral.

Hedon nodded and switched his gaze to the tactical display as the ships moved into position.

"No trace of enemy ships," Clarissa added as she checked the ship's powerful sensors.

She was standing just behind the admiral, her deep blue eyes gazing with pleasure around the large Command Center. Since Katie had given her the ability to appear as a hologram, she very seldom missed an opportunity to do so. It had made her ability to communicate and interact with the crew far better than ever before.

"The supply fleet?" Hedon asked as the main viewscreen switched to show one of the other ships in the fleet. It was the Conqueror class battle cruiser Matterhorn.

"It will be arriving in five more minutes," Clarissa reported in her contralto voice, which sounded like an attractive young woman. Clarissa was wearing her blonde hair cut short closer to Fleet regs, but it was still longer than most of the women on the ship. She liked her long hair and had decided to compromise and not cut it back completely.

Admiral Streth leaned back in his command chair and gazed speculatively around the large Command Center. There were two tactical holo displays to his right and two more on his left, which allowed him to see and direct any battle or needed fleet deployment. Two fleet officers manned each one.

In front of him, in a gentle arc, were the rest of the ship's major control stations. Communications, Helm, Navigation, Sensors, Damage Control, Tactical, and Life Support. Tactical was the largest, with six officers sitting in front of the massive control console. Other stations and control consoles were set up against the walls with numerous controls and viewscreens. On the front wall of the StarStrike was a massive center viewscreen with secondary viewscreens on both sides of it.

"Supply fleet emerging now," Clarissa informed Hedon as the main viewscreen switched to show numerous blue-white vortexes forming a short but safe distance from First Fleet.

Hedon watched as over the next two minutes. Another one hundred and fifty three ships blinked into existence as they exited the swirling spatial vortexes.

"Rear Admiral Kimmel is reporting everything normal," Colonel Trist said as he spoke to the admiral over his mini-com. "He is requesting that we stay in this system for an extra two hours as several of his supply ships are reporting a slight harmony discrepancy in their FTL drives."

Hedon nodded as this was not unexpected. "We can do that. We were going to stop in the next system to retune the FTL drives anyway. Captain Duncan, inform all fleet units that we will be staying in this system for eight hours."

There were six fleets taking part in Operation First Strike. They were currently traveling in three separate task groups so if the Hocklyns detected one group they wouldn't realize the full extent of the forces coming toward them. All six fleets were scheduled to make rendezvous in a double star system a short distance away from Hocklyn space.

"Four days and no sign of the Hocklyns," Colonel Trist commented as he walked over to stand next to the command console. It was located on a slightly raised dais so the commanding officer could have a good overall view of the Command Center.

"The risk of discovery will be higher as we near Hocklyn space," Clarissa reminded him as she stepped over closer to the colonel. "The Hocklyns are bound to have a few escorts cruisers and armed scouts on patrol as we get nearer to their empire."

"That's why we have the stealth scouts with us," remarked Hedon, looking over at Clarissa and Colonel Trist. "They will continue to reconnoiter ahead of our line of advance and report if any Hocklyns are waiting for us."

"Commander Layton is launching the scouts now," Captain Janice Duncan reported. She was from the planet Horizon in the Tau Ceti system.

Hedon glanced at the tactical display nearest him where the battle carrier Columbia was located. It depicted half a dozen green icons leaving the carrier, but Hedon knew the small scout ships were nearly undetectable. A few moments later, the large viewscreen showed six blue-white spatial vortexes form as the scouts made their jumps to check on the nearer star systems and then on to the Fleet's next planned destination.

"Carrier Challenger is launching a full CAP," Captain Reynolds added as twenty Talon fighters launched from her flight bay. Due to the size of the two fleets, a full squadron of fighters was being used for patrol.

"Final scans of the system are in," Clarissa reported as her eyes seemed to focus on a faraway point. "System is clear of any artificial emissions."

Hedon breathed a relaxed sigh of relief. There was always the chance they could stumble across a Hocklyn escort cruiser that the stealth scouts had missed, but so far their luck was holding. Turning back to the main viewscreen, which was now focused on one of the battle carriers, Hedon thought about what this mission meant. To him, it was the first step to someday returning home. He knew the odds were against him, but he fully intended to return to Maken someday. To rebuild that cabin by the lake was a burning desire if not for him, for the memory of his brother and his brother's wife Lendle. The cabin had become a symbol to him of what it would mean to defeat the Hocklyns.

Jeremy breathed a heavy sigh of relief as the Avenger re-entered normal space. Every day they came nearer to Hocklyn occupied territory. Prior to each emergence from hyperspace, he could feel the nervous expectation in the command crew. Each exit out of a spatial vortex could find a Hocklyn escort cruiser or even a fleet waiting for them.

"All ships reporting successful jumps," Kevin spoke from his sensor console as he watched the twenty-eight green icons on his sensor screen. "Fifth Fleet should be appearing shortly." Looking at the screen, he noted that even with Ariel's help the average ship was still separated by a minimum of ten kilometers.

"Four more days until we arrive at the rendezvous," Ariel commented from where she was standing next to Jeremy.

She looked over and smiled at the young admiral, knowing his father would be extremely proud of his son. Ariel's eyes glazed over in remembrance; she had lost so many friends over the years. The entire crew of the first Avenger, Katie and Jeremy's parents, and there were others. She also knew that if not for Katie, she wouldn't be here either.

"Fifth Fleet emerging," Colonel Malen reported as more friendly green icons began appearing on her tactical display above the plotting table. After a few minutes, sixty-two more Federation ships were in the system.

"We're getting closer," Angela spoke to Kelsey over her mini-com as she looked up at the main viewscreen, which at the moment was focused on a sea of unwinking stars. The star patterns were not familiar as they had moved far away from Federation space.

"I know," Kelsey replied as she entered hyperspace equations into her computer; she was already plotting the next jump. "I talked to Ariel last night, and she has all the confidence in the world in Jeremy. She won't admit it, but I think Ariel is anxious to attack the AIs."

"They destroyed my home worlds," Ariel spoke over the girl's mini-com. "The first crew of the Avenger died without getting a chance for revenge for the destruction and death the Hocklyns brought upon us."

Kelsey sighed; sometimes she forgot that Ariel could hear everything they said. They had all agreed before the start of the mission that Ariel would be allowed to listen to everything they said over the mini-coms. The only place they had complete privacy were their quarters and then only if they asked for it.

"Revenge is not a good reason to go into battle," Katie suddenly spoke. "We are fighting to preserve the new Human Federation of Worlds, and perhaps someday we can even retake the old Federation planets."

Ariel was silent for a moment. While she did have and understood human emotions, they were still very difficult for her to handle at times. "You're right, Katie," she replied. "I just hope to see that day come. Clarissa and I both would like to return home someday. I think all of the Federation survivors want that."

Kelsey nodded her head in understanding. Her parents were over two hundred years in the past, and there were days she truly missed them. Not hearing her father's strict voice as he instructed her how to fly a shuttle, her mother reminding her that Admiral Anlon only had his daughter's best interests at heart. She was glad that she had her friends with her or this would be almost unbearable.

Katie was busy at her computer system's control console. She became aware of a presence behind her and turning saw Ariel standing there. She had come over from where she had been standing by the admiral.

"Emotions are very difficult to handle," Ariel confessed with her hands on her shapely hips. "Even more so since I can now use this hologram to project my feelings."

"You are becoming more human every day," Katie responded with a friendly smile. "You're my best friend, Ariel."

"And you are mine," Ariel replied with a pleased glint in her eyes. "I have never regretted the day I first made my presence known to you."

"Not even after I used our friendship to sneak aboard the New Horizon?" Katie reminded her. After the New Horizon incident, Ariel had given Katie a very strict lecture about friendship.

"Not even then," Ariel admitted. "All friendships have their bad moments."

Katie nodded, even now she could sense the care and concern in Ariel's computer generated voice.

-

Rear Admiral Sheen was studying the tactical display and all the green icons floating there. Second and Third fleet had jumped into the next system on their way to the rendezvous with Fleet Admiral Streth.

"All ships reporting normal status," Colonel David Bryson the ship's executive officer reported. On the tactical display, one hundred and twenty Federation warships were shown.

"Two more days," Commander Samantha Evans commented as she stepped over closer to the admiral. "Still no sign of the Hocklyns."

"The odds of us encountering a Hocklyn ship or even one of their scouts increases as we near their space," Amanda reminded the ship's commander.

"Sensors report no threats in our immediate area," Lieutenant Stalls informed them.

"Still no Hocklyns," Lieutenant Trask commented over her mini-com to Benjamin. "I get more nervous every day."

"We will find them soon enough," Stalls replied. This wasn't like the old days aboard the old StarStrike. They were actually going on the offensive to take the fight to the Hocklyns.

"I just worry about what we will find," Lieutenant Ashton added, her voice sounding concerned. The young blonde navigation officer had already finished plotting the next jump. "Remember what happened when we went into Hocklyn space and then returned? I don't want that to happen again."

"It won't," Angela Trask promised. "We are laying communication buoys between us and the Federation. If anything were to happen we would know about it and return."

"I think it's the Hocklyns that should be worried," Benjamin said in firm voice. "The new Human Federation of Worlds has had over two hundred years to prepare for this. The Hocklyns are in for a rude awakening, and for once it will be them losing worlds, not us."

-

Amanda sat back in her command chair and looked around the bustling Command Center. She felt some comfort at seeing Lieutenant's Trask, Stalls, and Ashton at their consoles. They had been with her from the very beginning, and she had all the confidence in the world in them. She just hoped they all lived to see the end of this. She closed her eyes briefly and thought about Richard and his concerns about this mission. He understood its importance and her role, but it was always difficult for a husband and wife to be separated in these circumstances. Amanda understood there was a chance she wouldn't make it back. If that occurred, she had left a message for Richard with Fleet Admiral Johnson. She hoped that Admiral Johnson would never have to deliver it.

-

It was rendezvous day, and Fleet Admiral Streth watched as his various commands put in an appearance. In the past six hours, all of the separate task groups had dropped out of hyperspace and reported in. Four hundred and thirty-two friendly green icons were represented on one of the large tactical holo displays. This included the supply ships and other non-combat vessels, but it was still a massive amount of firepower the Hocklyns were about to be hit with. Far greater than anything the old Federation had possessed.

"When we hit their bases, they will know they are up against a large and advanced civilization," Clarissa commented as she checked on the status of all the ships in the various fleets.

She was also speaking to Ariel over on the Avenger. The two liked to keep each other updated on what they were learning, especially with their new hologram images.

"From what we know of Hocklyn history, they have very seldom had to fight against a well organized opponent," responded Hedon, recalling what they had learned on First Fleet's clandestine mission into Hocklyn controlled space so long ago.

"The only problem is whenever they have, they call in the AIs," Colonel Trist commented with narrow eyes. "We can only hope that there are no AI ships close by when we launch our attack."

"From what we know of the AIs, they only put in an appearance after the Hocklyns report that they have run into an advanced civilization," added Clarissa, folding her arms across her ample chest.

One of the things she had done was increase her breast size for the hologram. She felt it made her more attractive and drew more attention. She wasn't quite sure why, but the males of the crew seemed much more attentive. Katie though had given her a lecture about not going to the extreme and had limited what she could change.

"I guess the big question is how soon after our attack will the Hocklyns scream for help and when will the AIs show up?" asked Colonel Trist, looking over at Clarissa and wondering if she had any insight into this.

"Unknown," responded Clarissa, shaking her head. "We don't know the capability of the AI's jump drive other than it is very advanced. We should have a few months at the minimum before they can respond."

"They will come with a Hocklyn war fleet," added Hedon, recalling how they had attacked the original Human Federation of Worlds. The AIs had wiped out the Federation fleets and then left the Hocklyns to do the dirty work of eliminating the civilian population. "It will take them a while to gather a sufficient fleet to drive us out of their territory."

"Then what?" Trist asked.

"We fall back to New Tellus and lure them into that system's defenses. If we can annihilate the first attack by the AIs and the Hocklyns, we can buy the Federation some much needed time."

All three became quiet as they mulled this over. This was going to be a long war, but this time the Federation had some allies. The Hocklyns and their masters the AIs would find this new Human Federation of Worlds to be no pushover.

Finally, Admiral Streth turned to the other two. "All fleets have sixteen hours to make ready for battle. We will split the fleets in the morning and set off for our individual target systems. Our attacks will be coordinated, and we will launch our initial assault in seventy-two hours."

On Earth, President Kincaid was meeting once more with Fleet Admiral Johnson.

"Karla, how much longer before Admiral Streth launches his attack?"

"Another forty-eight to seventy-two hours," she replied. She looked down at a computer pad she was holding in her right hand. "Admiral Streth and his fleets should have reached the outskirts of Hocklyn controlled space by now. Our latest message from the admiral indicated he would take a short time to retune all the drives of his fleet before moving off to their pre-attack coordinates."

"So this is it," spoke Kincaid, standing up and striding over to the large wall map, which displayed the Federation. "We are about to be officially at war with the Hocklyn Slave Empire."

"We have been at war for centuries," the Fleet Admiral reminded him. "The Hocklyns just didn't know it."

Kincaid ran his fingers over the map. Tau Ceti, Alpha Centauri, Epsilon Eridani, 61 Cygni, Epsilon Indi, Goombridge 1618, Procyon A, New Tellus, and Sol contained all the heavily populated worlds of the Federation. He would be going on the air tomorrow to announce that the Federation was now in a state of war, his words would be broadcast to every civilized world and mining colony in the Federation. He had a meeting later in the day with their three alien allies. They too would be making the same announcement.

He turned back and looked at Fleet Admiral Johnson who was standing there watching him. "So now it begins," he stated in a level voice, feeling the sudden weight of war upon his shoulders.

"Now it begins after nearly four hundred years, the Great War is finally upon us," replied Karla, calmly.

They both turned to look at the wall map of the Federation. The Federation was humanity's last hope for survival. They would do everything in their power to make sure it continued to exist.

Chapter Fourteen

High Leader Ankler gazed out the viewport of his council shuttle as it neared Mirrin, a ten-kilometer long artificial space habitat that belonged to his family. Ankler wondered with growing concern if this would be the last time he returned to his home as High Leader. In three more days, another vote would be held about the humans and notifying the AIs. From his latest words with Nartel earlier in the day, he knew he would lose the vote.

"Docking in ten minutes," a senior Protector spoke, stepping into the small stateroom of the shuttle. The Protector had regular battle armor on but was only armed with a high caliber pistol and a long knife in a highly decorated scabbard. "Your wife and children are waiting."

"Thank you, Clyston," responded Ankler, letting out a long rasping breath. Then, looking at the senior Protector, he asked, "Clyston, you have been with me for nearly twenty years, why have you stayed? There are other positions where honor could have come far more swiftly."

Clyston was silent for a long moment as he thought over his answer. "It is difficult to get a posting in one of our home systems," he responded, his large dark eyes gazing at the High Leader. "While it is true, due to a lack of combat, honor in the home systems comes slowly; it is what I wanted to do."

"You have protected by family with honor," Ankler responded with an acknowledging nod. "For that I am grateful."

"Serving you has been an honor, and you have allowed the empire to steadily grow," Clyston continued. It was seldom the High Leader addressed him. "Now you have given us four more systems to move our people to as a result of your negotiations with the AIs. I hope to serve you for many more years to come. May you continue to serve our people with honor."

Ankler nodded and watched as Clyston left, going back to the cockpit of the shuttle. He knew that Clyston's opinion of him might change shortly. Looking back out the viewport, he saw the small flight bay on the end of the habitat open. The habitat was rotating slowly to create gravity on its interior surface. Nearly 60,000 Hocklyns lived and worked inside. Granted, due to the fact that he was High Leader, most of the menial work was carried out by slaves with careful Hocklyn oversight. His family was also very wealthy from their acquirement of honor over the long years. Normally a habitat of this size would hold closer to 300,000 Hocklyns.

They were in the Anlesh star system, whose fourth planet out was inhabited by nearly twenty billion Hocklyns. Space around the planet was full of shipyards and other habitats. Two massive construction docks labored twenty-four hours a day building new ones. Each month, two new habitats would exit the massive construction bays to be towed into their permanent orbits.

Space freighters were constantly coming and going, bringing supplies and raw materials from hundreds of slave worlds. This was the same in all ten of the Hocklyn home systems, but even at this construction rate, the population growth was outstripping their ability to build new habitats. Despite newer and stricter population controls, the population was still growing too fast.

Each year the demands on the numerous slave worlds grew. More food, raw materials, finished products, and the list continued to lengthen. Some of them were beginning to slip back into intense poverty as their populations were overworked to meet their quotas. Extra Protectors and even military ships had been assigned to ensure these planets continued producing what the Hocklyn worlds so desperately needed.

The lives of menial slaves were meaningless since others could always be brought in to work their worlds and operate the factories. The Hocklyn Empire consisted of sixteen thousand slave worlds with over three trillion slaves from which to pull supplies.

Once the shuttle was docked, Ankler stepped out to be greeted by his wife and his two oldest sons.

"High Leader," his wife spoke, bowing deeply. "We are honored by your presence." His wife was of smaller stature and her body more supple and curved.

His sons also bowed in respect for the position their father held.

"It is good to be home," responded Ankler, allowing himself to relax. "Honor has served us well."

"We have prepared a feast to celebrate your homecoming," Jaseth, his youngest son spoke.

He was in his early twenties and was wearing gray body armor as was customary. Jaseth was studying to be a War Leader and had already been assigned a commission as Second Leader on a dreadnought.

His brother Hangeth nodded his head in agreement. "It will be a good feast, father. We are celebrating your skill in bringing us four more worlds to settle our people on."

"It is good," responded Ankler, returning the bow. "Now, let us go eat and not speak of work. This is time for family."

He didn't want to mention his growing fear. No word as of yet from War Leader Bisth. Fleet Commodore Resmunt had sent another request only yesterday asking for more ships. The High Council was becoming uneasy, and the next vote would require that he notify the AIs about the humans. Once that occurred there would be a full scale investigation by selected members of the High Council, probably led by High Councilor Ruthan, as to where these new humans had come from.

Once that investigation was completed, there was no doubt in Ankler's mind that he would be removed as High Leader and his family would suffer accordingly for the loss of honor. Even their habitat might be taken away.

Walking down several long corridors, they reached the interior of the artificial structure. They stepped out on a large veranda that overlooked their home. The air was fresh and sweet as it once had been on the home world, free of pollution and industrial contaminates. Trees and flowing streams were everywhere. The habitat was a literal paradise. Looking upward, he could see a few white clouds drifting in the center of the long cylinder. Above them, he could barely make out other buildings and structures. Inside a habitat, there was no true up or down, just living space.

He knew that other habitats were suffering from overcrowding. As the population in the habitats grew there often was nowhere for the excess population to go to. Homes built for a family of four soon found eight or more living inside. The population pressure had been building for years, and Ankler knew that soon something drastic would have to be done. Even the four new star systems would not be enough. He sighed deeply, knowing that some very unpopular decisions would soon have to be made and enforced.

"Let us go eat," he spoke finally as he took one last long look around. He knew that shortly, all of this might come to an end. All because of the humans and his ancestor that had dealt with them so long ago.

Fleet Commodore Resmunt was still in his flagship, the dreadnought Liberator, weighing his lessening options. War Leader Bisth and his fleets were gone! There was no longer any doubt in his mind about that. His requests to the High Council for additional fleets to guard this sector were being ignored. Yesterday, he had sent out all of the armed scout ships he had at his disposal to scan the star systems between Hocklyn space and presumed human space. They had instructions not to venture further than 100 light years out. Resmunt knew the odds of detecting an inbound human fleet were negligible, but he felt he had to do so.

"You still think the humans are coming?" questioned First Leader Ganth, stepping over close to the command pedestal.

"Yes, First Leader, I do," Resmunt responded in a cold and concerned voice. He turned and his eyes focused on Ganth. "We attacked their worlds, or at least Bisth did. I have spent some time studying the history of our original conflict with them. These humans are a race of warriors, or at least their military is. They will not allow our attack to go unpunished. They will come if only to test our resolve and our honor."

First Leader Ganth nodded slowly. If they came, then the fleets they had gathered above this planet would smite them down. Honor would come swiftly to the Liberator and her crew. "If they come here, we will destroy them!"

"Let honor be served," spoke Resmunt, hoping his second in command was correct; he wasn't quite so certain. He feared their doctrine of honor that was so rigidly enforced could someday be their undoing. It required sacrifices at times when sacrifices were not necessary.

"War Leader Osbith of the dreadnought BattleHand is requesting a meeting with you later today."

Resmunt shook his head in aggravation. It was the same every day. War Leader Osbith had arrived with one of the two reinforcing fleets. He was now officially second in command of Resmunt's forces in the system due to his seniority. Unfortunately, Osbith had very little battle experience because he had come from a rear area of the Hocklyn Empire. Commodore Resmunt was not certain how useful he would be in an actual battle. He had additional War Leaders stationed at the other five forward fleet bases that would have been better suited. He was tempted to call one or two of them forward and place one of them in charge of Osbith's fleets.

"Agreed," responded Resmunt, letting out a long hissing breath. His dark, wide eyes focused on Ganth. "It will be a short meeting as I plan to return to the planet later. I want to make a final inspection of the defenses around the spaceport."

His eyes turned to the large sensor screen, which showed the fleet he had gathered above his world. There were eighty-four ships in the formation, all within the protective gravity well of the planet. He glanced at a data screen, which showed the makeup of his fleet. He had ten dreadnoughts, eighteen war cruisers, and fifty-six escort cruisers.

In normal times, he would feel confident with this force, but Bisth had taken ninety-six ships with him and failed to return. However, he also had the heavily armed shipyard that was floating in orbit, the defensive railgun satellites and missile platforms, as well as the heavy weapons down on the surface around the spaceport. Surely, if the humans came he could stop them.

Fleet Commodore Resmunt allowed his thoughts to wander briefly. If he could defeat the humans, then much honor would come his way, perhaps enough to even return to the home systems and move into the hierarchy of government. He had heard that the High Councilors lived a life of ease and luxury.

-

Hedon gazed with growing concern at the latest data from two of his stealth scouts that had just returned. First Fleet was floating in empty space in a small binary star system just twelve light years from their primary target, the main Hocklyn fleet base for this entire sector.

"They have to be expecting us," Colonel Trist informed the admiral after studying one of the large tactical displays. He arched his eyebrows in dismay; it showed the planet the large enemy fleet base was built upon. "They have gathered eighty-four warships above the planet. Not only that, but they have a very powerful satellite defensive grid to cover their base as well as that shipyard. How could they know we were coming?"

"Second, Third, Fourth, and Fifth fleets are all reporting in position and ready to strike," Captain Duncan reported from her communications console. FTL transmission booster buoys had been spread out behind the fleets to allow them quick communication with each other.

"What are they reporting about the Hocklyn bases they are targeting?" asked Hedon, looking over at his communications officer.

"Hocklyn fleets at the two bases are smaller than expected," she replied as she listened to the additional information coming over her com system. "I am transferring the latest data over to the tactical displays."

Instantly, the data currently being displayed on several of the screens was replaced with the new information of the other two preliminary target systems.

"That's where the ships came from, or at least some of them," Colonel Trist spoke as he gazed at the fleet makeup. "There is a dreadnought missing from each fleet, and I suspect some of the other ships were pulled from their rearward bases."

"This is a shrewd Fleet Commodore," Hedon admitted as he weighed his tactical options. He stood up and walked over to stand directly in front of the tactical display, examining it closely. "The failure of their four attack fleets to return or send back word of the battle must have tipped him off that something was wrong."

Unfortunately, stealth scout missions had been halted once Operation First Strike was launched. They had been concerned about tipping their hand if the Hocklyns detected or managed to destroy one. Now it looked as if that might have been a mistake. It seemed as if in the last ten days some major fleet movements had occurred in their primary target system.

Looking at the other tactical displays Hedon noticed that each of the two targeted forward fleet bases had one dreadnought, six war cruisers, and sixteen escort cruisers at their disposal. Second and Third Fleet were targeting one, and Fourth and Fifth fleet were targeting the other. His fleets had a superior advantage in both firepower and numbers. The plan could still work; he just needed to make some slight modifications. He let out a long deep breath. This was war, a constantly flowing and changing situation.

"We launch the attack in four hours," ordered Hedon after a moment. They hadn't come this far to pull back due to a wary Hocklyn Fleet Commodore. "Inform the other fleets they have a go. Colonel Trist, I want to move First Fleet to this system here." Hedon indicated a system just 3.6 light years from their primary target. "When our other fleets launch their attacks, I want the Hocklyns to become aware of our presence so they won't send reinforcements to their fleet bases."

"Yes, Admiral," replied Trist, relieved that the attack was going to commence. "What about their main fleet base. Do we attack?"

"No, at least not yet." Then, with a cunning smile, Hedon added. "We will send in half a dozen light cruisers just to ensure that they know we're here."

–

Fourth Fleet was carefully maneuvering into their attack positions. Jeremy knew from the latest data from their stealth scouts that all of the Hocklyn warships were inside the gravity well of the planet at which they were based. Fourth Fleet would jump in first in a bid to keep the Hocklyns pinned against the planet, and then the larger Fifth Fleet would come in and enter the gravity well to destroy them. Jeremy's fleet would stay just outside the gravity well in case it was required to meet any Hocklyn reinforcements.

"I guess this is it," Kelsey spoke nervously over her mini-com to the others. "This is what our parents worked for all of those long years ago."

"I just wished they were here to see it," Katie added in a very subdued voice.

She could remember her father, Greg Johnson, speaking to Jason Strong about how in some ways he would like to be around when the Hocklyns and humans tangled once again in the future. But their destiny had already been set in creating the new Human Federation of Worlds.

"I suspect they are," added Angela, wistfully. Angela was very religious, and there was no doubt in her mind that they were indeed being watched.

"This first battle shouldn't be too bad," pointed out Kevin from his console where he was keeping a vigilant eye on his sensor screen. At the moment, it just showed ninety friendly green icons and a few Talon fighters flying CAP.

"This is only the first of many," Ariel pointed out to the group. She was feeling excited about the coming battle and was standing just behind Jeremy, her voice coming only over the mini-com.

"Yes, the first of many," Jeremy reminded all of them in a serious tone.

"I think I would prefer to be back on that beach resort on New Tellus," Angela commented as she thought about what was ahead of them.

"Just do your jobs and we will come through this okay. If we do, I promise that when we get home we will go back to that resort."

"You just want some more of those wild fruit drinks," teased Kelsey, feeling her mood lighten.

"That works for me," answered Katie, enthusiastically. The resort had been a blast, especially when she had returned and talked Kevin into going parasailing with her over the ocean. It had been the most fun she had ever had! She would love to return there.

It was at that moment that a warning alarm suddenly sounded on Kevin's sensor console. A dark red threat icon had suddenly appeared less than twenty million kilometers from the fleet.

"Crap!" Kevin uttered as his hands flew over the touch screen and he looked back at Jeremy. "We have a Hocklyn armed scout within easy scanning range of us!"

-

Aboard the 300-meter Hocklyn ship, First Leader Calyss looked on in shock at what his sensor operator was putting up on the screen. He had thought Fleet Commodore Resmunt was insane when he had demanded that the armed scouts be used to search for an invading human fleet. Now, here it was upon his screens!

"Numbers and types," he demanded as he ordered the ship ready to jump back to the base.

His communications were already being jammed, and he knew he would be under attack in moments. Jumping back this quickly without letting his drive core cool down would probably seriously damage his ship, but there was no other choice. Honor demanded that he return to the base and spread the warning of this threat. For the first time in their long and glorious history, the Hocklyn Empire was about to be invaded.

Before his sensor operator could reply, two human light cruisers micro-jumped to within ten thousand kilometers of his ship and began accelerating. The ships appeared on the main viewscreen. Already, he could see flashes of light indicating missiles were being launched.

"Jump us, now!" he oathed as he realized his ship was about to be destroyed if he didn't do something.

Moments later, the armed scout vanished, and the missiles passed harmlessly through the location it had just occupied.

-

"They jumped!" reported Kevin, worriedly. "Now what?"

"Get me Admiral Gaines," ordered Jeremy, swearing under his breath. "Angela, send a message to Admiral Streth and inform him that we have been detected."

After a quick consultation with senior Admiral Gaines, it was decided they would launch their attack immediately. After being detected by the armed scout, there was no sense in delaying it.

Jeremy looked around the busy Command Center as the excitement of approaching battle swept over the crew. "Colonel Malen, take us to Condition One and prepare for battle."

"Yes, Sir," Malen replied as she pressed several buttons on her console at the plotting table. Instantly, red warning lights began flashing and alarm klaxons began sounding throughout the ship. "All crew go to Condition One, this is not a drill," she spoke over the ship's com system. "Condition One is now set."

"Helm, prepare to jump," Jeremy ordered, his eyes narrowing.

"Ship is ready," Ariel reported as she stepped up to stand closer to Jeremy.

-

The armed scout had jumped back to its forward base, but First Leader Calyss was having a hard time convincing the War Leader of the orbiting fleet of his discovery. The War Leader was convinced that it had to be a sensor error and was demanding that Calyss return to the system for additional scans. No one attacked the Hocklyns, it was unheard of!

Calyss was about to retort that he would not have his honor challenged in such a way when his sensor operator reported numerous red threat icons appearing behind them. Calyss glanced at the screen and knew he was too far out from the gravity well of the fleet base for protection. His ship was doomed.

"Turn us around," he ordered grimly with his right hand touching his battle armor across his chest. "Honor is before us."

"Honor is before us," his Second Leader responded in understanding. Instantly, the small 300-meter Hocklyn scout turned to attack the war fleet that was appearing behind it.

-

Jeremy looked on in surprise as the small armed scout turned to attack his fleet.

"What's he doing?" Kevin asked in shock. "That's suicide!"

"They're Hocklyns," Colonel Malen responded, her eyes focused on the rapidly approaching ship. "He attacks to protect his ship's honor." Colonel Malen had studied Hocklyn psychology at the Fleet Academy.

"The Monarch cruiser Reprisal is firing," reported Tactical.

On the screen, several missiles flew toward the Hocklyn scout and then detonated against its screens. One of the missiles was a Devastator ten-kiloton nuke, which erased any trace of the Hocklyn armed scout.

"Admiral Gaines and Fifth Fleet are jumping in," Ariel reported as her sensors detected the numerous spatial vortexes forming four million kilometers away.

"Take us in closer to the planet, but stay outside the gravity well," Jeremy ordered as he focused his eyes on the tactical display. It was time for his fleet to take up its position for the battle.

He watched an hour later as Fifth Fleet began entering the gravity well of the planet and the twenty-three ships of the defending Hocklyn fleet surged forward to meet it.

Fleet Commodore Resmunt had just returned to his office from his inspection tour when his aide came rushing in. "They're here!" the aide reported, breathing heavily, his large black eyes even wider than normal. "A human fleet is attacking the fleet base at star 7712!"

Resmunt eyes immediately moved to the large map of the sector on the wall. Fleet base 7712 was one hundred and ninety light years away.

"How large a force?" he demanded. If this was the human attack, it might be wise to take his own force here at his base and respond. Then he paused as he calculated the time to get there. At maximum jumps of thirty light years, it would take him forty hours to arrive, by then the battle would be over.

The aide paused as he passed on the news. "Base 7712 is reporting that it is under attack by over ninety heavily armed human warships!"

"Honor be served," Resmunt muttered quietly as he realized the fleet at the base would be annihilated.

"Honor be served," his aide replied, taken slightly aback at the Fleet Commodore's response. "Are we not going to send our fleet to aid them and destroy these humans?"

It was at that moment that a warning alarm sounded on his desk. Stepping over, he activated the blinking com system and listened to First Leader Ganth on the flagship.

"That won't be necessary," replied Resmunt, looking at his aide with a hint of sadness in his eyes. "The humans are coming for us also. That was First Leader Ganth, and he reports that six human light cruisers have just jumped into the system and are conducting scans of our defenses. I believe in the next few days, many of us will be finding honor."

"What should we do?" his aide asked. He was not afraid to die, but it was unthinkable that a human victory was possible, not against the Hocklyn Empire!

"Send a message to the High Council that we are under attack by human ships of unknown power and numbers. It is my belief that these same humans are also responsible for the destruction of all four of War Leader Bisth's fleets."

Fleet Commodore Resmunt watched as his aide rushed away to carry out his orders. Activating his com unit again, he sent word to have his shuttle prepared. He would be returning to the Liberator to conduct the upcoming battle.

-

A few hours later, Admiral Streth watched without surprise as a Hocklyn armed scout jumped into the small red dwarf star system First Fleet was occupying. He knew the Fleet Commodore in charge of the Hocklyn fleets had probably sent out every armed scout he had in an attempt to find the human fleet that was endangering his world.

Under his orders, no efforts were made to prevent the armed scout from scanning First Fleet. Hedon fully intended to use First Fleet to hold the main Hocklyn forces at this base, which would allow the other four fleets of Operation First Strike to destroy the Hocklyn forces at their remaining five forward fleet bases. Once that was done, he would call forward Second and Third Fleet to eliminate the main Hocklyn force.

"They're gone," Colonel Trist reported as the small red threat icon on the tactical display vanished. He turned toward Hedon. "From our latest reports the attacks by our other forces are proceeding as planned. Fourth Fleet was detected, but they launched their assault upon the Hocklyn base immediately. That battle should be nearly over with by now."

Hedon nodded. He let out a weary breath hoping this all ended well. So far there had been no reports of AI ships. That was the big danger; an AI ship could seriously damage his fleet. It still wasn't known if the new Devastator Three missiles could take one out.

Looking around the busy Command Center, Hedon felt the weight of responsibility knowing that tens of thousands of Fleet personnel were depending on his decisions. He just prayed that he made the right ones. Unexpected developments occurred in war, nothing could be taken for granted. He recalled his brother Taylor mentioning that to him one evening while they were at the cabin by the lake. His brother had been a major in the Federation marines at the time and had studied military tactics.

Taylor had said that war was a steadily evolving process with constant flux on the battlefield. He had warned Hedon to be cautious. What might work today could fail miserably tomorrow. Hedon had always taken his brother's advice seriously. He would never take combat against the Hocklyns for granted!

-

Jeremy watched as the Hocklyn dreadnought put up a valiant fight against the inbound Anlon bomber strike. He cringed as two, four, and then six of the bombers exploded from defensive fire before the rest of the four squadrons delivered their nuclear tipped Shrike missiles. When the nuclear fire cleared, all that was left of the dreadnought was a crumbled mass of glowing wreckage, which blew apart when several of the ship's remaining nuclear self-destruct devices went off.

"That's the last of them," Colonel Malen reported as the final red threat icon on the tactical display vanished.

"What were Fifth Fleet's losses?" Jeremy asked. He had watched more than one green icon flare up and vanish during the brief but intense battle.

Colonel Malen frowned as she studied the data. "One Monarch cruiser, two light cruisers, and four destroyers."

"In exchange for twenty-three Hocklyn warships," commented Jeremy, frowning. "What were the bomber and fighter losses?"

"Twenty-two Anlon bombers and sixteen Talon fighters."

Jeremy had watched with intense interest as the Anlon bomber strike had gone in. Two of Admiral Gaines battle carriers were carrying the new shielded bombers and their attack had been devastating against the Hocklyn fleet after Fifth Fleet had battered down their defenses. Not a single Hocklyn ship had managed to make a suicide run.

"Admiral Gaines is currently going into orbit and is preparing to send his assault shuttles down from the carriers to mop up the base."

Jeremy nodded toward Colonel Malen. "Keep us in position just outside of the gravity well; we don't know what might pop in. By now, this entire sector of the Hocklyn Empire knows it's under attack. Take us to Condition Two."

Kelsey glanced over where Angela was sitting in front of Communications and saw that her friend looked extremely pale. "What's wrong, Angela? This battle is nearly over."

"I know," she spoke, trying to force a smile upon her face. "But a lot of people just died and a lot more will before this is over. I just keep thinking about how their families will feel when we get back home and they find out their loved ones didn't make it."

Kelsey was silent for a moment before replying. "This is going to be a long war, Angela, and there will be many Fleet personnel and others that will lose their lives before this is over. All we can do is pray for them and hope they understand the sacrifices that must be made if the human race is to survive."

"This is about survival," Ariel broke in. She walked over to stand between the two women. "The Hocklyns will destroy the Federation and everyone in it if they get the opportunity. We are here to ensure that doesn't happen. I watched them destroy the original Human Federation of Worlds. They nuked the planets without mercy, killing billions of innocents. They would not accept surrender or spare even a child. They may have this honor system in battle, but they are cold of heart and quite merciless toward other races."

Angela and Kelsey looked at one another, knowing the AI was correct. This war was about one thing and one thing only and that was survival. At the end of it, either the human race would be gone or the Hocklyns would.

Chapter Fifteen

High Leader Ankler stared in open shock at the com message that had just been handed to him. He was still at his family's habitat and had been preparing to return to the High Council on Calzen. It had been three days since he had returned home and the next council meeting was scheduled for later today. He let out a deep sigh of frustration, knowing that everything was coming to a head. Years of hard work and labor were about to be brushed aside due to a mistake by Sigeth, his distant ancestor and the lies he had told about the destruction of the humans.

"I don't understand," his youngest son was saying. Jaseth had been with Ankler when an aide had rushed in with the message. "Why are you returning to the High Council chambers today? Can't you stay longer?"

Ankler stood up from where he was sitting behind his large, ornate desk. Looking at the message once more, he knew this was the end. Resmunt had been correct about the humans; they did pose a deadly and serious threat to the empire. If this message was accurate, the humans were attacking Resmunt's support bases in calculated fury, wiping them out one by one. For the first time in Hocklyn history, they were under attack and losing. Briefly, he explained to Jaseth that the Hocklyn Empire was under attack and by whom.

"Who are these humans?" Jaseth asked, his eyes focusing on his father and seeing worry and possibly even fear in his eyes. He couldn't ever recall seeing this before. What was wrong? He wanted to know more about these humans who were attacking the empire.

Ankler walked over and stood before his son. Perhaps someday Jaseth could restore the family's honor. "Long ago one of our ancestors was responsible for attacking and destroying the human home worlds. At that time, they were known as the Human Federation of Worlds. When the battles were over, he reported that all the human ships and their people had been annihilated."

"If that's true, then where are these humans coming from?" asked Jaseth, feeling confused.

Ankler let out a deep, rasping breath. There was no longer any point in hiding the truth. He suspected the High Council would be sending for him shortly. His family's honor was about to come to an end.

"He lied," answered Ankler, his eyes gazing intently at his son.

"Lied?" Jaseth echoed in disbelief. A Hocklyn did not lie about such things, surely his father was mistaken.

"Yes, he lied," his father replied with a tired and worried look crossing his face. "War Leader Sigeth faked documents which indicated the remaining human ships that escaped the destruction of their worlds had been destroyed. In reality, these ships, and possibly numerous others, escaped and established a new human colony far away from our empire. They have grown in power and numbers and may now pose a serious threat to us."

"War Leader Sigeth," Jaseth stammered suddenly realizing the ramifications of what his father was saying. "It was from the conquering and destruction of those human worlds that much of our family honor came."

"Yes," agreed Ankler, reaching out and putting his powerful hand on his son's shoulder. "The High Council will be sending for me shortly. I fear our days of basking in our past honor is about to come to an end."

"We will lose everything!" Jaseth spoke in sudden understanding, his large, dark eyes growing wide.

"I fear so," Ankler replied as one of his aides entered and handed him another message. Glancing down, Ankler saw it was from High Councilor Nartel demanding his immediate presence at the High Council chambers. It was also mentioned that there would be a vote against Ankler for possible treason to the empire.

"Jaseth, you are in the military, and any honor you have earned from your duties will stay with you," Ankler spoke in a soft voice, knowing this could be the last time he saw his son. "It may be up to you someday to restore our family's honor."

Later that afternoon, High Leader Ankler stepped into the ornate chamber of the High Council. The large room became quiet upon his arrival.

"What have you done!" roared High Councilor Ruthan, striding up to stand challengingly in front of him. "You said these humans were not a threat!"

"I didn't believe they were," replied Ankler, stepping around Ruthan and walking to the head of the council table to take his seat.

Ruthan followed him and slammed down a series of messages on the table in front of him.

"All five of Resmunt's forward fleet bases have fallen or are under attack," he spoke, accusingly. "Resmunt asked for six fleets to reinforce his sector and you turned him down, sending only two! Resmunt knew there was a danger and you refused to listen."

"I felt two were sufficient," Ankler replied in a steady and calm voice, refusing to let Ruthan get the best of him. "War Leader Bisth should have been able to conquer the humans. It was Bisth's incompetence at command that has brought us to this point."

"I think not," High Councilor Nartel spoke, standing up and gazing intently at High Leader Ankler. "I have been doing some research into the battles with the humans above their original worlds. It seems that a large number of human ships escaped the last battle and were supposedly hunted down later. It seems strange that the only reports that indicate these human ships were destroyed came from your own distant ancestor, War Leader Sigeth."

A low disgruntled rumbling came from the other High Councilors as they realized the significance of this statement.

"War Leader Sigeth," High Councilor Jarles hissed as he recognized the name. He stood up demanding to be recognized, looking at High Councilor Nartel. "Why are these reports in question? They are part of our empire's history!"

"None of his subordinates or First Leaders indicated any human ships being destroyed after the final engagement in their home system," explained Nartel in an accusing voice, and then, turning back to toward Ankler, he continued. "High Leader Ankler, this was your ancestor. For honor, were these reports by War Leader Sigeth lies?"

All the High Councilors gazed intently at High Leader Ankler. This was the same as accusing him of treason. Never in the history of the Hocklyn Slave Empire had such charges ever been leveled at a High Leader. There was absolute silence in the council chambers as they waited for an answer.

Ankler was silent for a long moment. He let out a heavy rasping breath, knowing it was useless to deny the charges. Once the High Council started looking, they would find that the reports were false.

"Yes, they were lies," he confessed, his hand going to his blade at his waist. He could end his life now and perhaps save some of his family honor. He could see in the eyes of the entire council that he had lost their support.

Ruthan nodded his head in satisfaction, recognizing Ankler's end. "I have already sent word to the AIs about the humans. They will not be happy with what you have withheld from them."

"The AIs," muttered Nartel, turning to face Ruthan, his large eyes narrowing in concern. "You should not have done so without the approval of the rest of the council."

The large doors to the council chamber suddenly swung open. A senior Protector stood there, his eyes sweeping over the councilors. "An AI ship has just jumped into the system. It will be in orbit of Calzen shortly."

"Thank you," responded Nartel, dismissing the Protector. He looked around the council table. "The AIs are coming. I suspect we will suffer serious punishment for the lies that High Leader Ankler's ancestor told. This will not be a good day for honor in our empire."

Two hours later, the council chamber doors swung open and a monstrosity entered. It was difficult to see what the AI was made of. Part of its body resembled a cube with irregular lines and multiple tentacles attached with a glowing white orb on top. It was impossible to tell if the orb was made of pure energy or of some type of highly advanced material. The AI's body seemed to float just above the floor of the council chamber. It came to a stop at the edge of the table and then a powerful voice spoke.

"We have become aware of the failures of this council," the voice said, sounding highly displeased. "You have hidden from us that more humans exist. Why was this done?"

"I felt we could handle the humans ourselves and bring them into our empire," responded High Leader Ankler, standing up to face the AI. "They will make excellent slaves for us."

"The humans are too dangerous," responded the AI, unsympathetically. "They must be destroyed."

"Why are the humans such a threat?" High Councilor Nartel asked, daring to speak. "Surely, they could be better used to serve the empire?"

"No," the AI responded in a firm voice, the glowing light on top of the AI growing even brighter. "The humans are a danger to all of us and must be eliminated."

High Leader Ankler listened to the AIs words in amazement. It almost sounded as if the AIs were afraid of the humans. How could that be?

"The humans can only have a few worlds at the most," responded Ankler, carefully. If he could talk the AIs into allowing him to conquer these few worlds, perhaps he could still salvage the situation and save his family's honor.

"That is incorrect," the AI responded, moving closer to Ankler, almost hovering over him. "The original humans of the Human Federation of Worlds were brought to those worlds from another, which we now believe is located in the area of space that War Leader Bisth went to. They may be much more numerous than you believe."

"Brought to the Human Federation of Worlds? Why, and by whom?" demanded Nartel, forgetting for a moment it was an AI he was addressing.

"That information is classified," replied the AI, sounding aggravated at such a question being asked.

"What are your orders?" asked Nartel finally, seeing that High Leader Ankler was only standing there, gazing uncomprehendingly at the AI.

"Your High Leader's life is forfeit," the AI spoke as a beam of light reached out and touched Ankler, reducing his body instantly to dust and ashes. Only his body armor and blade survived, falling to the floor with a rattling clang. "The four new star systems for colonization are also forfeit."

High Councilor Nartel nodded in understanding. This was what they had all been afraid of. The AIs were not forgiving. He let out a deep sigh of frustration; High Leader Ankler had cost them so much.

"We have two of our ships currently in that section of the galaxy," the AI continued as it floated away from Ankler's ashes. "They will be directed to stop this current attack against your empire."

"What are our orders?" Nartel asked now knowing that the human attack would be dealt with by the AIs.

"Prepare a fleet of your most powerful warships," instructed the AI as it moved slowly along the council table, hovering briefly near every councilor as if it were reminding each of them who was actually in charge of their empire. "There will be five of our ships going with you. We will find the human worlds and destroy them. This time all the humans will be eliminated. You will be sent a time and place to meet our ships. Do not fail us again!" The AI turned and left the chamber without another word.

Nartel stood for a moment as the massive doors swung shut behind the AI, and then he stepped to the front of the council chamber and sat down in the High Leader's chair. No one questioned his authority to take it.

"There is something about these humans that frightens the AIs," he spoke as he gazed at the other eight councilors.

"They have never used five of their vessels against a civilization before," Ruthan added still shaken at being so close to an AI. He had seen them from a distance before, but never like this. "If we want to regain those four systems for future colonization, we must destroy these humans!"

Nartel nodded in agreement. "We will gather the largest fleet possible for the attack. It will take a while, but we must not fail in this or all of our lives could be forfeit."

The other council members looked at the dust and ashes of what remained of their former High Leader in understanding. The AIs were even more merciless than the Hocklyns were.

"What about High Leader Ankler's habitat?" asked Ruthan, gazing inquiringly at High Leader Nartel. "What is to become of it?"

"His family's honor will be substantially reduced," responded Nartel, looking at Ruthan with his cold, dark eyes. "Order seventy percent of their wealth to be ceased, and then send another 200,000 Hocklyn civilians to their habitat. I believe they have the room."

-

Fleet Commodore Resmunt stood upon the command pedestal of his flagship gazing with deep concern at the gathering of red threat icons forty million kilometers from his fleet base. In desperation, realizing that a massive battle was soon going to take place, he had called up all the ships from the rearward bases as well as the older escort cruisers garrisoning eighteen of the conquered worlds in his sector. In response, he had gained another six war cruisers and twenty-two escort cruisers. There was nothing else that could reach him in time before the humans launched their expected attack.

"What's the latest report from our last two forward fleet bases?" Resmunt asked First Leader Ganth. "Did the dreadnoughts manage to escape?"

Once Fleet Commodore Resmunt had realized that the humans were systematically reducing his supporting bases to impotency, he had ordered the dreadnoughts to jump to the main fleet base to give Resmunt more experienced War Leaders as well as heavier firepower. None had showed up.

"We have now lost contact with all five fleet bases," Ganth reported as he came back from Communications. "The last report was from War Leader Daseth in system 7734. He was under heavy attack and did not believe he could escape from the gravity well of the planet."

Resmunt nodded, folding his sinewy arms across the light battle armor he wore. He gazed ponderingly at the main sensor screen. What were the humans up to? If they could destroy his fleet, they could push back the Hocklyn Empire for hundreds of light years in all directions. He knew the humans were using at least three large war fleets to attack the empire. Their superior weapons and tactics so far had been devastating to the defending Hocklyn forces. Many brave Hocklyns had met their honor in the last several days.

At last, the red threat icons on the main sensor screen seemed to stop growing, and after a few minutes, Resmunt knew this was the fleet he would have to face. "What are their numbers and makeup?" he demanded, looking over at First Leader Ganth.

"That information is coming in now over the main sensors," Ganth responded, his eyes widening upon seeing the data. "We are detecting one hundred and twenty warships. At least thirty-eight are of capital ship size."

Resmunt nodded, not really surprised. The humans would not be attacking unless they thought they could win. "They hope we will leave the gravity well of the planet and engage them in open space, but that will not be so. Contact War Leader Osbith. He is to position his fleets directly over the fleet base and beneath the defensive satellites. I want him in such a position so he can add his firepower to the satellites or the fleet base as needed. We will move the remaining ships and take up a position around the shipyard; its weapons are as powerful as four dreadnoughts."

"Yes, Fleet Commodore," First Leader Ganth responded as he turned to begin carrying out his orders. He felt great excitement at the coming battle, confident that the commodore would defeat the humans and achieve much honor in his victory. That honor would be shared by all the crewmembers of the dreadnought Liberator. "May honor be with us today."

"May honor be with us," Resmunt replied with a nod.

His gaze turned back to the main sensor screen. He did not trust these humans, and wondered just what their Fleet Admiral was up to. With a deep, rasping sigh, he turned to go send an FTL message back to the High Council. Fortunately, the FTL transmitter on the fleet base was so powerful it was immune to human jamming. He would send a message on estimated human fleet strength and what the potential danger from these humans were. Resmunt knew the High Council would not like what he was about to say.

Rear Admiral Sheen gazed speculatively at the tactical holo display as she studied the Hocklyn fleet movements. She watched as the Hocklyn ships carefully positioned themselves into several defensive formations, one directly over their fleet base and the other around their shipyard.

"Interesting move," Commander Samantha Davidson commented from Amanda's side, gazing thoughtfully at the tactical display. "I expected them to come out and meet us in open combat due to that honor system of theirs."

"Admiral Streth believes the commodore, or possibly Fleet Commodore, in charge of this base is unique. He has not done what previous Hocklyn War Leaders have in the past. These ship movements only prove Admiral Streth to be correct."

Amanda pressed a button on her command console and was instantly in contact with Admiral Adler on the battle carrier Wasp. "Jacob," Amanda spoke as she continued to gaze at the tactical display. "I don't see any point in delaying this any longer. I will take Second Fleet into the planet's gravity well and engage the ships defending the shipyard. Follow us in, but keep at a safe distance. When I feel we have caused enough damage it will be time to send in the bomber strike."

"You're going to lose some ships," Jacob warned. "That Fleet Commodore is shrewd. It's going to be tough going against those defenses."

"I know," Amanda replied with a heavy sigh, knowing a lot of good people under her command were about to die. "But what other choice is there?"

"You could use the Devastator Three missiles," suggested Jacob, cautiously "That would significantly weaken their defenses."

"You know we can't do that," Amanda replied. She had direct orders to save the Devastator Threes for use against the AIs if they showed up. They only had a limited number of the super powerful missiles. They were also extremely expensive and complicated to build.

"Only a few, Amanda," suggested Jacob, softly. "It would only take a couple to allow the bomber strike to be successful."

Amanda was silent for a long moment. She knew she could contact Fleet Admiral Streth and ask permission, but he had made her an admiral. This was her decision to make. "I will take it under advisement, Jacob. Second Fleet will micro-jump to just outside of the planet's gravity well and begin the attack. Good luck."

"Same to you, Amanda," Admiral Adler replied.

-

Fleet Commodore Resmunt sent off his final reports to the High Council. Due to the communication lag, he knew he would not hear back a reply before his forces were engaged by the humans. By the time a reply arrived, he strongly suspected this battle would be over.

On the main sensor screen, he watched impassively as a large part of the threatening red icons vanished, only to reappear scant moments later just outside the gravity well of the planet. "Here they come," he spoke as he gazed around the busy War Room. Every Hocklyn was at their post ready for the coming battle. "May honor be with us!"

First Leader Ganth felt his excitement rising. At last, the humans were here, and he could find new honor in combat. He couldn't wait to send his first missile and energy beams against the approaching enemy.

-

Second Fleet entered the gravity well and accelerated toward their target. Light cruisers and destroyers screened the heavier ships. The crews were at their battle stations, knowing this was the first real battle of Operation First Strike. The other bases had been pushovers because the human fleets had possessed superior numbers and firepower; however, that was not the case here.

"Battle carriers are launching their fighters," Commander Evans reported as numerous green icons began leaving the two battle carriers to take up a defensive position around the fleet.

"Hocklyns are launching fighters also," Lieutenant Stalls reported as his sensor screen bloomed with numerous small red threat icons leaving the Hocklyn ships. "We're going to be badly outnumbered."

"All ships launch fighters," Amanda ordered over her ship-to-ship com. She knew that would help to even the odds. She also knew her capital ships had nothing to fear from the Hocklyn fighters. They only carried small missiles that could be a threat to a destroyer but nothing larger.

"Third Fleet has jumped in," Lieutenant Stalls added as more friendly green icons appeared just behind Second Fleet.

"Twenty minutes until we reach optimum firing range," Lieutenant Mason from Tactical reported.

"All ships, concentrate on destroying the Hocklyn defensive weapons, particularly their short range railguns on their war cruisers and escort ships," Amanda ordered in a calm voice. "Our primary objective is not to destroy their ships but to partially disable them so we can send in an Anlon bomber strike."

"I just hope this works," Colonel Bryson the executive officer spoke with worry showing on his face. "I still think we should go for their dreadnoughts."

"It will, Colonel," promised Amanda, glancing over at the colonel. "We will just get the dreadnoughts a little later."

Amanda leaned back in her chair and watched the tactical display. In many ways, she wished Richard were here to tell her she was making the right decisions. But it also gave her comfort knowing that he was safely back at New Tellus in a monstrous asteroid that was heavily armed and armored. At least one of them was safe.

Second Fleet continued to close, and soon the first missiles began to be fired. Bright flashes of light roared across the Hocklyn formation, smashing into their shields.

"Power beams are to target their dreadnoughts," Amanda finally ordered as the WarStorm shuddered as increasing Hocklyn ordnance began to strike her shields. The first few rounds of weapons fire had been aimed at reducing the Hocklyn's defensive fire, but the heavy weapons fire from their dreadnoughts was proving to be too deadly. Already, a number of her warships were reporting heavy battle damage. She knew there were ten dreadnoughts she had to destroy if her attack had any chance of success.

It was at that moment the weapons on the Hocklyn shipyard began to fire. Her face blanched when she saw one of her destroyers and a light cruiser flare up and vanish from the tactical display.

"Heavy weapons fire from the shipyard," Colonel Bryson reported as he studied the data. "They have heavy missiles, railguns, and energy beams."

"Damn!" Commander Davidson swore as she looked over at the admiral. "This Hocklyn War Leader or Commodore isn't taking any chances."

In space, missiles, railgun rounds, laser beams, energy weapons, and power beams crisscrossed between the two opposing fleets. They struck energy shields, causing them to waver and occasionally fail.

When that occurred, a well placed heavy missile or nuke would either cause serious damage or destroy the helpless ship. Space was full of exploding ordnance as interceptor missiles and railgun defense systems intercepted incoming weapons. On the heavier human ships, defensive laser batteries blasted apart missile after missile before they struck the shields. Even as intense as the defensive fire was, numerous missiles and railgun rounds were still getting through.

"Status!" barked Amanda as she saw two more of her light cruisers vanish from the tactical display. She wasn't hurting the Hocklyns enough; she couldn't afford to trade them ship for ship. The weapons on that heavily armed shipyard were tearing her ships apart.

"We've taken out two of their war cruisers and eight of their escort cruisers and damaged others, but not enough for a bomber strike," Commander Evans reported. "That damn shipyard has too many heavy weapons on it, and we can't seem to be able to penetrate its energy screen."

"Then we must eliminate it," Amanda said with fire in her voice as she watched another of her destroyers blaze up and vanish on the tactical display. "I am authorizing a Devastator Three missile launch. Load two of them into the missile tubes and target the Hocklyn shipyard." She then switched over to Third Fleet's frequency. "Jacob, I am authorizing a Devastator Three strike against the shipyard, we're taking too much damage. I want your bomber strike ready to go."

"Give me two minutes, Amanda," Jacob replied as he passed on the orders to move his fleet up closer to Second Fleet and to launch the bombing strike. "What about the Hocklyn fighters, how many remain?"

"Quite a few," answered Amanda, looking at the tactical display that showed the massive fighter dogfight going on around the fleet. "They're rather occupied at the moment."

"Just tell me when, Amanda, we will be ready."

-

Fleet Commodore Resmunt grinned in satisfaction as another human warship fell to the massed fire of his fleets and the shipyard. He knew now it had been the correct decision to fall back to it. With its heavy weapons and powerful energy shield, it was almost impervious to damage from the attacking humans. As long as he held his ships close to the shipyard, he could destroy this arrogant human fleet.

"We are winning," First Leader Ganth spoke with pride as another human destroyer fell to the weapons fire from the flagship. More honor for the crew.

"We will continue to let them come to us," instructed Resmunt, knowing if he could continue this heavy bombardment of the human fleet, he might very well manage to hold his base.

-

The two minutes were up, and Amanda nodded at Commander Evans. "Initiate Devastator Three launch. All ships to fire upon the shipyard after Devastator strike."

Commander Evans stepped over to the tactical officer and, inserting her command key, gave the order.

Two metal hatches slid open on the WarStorm and, for a moment, there was the barest flicker of movement. Due to the sublight drive and inertial dampening systems on the Devastator Three missiles, they literally left the tubes and arrived at their target simultaneously. The first missile struck the Hocklyn shipyard's powerful energy shield, knocking a hole in it. The second missile shot through and detonated against the heavily armored hull.

-

Fleet Commodore Resmunt gazed in shock as two powerful explosions struck the shipyard. The first was a brilliant light and EMP pulse that shut down the weapons of many of the ships closest to the explosion. The second explosion was against the heavily armored hull of the shipyard itself. He looked up at the War Room's main viewscreen and, when it cleared from interference, saw that a good quarter of the shipyard was a mangled wreck and its energy shield was down. Human weapons were raining down upon it and in less than a minute, what had taken months to construct was a tangled, giant mass of expanding gases and burning and glowing metal.

"What was that?" First Leader Ganth oathed as he saw the shipyard destroyed. "What type of weapon did they use?"

"I don't know," Resmunt responded as he played the image over and over in his mind. "It some type of new weapon we've never seen before."

Ganth gazed at the commodore, knowing that the battle had now turned. "Honor is before us," he intoned respectfully.

"Honor is before us," Commodore Resmunt replied as he saw hundreds of small new threat icons leaving the human carrier ships. He watched the new threat with worry. What were the humans up to now?

"Jacob, hit the Hocklyn ships that were closest to the shipyard. Some of them may not have had time to restore their systems after the EMP blast," ordered Amanda, breathing a sigh of relief now that the shipyard was gone. The entire Hocklyn fleet seemed to be in disarray from the sudden destruction, now was the time to strike them. "Send me your light cruisers; I want them going in with Second Fleet."

"On their way," Jacob replied. "Go get them, Amanda!"

-

Commodore Resmunt felt his flagship shake violently as another human nuclear missile struck the energy shield. Looking over at the damage display console, he saw more lights turn a glaring red. Already, the War Room was full of smoke and the ventilation system was struggling to keep it clear.

"Fleet status," he demanded in a hard voice, knowing he was now losing the battle.

The small ships had been armed with numerous nuclear tipped missiles, which had ravaged his fleet, causing damage beyond belief. Ships that had been too close to the shipyard had been easy targets and had died before their shields could be restored. Other ships that had been damaged previously had been the target of multiple missile strikes, which had created holes in their energy shields, allowing missiles to strike the hulls of the ships. In just a few minutes, over forty Hocklyn ships had been destroyed.

"Only four dreadnoughts remain, as well as seven war cruisers and sixteen escort cruisers," Ganth snarled in anger as he saw victory slipping away.

"Pull us back to War Leader Osbith's fleets, perhaps by adding his ships to ours and using the defensive satellites we can still hold the humans at bay," ordered Resmunt, feeling desperate.

He also knew it would buy some valuable time to repair his damaged ships. He doubted if the humans would follow his ships into the satellites, at least not at first. He also knew he had his heavily armed fleet base to fall back to if necessary. If he had to fight these humans hand to hand down on the surface then that's what he would do.

-

"They're falling back," breathed Commander Evans in relief as the bomber strike swept past them on its way back to the carriers. "We hurt them badly with the Devastator Three strike and the bombers."

"Follow them in, but stay just out of range of those defensive satellites," Amanda ordered. "We need to initiate some ship repairs across the fleet before we tackle that defensive satellite grid."

Amanda leaned back in her chair and allowed a moment of calm to overtake her. The adrenaline from the battle was still pumping through her veins. She closed her eyes briefly and waited for her breathing to return to normal. Opening them, she saw the main viewscreen was focused on the planet below. It was a beautiful Tellus type planet with massive oceans and small landmasses.

Amanda stood up and walked over to the communications console where Lieutenant Trask was sitting. "Contact Admiral Streth and inform him that phase one of the battle is complete. The Hocklyn shipyard has been destroyed and their fleet driven beneath their defensive grid."

Angela nodded and sent the transmission. She had been frightened the entire battle, particularly when she had felt the WarStorm shudder violently from nuclear missiles detonating against her powerful shields.

"We survived that," a friendly voice spoke over her mini-com.

Looking over, she saw Benjamin smiling at her from his sensor console.

"But what comes next?"

"We take the planet," Lieutenant Ashton commented from Navigation. "It's going to be our main base for this sector."

All eyes turned toward the viewscreen as they wondered what was still ahead of them. Operation First Strike was well on its way to success, and only the planet below and the remaining Hocklyn forces in orbit stood in its way.

Chapter Sixteen

Resmunt gazed uneasily at the main viewscreen from the War Room in his flagship, the Liberator. For the past five days, he had watched with growing trepidation as the humans used their small bomber and fighter craft to degrade his satellites defenses. Looking at the main sensor screen, he saw that the latest attack was even now withdrawing. His dwindling fighter forces had met each human attack wave until now none remained.

"They have eliminated seventy-two percent of the satellites," First Leader Ganth reported in frustration. They had only managed to destroy twelve of the small enemy craft out of the sixty that had just finished making their attack run on the remaining satellites. The larger human war craft were staying outside the satellites weapons range as well as the defending warships floating beneath.

"They will be coming for us soon," Resmunt spoke as he looked at the numerous red threat icons hovering just out of reach of his ship's weapons. He had accepted that he would soon be finding honor above this distant and lonely planet so far away from their home worlds.

"How are the repairs coming on our remaining ships?"

"Repairs have been completed," replied Ganth, looking over a data screen. "The ships are not at 100 percent. Some of the damage can only be repaired at a shipyard, but they are all combat ready and capable of bringing honor to their crews."

Resmunt let out a deep breath as his eyes returned to another viewscreen showing the blue white world beneath them. He had sent most of his Protectors down to the surface to defend the fleet base. With the defenses he had put around it, he knew the humans would suffer heavily when they tried to take it.

It was also frustrating that the AI FTL transmitter was still offline. His technicians were not sure what was wrong with the device, other than it had failed when the new human weapons had destroyed the orbiting shipyard. The humans were still jamming normal FTL communication so there was no way he could get a message out to the High Council to report on his current situation.

He looked back at the sensor screen and the green icons that represented what remained of his fleet. War Leader Osbith's fleets were still intact with four dreadnoughts, eight war cruisers, and twenty-four escort cruisers.

Resmunt's own survivors from his battle at the shipyard were four dreadnoughts, seven war cruisers and sixteen escort cruisers. He had sixty-three ships to oppose a fleet of over one hundred. In normal times, he would have been quite pleased with a fleet of this size. But this situation was anything but normal for the Hocklyns. He also knew that the humans had other fleets that were probably in the process of still attacking the empire. Without FTL communication, he could not be sure what was occurring in his sector, but he had a suspicion that other worlds were still falling, particularly the slave worlds.

Jeremy watched from the Command Center of the Avenger as they jumped into their next target system. From the information his stealth scouts had brought back, this star system contained a heavily industrialized planet that the Hocklyns had conquered.

"Jump complete," Colonel Malen reported from where she was standing in front of the holographic plotting table.

"Sensors coming online," Kevin added as his screens gradually began clearing of static.

"All systems online and functioning normally," Ariel reported from his side where she normally was after a jump.

The main sensor screen quickly cleared, and the other twenty-seven ships of his command appeared as friendly green icons.

"All ships are in their projected positions," Ariel responded with a pleased tone.

Jeremy had been letting her direct all of the fleet's hyperjumps so as to better coordinate their emergence into a fleet formation ready for combat. She was immensely satisfied that all the ships were within just a few kilometers of where they were supposed to be. She would get with Kelsey later and refine the jump equations slightly. Perhaps if they carried them out to twelve decimal places the jumps would be dead on.

Ariel placed her hands on her shapely hips and looked around the busy Command Center. She had modified her body only slightly after Clarissa had commented about the extra attention she had gotten from just enlarging her breasts by one cup size. Ariel had stayed away from that, knowing that it might aggravate Katie, but she had made her hips look a little more feminine with more curves in the right places.

"Battle carrier Cygnus is launching a CAP," Malen reported as half a dozen small green icons left the massive carrier. "All ships reporting normal status."

"What do we have?" Jeremy asked as his gaze turned toward the holographic tactical display. This would be the first system his fleet had jumped into that possessed an inhabited planet.

On the display, a solar system appeared. There were ten planets, with two in the liquid water zone. The outer three were large, Jupiter-sized gas giants. There were also several small asteroid fields as well as numerous moons.

"The fourth planet is the inhabited one," Colonel Malen informed Jeremy as she studied the data now coming in over the long-range sensors. "It has high power emissions and all the evidence of a highly advanced industrial civilization."

"Hocklyn forces?" asked Jeremy, raising his eyebrows. He knew that there should be at least one or two escort cruisers in the system.

"There is a large space station in orbit," Malen continued. "A number of ships are docked to it, but from this range our sensors can't make them out."

"Ariel?" asked Jeremy, glancing over at the AI.

"Two escort cruisers and six freighters are docked to the station," Ariel reported as she ran the scans from the station through her computer systems. "There are also another ten freighters moving in the system. I am detecting several mining operations in the small asteroid fields as well as upon several of the smaller moons."

"This race still has their full tech base," commented Malen, narrowing her eyes. "I thought the Hocklyns normally eliminate a big part of that?"

"They do," Ariel replied as she continued to study the data. "This bears some investigation into the aliens that inhabit this system."

"What are your orders, Admiral?" Colonel Malen asked, turning to face Jeremy. "It's obvious from the two Hocklyn escort cruisers docked to the space station that this is a Hocklyn controlled system."

"Then we take this planet from the Hocklyns and make it ours," Jeremy spoke, his eyes narrowing. "Perhaps the inhabitants of this world will become allies. Helm, take us in system at sixty percent sublight."

Katie watched Ariel with a slight smile tugging at the edge of her lips. Both Clarissa and Ariel had taken advantage of their new holographic figures to enhance them, Ariel's not near as drastic as

Clarissa's, but both were now definitely more feminine. Both AIs seemed to be interacting with the crew better, and everyone had easily accepted their holographic images. It was exciting seeing the two AIs continue to grow.

"Still watching, Ariel," Angela spoke over their private mini-com. "I think these holograms you made for Clarissa and Ariel are working out great."

"They both seem to like them," Katie agreed as her green eyes played over the screens on her large console, making sure all of the ship's computer systems were running at peak efficiency. "I'm just glad I was able to do it."

"It makes speaking to Ariel a lot easier and more personal," Angela added as she listened to a message coming in over her com system. It was just a status report from the Monarch cruiser Reprisal.

"Ariel has been my friend from the time I was fifteen," responded Katie, recalling that first frightening meeting in Admiral Strong's office where Ariel had revealed herself. "She always will be."

Ariel smiled to herself. She had been listening discreetly as always. It made her feel good inside hearing what Katie had just said. Sometimes, she was glad she could feel human emotions, and this was one of them.

-

It took nearly four hours for Jeremy's fleet to maneuver into an attack position. He could have micro-jumped his fleet in closer, but he preferred this slower approach which gave his fleet more time to scan the system.

"I'm impressed," Colonel Malen finally said as she finished studying the latest scans. "They have a highly developed mining operation in two of the small asteroid fields as well as on six of the system's smaller moons. There is also some type of construction being done on one of the larger moons of the eighth planet, which is a gas giant."

"I'm also not detecting any signs of recent nuclear detonations on the planet's surface," Ariel reported with a hint of surprise in her voice. "I would estimate this planet was conquered no more than twenty to thirty years ago, and their population has not been reduced. Population density on the planet indicates a thriving population of over one point two billion."

"Strange," commented Jeremy, quizzically. "The Hocklyns normally reduce their slave populations to a more controllable size. Why didn't they do that here?"

"Only one way to find out," responded Colonel Malen, gazing at the tactical screen. "We go down and ask."

Jeremy nodded, that was exactly what he intended to do. But first, the two Hocklyn escort cruisers needed to be eliminated. The two cruisers had already undocked from the station and were making their way out toward the edge of the planet's gravity well. Jeremy did not intend to allow them to escape if that was their intention. He pressed a button, which changed his mini-com in his right ear to ship-to-ship. "Commander Adams, Commander Kendrick, I want you to take out those two escort cruisers. Do it from long-range as they may attempt to ram."

"Yes, Admiral," Commander Adams of the Monarch cruiser Reprisal replied. "Consider them dead!"

Jeremy watched as the two Monarch cruisers accelerated away from the fleet and entered the edge of the planet's gravity well. As soon as they were within weapons range, they opened up on the two Hocklyn escort cruisers. It was clearly one sided as the two powerful Monarch cruisers pounded the two Hocklyn ships with heavy weapons fire. It ended suddenly with both Hocklyn ships being destroyed as their self-destructs finally finished what the cruisers had started.

"I have a communications from the space station," Angela suddenly spoke with stunned surprise in her voice. "I have an individual calling himself Grayseth that represents the race that inhabits this planet. He is requesting a meeting with whoever is in command of our fleet."

"It could be a trap, Admiral," Colonel Malen cautioned, her eyes narrowing in concern. "They may be trying to lure us in. There are probably still some live Hocklyn Protectors on board that station."

Jeremy leaned back in his command chair, arching his eyebrows and thought for a long moment. The entire situation with this planet was unusual. If he could form some type of alliance with these people, a highly advanced and industrialized planet in this sector could be a godsend.

"We will take part of the fleet in," decided Jeremy, folding his arms across his chest. "The Cygnus, Nemesis, Reprisal, and Vendetta will go with us. The rest of the fleet will stay just outside of the planet's gravity well. Flipping his mini-com back to ship-to-ship, he contacted

Commander Susan Marks on the battle carrier Retribution. "Susan, I'm taking part of the fleet in to the space station, and you will be in charge until I get back."

"Yes, Admiral," Commander Marks replied and then she added, "Just be careful, we know nothing about these people."

"I will," Jeremy promised. He turned his gaze to the main viewscreen, which showed the orbiting space station. The large station was nearly two kilometers across. He wondered what type of people were on the station and inhabited the planet below.

Jeremy took his time moving his ships in closer to the space station. The Cygnus had two full squadrons of Talon fighters flying CAP as well as an additional squadron of Anlon bombers fully armed with nuclear tipped Shrike missiles. Jeremy felt that with the two heavy strike cruisers and the two Monarch cruisers he had very little to fear from the space station. Close scans had already indicated that it was unarmed.

"Atmosphere on the planet reads near Tellus normal," commented Ariel, walking over to Jeremy from where she had been standing next to Katie. "You should be able to breathe their atmosphere without any problems."

"They are asking us to come to a stop and send a party over in a shuttle," Angela reported as another message came over her com system. "They are guaranteeing the safety of anyone on the shuttle. They also say you can come armed if it will make you feel safer. They just want to talk about this current situation."

"Tell them I will be coming and bringing an armed escort," replied Jeremy, thoughtfully. "Also, inform them if there are any problems or signs of aggression we will destroy the space station."

Jeremy turned back to Ariel. "Are we picking up any transmissions from the surface that might indicate what type of species we are dealing with?" Jeremy knew better than to expect these aliens to be human. They might be similar, but they would not be Tellus or Earth norm humans.

"Actually, we do," Ariel said with a mischievous smile. "I will put a view of what our hosts look like up on the main viewscreen.

Instantly, on the screen a large figure appeared. Jeremy heard Kelsey and Angela gasp with surprise as their eyes widened at what they were seeing.

"Bear!" Kevin uttered aloud his eyes widening in recognition. "They look like great big brown bears!"

"Not quite," Ariel responded with a smile at Kevin's reaction. "If you look at them closer you will see that instead of having paws they have actual hands that are only slightly covered with hair. They are also of slimmer stature and walk upright. Their faces are flatter and their nostrils aren't so flared out."

Jeremy nodded as he gazed at the screen. From what he could see, the alien on the screen was a medium brown in color and didn't seem very threatening. This would definitely be an interesting species to meet.

"Prepare a shuttle," he ordered. "I want a squad of marines to come along also. Then, turning to Kevin, he asked, "Want to go meet the bears?""

Kevin hesitated only for a moment and then nodded. "Sure! Why not? It will give me a story to tell my children someday."

Thirty minutes later, Jeremy breathed a sigh of relief as the shuttle entered the flight bay of the space station without any problems. It passed through an atmospheric force field, which ensured that the flight bay stayed pressurized. Looking out the cockpit window, he saw a group of the aliens waiting. They were quite impressive. Jeremy guessed that they must stand a good two meters in height and would tower over most humans. They were powerfully built and of various shades of brown.

Already at a disadvantage, thought Jeremy, knowing he would have to look up at their hosts.

Stepping back to the shuttle's hatch, he watched it slide open. Sergeant McElroy indicated for him to wait as he took four of his marines down the ramp and set up in a defensive position. Looking around, he turned and motioned for Jeremy and Kevin to come down.

Reaching the bottom of the ramp, Jeremy and Kevin waited as the six aliens shuffled over to them.

"Greetings, slayers of the evil ones!" the largest bear spoke in a booming voice. "I am Grayseth, leader of this space station."

Jeremy noticed that the bear was using one of the Hocklyn's universal translators. Jeremy and Kevin had one also, except theirs were much smaller and rested on a small chain around their necks.

"Greetings, Grayseth," Jeremy replied in a strong and steady voice. "I am Admiral Strong of the Human Federation of Worlds." Then turning to Kevin, he added. "This is Lieutenant Kevin Walters who will be assisting me during our talks."

Grayseth nodded, acknowledging Kevin. "I have set up a room for us to meet in. There will be food and refreshments, though I am not sure what might be safe for you to sample."

Jeremy nodded. "I am sure it will be fine. What happened to the Hocklyn Protectors? There should have been a few still on this station even after their escort cruisers left."

"We killed them," Grayseth responded in a deadly serious tone. "We have waited for years for revenge over what they did to our colony worlds. They did not last long when it was time for them to die!"

"Perhaps we should speak of this in the room you have prepared," Jeremy suggested. Turning back to sergeant McElroy, he added, "I will only be taking two marines; I don't think we're going to have any problems here."

Sergeant McElroy nodded, and pointing to two of his marines, he instructed them to go with the admiral.

Jeremy was surprised to see how modern the space station was, it wasn't far behind what the Federation built. It was clean, the corridors were spacious, and occasionally crewmembers passed by them with a nod of acknowledgment as they went about their duties.

They passed through several levels, taking wide stairwells to each. It was becoming obvious to Jeremy that the bear-like aliens did not like cramped spaces. They entered a large room and Jeremy saw that a table had been set up with large chairs around it. Another table was set up with a number of different types of fruit and drink mixtures, including a large pitcher of ice water.

The bears took their seats and Jeremy and Kevin decided to stand so as not to look too ridiculous sitting in the oversized chairs.

Grayseth looked over at Jeremy and asked the obvious questions. "Who are you, and why have you come to our solar system?"

"We come from the Human Federation of Worlds, which is quite some distance from here," Jeremy began. He knew he had to be careful and not reveal too much information. "We came to fight the Hocklyns who are a threat to the entire galaxy."

"A worthy task," Grayseth rumbled in his deep voice. "A task that may be very difficult, considering they already control much of the galaxy."

"It will be difficult," admitted Jeremy, nodding his head slowly. "We have already freed much of this sector of space, destroying many of their ships."

"They will return in even greater numbers," warned one of the other bear-like aliens. "I fear no matter what you or we do, we will not be able to escape their grasp."

"You mentioned earlier that they destroyed your colonies?" asked Jeremy, raising his eyebrow. "What happened?"

"It was twenty years ago," responded Grayseth, his large dark eyes taking on a heavy look. "We had set up two flourishing colonies in nearby star systems. Nearly two million of our people had been transported to them when the Hocklyns came. They nuked both of the new colony planets and then came here. They gave us an ultimatum, either work for them or they would do to our home world what they had done to our colonies. We chose to work for them to protect our families."

"We cannot guarantee your continued safety," Jeremy finally spoke. He wanted these bears to know what might be ahead. "We expect the Hocklyns to counterattack heavily in an attempt to drive us back to our own sector of space."

Kevin's mini-com sounded and Ariel's voice came over it. Only Kevin could hear the AI. "Kevin, I am detecting numerous shuttle and freighter launches from all over the planet. You need to warn Jeremy. I'm not sure what is happening. Colonel Malen has put the Avenger and the other ships at Condition One as a precaution."

Kevin looked over at Grayseth and decided he needed to interrupt Jeremy. "Why are you launching so many shuttles and ships from the surface of your planet?"

Grayseth and several others looked surprised and uneasy at the question. Then Grayseth straightened his powerful shoulders and answered. "For years, we have prepared secretly for the day when we could take our planet back. Those shuttles and freighters contain weapons for this station as well as a full planetary defensive grid of satellites."

Kevin nodded and quickly passed on the information to Ariel. He didn't want Colonel Malen shooting down the shuttles and ships. It would not be a good start toward establishing relations with the bears.

"You risk much," cautioned Jeremy, knowing the Hocklyns might very well nuke the planet for such behavior.

"The Hocklyns took much away from us," one of the others responded in a grave voice. "We have built new cities deep beneath the surface of our planet. Even if the evil ones nuke the surface, many of us will survive. We will no longer be slaves to the Hocklyns!"

"They refused to let us explore our culture and heritage," Grayseth explained with a pained look in his eyes. "They limited the number of children our families were allowed. There was no more research or advancement allowed in any of the sciences. They were gradually destroying our culture. Without our culture, we are nothing."

Jeremy nodded in understanding; he could well see their point. The Hocklyns had forced the bears into living an intolerable existence, now they were ready to end it no matter what the risk.

"We will do everything we can do to help," promised Jeremy, knowing he would have to have a long talk with Admiral Streth. "I will contact our Fleet Admiral and see what resources can be allocated to help defend your planet."

Grayseth nodded pleased with the offer of assistance. "You sound like an honorable people, Admiral Strong. I will be speaking to our planet leaders and strongly suggest an alliance. Together we can grow strong and resist the evil ones."

Jeremy nodded; he was beginning to like Grayseth.

-

Several hours later, they were back over on the Avenger. The talks had gone smoothly, with the bears offering to give the humans a full list of their capabilities and weapon's technology.

"We need to help them," Kevin spoke as they walked back toward the Command Center. "This is a good race, the type of race that would be well received by the people of the Federation."

"I agree," Jeremy replied. He was already thinking about what could be done. "If we can fortify this planet so the Hocklyns can't retake it, it would make a great forward base for this sector in our war effort. They are highly developed with a solid tech base; it could make a huge difference."

"They seemed very friendly and open minded," added Kevin, recalling the recent meeting.

Jeremy nodded. "You just like bears," he said with a friendly smile. "I'll bet when you were a kid you had a teddy bear."

Kevin turned red and slowly nodded. "Yeah, I did."

-

Admiral Streth, Admiral Sheen, Admiral Adler, and Colonel Grissom were meeting on the StarStrike in a small conference room, which gave them a semblance of privacy. A large viewscreen was on one wall and a large picture of the original StarStrike was on the other. Hedon gazed over at the picture longingly; he really missed his old flagship. He wondered what his brother Taylor would think of his new one if he were still around. With a heavy sigh, Hedon brought his thoughts back to the present situation.

"I am dispatching two of the Fleet repair ships to the world of the Careth," Hedon commented as he reached a decision. "With their manufacturing and repair capability they can help the bears arm their space station."

"Intelligent bears," spoke Jacob, grinning. "Who knows what else is out there?"

"Admiral Strong says they are quite likable," Amanda added as she read more of the report.

"They have a high technological base and their planet is industrialized," Jacob continued. "For some reason the Hocklyns only destroyed their two colony planets and left their home world intact."

"Unusual for them," Hedon spoke through pursed lips, wondering why that was. "I don't know how long we have before the Hocklyns can launch a successful counterattack against us. The bears are willing to join us in our war against the Hocklyns. They are already in the process of arming their space station and putting a planetary defensive grid in place."

"What can we do to help them?" Amanda asked, her blue eyes looking at the other two. "Do we give them our advanced weapons? At some point in time, the Hocklyns are going to return, what will happen to the Carethians then?"

"I don't think we dare give them our most advanced weapons," Hedon breathed with a heavy sigh. "We can help them with railguns and possibly some missiles, but the Devastator Threes and Power Beams are restricted."

"Lasers," suggested Jacob, thoughtfully. "The Hocklyns are already familiar with them, and if we make them powerful enough they could be a formidable weapon for these bears to use."

"We could expand their space station and help to armor it," Amanda added. "Our Federation armor will be much more resistant to weapons fire than anything they have."

"We also have a freighter full of laser satellites," Colonel Grissom said as she looked over a list of what was in the supply fleet. "I would suggest turning them over to the bears for immediate defense of their world. It might not be a lot, but it would be a good start. I also agree that lasers and possibly even our Klave heavy missiles would be a good option. Neither contains technology that the Hocklyns are not already aware of."

Hedon nodded his head in agreement. "This might be a chance for us to build a forward base deep in Hocklyn territory. It could cause them a lot of problems in the future. I think this is an opportunity we dare not pass on. I will instruct Admiral Strong that he is to stay in the bear's system while we send more ships to support him. I will contact Admiral Kimmel and discuss just what can be done with what we have in the supply fleet to help the bears. Colonel Grissom, I would like you to accompany the ships we are assigning to this and see from a security standpoint what we can do. For now, this mission has the utmost priority."

"I think it's the right decision, Admiral," Amanda replied pleased with how this meeting was going. "We need more allies, and from what Commander Strong has indicated, these bears could be ferocious in battle."

Hedon leaned forward, placing his arms upon the conference table. "Unfortunately, we still have one issue that needs to be taken care of, and that is the planet below us." Looking over at Jacob, he asked, "How much longer will it take you to destroy the rest of the Hocklyn's defensive satellites?"

"I believe four more attack waves of our bombers and fighters and they will pretty much be eliminated."

Hedon looked over at Amanda with a nod. "Plan on a full scale attack in thirty-six hours. We have repaired all of our battle damage and its time to finish this." Hedon would also be notifying General Abercrombie that his marines would be needed shortly to capture the spaceport down below intact.

-

Later, Amanda entered her quarters on the WarStorm and sat down in a comfortable chair, which seemed to mold itself to her body. She let out a deep sigh of relief and looked over at the far wall, gazing reflectively at a picture of her parents in front of their beach house back on Aquaria on Krall Island. Idly, she wondered if the house was still there, or if time had removed all traces of it. Perhaps someday she would get to find out.

She needed to get some rest. First thing in the morning, she needed to plan her attack against the remaining Hocklyn ships. Her fleet had taken more damage than expected in the first battle, this time it would be different.

Raymond L. Weil

Chapter Seventeen

Admiral Johnson was meeting with Admiral Telleck, Admiral Freeman, Governor Malleck, President Kincaid, and Admiral Andrews in the command asteroid in orbit around New Tellus.

"This asteroid is impressive," President Kincaid commented as they used a transit shuttle to travel deep within the asteroid. "The entire surface seems to be covered with weapons." This was the first time he had actually been inside the massive asteroid command base.

"It is," Admiral Johnson agreed. "It took us years using lasers and blasting to form the asteroid into a sphere, then decades more to add all the tunnels and power stations. We placed every weapon we could think of on the surface. This asteroid has a crew of over twenty thousand."

"Including numerous power beam installations," added Admiral Andrews, smugly. "If the Hocklyns attack this installation they will be destroyed. We have eight asteroid fortresses orbiting New Tellus and all are heavily armed and shielded."

President Kincaid looked over at Richard and Admiral Johnson with a questioning look in his eyes. "What about an AI ship? Can you destroy one of those?"

The admirals looked uneasily at one another as the transit shuttle began to slow down, indicating they were nearing their destination.

"We don't know," Admiral Johnson finally admitted. "This asteroid is equipped with both regular Devastator missiles and the newest version of the Devastator Three. With the heavy weapons fire the asteroid is capable of and coupled with a missile attack, we believe we can knock their shields down. We won't know for sure until we try."

After another few minutes, they reached the heart of the asteroid, which contain the massive Command Center. They stepped out onto a small balcony and looked out over the room, which oversaw the eight massive asteroid fortresses.

"Impressive," President Kincaid spoke, his eyes sweeping over everything. The Command Center contained dozens of large computer consoles and hundreds of massive viewscreens. "Can you command the entire defense of the system from here?"

"Just the defenses around New Tellus," responded Admiral Andrews, looking over at the Federation president. "The planetary defense grid and the asteroid fortresses can be controlled from this Command Center. It allows us increased coordination in allocating our defensive assets."

"There are also two thousand Talon fighters and sixteen hundred Anlon bombers based on the asteroids," Admiral Johnson added with a pleased smile. The fortresses were a very stable fighter and bomber launching platform.

"Where will the actual command of the battle be run from if the Hocklyns attack?" President Kincaid asked. He had assumed it would be from the asteroid command fortress.

"From New Tellus Station," Admiral Johnson answered as she turned to face the president. "We have equipped it with the heaviest possible energy shield we could design, and it is massively armored. It has the firepower of twenty battle cruisers. Also, being inside the gravity well of New Tellus helps. We can coordinate the movement of our fleet units to repel or destroy any Hocklyn attack."

Indicating for the group to follow him, Richard led them into an immaculate briefing room that held a long conference table as well as numerous viewscreens on the wall. The room had been specifically set up for this meeting. The screens showed views of the space around New Tellus as well as on New Tellus itself.

President Kincaid stood gazing at the viewscreens for several moments, amazed at all the information that was available to Admiral Andrews. "I must say, I'm impressed."

"I was amazed also when I first saw the asteroid fortresses," Richard confessed. "This is something we never even considered back in the old Federation."

They all took a seat and then President Kincaid looked around the assembled group. "Admiral Johnson, what is the latest status of Operation First Strike?"

Karla took a deep breath. Reaching forward, she activated a computer screen, which displayed the most recent messages from Admiral Streth. "They have successfully destroyed five of the six forward fleet bases of the Hocklyns and eight secondary bases. They have also freed twelve of the known slave worlds in that sector."

"What about losses?" President Kincaid pressed. "How badly have we been hurt?"

Karla called up the latest numbers. "Two battle cruisers, eight Monarch cruisers, eighteen light cruisers, and thirty-two destroyers."

President Kincaid turned pale at hearing the losses. "Will those losses endanger Operation First Strike?"

"No," Karla responded with a shake of her head. "Most of the losses can be made up from the reserves in the supply fleet."

"Admiral Streth still needs to take out their main base though," added Admiral Telleck, looking over at the president.

"They have already substantially damaged or destroyed the fleet that was protecting it," continued Karla, nodding her head in agreement. "For the last several days they have been using their fighters and bombers to take out the planet's defensive grid." Looking down at her screen once more, she added, "Admiral Sheen and Admiral Adler should be launching their final attack on the remaining Hocklyn ships and the base within just a few more hours. Then, for all intents and purposes, that entire sector of space will be under our control."

"Which brings up the main reason for this meeting," President Kincaid spoke, his eyes taking on a serious look. "What are we to do about this new alien race that Admiral Strong has contacted? They have formally sent a request to join our alliance and are asking for military aid to defend their planet."

"I say we help them," Governor Malleck spoke up for the first time. He had been patiently listening to the conversation waiting for this to be brought up. "According to Admiral Strong, this is a very advanced race with a high technological level. If we can set up a base in Hocklyn space to use against them in the future, then I say we do it."

"This race of bears is over seven hundred light years from the Federation," President Kincaid reminded the governor. "It will take our supply ships twelve to fourteen days just to reach them. Is that even practical?"

"It is," replied Admiral Freeman, joining the conversation. "We have a new class of military supply ship that can make the trip in ten days. The ships are the size of a light cruiser, with energy shields and defensive weapons. They would be ideal for this type of operation."

"I would make another suggestion," Governor Malleck added. He was about to propose something that Admiral Telleck had suggested. "We know that our defensive satellites have a flaw because they are too easy to destroy."

"Yes, we've had to make some adjustments in our fleet deployment to ensure their survivability," answered Admiral Johnson, unhappily. She had been forced to assign more destroyers to picket duty by moving them into all of the defensive satellites grids over the planets to prevent the satellites from being picked off so easily.

"We have a new development that will solve that," spoke Governor Malleck, indicating for Admiral Telleck to explain their proposal.

Admiral Telleck stood up and walking over to a holographic image projector inserted a computer chip into it. Instantly, an image of a small metallic sphere appeared floating directly above the display table.

"This is our new satellite defensive battle station," he announced as the others gazed on. "It is 120 meters in diameter and fully self contained. It has an energy shield, defensive lasers, railguns, and interceptor missiles with a standard crew of forty."

"By placing them either in or just above our defensive satellites we can increase the grid's survivability. Not only that, but these installations can also serve as Command Centers for their section of the defensive grid."

Admiral Johnson stood up and walked over to gaze closely at the image. "How soon would these be ready to deploy?" She could already see their usefulness. She had suggested something similar, but the construction time to implement such a program wasn't there yet.

"Immediately," Admiral Telleck said with a smile. "We have already started construction inside several of the construction bays in Ceres. We have twenty-four of these ready to deploy and would like to send all of them to help in the defense of these new aliens."

"What?" President Kincaid stammered in surprise. He didn't know if it was wise to deploy such a new weapon system to these aliens. "How would you get them there? I don't believe we have anything that can handle something of that size and jump into hyperspace."

"It's quite simple actually," responded Admiral Telleck, looking around the small group. "We attach them to our battle carriers and take them to these aliens. We estimate we can attach four to each one."

"Won't that be dangerous on the ship's systems?" asked Admiral Freeman, thinking about the energy that would be needed to open a spatial vortex to take something so large into hyperspace.

"Not if we make the jumps shorter," Admiral Telleck responded. "We believe we can make it to the bear's planet in sixteen days."

"Where will the battle carriers come from?" Admiral Johnson asked. She hated sending any more ships in Admiral Streth's direction. It was all she could do to ensure she had sufficient forces to defend the Federation with in case of a Hocklyn attack.

"We will furnish the battle carriers," Governor Malleck answered as his eyes swept over the group. "In this instance, we agree with Admiral Strong and Admiral Streth's assessment that helping these aliens is in the best interest of the Federation."

What Governor Malleck didn't mention was that the world of the Bears might someday be used to launch an offensive to retake the old Federation home worlds. It was primarily for this reason they were willing to allocate the resources. The Federation survivors were determined to drive the Hocklyns from their old worlds and return home someday.

After more discussion, the group finally agreed on Admiral Telleck and Governor Malleck's plan. It was also decided to send additional laser satellites as well as missile platforms to the bears.

-

Later, Admiral Johnson was alone with Admiral Andrews in a small office just off to the side of the Command Center. The two would be traveling to New Tellus later to eat with the president and for further discussions.

"Do you know why Governor Malleck and Admiral Telleck are so determined to help these new aliens?" Karla asked as she sat down.

"Yes, they want to retake our home worlds someday," replied Richard as he poured both of them a glass of cold water. Handing one glass to Admiral Johnson, he sat down behind his desk and leaned back, still holding his glass in his right hand. "It could be a good plan; at the worst it will cause the Hocklyns a lot of problems having a heavily armed and defended hostile planet in their own backyard."

Karla was silent for a moment and noticed the picture of Admiral Sheen on Richard's desk. "Miss your wife, don't you?"

"Of course," Richard replied with a heavy sigh. "She's gone off to fight a battle and I worry. What husband wouldn't?"

"She's very resourceful," responded Karla, wondering if she were in the same position if she could have allowed her husband to go off like that. Sometimes she regretted choosing the military over a family. Perhaps someday she would change her mind.

"She always has been," Richard replied with a smile, recalling their trip to the resort on New Tellus. "She always manages to come up with something to surprise me."

Admiral Johnson nodded and then said. "I'm going to go ahead and give the approval to send tactical nukes to the bears to be used on the Shrike missiles the missile platforms will be equipped with."

Richard nodded his approval at this decision. "I wonder what effect Operation First Strike is having on the Hocklyn Empire? By now, word of our assault has to have spread. Even their High Council must know what's happening."

Karla nodded and then, with a serious and worried frown, she added, "The AIs will learn of our attack shortly. That's what concerns me the most."

-

High Leader Nartel gazed in growing worry at the reports coming in from Fleet Commodore Resmunt's sector. The humans were sweeping through the sector, destroying base after base and freeing numerous slave worlds. It would take years to repair the harm to the empire the humans were causing.

"This is all High Leader Ankler's fault!" Councilor Ruthan roared as he studied the reports before him in disbelief. "His ancestor should have destroyed these humans centuries ago."

"But he didn't," responded High Councilor Jarles, standing up to be heard. "The two AI ships will arrive in Resmunt's sector shortly and destroy the human war fleets. In the mean time, we have two operations that need to be organized."

"Prepare a large fleet to meet the five AI ships two months hence and gather another large fleet to pacify the area the humans are freeing," spoke High Leader Nartel, knowing what Jarles was referring to.

"How large a fleet?" asked High Councilor Berken, rising to his feet. "Our fleets are scattered throughout the galaxy, expanding the empire. It will take months to assemble a fleet the size the AIs are demanding."

"Not necessarily," responded High Leader Nartel, striding over to a large viewscreen, which depicted Hocklyn controlled space. He had already spoken to several Fleet Commodores and War Leaders about what could be done to free up the necessary ships. He made several adjustments and the three sectors around Resmunt's sector of space flashed up.

"If we strip all the support bases in these three sectors and stop their expansion of the empire, we can pull sufficient ships to satisfy the AIs."

"How many?" demanded Ruthan, doubtfully. The AIs frightened him by what they could do to the empire. "We dare not infuriate the AIs anymore than they already are."

"Sixteen Dreadnoughts, forty war cruisers, and eighty-six escort cruisers," High Leader Nartel responded in a steady voice. "We can have them at the rendezvous point in two months."

"That still may not be enough to satisfy the AIs," High Councilor Berken responded dubiously as he studied the numbers. "We can't take the risk of anything going wrong."

High Leader Nartel paused for a long moment as he thought about his only other option. Several of the more experienced Fleet Commodores had recommended it instead of the one he had just proposed. "We have the main fleet base at Kenward Seven that could be stripped and all of its forces sent to Resmunt's sector."

"Kenward Seven," echoed Ruthan, frowning heavily. It was one of the main fleet bases that protected the heart of the empire from attack. Granted, an attack had never occurred until now. "How many ships?"

"Twenty additional dreadnoughts, sixty war cruisers and one hundred and thirty escort cruisers," High Leader Nartel responded. "These forces, along with the others, should be able to easily subdue and destroy these human worlds."

"There will be five AI ships with them," High Leader Berken added with a nod of his head as he considered the suggestion. "We should suffer few losses once the AIs destroy the majority of the human ships. Our forces will complete the mopping up of stray warships that might have escaped the AIs and then destroy the human worlds."

"Then we send the fleet from Kenward Seven as well?" High Leader Nartel asked, his cold eyes meeting those of the rest of the council.

The council voted unanimously to do so with the stipulation that the Fleet Commodore in charge of the fleet ensure that not a single human escape!

-

Later, High Leader Nartel was in his new office high above the Council Chambers gazing out of the open window at the distant streets below. The streets were crowded, even here at the center of government of the empire.

Once this crisis with the humans was over, he had a new rule he needed the High Council to pass; it would not be a popular one and would meet considerable resistance. This was something that High Leader Ankler should have enacted years ago. The rule was designed to deal with the Hocklyn overpopulation. For the next two generations, childbirths would be limited to one per couple and then moved to two, permanently. To violate the rule would have a serious impact on one's honor.

Nartel also knew he would probably need the military to enforce it as many Hocklyns preferred large families. He didn't know how the general public would feel upon seeing armed Hocklyn Protectors marching across their worlds and habitats ensuring the new regulation was followed. Nartel suspected that the Hocklyn race was in for some very hard times, but it would be necessary to preserve their empire and to continue to live under the rule of their masters, the AIs.

-

Second Leader Jaseth was breathing hard as he warily watched his opponent. This was his third honor duel in the past three days. Since his father had been killed by the AIs for his failure as High Leader, the challenges had begun.

Taking a deep breath, he stepped slowly to his right and feinted with his knife, drawing his opponent in. Flipping the knife to his left hand, he slashed downward, feeling the knife encounter skin and cutting deeply into his opponent's leg.

"Honor cut," called out the duel master. He raised his right hand, indicating the match was over.

Jaseth's opponent just glared at him without acknowledgment and turning, left without a word.

"It's time to go, Second Leader," War Leader Versith of the dreadnought Viden spoke, his eyes gazing intently at Jaseth. "You can do no more here. Your personal honor has been redeemed by your actions in these duels."

Jaseth nodded in agreement as he stepped to the side of the honor duel arena and drank a large amount of cold water. He stood there for a moment, feeling the aches and pains from fighting three duels. He had a number of unhealed wounds that were still seeping blood. "Honor has come my way, now it is time to return to my duties."

"We will treat your wounds on the ship," Versith commented as they left the dueling arena. "How is the rest of your family?"

Jaseth stopped and looked over at the War Leader, who was also a close family friend. "My mother is still in the Mirrin habitat. Fortunately, we were left with enough to keep our home and the area immediately around it, but very little else."

"It was Councilors Ruthan and Nartel," Versith muttered in a raspy voice. "They have always wanted to depose your father as High Leader."

"The AI took care of that," spoke Jaseth, letting anger appear in his voice.

"We cannot blame the AIs," Versith cautioned the young Second Leader. "There are times when we must pay for past mistakes. This was one of them. What about your brother, Hangeth?"

"He will be staying with my mother for now," spoke Jaseth, noticing for the first time how blood soaked his side was. "Now let us return to the ship. I have much to learn from you."

"Yes," Versith responded, his large dark eyes gazing upon the younger Hocklyn. "Someday you will be a great War Leader and will bring much honor to our people."

"Perhaps," Jaseth replied as they started walking again. "I just hope the humans are still around. It is because of them my family has fallen into disgrace. My honor will not be satisfied until I see the last one of them die!"

-

Jeremy was meeting with Grayseth aboard the Fleet repair ship Osborn. He had taken the bear on a quick tour of the ship, explaining to him what its capabilities were.

"You offer us much," Grayseth spoke as the two entered a small conference room that had been set up for the occasion.

"We will be allies," Jeremy said as he poured Grayseth a large cup of ice-cold water. He poured a smaller one for himself. "The Hocklyns are our mutual enemy, and I believe my government will fully agree to give you all the assistance we can."

"You have already furnished us with much," Grayseth replied as he sat down in the large, comfortable chair that had been provided. "Already, work has begun on the space station and the new defensive grid is being put into place. The evil ones will not like what they find here when they return."

"Speaking of the defensive grid, one of the supply ships that arrived today has sixty of our new laser defense satellites on board," Jeremy said with a smile. "I have been instructed to turn them over to you for the defense of your planet."

"Laser satellites," Grayseth spoke in a pleased voice. "We have talked of such, but the power requirements have always been beyond our reach."

"That too will not be a problem," Jeremy continued. "I have also been authorized to furnish some of our Type Two fusion reactors for use on the space station to be used as its primary power source."

Grayseth nodded graciously. "Your race is truly powerful and has much knowledge. We have many things to learn from one another. Let us always be friends and hunt together."

"Always be friends and hunt together," Jeremy replied. He had already decided he would do everything in his power to protect the bears. Now he just needed to figure out how he was going to do it.

-

Several hours later, Jeremy was eating a relaxing meal in the officer's mess with his friends. Ariel was even sitting at the table, listening.

"I love these bear people," Kevin was saying with a gleam in his eyes. "They are so friendly and polite."

"It's their culture of respect for others," Jeremy explained. Grayseth and he had discussed this in great detail over the last few days. "It is one of the things that was being eroded by the Hocklyn occupation. I also wouldn't consider the bears to be harmless. Do you know that there were forty Hocklyn Protectors on the space station and another six hundred on the planet when we attacked the two escort cruisers? They all died within minutes of each other in hand-to-hand combat with the bears."

Kevin nodded as he considered what Jeremy had just said. The bears didn't look that dangerous.

"They're Carethians," Angela put in, looking at the others. "We need to quit calling them bears."

"I don't think they mind," Kelsey said as she used her knife to cut a slice of roast beef that was on her plate. "I think they were quite pleased to learn we have several primitive species of bears living on Earth."

"So," Katie said, her green eyes glinting mischievously. "What's this about a teddy bear you used to sleep with, Kevin?"

Kevin looked accusingly at Jeremy. "I can't believe you told her that."

"It wasn't me," Jeremy pleaded hastily, his eyes widening. "I would never do that to you."

"It was me," Ariel confessed not understanding the problem. "From what I have learned many young children sleep with stuffed animals. I am sure you did also, Katie."

Katie was silent as she recalled some of her favorite stuffed toys, then she turned back to Kevin. "So did this teddy bear have a name?"

Kelsey shook her head as she listened to the two. It was nice for them to be able to get together and act like friends occasionally. The five of them, actually six counting Ariel, had a special friendship and bond that nothing would ever be able to break.

"Admiral Strong, report to the Command Center!" suddenly blared out of the ship's com system. At the same time, the ship's Condition One warning lights and klaxons began going off.

"What's going on?" exclaimed Kevin, standing up and looking down unhappily at the hamburger and fries that were still lying uneaten on his plate.

"I don't know," Jeremy responded as he got up and turned to exit the mess hall. "But I don't think it's going to be good or Colonel Malen wouldn't have taken us to Condition One so quickly."

"It's the AIs," Ariel suddenly announced as she accessed what was occurring in the Command Center. "One of our stealth scouts has detected two AI ships in a nearby star system."

The five paused and looked at each other with growing concern, feeling a sudden cold chill. It had been hoped it would be several months yet before the AIs showed up; evidently, that was not going to be the case. This could endanger the success of Operation First Strike as well as the bears.

A few minutes later, all five hurried into the Command Center and took their places, relieving the junior officers that were in charge.

"What do we have?" Jeremy demanded as he sat down at the center command console and looking over at Colonel Malen.

"One of our stealth scouts detected two AI ships in this system," the colonel said, indicating a star that began blinking in red on the tactical display. "That's sixteen light years from our current position."

"I wonder where they're going?" Kevin uttered in a quiet voice that Jeremy still managed to hear.

"They're going to their main base in this sector," Jeremy commented as he studied the tactical display. "They know that's where our primary fleets are located and they can do the most damage. Angela, send an urgent message to Admiral Streth that we have made contact with two AI ships and that they may be inbound toward his location."

"What are we going to do?" Colonel Malen asked, her eyes focusing on Jeremy. "We could also be their target."

"We know that AI ships can jump into the gravity well of a planet unharmed," Ariel informed Jeremy, recalling what had happened in the old Human Federation of Worlds. She felt uneasy knowing the AIs had suddenly arrived; it was one of her deepest and darkest fears. She wasn't sure she could defeat an AI ship, even with the new Devastator Three missiles and power beams. "The gravity well won't protect us."

"I have a priority message from the stealth scout," Angela spoke suddenly as she focused intently on the message. "They managed to get close enough to take a course reading when the AIs jumped. They are ninety percent certain the AI's target is Admiral Streth."

Jeremy leaned back and thought deeply. All of the fleets combined only had fourteen of the new modern strike cruisers that had been specifically designed to take on an AI ship. Of the fourteen, Jeremy had four of them. He also had the only one equipped with an AI. Jeremy looked over at Ariel for a long moment before reaching a decision. "Kelsey, plot an emergency jump to Admiral Streth's location. Colonel Malen, contact the Nemesis; I want both ships out of the planet's gravity well ASAP. Once we're out of the gravity well we will be making an emergency jump to First Fleet's location."

"What are you doing, Jeremy?" Ariel asked in a worried and concerned voice over their private mini-com. Jeremy noticed that Katie, Angela, Kevin, and Kelsey were all looking at him.

"We're going to attack those two AI ships," Jeremy responded in a determined voice. "Ariel, I want you working on special tactics using all of our weapons, including the Devastator Three missiles."

"Yes, Jeremy," Ariel replied in a meek voice. For once, she was not excited about going into combat.

Chapter Eighteen

Admiral Sheen was just preparing to launch her attack on the remaining Hocklyn fleet when she received an emergency hail from Admiral Streth on the StarStrike.

"Bad news, Amanda," Hedon reported over the mini-com. "We just received word from Admiral Strong that two AI ships are inbound."

"AIs," repeated Amanda, feeling a cold chill of fear run down her back. She knew full well what the AIs had done to the fleets of her home worlds. There were not supposed to be any AI ships nearby. "Where the hell did they come from?"

"Unknown," replied Hedon, trying not to sound concerned. "But one of Admiral Strong's stealth scouts stumbled across them and managed to take a reading when they made their hyperjumps."

"How much time do we have?" asked Amanda, knowing that it probably wasn't much. An FTL message didn't travel much faster than a ship did in hyperspace. The two AI ships could arrive at any moment.

"Probably less than twenty minutes," Hedon responded.

"Not enough time for us to escape the gravity well," commented Amanda, knowing the AI ships would have her and Admiral Adler's fleets at a disadvantage. She carefully weighed her options and none of them were good. "What are we going to do?"

"I'm ordering Admiral Kimmel to jump the entire supply fleet to Admiral Strong's coordinates except for his two strike cruisers, which I am temporarily reassigning to First Fleet. I am also sending all of my lighter units along as well. They will be ineffective against an AI ship and there's no point putting all of them in jeopardy."

"What about us?" Amanda asked as she looked at the tactical display. They were less than ten minutes out from engagement range of the remaining Hocklyn fleet units. If they turned now, they could reach the edge of the planet's gravity well in a little less than twenty. She had four strike cruisers, which could be used against the AIs.

"Pull back and set up in a defensive formation," Hedon ordered. "We know the AIs can jump inside a planet's gravity well, so be prepared for that. Use of Devastator Three missiles is authorized. Good luck, Amanda."

"Yes, Admiral," responded Amanda, letting out a deep breath. She turned around and looked over at Commander Evans. "You heard?"

"Yes," Evans replied her eyes narrowing. "The AIs are coming; how should we position the fleet?"

Amanda examined the tactical display for a few seconds before responding. "We will hold our position here. We have four strike cruisers and six battle cruisers that are equipped with Devastator Three missiles. Admiral Adler has two additional battle cruisers, which gives us twelve ships to use against the AIs. We will put six groups of two around the periphery of the two fleets and wait. There is nothing else we can do."

"Do you think we can destroy two AI ships?" Commander Evans asked, her eyes showing worry. "I watched some of the videos from the first war, and they were unstoppable."

"I know," admitted Amanda, recalling those terrifying videos that showed the AI ships blasting apart Federation warships with impunity. "But we have better and more powerful weapons this time around."

Commander Evans nodded. She looked around the Command Center and took note of the sudden quiet. The crew knew that surviving the AIs would be highly questionable. Evans could feel her own heart beating faster, and she took several long, deep breaths. She had a ship to command and a job to do. She would let Admiral Sheen worry about the AIs.

-

Admiral Streth watched as the supply fleet and his lighter units jumped out. At least if they made it to Admiral Strong they would still have a fighting chance of survival if the AIs could not be defeated by First Fleet. Hedon let out a heavy sigh. First Strike had been succeeding beyond his wildest expectations and now this. He had not been expecting to face any AI ships for a long while. He realized that they must have been on patrol somewhere in the local area of space. It had always been a possibility as they had no intelligence about just how many AI ships were being used to watch their steadily expanding empire.

On the main viewscreen, Hedon watched as multiple blue-white spatial vortexes opened and then collapsed as a major portion of his fleet fled the expected battle with the AIs. When the last vortex faded away, the StarStrike was setting just outside of the gravity well of the Hocklyn's fleet base with six battle cruisers, two battle carriers, and four strike cruisers. He had kept back the two battle carriers and had ordered their Anlon bombers set up for a Shrike nuclear assault against the AI ships. If he could put enough nukes, including Devastator Threes, against their shields, surely they would fail.

"No sign of the AIs yet," Clarissa reported as she walked over to Admiral Streth and Colonel Trist. "I estimate we have six to twelve minutes before they make an appearance."

"I guess we find out just how well the Federation built this battleship," Colonel Trist commented as he glanced over at one of the tactical displays.

"It's the only thing we have that is comparable in size to one of the AI ships," Hedon spoke. He was glad the Federation had built the StarStrike. It had the screens and the punishing power to stand toe to toe with an AI ship, at least for a while.

He had never fought an AI ship before, though he had seen numerous videos of what had happened when the AIs attacked the original Human Federation of Worlds. They had been unstoppable as they annihilated the human fleet to make way for the Hocklyn nuclear bombardment of the Federation worlds. Over fourteen billion people had died after the fleet was destroyed.

Clarissa listened for a moment more and then secretly transmitted a message to a point several light years away. Admiral Stillson needed to be apprised of what was about to occur. The Ceres Fleet might be needed.

-

Admiral Stillson looked stone faced at the message that had just been received from Clarissa aboard the StarStrike.

"Two AI ships," his second in command Colonel Jarvington muttered, worriedly. "Do we go in?"

"I don't think we have much of a choice," Stillson answered as he thought about the ships he had at his disposal. "We will take all eight battle cruisers, one of the carriers, and the four strike cruisers. That will give us the heavy hitting power we need as well as the Devastator Three missiles. Clarissa reported that Admiral Streth has tasked both of his remaining carriers for Shrike nuclear strikes. I suggest we do the same for the carrier that will be going with us. Prepare the fleet for a jump as soon as Clarissa reports the arrival of the AIs."

"Yes, Admiral," Colonel Jarvington replied. He quickly turned and began implementing the admiral's orders.

Admiral Stillson sat at his command console thinking about the coming battle. They were about to learn very quickly if they could destroy an AI ship.

Fleet Commodore Resmunt looked with confusion at his main sensor screen. The humans had been about to attack, then stopped, and were now scrambling to get into a defensive formation. Something was going on.

"Many of the human ships in the outer system have jumped out," First Leader Ganth reported. "Only their heavy units remain."

Fleet Commodore Resmunt studied the sensor screen for a long moment trying to figure out what the humans were up to. They acted as if they were expecting an attack, but from whom? Then, with dawning realization, Resmunt understood what was happening.

"It's the AIs," hissed Resmunt, turning his dark eyes to face Ganth. "They are coming." He realized this might be his best opportunity to strike the humans. If he waited until the AIs arrived and then launched an assault against the human fleet, surely the AIs would recognize his efforts and give him honor. "Honor awaits," Resmunt spoke in his rasping voice. "We attack when the AIs attack."

"Honor is before us," First Leader Ganth agreed. "I will ready the fleet."

Two massive white spatial vortexes suddenly formed on the outskirts of the system, and out stormed two massive spheres. The AIs ships were 1,500 meters in diameter and wrapped in a powerful energy shield. The surface of the spheres were covered with weapon emplacements and other constructions. The powerful AI ships had been built with only one purpose in mind, to destroy any civilization that could ever be a threat to the AIs and their plans for the galaxy. The two AI ships slowly orientated themselves and began scanning the system. Power systems were brought online and the weapon systems powered up.

"They're here," reported Clarissa, trying to keep her voice calm.

She was frightened as the two AI ships were obviously a very serious threat to the StarStrike. If the StarStrike were destroyed, Clarissa would die with it and her long life would be over. She wondered if she should send a farewell message to Ariel. She did however send a message to Admiral Stillson notifying him of the arrival of the two AI ships.

"All ships stand by," Admiral Streth ordered over his mini-com, which was set for ship-to-ship communications. "We have to let them jump in, and then we will launch our attack."

Hedon took a long breath. He knew that no matter what he did he was about to lose some ships. He just hoped he could stop these two AI ships with the forces he had. If not, then once his fleet was destroyed the AIs would move in and destroy Admiral Sheen and Admiral Adler's fleets. Both were trapped in the gravity well of the planet.

"All ships have Devastator and Devastator Threes loaded in their tubes," Colonel Trist reported as he gazed at the tactical display, which depicted the two AI ships. The display next to it showed the thirteen green icons of the remaining First Fleet ships. From two of the icons, numerous smaller icons began appearing.

"Commander Layton and Commander Bixby are launching their bombers," Captain Reynolds reported from sensors.

Hedon nodded. It was essential that he hit the two AI ships as hard as he could as soon as they jumped into attack range. Hedon watched with calm nerves as the Command Center around him buzzed with increased activity.

"Vortexes forming in front of the AIs," Clarissa informed them as she walked over to stand next to the admiral. She was growing more frightened every minute. For the first time since she had become the AI on the new StarStrike, she wondered if she would survive the next few hours.

"AIs have entered the vortexes," she reported. She had barely spoken the word when two white spatial vortexes formed less than twenty thousand kilometers from the StarStrike, and the AI ships were here!

"All ships form up on the StarStrike, formation Delta Bravo Two," Hedon ordered swiftly. "Helm, close with the AIs at max combat speed. Tactical, prepare to fire upon my command."

The StarStrike and her twelve protectors charged forward. Weapons were readied and targeting systems locked on. The last admiral from the former Federation of worlds was attacking his enemy; the very enemy that had destroyed the worlds he had loved so much.

-

Admiral Sheen's face turned white when she saw how close the AIs had jumped to Admiral Streth's fleet. Even as she watched, she saw the admiral adjust his fleet formation and move rapidly to engage.

"Hocklyn fleet is breaking orbit and moving to intercept us," Commander Evans spoke suddenly as she saw the sudden movement from the remaining Hocklyn ships.

"Of course," Amanda replied with a sigh. "They see that their masters have arrived. It's the opportune time for them to attack us. They figure once the AIs have destroyed Admiral Streth's fleet they will jump in and begin to destroy ours."

"The Hocklyns will be in weapons range in four minutes," Lieutenant Stalls reported from his sensor console.

"Let's go get them," ordered Amanda, knowing she had no other choice. There was nothing she could do to help First Fleet and Admiral Streth.

She quickly contacted Admiral Adler and told him to prepare his Anlon bombers for a nuclear strike. They needed to finish off this Hocklyn fleet before the AIs could come to its rescue. She looked back wearily one last time at the main tactical display, which showed the StarStrike and the rest of First Fleet charging toward the two deadly AI ships. "Go get them, admiral," she said softly.

-

"Stand by to fire," Hedon ordered as they reached optimum weapons range. Before he could say another word, two massive energy beams leaped out from the AI warships, striking the battle cruiser Deliverance and the strike cruiser Hunter. Massive explosions covered the main viewscreen.

"Deliverance is down," Captain Reynolds reported, his face turning ashen at the sudden destruction of the powerful warship.

"The Hunter is reporting her shields held, but just barely," Colonel Trist added. "They can't take another hit like that!"

"All weapons, fire!" ordered Hedon, grimly.

From the remaining twelve warships energy beams, Devastator missiles and Devastator Three missiles launched. Space lit up with energy beams and missile trails.

The two AI ship's screens suddenly blossomed with a multitude of brilliant flashes as the nuclear ordnance and the energy beams struck. The screens wavered in a couple of areas, but refused to go down.

"AI ship's shields are holding," Colonel Trist oathed worriedly, looking over at the admiral. "Even the Devastator Threes are failing to get through."

"Anlon bombers going in," Captain Reynolds reported. On his sensor screen, 280 bombers each equipped with four nuclear tipped Shrike missiles hurtled determinedly toward the two AI ships.

"AIs are opening up some type of defensive fire," Tactical reported.

Hedon watched in horror one of the large tactical displays showing the bombers. In multitudes, they were being wiped out.

"Bombers launching their missiles," Colonel Trist reported, his throat suddenly feeling very dry. "They are attempting to withdraw."

In seconds, more nuclear explosions covered the powerful energy screens of the two AI ships. The screens were glowing a steady white from all the energy that was being released. Another AI energy beam leaped out and the strike cruiser Hunter vanished from the screen as her weakened shields were penetrated and her hull exposed. The energy beam shot completely through the ship, cutting her into.

The StarStrike suddenly shuddered violently, and the lights in the Command Center appreciably dimmed.

"We got hit by an energy beam," reported Clarissa, nervously. "Shields are holding at eighty percent."

Hedon nodded and took a deep breath. "Continue to close," he ordered unwaveringly He would ram one of the AI ships if he had to. His eyes focused intently on the main viewscreen, which now showed the two AIs. He was determined that these two AI ships would not be leaving this system, no matter what the cost.

-

Fleet Commodore Resmunt allowed himself to smile, knowing that victory was once more within easy reach. The remaining ships in his fleet were nearly within engagement range of the humans. He had sixty-three warships still under his command, including twenty-three capital ships. It was time to make the humans pay for what they had done to his shipyard and fleet a few days earlier.

"Honor is before us," he spoke as he prepared to give the word to fire on the two human fleets before him.

"Honor is before us," First Leader Ganth agreed. Ganth was feeing jubilant. He reached down and ran his right hand over the jeweled hilt of his knife. With the AIs here, victory was assured. Much honor would soon be coming their way.

Admiral Stillson had jumped his fleet into the outer periphery of the system. Long-range scans already showed Admiral Streth was already heavily engaged with the two AIs ships.

"Status of First Fleet!" he demanded as he gave the order for the navigation officer to plot a jump as close to Admiral Streth's position as possible.

"First Fleet has already lost three battle cruisers and one strike cruiser, other ships are damaged, and the StarStrike is under heavy attack," Colonel Jarvington replied in a stunned voice as he studied the scans that were coming in. "I think Admiral Streth intends to ram one of the AI ships!"

"Prepare to jump," ordered Stillson, worriedly. He couldn't let Admiral Streth sacrifice himself. The drive core could still handle a short micro-jump, and he intended to jump directly into the fire. "All weapons to target the AI ships as soon as systems come online. Use of Devastator and Devastator Three missiles is authorized."

"Jump plotted," the navigation officer reported.

"Jump!" Stillson ordered. He had to save Admiral Streth! The Federation couldn't afford to lose its greatest hero.

Hedon felt the StarStrike take another heavy blow. Smoke was drifting across the Command Center as the ship's systems were pushed to their limits.

"Shields are at forty percent," reported Clarissa, worriedly. She was hurriedly shifting power feeds and cutting out what she considered non-essential systems all in an attempt to strengthen the weakening energy shield.

"Battle cruiser Matterhorn is reporting heavy damage, their shields are down," Colonel Trist spoke, his face drained of color

"New contacts!" yelled Captain Reynolds. "Its Admiral Stillson from New Tellus, he's brought eight battle cruisers, four strike cruisers, and one carrier!"

"He's turning to engage the AIs," Trist reported as he gazed with relief at one of the tactical screens. It should take some of the pressure off the StarStrike, at least enough to allow them to recharge the ship's shields.

Clarissa felt the attack ease. With the advent of the new ships, the AIs were shifting their fire. She could sense the energy screen on the StarStrike quickly strengthening. She would live a little bit longer.

Trist looked over at Admiral Streth. "Where the hell did Admiral Stillson come from?"

"I don't know," Hedon replied confused by the appearance of the new ships. "But we need to press the attack. This might be our only chance to destroy these two AI ships." Hedon quickly contacted Admiral Stillson, directing him to focus all of his firepower on just one of the AI ships.

-

Amanda felt the WarStorm shudder again as a Hocklyn missile managed to penetrate the energy screen and detonate against the hull. Space between her fleet and the Hocklyns was full of exploding ordnance and missile trails.

Both sides were losing ships, but Second and Third Fleet had nearly a two to one advantage in ships and were rapidly wearing the Hocklyn fleet down. If the AIs didn't intervene, this battle would be over in another few minutes. She tapped her mini-com, putting her in contact with Admiral Adler. "Jacob, launch your bomber strike, its time we finished this."

"On their way, Amanda," Admiral Adler replied.

As Amanda watched, the bombers launched. Turning her attention back to one of the sensor screens, she saw that more Federation ships had arrived to help First Fleet. She also noticed that nearly half the First Fleet icons were missing. Forcing herself to focus, she turned back to the battle at hand. She needed to deal with the Hocklyns first and then worry about the AIs. She also didn't have the time to figure out where the additional Federation ships had come from.

-

Resmunt snarled in anger as another of his war cruisers vanished from his sensors as its self-destructs went off. The battle was not going well. He had hoped the human fleets would be distracted by the arrival of the AIs. He now realized he should have waited longer to launch his attack. The AIs were still engaged with the human fleets outside of the planet's gravity well. He had thought by now it would have been over and they would have jumped in to engage the human fleets he was attacking.

"Move us in closer to the human fleet," he ordered, wanting his weapons to be more effective. "If honor is to come our way today, we will meet it with the deaths of these humans."

"As you order," First Leader Ganth responded as he moved to comply. Even as ordered the fleet to move closer, he saw another human destroyer vanish from the sensor screens as the Liberator's energy beams annihilated it. With each destroyed human ship, more honor came to the crew of the flagship.

-

Amanda winced as the destroyer Albright disappeared in a blaze of light on the main viewscreen. Too many of her ships were dying. Looking over at the damage control console, she saw a number of red lights burning steadily. The WarStorm was still taking damage.

"Shifting fire to Hocklyn war cruiser," Lieutenant Mason at tactical reported.

From the WarStorm, its twin power beams leaped out, striking the war cruiser's energy screen. The screen wavered, and then it was struck by a combination of Klave high explosive missiles and four ten-kiloton Devastators. The shield collapsed in several areas and railgun rounds as well as missiles struck the armored hull. Massive gashes were torn in the hull and explosive decompression ran through the outer edges of the Hocklyn ship. Then a Devastator missile penetrated and blasted the Hocklyn war cruiser into burning wreckage. Seconds later, its self-destructs went off and the ship was gone.

"War cruiser is down," Lieutenant Stalls reported in a satisfied voice.

"Bomber strike is going in now," Commander Evans informed Admiral Sheen as the Anlon bombers swept past the WarStorm in their squadron formations.

Amanda nodded. The bomber strike would deeply hurt the Hocklyns and then her warships could move in and finish them off. This part of the battle was almost over, but the battle against the two AI ships might just be beginning. Her eyes shifted over to one of the sensor screens, and with relief she saw that the StarStrike was still fighting.

-

The Avenger and Nemesis exited two blue-white spatial vortexes just 20 million kilometers from the AI ships.

"Status," barked Jeremy as the systems quickly came back online and the main tactical display lit up.

"Both AI ships are still intact," reported Ariel, uneasily. "First Fleet has lost nearly seventy percent of their heavy units. There is also a Ceres Fleet under command of Admiral Stillson in the system attempting to take on the AIs. According to Clarissa, Admiral Stillson has lost thirty percent of his relief fleet in the last four minutes. She also reports that their weapons, including the Devastator Threes, have been ineffective in knocking down the AI's energy shields."

"Suggestions?" Jeremy asked, his face showing deep lines of worry. He knew if they could not destroy these two AI ships then Operation First Strike would be a failure and the AIs would turn immediately and attack the Federation. There had to be a solution!

"In a moment," Ariel responded as she studied the data coming in from the sensors.

She began running numerous attack simulations on the ship's main computer. She was also deeply worried about the StarStrike. Clarissa had just informed her that the ship was suffering heavy damage and that she was afraid Admiral Streth was going to attempt to ram one of the two AI ships. Ariel had never heard fear in Clarissa's voice until now.

"Quickly, Ariel," urged Jeremy, seeing another battle cruiser vanish from the tactical display. "We're losing a lot of ships!"

Angela and Kelsey looked fearfully at the main viewscreen, which Ariel had focused on one of the two AI ships.

"They're destroying First Fleet," Angela cried in anguish, looking over at Kelsey. "What are we going to do?"

"I don't know," Kelsey replied her heart beating rapidly. "We have to find a way to defeat them."

"Give Aerial and Jeremy a chance," Kevin spoke hesitantly over their mini-com. They will come up with something."

Suddenly Ariel froze, and then ran the data one more time in a simulation.

"I have it," she spoke triumphantly a satisfied smile crossing her face. "Give me complete control of the Avenger and the Nemesis and I can destroy the AI ships."

"Are you certain?" Jeremy demanded, his eyes widening. "How?"

"First Fleet and the Ceres Fleet are still using Devastator Threes, and I am detecting a slight weakening of the shield whenever one hits. I intend to place four Devastator Three missiles within twenty meters of each other and detonate them simultaneously. It should knock a brief small hole in the shield where another Devastator can be fired through. My simulations show a ninety percent probability of success."

"What timeline do the missiles have to be detonated in?" asked Jeremy, listening intently to Ariel.

"Within microseconds," Ariel admitted. "That's why either Clarissa or I will have to handle it."

"Do it," Jeremy ordered grim faced as another Ceres strike cruiser vanished from the tactical screen. "Let's go destroy some AIs!"

-

"Admiral, the Avenger and Nemesis just jumped into the system," Colonel Trist reported, his eyes growing even more worried as additional red lights flared up on the damage control console. The StarStrike was starting to take damage again. Already, numerous departments had been ripped open to the deadly vacuum of space. There were also several uncontrolled fires burning further within the ship's hull where AI energy beams had penetrated.

"What!" Admiral Streth roared with deep concern in his eyes. Admiral Strong was essential in the negotiations with the bears. He couldn't be risked in this battle. "Order him to jump out immediately!"

"Hold," Clarissa suddenly spoke her holographic image appearing next to the admiral. "Ariel has figured out a way to destroy the AI ships, Admiral. She has transmitted the information to me. I need full control of the StarStrike and all of her weapons systems. This is something that only Ariel or I can do."

Hedon looked critically over at the AI. He knew he had no other choice. They were losing the battle. "Very well, Clarissa, the ship is yours. If this fails, then I intend to use the StarStrike to ram one of the two AI ships."

Clarissa nodded her understanding, but she had no intention of failing.

-

The Avenger and Nemesis suddenly exited two blue-white spatial vortexes less than ten thousand kilometers away from the two AI ships.

"Target lock on sphere one," Ariel reported as she turned both ships toward the two AIs. "Firing Devastator Threes."

On the outer hulls of the Avenger and Nemesis, four hatches opened on each ship and, after a brief flicker of movement and a slight flash, were still.

"Impact on target one," Ariel reported, her sensors reaching out and tracking the sublight missiles and their twenty-megaton warheads. "Detonation."

Four massive nuclear explosions roared against the energy shield of the designated AI ship, creating a hole less than ten meters across. But that was all Ariel needed. Two of the remaining four Devastator

Three missiles impacted on the side of the shield, but the other two flashed through and two twenty-megaton warheads struck the armored hull of the AI ship. The AI ship was thrown to one side as its armor was ravaged and peeled away by the powerful blasts. The energy shield wavered and then failed completely.

"All weapons, fire!" Jeremy ordered as Ariel drove the two strike cruisers toward their target. More missiles left the launching tubes, both Devastator and Devastator Threes. Underneath their withering fire, the AI ship burned.

-

"They got it!" Colonel Trist yelled excitedly at the top of his voice as the AI ship writhed on the main viewscreen. "The Avenger and Nemesis have done it!

"Take us in, Clarissa," ordered Admiral Streth, knowing now they had a real chance. "Now it's our turn."

Clarissa quickly took over all of the ship's key systems and made ready to fire their last nine Devastator Three missiles. She had additional data from scanning Ariel's attack. Ariel was also speaking to her, offering suggestions.

The hatches slid open, and the missiles launched. She used six missiles to blow a larger hole in the AI's shield, allowing the other three missiles to flash through the twenty-meter wide opening. All three detonated against the hull of the AI warship, causing massive damage, and then secondary explosions began going off, hurling entire sections of the AI ship into space. The shield failed and the remaining First Fleet and Ceres Fleet ships began pouring heavy weapons fire upon the AI. In just a short few moments, it was over, and both AI ships were nothing more than burning husks.

"We got them," Colonel Trist spoke with a big, satisfied smile breaking out on his face. "We just destroyed two AI ships!"

"Thanks to Admiral Strong and Ariel," responded Hedon, forcing his breathing to slow back down. He stood up and walked over to where Colonel Trist was standing next to one of the tactical displays. He then became aware of a strange sound. The entire command crew was standing up, clapping their hands, and slapping each other on the back. He could hear cheering and loud screams of joy over his mini-com. Hedon allowed himself to smile. A lot of good people had just died, but they now knew how to destroy the AIs.

-

Fleet Commodore Resmunt looked on in shock as the humans destroyed the two AI ships with their powerful missiles.

"That's impossible!" First Leader Ganth uttered in a stunned voice as the two AI ships succumbed to the human attack. "The AIs can't be destroyed!"

"Until now," Resmunt replied in a low voice, his large eyes growing wide at what he was seeing. Never in all the history of the empire had an AI ship even been damaged in battle. And now, here, in front of his very eyes, two had just been destroyed!

The enemy's bomber attack was in the process of withdrawing after letting loose numerous nuclear tipped missiles against his fleet. Resmunt had fired a good twenty percent of his available nukes, detonating them in and around the small enemy bombers and destroying many of the missiles as well as hundreds of the small ships. Even so, the attack had been devastating against his remaining ships.

"What do we have left?" he demanded, turning toward First Leader Ganth.

"Four dreadnoughts, including the Liberator and eight war cruisers. All of the escort cruisers are either too damaged to continue or have been destroyed."

"Have all our remaining ships form up on the Liberator and set a course of 776 by 212 axis 31," he ordered.

"That's away from the battle!" protested Ganth. "We can't withdraw, honor is at stake."

"You don't understand," hissed Resmunt, motioning toward a viewscreen that showed one of the now smoldering AI ships. "We must get word back to the empire that the humans know how to destroy an AI ship. That report alone will bring honor to us for revealing this threat to the AIs."

Ganth hesitated and then passed on the order. He knew Fleet Commodore Resmunt was right. The word must be spread that the humans could defeat an AI ship; that information would shake the empire.

–

Amanda watched in frustration as the remaining Hocklyn ships turned and fled from her fleet. "Can we catch them?" she demanded, looking over at Commander Evans.

"No, Admiral," answered Evans, shaking her head. "They are already accelerating and will be at full sublight shortly. We can't get back into effective weapons range soon enough."

Amanda leaned back in her command chair and let out a long breath of disappointment. She then gazed back at the main viewscreen, which showed one of the destroyed AIs ships. She didn't know how, but someway Admiral Streth had managed to figure out a way to destroy the AIs. It was a partial victory at least. She knew now with confidence that Operation First Strike would continue.

-

Fleet Commodore Resmunt had his remaining fleet jump immediately after they cleared the planet's gravity well. The rest of the human ships were too disorganized and damaged by their battle with the two AI ships to prevent him from escaping with the news of what they had done.

"Honor was with us today," First Leader Ganth spoke as the Liberator jumped into the safety of hyperspace.

"Honor was with us indeed," Fleet Commodore Resmunt agreed as he thought about what this would mean to the empire.

The humans had arrived on the scene, and they were much more powerful than any enemy the empire had ever faced before. Resmunt suspected the empire was about to embark on a long and dangerous war with a determined enemy who would not show the Hocklyns any mercy. Resmunt knew the empire's years of dominating slave races and treating them as resources to be used and discarded was about to come back to haunt them. The humans were coming and the empire, as well as the AIs, had better be ready.

Chapter Nineteen

A full week had passed since the two AI ships had been destroyed. Admiral Streth was down on the planet touring the recently captured spaceport with General Abercrombie. Numerous slaves still walked around, not sure what their new status of being free meant exactly.

"Most of these aliens come from nearby star systems that the Hocklyns conquered," explained General Abercrombie as they passed a group that obviously had a feline background. The aliens looked away and continued working.

"Why are they still working?" Hedon asked as he paused and watched a group that were painting a large hanger that contained small Hocklyn shuttles. Already Federation techs were going over them as well as other captured technology.

"They know nothing else," explained Abercrombie, pursing his lips. He was still perplexed at the situation. "We can talk to them with the universal translators, and they understand that they are now free, but many are uncertain if they want to return home. They are afraid if they leave the Hocklyns will return and kill them as well as their families who are still back on their home worlds."

"So what do we do?" asked Hedon, raising an eyebrow. He didn't like the idea of having a slave work force, even if it was a voluntary one. "We can't continue to allow them to work like this."

"They have elected a group of leaders to represent them, one from each of the races that is present here. Some will return home, but many prefer to stay. We will set up some type of wage scale and make sure they have reasonable accommodations. They can continue to operate this spaceport with some supervision from us. I don't know what else we can do."

Hedon nodded. There were no longer any Hocklyn Protectors on the planet. The marines had fought a long pitched battle on the outskirts of the spaceport, killing the last few as they made a charge with knives at the advancing marine lines. The fighting had been ferocious, and numerous marines had lost their life. It had been necessary to use railgun rounds from orbit to take out the numerous weapons emplacements that had surrounded the spaceport. They were fortunate that a destroyer had flown low over the spaceport, drawing fire before the marine assault shuttles had been launched. If not, then the marine casualties would have been much higher.

A few minutes later, they were in the former Fleet Commodore's office. Hedon gazed around at the large map on the wall as well as the furnishings. Admiral Sheen and Admiral Adler were there, waiting.

Hedon walked over and sat down behind the desk. Someone had been thoughtful and brought human-sized chairs into the room. He looked over at Amanda first. "What's the current status of Second Fleet?"

"We lost two battle cruisers, four Monarchs, seven light cruisers and twelve destroyers in the final battle," she reported with a shake of her head. "In return we destroyed fifty-one Hocklyn warships. Our weapons may be better, but their energy beams are still deadly."

"From what intelligence we have been able to gather, we are fairly certain their Fleet Commodore and his flagship were one of the twelve ships that escaped," Jacob commented as he walked over and gazed out the large, reinforced window at the spaceport below. From this height, it provided a grand view of the spaceport and the local countryside. There was still some smoke rising where the Hocklyn weapon emplacements had been destroyed.

"First Fleet suffered heavily as well," Hedon confessed still feeling pain at the horrific losses caused by the two AI ships. "We lost four battle cruisers, one carrier, and three of the four strike cruisers. Admiral Stillson's fleet lost three battle cruisers and two of his strike cruisers."

"A lot of good capital ships," Jacob said with a sad look in his eyes, knowing it had taken a high cost in lives and ships to destroy the two AI ships. "We were just fortunate that Ariel was able to figure out how to destroy the AIs."

"What about the rest of Admiral Stillson's fleet, what is to become of them?" Amanda asked.

There had been a moment during Admiral Streth's battle with the AIs that she thought he was going to ram one of the ships with the StarStrike. She was glad that had been averted. There was no doubt in her mind that if that was the only option he had left to destroy one, he would have done it without hesitation.

"I'm still a little aggravated at Admiral Telleck for sending this fleet in secret to watch over us," Hedon responded with narrowed eyes. He let out a deep sigh and continued. "I understand why, but they still should not have done it. I have assigned him to assist Admiral Strong in the bear's system setting up the planetary defense grid and their space station. For the time being, both fleets are being assigned permanent duty in that system."

"What about the StarStrike?" asked Jacob, turning around to face Hedon. He knew the flagship had taken a lot of damage from the two AI ships.

"Two of the repair ships are working on her," replied Hedon, wincing at the memory of how badly the battleship had been damaged. A less powerful ship would have been destroyed. "It will be another four weeks before she is completely repaired."

Amanda nodded in understanding. Her own ship, the WarStorm, had just finished its repair stint with one of the repair ships. She had also sent a long message to Richard about the battle and how she wished he were here with her. The nights were very lonely as she lay in bed, so far from home.

Standing up, she walked over to the window and gazed out. Then, glancing over at Jacob and Admiral Streth, she asked. "Do you think all of this was worth it?"

"If we want to return home someday, Amanda," Hedon said in a softer voice. "I want to return to Maken."

"You want to rebuild your brother's cabin on the lake," said Amanda, knowing what Hedon was thinking. They had discussed it in the past.

"Yes," he replied. "Someday, I want to free our home worlds."

"A worthy quest," General Abercrombie commented with an understanding nod.

A few moments later, they all standing together looking out the large reinforced window at the world they had liberated. They still had much to do.

-

Jeremy was down on the bear's planet with Kelsey, Kevin, and Katie. Angela had drawn command duty and had not been able to accompany them.

"I can't believe this!" Katie squealed in enjoyment as she walked along the beach, feeling the sand squish up between her toes. "This is just like New Tellus!"

"No fruit drinks though," Kelsey spoke with a relaxed smile. She glanced along the beach, seeing a few other crewmembers out for a stroll or taking a swim in the shallow water near the shore. This area had been restricted by the bears for use by crews of the human fleets.

"The bears have agreed to allow our people to come down on leave," Jeremy explained as he watched a multicolored bird fly low over the ocean. "They will be building some suitable accommodations along this section of beach for us to stay."

"This will be a great place to relax and get away from the war," Kelsey said, nodding her head in excitement at the thought of having this beach available to them.

"The bears are going to be great allies for the Federation," Kevin added as he bent down and picked up a seashell. It was a bright white with a slight pink tinge on the inside, just like what one would find back home.

"I can't believe how much you like these bears," teased Katie, reaching out and taking Kevin's hand. "I wonder if they have parasailing here?"

"Oh, God," Kevin moaned, but he left his hand in Katie's.

"Well, Admiral," Kelsey spoke with a big smile. "What's next on the agenda?"

Jeremy stopped and stood at the water's edge, gazing at the small waves coming toward the shore. He put his arm around Kelsey and pulled her close, it was private enough here that no one would notice. "We get the bears ready for war. I believe someday we will see its end. We just need to have faith in each other and be prepared for what's ahead."

"Sounds like a speech your father would have made," Kelsey said, leaning her head against Jeremy's shoulder.

The four stood quietly, watching the slowly sinking sun. The sunset was gorgeous, and they reveled in their friendship and love for one another.

-

High Leader Nartel stood at the front of the large, ornate conference table of the Hocklyn High Council. His cold gaze swept over the other nine High Councilors.

"It's impossible," High Leader Ruthan stammered in his deep rasping voice. "The humans could not have destroyed two AI ships!"

"It's true," High Councilor Desmonde spoke, his large dark eyes looking worried. "Fleet Commodore Resmunt escaped and has sent back both video and sensor scans of the destruction."

"We must accept what has happened," snapped Nartel, wanting this senseless bickering between the High Councilors to come to an end. "We should be more concerned with what the response from the AIs for this failure will be."

"Surely we won't be punished for this!" responded Ruthan, looking at Nartel in disbelief. "It was the humans that destroyed the two AI ships, not us."

"I fear the AIs may not see it that way," High Councilor Berken interrupted as he stood and looked around the conference table. "They may indeed hold us responsible because it was High Leader Ankler's ancestor who allowed these humans to escape. Sigeth was a Hocklyn, and that will be the only consideration of the AIs."

The meeting continued for quite some time. They were just about to adjourn when the large doors to the conference chamber suddenly swung open, and a senior Protector stepped in. "Four AI ships have just jumped into the system, and they will be in orbit of Calzen shortly. So far, the AIs are refusing to communicate with us. What are your orders?"

High Leader Nartel sat back down, letting out a deep and worried breath. Four AI ships, that wasn't a good sign. "Do nothing," he ordered, his eyes deadly serious. "We must do nothing to offend or cause the AIs to doubt us."

"Yes, High Leader," the senior Protector replied as he turned and left, shutting the massive wooden doors behind him.

"What do they want?" Ruthan asked, his large dark eyes growing wide in fear.

"I don't know, but I suspect we'll soon find out," High Leader Nartel replied as he settled back to wait.

-

The four AI ships swept into orbit above Calzen ignoring all of the Hocklyn warships that were present. The Hocklyn ships moved rapidly to put distance between themselves and the AIs. The space above the Hocklyn home world was thick with orbital shipyards, factories and hundreds of habitats. In between, numerous shuttles, freighters, and warships moved constantly. The space around the four AI ships quickly became empty of ships as they scattered.

The AIs didn't hesitate as they considered their options. Never in their long history had they lost a warship, the Hocklyn leadership needed to be taught a lesson. Their failure to destroy the humans in the first place had led to this situation. Now they had lost two valuable ships as well as the irreplaceable AIs that had been on board!

Targeting systems locked onto the habitats above the planet and then the energy beams flicked out. The habitats were defenseless without armor or any type of energy shielding. The beams cut through, blasting into the interiors causing massive decompression explosions. For ten minutes, the four AI ships ruthlessly eliminated habitat after habitat. The space above Calzen became filled with wreckage. When it was over, forty habitats were gone, and so were twenty million Hocklyn civilians.

—

High Leader Nartel and the rest of the council were outside on a large balcony watching the ruthless destruction above them. Nartel had already given orders to the Fleet Commodores and War Leaders not to resist. Unlike the humans, they had nothing that could damage an AI ship. When the last flash of light faded away and the AIs stopped firing, Nartel turned and led the councilors back inside.

"Why?" Ruthan demanded his eyes flushed red with anger. "Why did they destroy the habitats?"

"Because they can," snarled Nartel, wishing Ruthan would develop a backbone. He wondered how someone so pathetic had ever become a member of the High Council. "They are our masters, and we failed them with the humans. This was an abject lesson to remind us that they will not accept failure in the future."

"What are we to do?" Ruthan asked.

It was at that moment that the large conference room doors opened again, but instead of a senior Protector entering, two AIs appeared. They floated above the floor, their bodies a mixture of smooth and sharp lines. The two AIs stopped near the head of the conference table, the glow from the orb on top of the AI becoming so bright it was difficult to look at.

"You have failed us with the humans," one of the AIs spoke in a commanding voice. "For that failure, you have been punished."

Nartel wondered if he were about to die in the same manner High Leader Ankler had. For a brief moment his hand touched his knife, then it dropped away to hang limply at his side. "What are your orders?"

The AIs were silent for a long moment as if pondering the question. "The attack against the humans will have to be delayed," one spoke. "The ships at Kenward Seven will have to be upgraded with more powerful energy weapons and shields. Once the upgrades are complete, a fleet of our warships will join yours to destroy these human vermin."

Nartel nodded. If the AIs were willing to provide weapons that were more advanced, it would be well worth the delay. "Send us the technical details and we will begin the upgrades immediately."

"It will be done," one of the AIs responded. The two AIs then turned and left the council chambers.

High Leader Nartel looked around at the other councilors. "I will be contacting Fleet Commodore Resmunt shortly and ordering him to take his surviving ships to Kenward Seven to be upgraded."

"Resmunt has already failed us once," Councilor Ruthan objected, his voice rising in ire. "He should be stripped of honor and sentenced to menial tasks for the empire."

"On the contrary," responded Nartel, folding his powerful arms across his chest. "Commodore Resmunt has done well. If not for him, we would not know that the humans had destroyed two AI ships. He is also the only Fleet Commodore we have that has faced the humans in combat. He will be promoted and continue to serve the empire."

-

High up in orbit in the dreadnought Viden, Second Leader Jaseth gazed at the main viewscreen at the wrecked and destroyed habitats that littered this section of space. The Viden and several other ships were in the process of searching for survivors. The humans caused this, Jaseth thought with burning anger. Someday, he would make them pay for what had happened to his family as well as for the destruction he had just witnessed. He would not be satisfied until the last human was dead!

-

Thousands of light years away were the former Human Federation of Worlds. One of those was the planet of New Providence. Two Hocklyn escort cruisers were passing through the system and their First Leaders were discussing the recent developments with the humans and the AIs. Unbeknownst to them, a small stealth satellite picked up their communication transmissions and passed them on to its base.

Deep beneath New Providence, General Whitmore was in the primary Planetary Command Center. With him were President Brice and the head of Planetary Intelligence, Colonel Dickerson.

"Are we certain about this information?" President Brice demanded, his face showing disbelief at what he was being told.

"Yes, Sir," Colonel Dickerson replied. "Humans have attacked the Hocklyn Empire and even managed to destroy two AI ships that were sent to stop them."

The president sat down and looked at the others. "You know what this means?"

"Yes," General Whitmore responded as an aide walked up and handed him more communication intercepts. "Admiral Streth succeeded beyond our wildest dreams. He established a new colony, and now they are attacking the Hocklyns."

"The ship that appeared in our system several centuries ago was legit, it was one of ours," President Brice said. For years after the mysterious cruiser had appeared it had been speculated that it had been a trick by the Hocklyns to lure any remaining humans out of hiding. "What are your recommendations, General?"

Whitmore paused for a moment before responding. "We have a number of stealth destroyers at our disposal. From the communication intercepts, we know where the human fleets have struck. I propose we send one of the destroyers to this area and make contact with these humans. If they are indeed survivors from our original worlds, then it may be time for us to come out in the open and join them in a new alliance."

"It will be risky," Brice commented as he carefully weighed his options. Then he stood up. "We have hidden long enough, send the destroyer. Once we have made contact we can decide how best we can serve in this war."

Whitmore nodded. There were over sixty million people living in the deep underground cities on New Providence. If this mission were successful, it would be time to go back up and reclaim the surface of their world.

-

Admiral Johnson was meeting with Admiral Telleck and President Kincaid back in the Federation Council Chambers on Earth.

"They destroyed two AI ships," the president repeated, thrilled to hear the news. "So the new ships and weapons worked."

"Yes and no," answered Admiral Johnson, recalling what Admiral Streth had requested. "It was only our AIs, Clarissa and Ariel that were able to use our ships and the Devastator Three missiles to destroy the two AI ships. Lieutenant Katie Johnson says she can design a new computer program that will allow the rest of our strike cruisers to operate in the same manner. Admiral Streth is also recommending that we increase the yield on the Devastator Three missiles to forty megatons."

"What about the AIs?" Kincaid asked with worry lines appearing around his eyes. "What will their reaction be to our destroying two of their ships?"

"Unknown," Admiral Telleck responded in a grave voice. "We have never seen an actual AI. Admiral Streth also reported that they found nothing in the ruins of the two AI ships."

"He's bought us some time," Karla continued in a positive voice. "It will be months before the Hocklyns and the AIs attack again. By destroying two AI ships, we have demonstrated that the AIs are not invulnerable. That is going to shake the Hocklyn Empire and may give the AIs reason to pause before they move against us."

"What about Admiral Stillson's fleet?" President Kincaid asked, his eyes narrowing. "Is it returning home to Ceres?"

Admiral Telleck looked over at Fleet Admiral Johnson before replying. "No, it has been permanently assigned to Admiral Strong and Fourth Fleet, and they will be providing support to the Carethians. Governor Malleck has volunteered Ceres to provide logistical support to the bears. A new supply fleet is already being prepared, and Admiral Streth has approved of the plans."

"I guess I am not surprised," Kincaid commented as he sat down behind his desk, indicating for the others to sit down also. "Sometimes I wonder who is in charge of this war, us or Admiral Streth?"

No one answered, but they all knew what the truth was. They had all been taught since grade school that the great Admiral Hedon Streth would someday awaken to save the Federation from the Hocklyns. That day was here and Admiral Streth had already won the first battle. They could only hope and pray that he continued to do so.

The End

If you enjoyed The Slaver Wars: First Strike and want the series to continue, please post a review with some stars. Good reviews encourage an author to write and help books to sell. Reviews can be just a few short sentences describing what you liked about the book. If you have suggestions, please contact me at my website listed on the following page. Thank you for reading The Slaver Wars: First Strike and being so supportive. Current plans call for there to be at least two more Slaver Wars books if the interest continues.

Coming soon! The Slaver Wars: Retaliation

Admiral Jeremy Strong is working frantically helping the Carethians prepare for the impending attack of the Hocklyns and the AIs. Jeremy has also heard a rumor about a mysterious ship that appeared at Admiral Streth's new base. Supposedly, the ship had been hurriedly escorted back to the Human Federation of Worlds. No one was saying where the ship had come from or why it had been sent back home under heavy escort.

In Hocklyn space, Fleet Commodore Resmunt is preparing for his return to the worlds the humans had driven him from. He has assembled the largest war fleet in Hocklyn history. The fleet has new weapons and shields, but even more important are the ten AI ships that will be going with him. The AIs are demanding that the humans be annihilated and their home worlds destroyed.

Books in the series should be read in the following order.

Moon Wreck:
The Slaver Wars: Alien Contact
Moon Wreck: Fleet Academy
The Slaver Wars: First Strike
The Slaver Wars: Retaliation

For updates on current writing projects and future publications go to my author website. Sign up for future notifications when new books come out on Amazon.

Website: http://raymondlweil.com/

Other Books by Raymond L. Weil
Available at Amazon
-

Dragon Dreams: Dragon Wars
Dragon Dreams: Gilmreth the Awakening
Dragon Dreams: Snowden the White Dragon

-

Star One: Tycho City: Discovery
Star One: Neutron Star
Star One: Dark Star

-

Star One: Tycho City: Survival
Coming November 2013

-

The Slaver Wars: Retaliation
Coming January 2014

-

Dragon Dreams: Firestorm Mount
Coming 2014

Turn the page for a brief description of Star One: Neutron Star

Star One: Neutron Star

It is the year 2044 on Earth. At the Farside observatory complex on the Moon, a startling astronomical discovery has been made. A survey for pulsars has found an x-ray source in a region of space where none has been detected before.

Upon further investigation, they find that this x-ray source is just outside of the solar system. The astronomers are paralyzed by what they have found knowing what its disastrous ramifications might be.

A neutron star is approaching the solar system. It appeared out of a small dust cloud that was shielding its approach. Armageddon has arrived; the star is on a trajectory that will take it through the center of the solar system. Life on Earth will not survive its passing.

The only hope for survival will be on the massive Star One space station at the Earth-Moon Lagrange point or possibly in Tycho City deep beneath the Moon's surface. It will be a race against time to save a fraction of the Earth's frightened population.

A power struggle will erupt on Earth over who is to survive. On Star One and at Tycho City they prepare for the worst, unfortunately, the threat from Earth might be just as dangerous as the approaching neutron star.

http://www.amazon.com/gp/product/B00860XMVU/ref=cm_cd_asin_lnk

Printed in Great Britain
by Amazon